LEGA
OF KINGS

One arrow pierced through Nasaan's upraised shield right next to his arm, gouging his bracer. Another struck a bolt on his shield with a sound like the crack of lightning and bounced off. He heard several of his warriors curse as they were struck, but no man fell, and no man faltered. They all understood the importance of getting inside the city gate before Jezalya had a chance to mobilize.

Even now the alarm must be sounding in all her barracks. The head of the night watch would be cursing his own inattention as the daylight officers staggered naked out of bed, fumbling for their armor, yelling for information. No doubt they would order the great city gate to be closed, unaware that Nasaan's men had taken control of it.

Closer and closer to that gate Nasaan rode now, desert blood singing in his veins. Then the first of his men passed through it, ululating in triumph as they entered the city. Nasaan's agents inside Jezalya had done their job well. He glanced back over his shoulder to make sure all was well behind him—

And saw death bearing down upon him.

BY CELIA FRIEDMAN

The Coldfire Trilogy
Black Sun Rising
When True Night Falls
Crown of Shadows

The Magister Trilogy
Feast of Souls
Wings of Wrath
Legacy of Kings

CELIA FRIEDMAN

LEGACY OF KINGS

3
MAGISTER
TRILOGY

orbit

www.orbitbooks.net

ORBIT

First published in 2011 in the United States by DAW,
an imprint of Penguin Group (USA) Inc
First published in Great Britain in 2011 by Orbit

A CIP catalogue record for this book
is available from the British Library.

ISBN 978-1-84149-536-1

Typeset in Adobe Caslon by Palimpsest Book Production Limited,
Falkirk, Stirlingshire
Printed and bound by CPI Group (UK) Ltd, Croydon, CR0 4YY

Papers used by Orbit are from well-managed forests
and other responsible sources.

MIX
Paper from
responsible sources
FSC® C104740

Orbit
An imprint of
Little, Brown Book Group
100 Victoria Embankment
London EC4Y 0DY

An Hachette UK Company
www.hachette.co.uk

www.orbitbooks.net

DEDICATION

This book is for Jen Kuiper:
Awesome role-player
Valued friend
Mensch

ACKNOWLEDGEMENTS

LITERARY THANKS go to Cordwainer Smith for his stunning story "The Game of Rat and Dragon" and Anne McCaffrey for her Pern series, for sparking my interest in the linkage of human and animal consciousness. While the theme has appeared in more books than one can count, the ways in which those two writers handled it raised questions in my mind that took on a life of their own over the years, until they helped give birth to this series. Those were benign relationships, of course, involving domestic cats on one hand and a species genetically altered to interact with humans on the other. Being of a much darker bent, I found myself wondering what such a relationship would be like if the species in question were one whose mind was not naturally compatible with the human psyche, but a truly wild creature with whom we had no common ground. And thus began the creative journey that culminated in this book.

Creative thanks go to Betsy Wollheim and Russ Galen, who helped me take that idea and mold it into a truly great story. No writer could possibly ask for a better editor or agent.

Revision thanks go to my reading team, who labored tirelessly to provide an answer to the writer's eternal question, "Hey, how do you think it's going?" That's Carl Cipra, Zsusy Sanford, David Walddon, Steve Rappaport, Paul Hoeffer, and Jennifer Eastman.

Research thanks go to Christian Cameron, Jon Herrmann, Aleksandra Kleczar, Dr. Julian Redditt, and Markus Ofner for providing the kind of information and assistance you just can't get from books.

Artistic thanks go to John Palencar for my beautiful covers. All I can say is . . . wow. Seriously. Wow.

And last—but definitely not least—very special thanks go to the people who helped keep me sane while I was writing this book. I have had a few speed bumps in my life during the last couple of years, and these people helped me overcome them and get back to the keyboard: James and Jenny Wood, Carmen C. Clarke, Jen Kuiper, David Williams, Anthony C., Jed Stancato, Cathy Wallin, Kristi Kelly, Hugh Montgomerie, Melissa Hendrix, Amanda Spikol, Chazz Mahan, and Tonya Druin. You guys were great. Thank you for being there when I needed you and for helping me stay grounded. (Well, as grounded as I ever get.)

What will future minstrels sing of the days leading up to the final battle?

They will sing of the Souleaters with their stained-glass wings, who feasted upon the life-essence of mankind and brought down the First Age of Kings. And of the army of martyrs that gathered to fight them, led by the world's last surviving witches. By fire and faith they herded the great beasts into an arctic prison, where the incessant cold and long winter's darkness would rob them of strength, and hopefully of life. And the gods themselves struck the earth with great Spears, it was said, erecting a barrier born of their Wrath, which would hold any surviving Souleaters prisoner until the end of time. For forty generations the Wrath held strong, so that the Second Age of Kings could thrive. But it was not truly a divine creation, merely a construct of witches, and when it finally faltered, the Souleaters began their invasion.

They will sing of the Magisters, undying sorcerers who wielded a power that seemed without limit, and of how they were bound by their Law to the fates of mortal men. But no minstrel will sing of the secret that lay at the heart of that dark brotherhood, for no mortal man who learned the truth would be allowed to live. The Magisters fueled their sorcery with the life-essence of human consorts, offering up the death of innocents to assure their own immortality. Perhaps that practice was what corrupted their spirits, so that they became innately hostile to their own kind . . . or perhaps there was another cause. Colivar alone seemed to know the truth, but even his most ancient and determined rival, Ramirus, had not yet been able to pry that information out of him.

They will sing of Kamala, a red-headed child destined for poverty and abuse in the slums of Gansang, who defied the fates and became the first female to learn the art of true sorcery. But her accidental killing of Magister Raven broke the brotherhood's most sacred Law, and even her reclusive mentor Ethanus dared not give her shelter any longer. Forced to masquerade as a witch, she traveled the world in search of some knowledge or artifact that she might barter for her safety, so that she could bear the title of Magister openly and claim her proper place in the brotherhood of sorcerers.

They will sing of Danton Aurelius, who ruled the High Kingdom with an iron fist until the traitor Kostas brought him down. They will craft lamentations for the two young princes who died alongside their father, even as they celebrate the courage of Queen Gwynofar in avenging her husband's death. Alas, it was not to be the end of her trials. For when prophecy summoned her to Alkali to search for the Throne of Tears, an ancient artifact that would awaken the lyr bloodlines to their full mystical potential, the gods demanded her unborn child in sacrifice, and later her beloved half-brother, Rhys.

They will sing of the Witch-Queen, Siderea Aminestas, mistress of Magisters and consort to kings, whom the sorcerers abandoned when her usefulness ended. And of the Souleater who saved her life, at the cost of her human soul. Vengeance burned bright in her heart the day she fled Sankara on the back of her jewel-winged consort, seeking a land where she could plant the seeds of a new and terrible empire.

They will sing of Salvator, third son of Danton Aurelius, who set aside the vows of a Penitent monk to inherit his father's throne, rejecting the power and the protection of the Magisters in the name of his faith. Songs will be crafted to tell how he was tested by demons, doubt, and the Witch-Queen herself, even while the leaders of his Church argued over how he might best be manipulated to serve their political interests.

And last of all they will sing of the confrontation that was still to come, in which the fate of the Second Age of Kings—and of all mankind—would be decided. And those who hear their songs will wonder whether a prince-turned-monk-turned-king could really save the world, when the god that he worshiped might have been the one who called for its destruction in the first place.

PROLOGUE

THE BATTLEFIELD was silent.

Bodies lay strewn across the blood-soaked ground, corpses of enemies intertwined like lovers. Thousands upon thousands of men who had once been the pride of their nations—strong and loyal soldiers—were now reduced to carrion. With death they had lost all dignity, all purpose. It no longer mattered who they had fought for, or how deeply they had believed in their causes. The ravens that were gathering over the battlefield cared nothing for such human niceties.

Silently, Colivar walked among the corpses. The battle had not brought him as much pleasure as it should have. The heady intoxication he had once experienced when he caused men to turn against their brothers, back when the sport was still new to him, was now dulled by familiarity.

All these men had died at his call or at the call of some other Magister. Oh, they'd thought they were dying to serve their kings—giving up their lives for a cause that was worthy of sacrifice—but the sorcerers knew better. By now the leaders who had ordered this conflict were dead, along with all their counselors. Perhaps their heirs as well. It might not even have been Colivar's opponent who had killed them all. Human conflict on this scale drew Magisters like flies. What greater exercise of power was there, than to cast an entire nation into chaos? Few could resist such temptation.

While Colivar's blood still became heated at the thought of such a contest—that perverse spark within him would probably never die—his human soul, a distant and wounded thing, remained cold. The kind of events that had once moved him to ecstasy no longer had that power. Did that mean that the ancient wounds were healing at last? Was it a sign that his humanity, rent to pieces by madness so many years ago, was slowly pulling itself back together? Or were the final fragments of his battered soul simply expiring from sheer exhaustion, starved to death by this cold, callous existence? If so, what would he become when they were finally gone? Uncomfortable questions, to be sure.

"This has to end." The voice came from behind him, shattering his reverie. "You know that."

The sudden awareness of another man so close to him triggered Colivar's most primitive territorial instincts. Whipping about, he called forth enough soulfire to defend himself from any manner of assault—or to launch an attack himself—and held it at the ready while he took stock of his visitor. That the man was a Magister himself was immediately apparent, from his bearing if not his dress. Hatred keened inside Colivar's brain, primitive impulses surging through his veins with undeniable force. *Drive the invader away! Tear him to pieces if he will not flee!* If Colivar had been a weaker Magister he might have lost the connection to his human self entirely at that moment and launched himself at the intruder like an animal. The sensation of what it was like to tear open an enemy's neck with razor-sharp teeth was not so distant in his past that he had forgotten it. Even as he struggled to fight back the tide of bestial instinct, part of him longed to surrender to it.

But finally, with effort, he recovered enough self-control to shape human words again. "Why are you here?" he demanded. His voice sounded strange in his ears, hoarse and halting. He did not talk much to anyone these days. "What do you want?"

"To speak with you," the stranger said calmly. If he felt the same territorial passions coursing through his veins he showed no sign of it. "Nothing more."

Magisters rarely socialized with one another. Once they were no longer students, but had fully established their independent identities, the territorial instinct in them became too strong to allow for it. Each sorcerer went his own way in life, and if the paths of two should happen to cross, thousands of morati might die as they competed for supremacy. Whole kingdoms had been swallowed up by such rivalries, knights and princes waging war for causes they believed to be their own, when in fact their hearts were manifesting the territorial rage of the sorcerers who controlled them. Not that it mattered what morati believed. Even if such men had known the truth, they could not have resisted.

But . . . a strange Magister was here now, in his domain, and Colivar had managed to resist the immediate impulse to destroy him. Perhaps the recent battle had drained his inner beast of strength, at least enough to make civilized discourse possible. It was an interesting concept. Perhaps worth exploring further.

He absorbed back into himself the power that he had conjured. No doubt the stranger knew how quickly he could summon it again if need be. "Speak," he said hoarsely.

The stranger was a tall man, solidly built, with fine wrinkles about his eyes and a hint of gray at his temples. Which might mean that he had undergone First Transition while in his 30s or 40s and ceased to age physically at that point. Or it might mean that he had been a gangly youth, or even an elderly cripple, who was now using his power to provide himself with more attractive flesh. There was no way to know. Using one's power to find out a Magister's true appearance—or true age, or true anything—was considered a mortal offense.

"You heard my words." The man's voice was quiet but compelling, in the manner of one who knows he does not need volume to make his point. "This has to end." A sharp, sweeping gesture encompassed the battlefield, as well as Colivar and the whole world beyond him. "All this."

"You mean . . . the war?"

"I mean what we bring to it. Our excesses. Our internecine violence. The price that the morati world pays for our boundless self-indulgence."

The corner of Colivar's mouth twitched. "So we should be more . . . considerate?"

"No. Simply more practical."

"For the sake of the morati?"

The stranger's eyes narrowed. "Once there were great kingdoms scattered across the earth. What is there now? Chaos. Barbarism. Barely a memory of great things and no energy left to restore them. Is that the world we wish to live in?"

"We were not the ones who caused the First Kingdoms to fall," Colivar pointed out.

"No. But we keep them from being rebuilt." The stranger's eyes were clear and bright, the pale blue color of arctic ice. It awakened shadows of memories in Colivar that he would rather forget. "Do you not wish to see the great towers rise up once more? To live in the kind of world that the First Kings once enjoyed? We, who feed upon death, will never create such things ourselves. We are too obsessed with destruction, too blinded by our instinctive hatred for one another. And in our madness we are dragging the morati down with us. Soon there will be nothing left in them that is capable of greatness. And that will be a loss for us all."

How arrogant this man was, Colivar thought, to lecture another Magister as if he were a schoolchild! In another time and place he might have been infuriated by such behavior. It might even have caused him to forget his self-control and end this interview in bloodshed, as the beast inside cried out for him to do. But there were other emotions stirring inside him also, strange and disturbing emotions, that spoke to his more human side. And so he denied the beast sovereignty. For now.

The stranger was right about the future of civilization, of course. No Magister knew that better than Colivar. He alone understood the full measure of what mankind had lost. He yearned for that ancient world in a way none of the others could possibly comprehend. He also understood enough of the Magisters' true nature to know that mankind would never reach those heights of greatness again. The Souleaters had simply destroyed too much. And now the Magisters were here. Mankind might recover from the first plague, but the second was far more dangerous.

"We are predators," he said harshly. "Not caretakers."

"And what good will that distinction do us when the world is swallowed up by chaos? For that is where it's headed right now; you know that. It may bleed but slowly from the wounds we have dealt it thus far, but it bleeds nonetheless. We must stanch the wound while healing is still possible. Else our very world will slip through our fingers, and not all the sorcery in existence will be able to restore it."

"You care about the morati," Colivar challenged. Not because he believed the stranger really did, but to stir up his inner beast and put him off his guard. Accusing any Magister of human compassion was a powerful insult. He was curious to see how this one would respond.

But the stranger did not flinch. "And you were once willing to die for them, Colivar. Or so the legends suggest. Is that true? Did the welfare of the common man once mean that much to you?"

Memories—true memories!—came welling up from the darkness where he had buried them long ago. They had been rent to pieces by the madness and suffocated by years of neglect, but even in their damaged and disjointed state they still had the power to shake him to the depths of his soul.

He looked away from the stranger, not wanting to meet his eyes, and gazed out over the battlefield. Ravens had come down to earth and begun to pick at the flesh of the fallen. Some of the soldiers were not quite dead yet, but they were too wounded to fight the birds off. Colivar was closer kin to those ravens, he knew, than to the morati. He accepted that. The beast that was within him would have it no other way. Once, long ago, he had tried to deny it, to pretend that he was still human. But the beast was a part of his soul now, wedded to him by his own willing submission, and was not so easily banished.

If you understood the true source of our power, he thought, *you would not question me thus.*

"There may once have been a morati named Colivar, who cared about this world." He kept his voice carefully neutral, so that this stranger would not guess at the maelstrom of emotion that his words had inspired. "Perhaps he would even have been willing to offer up his life for it. But that man is dead now." He turned back to the intruder. "We are what we are. Not all the sorcery in the world can change that."

"No," the visitor agreed. It was maddening to Colivar how calm he was. Was this man's inner beast weaker than his own, or was it just better disciplined? He had always wondered what the others of his kind experienced. Were their internal battles less fierce than his, because they were farther removed from the source? Or did they just hide them better? "Sorcery cannot change it."

"What, then?"

"Something more powerful than sorcery. Something that the morati, ironically enough, understand the value of . . . though we have forgotten it." He let Colivar consider that for a moment, then said, very quietly, "Law."

Colivar drew in a sharp breath. "You mean . . . what? Rules of engagement?"

"No. Those are for wartime. This must be something more basic. More primal. Something to help us curb our darker instincts when they arise, so that open warfare will no longer be necessary. Or at least . . ." A dry smile flickered across his lips. "Not quite so often."

"We are not morati," he said harshly.

"No . . . but that does not mean we cannot learn from their accomplishments. Rule of law is what separates the morati from the beasts. Perhaps it can do the same for us."

But a Magister's beast is part of his soul, Colivar thought darkly. *Divide the two, and you destroy both halves.* This stranger did not understand that, of course. None of the other Magisters did. And he was not about to explain it to them. "How do you propose to enforce these laws?" he demanded. Trying to focus upon the stranger's words, rather than the memories they conjured. "What manner of authority do you think that Magisters will accept?"

"Common accord would be required."

For a moment Colivar was speechless. Finally he managed, "An agreement by . . . *all* of us?"

The stranger bowed his head.

"Even the morati could not manage such unanimity."

"We are greater than the morati, are we not?"

Colivar shook his head in amazement. "There are some who would call you mad for even suggesting such a thing."

"Whereas I prefer to think of myself as practical."

We are incapable even of talking face-to-face with our own kind without bestial instincts taking control of us. What kind of law do you envision for us? How do you propose to punish transgressors?

But those words died on his lips, unvoiced. Because the suggestion, mad as it was, struck a chord deep within him. A *human* chord. And for a moment—just a moment—the beast within him was quiet, and he could think with unexpected clarity.

"This was your idea?" he managed at last.

The stranger shook his head. "Not mine alone. But few are capable of spreading the word as effectively as I, so I volunteered. The task requires . . ." A faint smile quirked his lips. ". . . unusual self-control."

What if all the others join together in this project, Colivar thought suddenly, *and I alone cannot?* He was suddenly acutely aware of the chasm that separated him from all the others of his kind. If this stranger knew the truth about him, would he have come here with the same offer? Would he even want Colivar to be part of this project?

"It will take a very long time," he challenged.

"Perhaps. But time is the one thing we have in abundance, is it not?"

"And the ultimate goal is . . . what? To bring us all together in one great assembly, so that we can collaborate on a set of rules?" He laughed harshly. "We would tear each other to pieces before the first word was set on paper."

"Ah." A smile flickered across the stranger's face; it was a cold and humorless expression. "But you see, that is the difference between you and me. I believe that Magisters can rise above their bloodier instincts, if they are convinced of the need to do so. Maybe someday, if we are determined enough, it may even be possible for a number of us to come together like civilized men and discuss matters of common interest without our darker instincts interfering. That would be a thing to marvel at, wouldn't it?"

"You really believe that establishing a set of rules can all make this possible?"

The stranger said solemnly, "It is not the law itself that will have power, Colivar. It is what we must become in order to establish it."

Ravens cawed in the distance. Somewhere amidst the bodies, unseen, a dying man groaned. Colivar shut his eyes and focused upon the sounds, trying to sort out the storm of emotions in his soul. He felt as if he were at a crossroads, peering into the darkness, trying to make out any hint of the terrain up ahead, to choose his way. But both paths were shrouded in fog, their features indiscernible. One must step forward in blind faith or not go forward at all.

All the assumptions he had made about his power—about his very soul!—were being challenged by this man. But what if his assumptions had been wrong? What if the other sorcerers, born in a simpler time, had a clearer understanding of what their true potential was? What if they could really change things?

And what if he, unique among Magisters, could not share in that change? It was a chilling thought, that made the more sensitive parts of his anatomy want to draw up into his body out of pure dread.

But if they could succeed in this mad plan . . . just imagine the potential of it! Not only for their society in general—if the ranks of Magisters could be called that—but for his own inner struggle as well.

I could be human again, he thought with wonder. It was a dream he'd been forced to abandon long ago. Now he was being challenged to take it up again. The concept was almost too much to process.

A raven cawed in the distance. He shook his head, trying to clear it.

"What is it you want of me?" he said at last.

Though the stranger had been impassive thus far, it was clear from the way his expression eased now that he had been far from certain about where the conversation was heading. Or who would come out of it alive, should it devolve into a less civilized discourse. "Simply your agreement that the task is worth attempting. That when the time comes to enter the next stage, you will consider playing an active role. How much will be possible, of course, no man can predict. But we mean to do our best, and your support would mean much to us."

Colivar raised an eyebrow. "Do not attempt to flatter me," he said darkly. "That is a morati trick."

The stranger shrugged. "Your word has much weight among our kind. That is not flattery, simply the truth."

"Because I am more deadly than most?"

"Because you have more knowledge than most." The sapphire eyes glittered. "Even though you hold that knowledge close to your breast."

Colivar drew in a deep breath. What lay within his breast was the soul of a beast, coiled, waiting. Did other Magisters perceive themselves in the same way, as if every moment they were caught in a tug-of-war between their human halves and some dark, animalistic master? Or did they believe that all their violent, territorial urges were simply human emotions gone awry? There was no way to ask; Magisters did not discuss such things with one another.

He had always perceived their ignorance as a weakness. But perhaps it might open doors for them, where his own knowledge of the past had closed them.

"Very well." Colivar nodded stiffly. "When the time comes that all the Magisters have agreed to this course—when they come together to determine what manner of law they will establish—then I will come to that place, also." A faint smile flickered across his lips. "And I will try my best not to kill them all."

The stranger bowed respectfully. "That is all we can ask."

And he turned away to leave. It was, in its own way, as powerful a statement of intent as a Magister could possibly offer. He had no way to know that Colivar would not strike him down from behind as soon as his back was turned. Yet he willingly took that chance. Was it optimism that motivated him, or foolishness? Or both?

"Wait," Colivar said.

The stranger turned back to him.

"You know my name, but you have not given me yours." He

raised an eyebrow. "Is that the way you wish to begin this *cooperative* effort?"

The cold blue eyes regarded him. There was power in a name, even one that was used in public circles. And there was much more power in receiving a name directly from its owner. Few Magisters would make such a gesture.

Prove how much you care about this project, Colivar thought. *Prove how far you are willing to go to bring it to fruition.*

"Ramirus," the stranger said. "I am called Ramirus."

Ravens cawed in the distance as he once more turned to leave. This time Colivar did not stop him.

BEGINNING

CHAPTER 1

THE ATTACK began before dawn.

Jezalya's population was mostly asleep, trusting to its sentries to sound an alarm if trouble came calling. But no one really expected trouble. The wall surrounding the desert city was tall and strong, with centuries of witchery woven into its substance; only a fool would try to break through it. Least of all during the night, when even the fiercest of warriors laid his weapons aside, leaving sovereignty of the sand to lizards and demons.

Their error.

Outside the city Nasaan waited, studying the great wall through a spyglass. He had a small but loyal army at his command, made up of tribal warriors from the most powerful desert families. Perhaps they were not as well armored as the soldiers of Jezalya, but they were ten times as fierce, and they were bound to him by ties of blood as well as political fealty. His witches were kin to him as well, which meant that they would be willing to lay down their very lives to assure him victory. They were a whole different species from Jezalya's witches, who provided the city's prince with power in carefully measured doses in return for carefully measured coinage. Oh, those witches would help out with a few small tasks, and maybe even scry for trouble now and then, but only up to a point. As soon as they became convinced that Jezalya was a lost cause they would bolt like frightened rats, and not waste one precious moment of life-essence trying to save her.

Or so Nasaan's spies had assured him, after months of reconnaissance.

A pale blue light began to spread along the eastern horizon, harbinger of dawn. Inside the city, Nasaan knew, people were just starting to stir. The grand market at the heart of Jezalya would open as soon as the sky was light, so the most ambitious vendors were already laying out their wares, lining up fresh vegetables and strips of newly slaughtered flesh in neat rows to entice buyers. Wagons were beginning to move up and down the narrow streets, transporting goods from one place to another in anticipation of a new day's business. Merchants who had sheltered in Jezalya for the night were gathering their parties together, preparing to return to the road. And along the top of the great wall sentries watched the sky lighten, unutterably bored. Once more, a night had passed without incident. They were not surprised. War was a creature of daylight, and if trouble came, it would not be on their watch.

Wrong again.

There was not yet enough light to see by, but Nasaan's spyglass had been bewitched so that it would magnify what little there was, facilitating his reconnaissance. He could see sentries walking along the top of the wall, their eyes scanning the barren plain that surrounded Jezalya. Nasaan tensed as one man looked his way, but his witches had crafted spells to keep the enemy from seeing him or his people, and apparently those were more effective than whatever spells Jezalya was using to watch for trouble.

His men were clearly anxious to begin the fighting, but it would do no good to rush the city's outer wall prematurely, Nasaan knew. His strategy inside the city must play out before he and his men could make their move. Otherwise they would be held at bay by the same great wall that had defeated greater armies in the past. Such a barrier could not be conquered from the outside.

With a whispered word he cautioned his men to stillness, and waited.

One of the sentries' lanterns suddenly went dark. Nasaan stiffened. A few seconds passed; then the light returned, and whoever held the lantern now bobbed it up and down: once, twice, three times.

Nasaan's signal.

There was no alarm sounding yet. No noise of combat from inside the city, carried to them on the dry desert wind. Nasaan held his breath, his hand closing tightly about his reins. The more that his agents in Jezalya could accomplish by stealth and trickery, as a prelude to all-out battle, the better it would be for everyone.

No man can breach the walls of my city, Jezalya's ruler had bragged. The words had been meant as a deterrent, but instead Nasaan had accepted them as a personal challenge. That was the day that he had known it was his destiny to claim the prosperous trade city for his own. Not with brute warfare, charging against the great wall as so many armies had done in the past, struggling to mount ladders and climb ropes while the city's warriors rained down hot oil and burning arrows on their heads. No. Such a strategy was doomed to failure before it began.

But a few dozen men inside Jezalya could accomplish more than a thousand men on the outside, if the desert gods favored their mission.

And Nasaan was on good terms with his gods.

What was the name of the city's ruler, anyway? Dervash? Dervastis? Son of a chieftain from a minor tribe that few men respected. It was amazing that the city had accepted the rule of such a man, given the weakness of his family line. Nasaan carried the blood of ancient kings in his veins, and with it the spark of their greatness.

Jezalya deserved such a leader.

Slowly, torturously, the massive gates finally began to swing open. Nasaan could see a wave of anticipation sweep through the ranks of his men as they tensed in their saddles, preparing to ride forward. *Not yet*, he thought. Raising his hand to signal them to hold their ground, cautioning them to have patience for a few moments longer. *Not yet!* His small army was positioned much closer to Jezalya than would have been possible during the day; his witches had drawn upon night's own darkness to augment their protective magics. But the greatest risk of the operation would be in its first moments of aggressive action, a mad dash across the open plain to the city's entrance. Not even all his witches acting in unison could obscure something like that. They needed to wait until Nasaan's men inside the city had finished their job and controlled Jezalya's main gate. If Nasaan's men tried to storm the gate before that had been accomplished . . . well, it would be one hell of a bloody mess, that was certain.

This prize is worth bloodshed, he thought. And he whispered a final prayer to the god of war under his breath, promising to build him a great new temple in the heart of Jezalya if the battle went well.

And then, at last, the gates of the city were fully open. The massive armored doors would not close quickly or easily, Nasaan knew; his first objective had been accomplished, and all of it without raising the city's alarm. So far so good.

But there was no way to manage the next phase of the invasion without alerting his target. Hiding a host of warriors from sight when they were moving stealthily in the depths of night, keeping to cover whenever possible, was one thing; masking the charge of an attacking horde riding noisily across open ground was another. Better to abandon witchery entirely, now, and claim whatever advantage speed and fury could buy them.

A tense silence fell over the armed company, punctuated only by the impatient snuffing of a few horses. They, too, could feel the tension simmering in the air. But no one was going to move without Nasaan's command.

And then his hand fell. And with a war cry so terrible it would surely strike fear into the hearts of the enemy, his men kicked their horses into sudden motion. Thundering across the dry earth, the beating hooves raised clouds of dust so thick that it seemed as if a sandstorm were bearing down upon the city, faceless and terrible. This was not merely a human army descending upon Jezalya, but the very embodiment of the desert's fury.

Fear us! Nasaan thought fiercely. Gripping his reins with one hand as he raised up his other arm, positioning his battle-scarred shield high enough that it would protect him from the enemy's fire. *Fear us so much that you choose surrender instead of risking slaughter at our hands. Choose life instead of death.*

He had agents inside the city who would tell its leaders that

this was their only choice. That they could either surrender to
the tribal army and know peace, or suffer the full fury of its
wrath. Nasaan himself hoped they would choose the first
option—it would leave more of the city intact for him to rule—
but he suspected that many of his men felt otherwise. They
lusted for the aftermath of military conquest as much as they
did for battle itself, hungering for the thrill of unbridled rapine
and destruction that would follow a lengthier siege. Nasaan's
greatest challenge, if the city surrendered, would be to keep his
own men from destroying it.

Of course, if the leaders of Jezalya did not surrender . . . then
he would rule over whatever was left once his men were finished
sacking the place.

A sudden sharp blow struck his shield from above. Then
another. Arrows were being launched at them from the upper
reaches of the wall. There weren't as many as normally would
be expected—Nasaan's agents had apparently taken control of
the nearer portions of the wall, denying Jezalya's archers
access—but still there were enough to send a thin steel rain
hurtling down from the sky, lethal in its velocity. One arrow
pierced through Nasaan's upraised shield right next to his arm,
gouging his bracer. Another struck a bolt on his shield with
a sound like the crack of lightning and bounced off. He heard
several of his warriors curse as they were struck, but no man
fell, and no man faltered. They all understood the importance
of getting inside the city gate before Jezalya had a chance to
mobilize.

Even now the alarm must be sounding in all her barracks.
The head of the night watch would be cursing his own inattention as the daylight officers staggered naked out of bed,
fumbling for their armor, yelling for information. No doubt they

would order the great city gate to be closed, unaware that Nasaan's men had taken control of it.

Closer and closer to that gate Nasaan rode now, desert blood singing in his veins. Then the first of his men passed through it, ululating in triumph as they entered the city. Nasaan's agents inside Jezalya had done their job well. He glanced back over his shoulder to make sure all was well behind him—

And saw death bearing down upon him.

A vast mounted force was coming up swiftly behind his men, and it did not look friendly. Where it had come from he did not know, but its witches must have been touched by the gods, to be able to obscure the presence of so many men. Judging from the cloud of dust this new army was raising, it was several times the size of his own, and it was bearing down upon them with the speed of a sand-spawned whirlwind. The bulk of Nasaan's strike force was about to be trapped between the great wall and this furious army. And now sounds of battle were starting to ring out from inside Jezalya's walls; without timely reinforcement, Nasaan's men inside the city would not stand a chance.

Even as he cried out a warning to his men, arrows began to fly at them from behind. Those who were holding shields had not positioned them to defend against a rearguard action; arrows pierced both human and equine flesh. One horse reared up as it took two arrows in its side, nearly throwing off its rider; another went down with its rider still in the saddle, and both were trampled underfoot. One of Nasaan's witches quickly cast a spell to protect them, but there was little she could do other than fend off the arrows one by one as they arrived. There were no natural obstacles here that could be manipulated to greater purpose, no sunlight to be angled into the enemy's eyes, not even cloudy skies to help provide a bolt of lightning . . . only an empty, barren landscape, devoid of any tool that a witch might use to lend added force to her efforts.

As the human whirlwind bore down upon them, Nasaan's rearmost ranks wheeled their horses about to confront it. Feverishly Nasaan prayed for the war god Alwat to favor him and his warriors as he braced to meet the enemy head-on. It was said that Alwat favored those who had the courage to fight against impossible odds; if so, then Nasaan's situation right now was sure to please him.

Suddenly something massive and dark swooped down out of the sky, right over the enemy's front line. The men attacking Nasaan seemed to falter, with no visible cause. It was a strange thing to witness, as if a wave of uncertainty were somehow rippling through the enemy ranks, man by man. Even the horses seemed to grow confused, and several stumbled, becoming dangerous obstacles to the men behind them. Never in all his life had Nasaan seen anything like it. But he was not one to question a gift from the gods. Voicing a war cry that echoed across the vast plain, he signaled for his men to charge.

Whatever the dark creature was, it hovered overhead as the battle was joined, its vast wings barely visible against the dark sky. Nasaan could not spare a moment to look up at it, but he could sense its presence overhead even as he braced himself for impact. It was watching them. Waiting. He knew that instinctively, just as he knew instinctively that this was not a natural creature, and that whatever it was doing to the enemy was not a natural act.

Steel continued to ring out against steel in the barren plain as the two armies fought, and dust arose in great plumes all about them. But there was clearly a sickness in the soul of the enemy now, and they could not stand their ground. The first man Nasaan engaged seem to move lethargically and could not manage to turn aside Nasaan's sword, nor could he swing his own powerfully enough to make his blow count. From what Nasaan could glimpse out of the corner of his eye as he dispatched the man, others were acting similarly. The enemy's horses were stumbling about like untrained colts who had never seen a battle before. Several reared up in panic and tried to flee the battlefield, colliding with others as they did so, fostering utter chaos. All semblance of military formation among the enemy had been lost. Even as Nasaan thrust his sword into the side of a third enemy warrior, he wondered what sort of terrible power could have caused such a thing.

And then he saw a vision. Or maybe it was not a vision. Maybe there really was a woman standing in the middle of the battlefield, in a circle of utter calm. Maybe the tides of violence really did part around her like a rushing stream, without any man being consciously aware of the process.

At first glance she appeared to be a woman of the desert, with the golden skin and the finely chiseled features of a tribal princess, but her bearing proclaimed her to be something more. Her body was wrapped in layered veils of fine silk, and the long sleeves beat about her body like restive wings as men fought to their deaths on all sides of her. And her eyes! They were black and faceted, like gemstones, as inhuman as they were beautiful.

She was staring straight at him.

Nasaan knew that there were demons of the desert called *djiri*, wild spirits who sometimes aided tribal warriors in battle. He also knew that their help did not come without a price. Tales were told around the campfire of warriors who had been saved from the brink of death by such creatures, only to discover that the price demanded was their firstborn child, a favored wife . . . or even their own manhood. The *djiri* were capricious and cruel, and notoriously unpredictable. One of Nasaan's own ancestors had supposedly received the aid of such a demon, back when he had led his tribe in battle against the Tawara, and the ancestral songs hinted at a price so terrible that he became a broken man as a result and ultimately took his own life.

None of Nasaan's men seemed to be aware that the *djira* was present, nor did the horses appear to see her. Yet the tide of battle parted as it approached her, like rushing water parting around an island. Men fought, bled, and died on all sides of her, but no matter how chaotic the battle became, they did not move into her space. Blood spattered across the ground not far from her feet, and clods of earth torn loose from the earth by pounding hooves came flying in her direction . . . but men and horses all turned aside as they approached, seeking bloodshed elsewhere. No living thing would come close to her.

All this Nasaan absorbed in a single instant, and then an enemy warrior engaged him, and he was fighting for his life once more. Not until he had dispatched the man—an easy task, given the enemy's confusion—was he able to look back at the woman.

She was still there. Untouched by battle.

Her eyes were as black as the desert night and filled with promise.

A wounded horse staggered by Nasaan. Its rider, a young man in brightly polished scale armor, took a swing at his head. Nasaan caught the blade on the edge of his shield and turned it aside easily; the man's blow was as weak as a child's.

She did this, he thought, as he gutted his opponent with a

quick thrust and watched him tumble to the ground. Overhead
the great beast was beating its wings steadily, driving dust down
into Nasaan's eyes. He blinked it away just in time to meet the
attack of another assailant, decapitating the man with a single
sweeping blow. Even as he did so, the man's horse fell to its
knees, so swiftly one might think it had been hamstrung.

Magic.

Even without looking at her, he knew that she was smiling.
He could feel her presence against his skin, cold fingernails of
promise pricking his spine. *You want Jezalya.* The words were
like ice against his flesh. *I can give it to you.* Had his ancestor
experienced something like this? Had the offer of his own *djira*
been simultaneously terrifying and seductive, casting his soul
into such confusion that he could barely think straight? The
touch of a desert spirit should not be cold; Nasaan knew that.
But that observation was a distant thing, and his focus right
now was the immediate picture. As he turned aside the blade
of yet another attacker, only her offer mattered.

I can give you victory, she whispered into his brain.

If he refused her, did that mean the enemy would suddenly
come back to its senses? Perhaps even gain a magical advantage
in turn? The thought of his own warriors being infected with
that strange mental sickness was daunting. Courage alone could
not shield an army from such a power. No human effort could.

He took advantage of a moment's respite to look out over
the battlefield. His men were doing well; they had taken advantage of the enemy's strange weakness to decimate its ranks,
despite the odds against them. They might be able to carry the
day even if the *djira* turned against them now. But time was
everything inside Jezalya, and every minute they wasted made
the situation more precarious for his people inside those walls.

Any minute now the great gate might start to close, so that his men in the city were left isolated. He could not allow that to happen.

Gritting his teeth, he looked back at the *djira*. Dead men and horses were piled around her in a perfect circle, like some ghastly siege wall. Fresh blood, gleaming blackly in the dim morning light, soaked the ground surrounding her feet.

He waited until she met his eyes, then nodded.

Go, then. The words resounded in his brain as clearly as if she had spoken them aloud. *Ride to Jezalya. Take the city.*

For a moment he hesitated . . . but only for a moment. Then he wheeled his horse about to face the city once more, and cried out for his men to follow him. A few looked at him as though he were mad, but something in his manner must have convinced them he was not. Or else they were just willing to follow him anyway. One by one they worked their way free of the battle's chaos to join him. Stumbling, confused, the enemy did not pursue them. The last living strength had been drained from their limbs, the last vital energy from their hearts. Whatever power the *djira* was using on them was truly fearsome, and Nasaan was glad he had not given her reason to turn against him.

Hooves pounding, his small army thundered toward the city, ranks reforming as they rode. This time there were fewer arrows to contend with; clearly Nasaan's agents within Jezalya had been dealing with the guards. The gate was still open, and through it he could hear the sounds of battle—human cries and collapsing defense structures and the ringing clash of steel-on-steel—while the sun breached the eastern horizon at last, sending lances of harsh golden light spearing across the plain, crowning his men in fire as they rode.

He passed through the city gate with his sword raised, the names of his ancestors a prayer on his lips. And Alwat's name as well, a prayer of gratitude for this improbable victory.

And he rode into the fires of Hell.

And glory.

———————

Jezalya's surrender was finalized in the House of Gods. Nasaan had disdained the splendor of Dervasti's palace as well as the grand plaza where his predecessor had staged official celebrations. The grandeur of such places seemed empty and artificial to him, bereft of true power. Here, in a windowless temple at the edge of the city containing all the gods of the region, was where the true power of Jezalya lay. And Nasaan meant to make it clear to all just who controlled that power now.

Standing in the House of the Gods in his blood-spattered armor, surrounded by several hundred idols, the conqueror of Jezalya received the city's leaders one by one. On all sides of him ancient gods watched silently, gold-chased statues sitting side by side with crude tribal totems, sacred rocks, and even a handful of artifacts whose precise identities had been forgotten long ago. Every tribe in the region had placed an image of its deity here at one time or another, every merchant his patron god, every pilgrim his protector-spirit. Jezalya honored all the gods of the world, and in return, it was said, all the gods of the world protected Jezalya.

Even now the priests would be struggling to work Nasaan's invasion into that narrative. Some were now whispering that the fall of the city must have been the will of the gods all along; Prince Dervasti had displeased the ancient deities, and so they had brought him down. Perhaps it was because he had moved the city's sacred business from the House of the Gods to his grand but soulless palace. Or perhaps he had offered some more subtle insult to the desert deities, out of sight of his subjects. One thing was certain, all the whispers agreed: The city would not have fallen if the gods had not willed it to happen. And if the gods had not wanted Nasaan to take over Jezalya, then he would not have been able to do so.

Nasaan had paid well for those whispers.

Now, as the city's leaders came to him one by one to offer their obeisance, he could feel the eyes of those ancient gods upon him. The fact that he was willing to handle this business in front of them should grant him legitimacy in the eyes of the locals, even if there had been no overt oracular signs in his favor. And he would garner the approval of the priests for choosing to stage his business here, rather than in the opulent, hubristic palace that Dervasti had built. Which was no small thing in a city that was the center of worship for hundreds of tribes. The setting could not possibly serve him better.

One by one his reluctant subjects entered the windowless chamber, bowed to him—with varying degrees of respect—and then approached. There would be no open defiance of him, of course. The row of heads on pikes just outside the city's main gate was a clear warning to anyone who did not like the current state of affairs that his opinion on the matter was not being sought. Whatever misgivings these men might have about the current situation, they would keep it to themselves. But it was not an easy thing to dissemble in the presence of so many gods, and those who had the most to hide from Nasaan were visibly on edge. He took note of their names for later, even while he accepted their formal protestations of loyalty. A newly conquered city was extremely volatile and he meant to watch this one closely.

You are a prince now, he told himself. The title felt strange to him, like ill-fitting armor. Maybe when he washed the blood out of his hair and picked the crusted gore out from under his fingernails it would seem more natural to him.

The lords of the city who had survived his initial purge offered him not only vows of loyalty but generous tribute as well. Some presented him with treasured heirlooms, empowered by generations of tribal reverence. Others brought rare perfumes, precious incense, aromatic spices. Still others placed hemp bags brimming with coins at Nasaan's feet, a simple but eloquent offering. They were all bribes, of course. Those in high office who had survived the conquest were anxious to keep their heads on their shoulders. Others whose positions were less precarious hoped to win the favor of the city's next administrator. And there were offerings from outsiders as well: merchants who regularly passed through the city, travelers who depended upon her generosity, tribal representatives who wanted to make sure that Nasaan did not add their ancestral lands to his military agenda. The new prince would keep half of all the treasure for himself, and the rest would go to his men, a reward for their courage in battle. And especially for their restraint afterward. Most of the city was still standing, and most of its women were unviolated. Such things did not come cheaply.

And then one of Nasaan's warriors stepped into the sacred chamber, glancing anxiously about as he did so. Many of the tribesmen were nervous about being in the presence of so many gods, and were clearly in awe of their leader for feeling otherwise.

"Yes?" Nasaan asked. "What is it?"

"There's a woman to see you." The man hesitated. "She came alone."

Nasaan raised an eyebrow. The few women who had come to see him thus far had all been accompanied by sizable retinues. When they'd been forced to enter the House of Gods without their attendants in tow they had done their best to mask their fear, but Nasaan could smell it on them. Would this new prince respect their status, their alliances, and their families, or consider them the spoils of war? Jezalya had been at peace for long enough that none of them had been through this kind of thing before. None of them knew what to expect.

Yet this woman came to him alone.

"Who is this maverick?" he asked.

"She would not give a name." The man paused. "She said that you would be expecting her."

A chill ran down Nasaan's spine. Only one woman would have reason to introduce herself like that . . . or one creature that was not a woman. Would the gods be angered by a *djira* entering their sacred space? Or would that be deemed an offense only if she claimed to be a god herself?

Drawing in a deep breath to settle the sudden tremor in his stomach, he waited until he was sure that his voice would not betray his unease before he nodded to the man and ordered, "Send her in."

She looked more like a woman now than she had on the field of battle, but he was not fooled by that. Her eyes were human in color and shape now, and the layers of silk that draped her frame lay still about her flesh like normal human garments, but the power that emanated from her person filled the chamber like a costly incense. Sweet, musky, intoxicating. He licked the taste of it from his lips and felt its power pass into his blood. Desire and dread combined, a heady intoxicant.

"You know who I am?" she asked.

The *djiri* did not have names, at least in their natural form. Only when they took on mortal flesh for an extended period of time did they bother with such human trappings. Was she testing him, to see how much he knew about her kind? Even the legends of these creatures—what few there were—offered little clue as to their true motives. Each *djira* was unique, with a nature as mercurial as the shifting sands of the desert. That was part of what made them so dangerous.

"I know what men call you," he answered.

She walked toward him, her dark eyes taking in the piles of gold surrounding them, a flicker of a smile playing across her lips. The presence of so many gods did not seem to concern her at all; her gaze passed over them briefly, then fixed upon the treasure at his feet. "So do you require an offering from me as well?" she asked. "Or is my past service enough?"

She was testing him, he realized. Daring him to haggle with her over the price of her aid. But he knew the ancient legends well enough to know where that would lead him. The *djiri* did not look kindly upon those who tried to wriggle out of their contracts. And he had seen what this one could do to mortal men if she wanted to; he had no desire to be at the receiving end of that kind of power.

"Your service is worth far more than merchant's gold," he said graciously.

"You owe me your victory," she said bluntly.

There was no way to deny it. Lips tight, he nodded.

"Your entire tribe is in my debt as well." The dark gaze was mesmerizing, merciless. "Had I not changed the course of battle, your men would have perished outside the gates of Jezalya. Your women would not have had warriors to protect them after that, when neighboring tribes moved in to claim their land, their wealth, their persons. Within a year your tribe would have perished, and within a generation all its proud history would have been forgotten. Do you not agree?"

He stiffened. "I am the one who made a bargain with you. The price is mine to pay. Leave my people out of it."

"Ah." Her eyes narrowed. "So the new prince is a man of honor. Little wonder that men are willing to die for him."

His expression tightened, but he said nothing.

"Surely such a prince must hunger for more than a single conquest. Surely this one city, no matter how well appointed, would not be enough to satisfy him."

After a long day of battle and bloodshed, Nasaan suddenly found that he did not have the energy for riddles. Not even from a demon. "If you came to name your price, then do so. If not . . ." A spark of defiance took root in his soul. "I have other business to attend to."

Was that anger in her eyes? For a moment it seemed he could sense the supernatural power that was coiled tightly within her, ready to destroy anything and everything in its path. But he was not going to roll over on his back for anyone.

She needs me for something, he thought. *Else she would not go to such effort to expand upon my debt.* Still, he had taken a risk in confronting her. The gods alone knew where that would lead.

"There are cities to the north," she said to him, "even more prosperous than this one. Roads that lead directly to Anshasa and beyond. Bodies of water so vast that you cannot see the far side of them, even on a clear day." Her voice dropped to a whisper, low and seductive, as her power wrapped itself around him; his flesh stiffened as if warm fingers were probing his manhood. "Do you not hunger for those things, my prince? Do you not dream of possessing them? I can help you establish an empire such as most men only dream of."

He drew in a sharp breath. "I imagine it would cost a man his soul to pay for such a service."

"Perhaps," she agreed. "For some. But I am a simple creature, with simple desires. I am content to ally myself with a man of power and bask in his glory." Irony was a black fire in her eyes. "Is that too high a price to ask?"

A shiver ran down his spine as understanding came to him. "You want to rule by my side."

"Every king must have a queen. Even if she is not openly acknowledged as such."

"And what will my people say when I give a creature that is not even human power over them?"

"Your people will know only that you found a woman who pleased you and took her in to serve as your counselor. Whether I appear to be your wife, your concubine, or your queen is irrelevant to me. Only you and I will know the truth. As for having authority over them . . ." A cold, dry smile flickered across her lips. "I offer you my counsel. Nothing more. Take it, and my power will be wedded to your ambition. Deny me, and you will fight your battles alone. That is my offer." *And my threat*, her expression added.

It was a strange offer, coming from a desert spirit. She could easily have demanded more. He was surprised she was not threatening him more openly . . . though the threat lurking between her words was no less powerful for being unvoiced.

"This will satisfy you?" he asked. "Even without public acclaim? It is enough to satisfy my debt to you?"

"To plant the seed of an empire and help it grow to strength? Yes, that will satisfy me." With a smile she stepped forward, closing the space between them. Her strange perfume filled his nostrils as she reached out to touch his chest, slender fingers tracing a thin line of blood that had spattered across his breast-plate. "Besides, I find a man of power . . . enticing."

A sudden rush of heat to his loins cut short his breath. Was it some *djir* spell that was stirring his blood, or just the female power of her presence? He had fought in enough wars to know that a man was quick to arouse in the hours following a battle. *What if she adopts the role of a prince's concubine? Will she play the part in private as well, in all its aspects?* For a moment it was hard for him to think clearly. Then, very slowly, he brought his hand up and closed it over her own. And lifted her hand away from his chest, putting distance between them once more.

"Your price will be met," he said quietly. Feeling the blood pound in his veins, not sure whether desire or ambition was the greater driving force. Never mind that he had just sold his soul to a desert spirit, whose nature and motives were a mystery. She had stirred up a more powerful desire in him than any simple lust. And proven, in doing so, just how well she knew him.

No, he thought. *Jezalya is not enough for me.*

Smiling triumphantly, she stepped back from him. "Then I will leave you to your other business. For now." Her eyes glittered darkly, reminding him of his vision of her on the battlefield. Faceted eyes, black as jet. Such secrets in their depths! Hopefully he would learn their true source before they consumed him.

It struck him as she walked to the door that he should have asked about the winged creature that was at the battle. Too late now. He would have to remember it for later.

"Oh. One thing more." She turned back to face him. "All the

tribes that make their home within your territory and accept your rightful authority, I will protect as though they were my own kin. Those outside your borders, however, are mine to do with as I please." She smiled coldly. "I trust that will not be a problem for you."

This time she did not ask for an answer, nor wait to hear one, but left him alone amidst the city's gods to make his peace with the price of victory.

CHAPTER 2

IT WAS raining by the time Salvator reached the monastery, which did not make his entourage very happy. The servants had managed to get a traveling canopy unpacked when the rain first began, and four of them now carried it high over Salvator's head so that he and his horse could remain dry, but other riders did not have such protection. The guards dealt with it well enough—they never expected to be pampered anyway—but the various courtiers who had come along on the journey in the hope of winning Salvator's favor were less than pleased. Out of the corner of his eye the High King could see one of them struggling to make sure that his cloak covered every single inch of his precious silken garments, lest a drop of water discolor them. Yes, he thought, God alone knew what the state of the kingdom would be if one of the High King's advisers got his clothing wet!

The young monarch was tempted to urge his horse to greater speed, to ride out into the rain ahead of them all, but he knew that the servants carrying the canopy would be mortified if he did so. Besides, he did not need Cresel lecturing him later on all the reasons he should bear himself with proper royal dignity. Or his mother. Even though the sensation of rainwater pouring down upon his head would refresh him body and spirit, washing away the suffocating formality of the royal court, that did not matter. Some things simply could not be allowed.

As the company made its agonizingly slow approach to the monastery gates, Salvator felt a pang of longing for the life that he had once lived within these walls, and for the utter simplicity of his former existence. IIis soul ached for the familiar rhythm of monastic duty, the moral clarity of a life devoted to spiritual ideals. It seemed like a lifetime since he had left those things behind. How long would it be before his spirit finally accepted the change, so that he no longer felt as if he were playing a part in some bizarre play, reading the part of a High King while everyone applauded dutifully?

Evidently the monks had seen his entourage approaching, for the heavy wooden doors opened before the first rider reached them. A robed brother came up to Salvator as he entered the courtyard, holding his horse steady while he dismounted, then leading the animal away. No words were needed, nor were any offered. Other monks tended to his entourage with equally wordless efficiency. Their silence was clearly disturbing to Salvator's courtiers, who were accustomed to a stream of incessant chatter. A few of them even asked the brothers pointless questions in a vain attempt to get them talking, but they received no more than a nod in response, or perhaps a single word at most. Finally the silken magpies settled for prattling amongst themselves, wondering aloud when the current weather might improve, commenting upon how miserable it was to be traveling on such a day, expressing concern that the rain might damage a particular garment. So at least the bad weather was keeping them occupied.

How unlike these chattering birds the brothers of the monastery were! An observer might have guessed them to be from a wholly different species. Nor did they offer up any more deference to their visitors than the absolute minimum that protocol demanded. Such behavior probably would have enraged Danton, who had insisted that all men bend to humble themselves before the Royal Presence. But to Salvator it was refreshing. The Penitents honored and obeyed mortal kings, but they refused to glorify them; true humility was reserved for the Creator alone. Not all rulers were comfortable with such a philosophy, but it suited Salvator well.

"I have come to see the abbot," he told one of the monks. The brother nodded and gestured for him to follow him into the heart of the monastic complex. A handful of royal guards moved to follow the pair, but Salvator waved them back. There was no danger for him in this place.

As he left the courtyard, he saw one of the brothers leading his courtiers to a cloistered walkway where they might escape the worst of the rain. The monastery would be hard pressed to accommodate so many visitors, he mused. Normally there were no more than a handful of pilgrims here at any one time. Well, at least his court peacocks would have something to complain about while he was gone.

He was led past herbal gardens, all too familiar; the fresh scent of rosemary and sage was muted by the rain but still discernable. A bouquet of memory. Salvator let the smells seep into his skin as he walked, and he welcomed the rain that was falling on him as though it were a ritual cleansing bath. There was power in this place—not the kind of power other princes would covet, perhaps, but a subtler thing, a quiet transcendence—and he wanted to drink it all in while he could. God knew, his usual environment was not conducive to meditation.

The abbot was waiting for him in the main cloister. He was a man of advanced age, his face as finely wrinkled as a crumpled sheet of parchment, with a fringe of short white hair balanced on the edge of his skull like an afterthought. Though he was in charge of the monastery and responsible for the spiritual well-being of its community, he had always refused to set himself apart from his charges in any way, and was indistinguishable in dress and manner from the other monks. *We are all brothers in the eyes of the Creator*, he had once told the local primus, disdaining to wear the special robes he had been offered. Humility was the most important lesson for him to teach others, he explained, and how could he do that if he did not embrace it with a full heart himself?

"High King Salvator." The abbot bowed his head stiffly, a formal acknowledgment. "You do us great honor by your visit."

"And you honor me by your hospitality," Salvator responded with equal formality. Suddenly he found himself at a loss as to how to interact with this man, whom he had worked with and prayed beside for four years of his life. His recent change in station had put them on different planes of existence, and he was not sure how to bridge the gap.

"Your people were well received?" the abbot asked.

"Indeed they were."

The abbot coughed into his hand. "And are you sure you brought a large enough company with you? Because I wouldn't want the High King to run short of servants."

The knot in Salvator's gut loosened. He chuckled softly. "I

can't even take a piss these days without a hundred people watching."

"And I am sure that such a custom contributes to the welfare of the nation. Though it is beyond the ability of a simple monk to understand how." A smile spread across his face, refreshing in its easy warmth. "It is good to see you, my son—excuse me, Majesty—though I worry about what sort of business might bring you to this place. I suspect this is not merely a social call."

"No." Salvator's brief smile faded. "Not a social call. But you don't need to call me by title when we're alone, Father. The priest who tamed a wild young prince, and brought him to know and love God, deserves better than that."

The abbot nodded solemnly. "Again, you honor me."

"Is there somewhere we can speak alone?"

He looked about in surprise. Neither the cloister nor its courtyards had anyone else in it. "We are alone here, are we not?"

"No. I mean . . . where we cannot be interrupted."

The abbot looked deep into his eyes, searching for clues there. Could he sense the burden that had driven Salvator to come here, could he guess at its name? If so he showed no sign of it, but merely nodded. "Come, then."

Salvator followed him out of the courtyard, falling into step behind him as naturally as he had back when he had lived here. It would take some time before the habits of those years began to fade, he reflected; in the meantime, it was strangely comforting to let another man lead the way, if only for this short distance.

Very few rooms in the monastery had doors. The abbot led him to one of them, ushered him inside, and shut the heavy oak door behind them. There were a few chairs set neatly along the wall, flanking a narrow window, but Salvator chose to remain standing. If not for the aura of serenity that permeated the entire monastery, he might have started pacing; as it was, his hands clenched and unclenched by his sides as he considered how to broach his business. The abbot waited patiently, his own hands folded inside his sleeves, the living embodiment of tranquility.

"I require counsel," Salvator said at last.

"A king has many counselors," the abbot said quietly. "I am sure they know more about ruling a country than I do. Have they all failed you?"

"This is not about royal business. It is about . . . spiritual matters."

The abbot raised an eyebrow.

"My court advisors are not Penitents," Salvator continued. "They cannot speak to the needs of my soul."

"There are scions of the Church ready and willing to attend upon you," the abbot pointed out. "I would imagine a Penitent king could snap his fingers and the local primus would drop everything to accommodate him."

"Aye, the local primus has come to me," Salvator said dryly. "As have a number of his peers. In truth, I did not know there were so many primi with an interest in my kingdom."

"Your ascension is a significant event for our faith," the abbot said. "They wish to celebrate it."

Salvator nodded tightly.

"So what better counsel could you possibly seek than that which a primus of our Church might offer you?"

A faint smile played upon the High King's lips. "Do you doubt your own capacity, Father?"

The abbot almost rose to the bait—almost—but instead drew in a deep breath and said, "I am what I am, a simple monk, whose experience has been limited to affairs inside this monastery for decades. If you want me to talk about the Creator and man's duty to him, I will be happy to do so. But a High King needs someone who understands the complexities of his office, his secular responsibilities. And I fear I may not be the best choice for that purpose."

Salvator shut his eyes for a moment, then turned away from the abbot. Walking over to the narrow window, he looked out upon the rain-soaked gardens beyond. It was a minute before he spoke.

"The primi are . . . ecstatic to have a Penitent king at last. Intoxicated by dreams of what the Church might become in time, if I would only help them make the most of this opportunity. That is their mission, you see. To determine how my reign can best serve the Church's interests, and to make sure I follow that path."

"You think they would not be objective in counseling you?"

He sighed. "I think that to ask them to be objective would dishonor their calling." Salvator turned back to him. "You may not have their worldly knowledge, Father, but I know you will speak to me from your heart. And that is what I need right now."

For a long moment the monk was silent. His expression revealed nothing of his thoughts. Finally, very slowly, he nodded. "Very well. I will do my best for you."

It was the moment Salvator had been waiting for, but suddenly he found that he did not know how to begin. He had rehearsed his words a hundred times at least, yet all those preparations now deserted him.

Drawing in a deep breath, he struggled to gather his thoughts. "What have you been told about the *lyr*?"

"You mean the recent correction to Church doctrine? That they are now revealed to be an ancient line of witches with some measure of immunity to the Souleaters' power, part of the Creator's overall plan for mankind rather than an unnatural race set apart from it. That the barrier called the Wrath of the Gods is not a curse, nor anything associated with false gods, but simply an ancient spell, imbued with the power of human self-sacrifice." The abbot blinked. "I admit I was . . . surprised . . . but then I heard that you had played a part in that revelation." He smiled faintly. "You have always been full of surprises."

"I was but a spectator," he said with genuine humility. "My mother risked her life to gain access to an ancient artifact that revealed the truth. At the cost of her own faith, I might add."

The abbot nodded. "That is the unfortunate risk of worshiping false gods. One single note of truth and the whole tower of lies collapses." He sighed. "I am glad to learn that the heritage you were so ashamed of has been exonerated. Such shame was never necessary in the first place, but I know it weighed heavily upon your soul."

"The Creator gives us puzzles sometimes," Salvator responded. "To test us. If we mistake their nature, our own error can then become a test in its own right. I do not understand the purpose of all He has done to my mother's family or why He left them in spiritual darkness so long, but I do understand that they are being tested now. What the end game will be, only God Himself can say."

"Do they see their past error now? Or cling to their ancient gods still?"

"Hard to say. Only a handful of *lyr* received my mother's

revelations with any clarity; others experienced only misty visions, easily misread. The Lord and Lady Protector of Kierdwyn—my grandparents—were among those who received the strongest images, but I am not sure how much of that they communicated to their people. They struggle now to find a way to reconcile these new discoveries with their ancient faith, so that when the truth is made public their people will be able to accept it. Whether that will be possible or not I do not know. It must be a terrible thing to suddenly discover that the legends you dedicated your whole life to have no more substance than a minstrel's romance, that your most sacred artifacts were erected by simple stonemasons, and that the greatest miracle of your faith was no more than a mundane witch's spell." He paused. "That said, their purpose has not really changed, has it? The *lyr* have spent a thousand years preparing for the day when the Souleaters would return. They believe they are fated to do battle with them, so that the Second Age of Kings will not collapse in ruin as the First did. Does it really matter who gave them those orders in the first place? The demons are in fact returning. The *lyr* will soon be tested. That much seems indisputable."

The abbot's eyes narrowed. "Has it been confirmed that the Souleaters are back? We've heard rumors that one was seen up north, but no more than that. The Primus Council has made no official statement on the matter."

For a moment Salvator did not answer. There was a black weight upon his soul, and giving its name to another man might lend it more substance.

"Aye," he said at last. His voice was solemn and quiet, the way one might speak at a graveside. "They have returned. We are sure of that. And I think there may be one in the High

Kingdom itself—at least one—though I do not know exactly where."

The abbot breathed in sharply. "I have heard nothing of such a creature in our lands."

Salvator nodded. "I may be the only one who knows about it."

The abbot raised an eyebrow.

Salvator ran a hand through his short black hair, a nervous gesture. "I seem to be . . . aware of its presence. As one might be aware of something just outside the limits of one's vision. Sometimes I awaken at night with a strange scent in my nostrils, as if the thing has actually been inside my chamber—a sweet and smothering scent, that my very soul reviles—yet even though I tell myself it was only a dream, I know deep inside that it was more than that. With the same sure instinct that my mother knew her visions at the Throne of Tears were true, I know that mine are as well." His hand fell back down by his side. "You see now why I have come to you."

"Does your mother know?" the abbot asked quietly.

Salvator shook his head.

"How long has this been going on?"

"I first sensed its presence the night of my coronation. Though I didn't know what it was at the time. Nor did it seem a particularly significant event back then; I thought I was just having bad dreams." He laughed shortly. "I was having a lot of nightmares in those days.

"But night after night the feeling persisted. It would come to me most often in that moment between waking and sleeping, when the soul is most vulnerable to supernatural powers. Something was in the High Kingdom that should not be, I was sure of it, and its nature made my skin crawl. Yet why had I become aware of its presence so abruptly? I had not developed any special powers between one day and the next. All I could think of was that the High Kingdom had become mine that day. No longer my father's territory, or my mother's, but my own. The thing that I was sensing might have been present in it for some time already, but that night it became a threat to me, personally. And so I had become aware of it. Without any idea of what it truly was or what its presence signified." He paused. "I was afraid that if I revealed such thoughts to others, they might deem me mad. I was afraid that I *was* mad. I dared not confide in anyone.

"Then came the Alkali campaign. I traveled up north and met with the Guardians, and they showed me the relics that Rhys had collected. Pieces of an actual Souleater." He shuddered, remembering that day. "As I touched them, as I felt their texture beneath my fingertips, I suddenly smelled that same sweet and foul odor that had come to me so often in the night. And it was as if that scent pulled aside a veil that had been blinding me. Suddenly I knew, with utter certainty, that the presence I had been sensing for so many nights was one of these ancient demons.

"So now I know it for a fact: There is a Souleater in my territory. It seems that I sense its presence as surely as a solitary predator can sense when a rival enters its territory. Animal instinct, visceral and pure." Again he paused. "You understand, Father, I have shared this with no one. Until today."

The abbot nodded solemnly. It was clear from his expression that he did not think Salvator was mad, which was at least a step in the right direction. "If the *lyr* are witches," he said thoughtfully, "then you bear the touch of their witchery in your veins. Given what we know about their history, one should not be surprised by such a manifestation."

"My mother's blood is especially powerful," Salvator provided. "I don't really understand all the details of that, but it's the reason they chose her for the Alkali mission. Apparently she has some special capacity that the other *lyr* don't, a gift that allows her to connect with any descendant of the Seven Bloodlines. That's how she was able to channel the visions from the Throne of Tears to all the other *lyr*."

"And you have inherited her blood. Perhaps her special capacity as well." He paused. "Maybe it's time you talked to her about your visions. She may be able to tell you more about them than I can."

For a moment Salvator shut his eyes. Then he said, very quietly, "It is not that simple."

"Why not?"

Salvator sighed heavily. "After I returned from Alkali, I asked my witches to search the High Kingdom for any Souleaters that might be there. They came up empty-handed. I know the Magisters have been searching for the creatures as well. One of them is bound in contract to my mother—she thinks I don't know that, by the way—and I'm sure she has asked him for help. Yet she is not aware of any Souleater in my Kingdom, so that means Ramirus has not found one either. This demon's mesmeric power protects it from discovery."

"But *you* sense its presence."

Salvator nodded tightly.

"Which implies . . ."

"That I am resistant to its power," he said solemnly.

"That's a good thing, isn't it?"

Steepling his hands upon his chest, Salvator stared down at them in silence for a moment. "When I came to this monastery four years ago, it was because I believed with all my heart that if enough of us did penance for the sins of mankind, the Souleaters would not return to us. That the Destroyer would be appeased by our sacrifice, and spare mankind His wrath. But we failed." His voice dropped to a hoarse whisper. "We *failed*, Father. And now the ancient demons have been sent to us again, to bring down the Second Age of Kings as they did the First.

"So what is our duty as Penitents now? To stand aside and watch the world be destroyed, offering nothing better than lamentations from the sidelines? Are we permitted to hide away the contents of our libraries, so that when human civilization finally collapses our knowledge will be preserved for future generations? Or would that be deemed blasphemy, an attempt to lessen the impact of divine justice? Are we allowed to do battle with these creatures in any way? Or is it our duty to stand aside in the name of the Destroyer, and watch as the most terrible prophecies of our faith are fulfilled?

"These questions are not addressed in our scripture. And I cannot ask the primi for answers. There is too much power in such questions for me to entrust them to any man who cares about power." He spread his hands wide. "So I have brought them here. To you, Father. To hear your thoughts upon these matters."

For a long time the abbot was silent. Finally, very quietly, he said, "I am humbled by your faith in me. But I cannot provide you with answers, you know that. Those you must find for yourself."

"I have not come for answers," he responded. "Only your wisdom, to shed light upon the questions." When the abbot said nothing, he pressed, "The Creator once led me to this place, to become a man of peace. Now He has placed a sword in my hand, such as no other man can wield. If I take it up, will I

betray my faith? I know that if I turn away from it, I may betray my kingdom."

The abbot turned away from him. In silence he stood, still as a statue, a beam of late afternoon sunlight washing over his sandaled feet. Though he did not speak aloud, Salvator knew that he was praying, and he waited.

"The Church has declared that the *lyr* are not abominations," the abbot said at last. "The power in their veins is a natural force, provided by the Creator. Or so we are now told. Would God have provided mankind with such a power if he did not mean for him to use it?"

"The Magisters have power as well," he pointed out.

"The power of the Magisters is an unclean thing, ripped from the heart of Creation and crafted into a foul form that goes against God and nature. Only the blackest of souls wield true sorcery, and any man who is touched by it will share in their corruption."

He turned back to Salvator. "I have read the ancient scriptures. Not only the *Book of Destruction*, which you know of, but other records as well. Forgotten texts, scribed on fragments of parchment so fragile that the touch of a breeze would render them to dust, or incised into clay tablets that have been shattered into a thousand bits, which generations of monks have struggled to reassemble. In all those records—in all the prayers of our ancestors—there is not one word of condemnation for those who fought against the Souleaters in the Great War. I have even seen fragments of an ancient psalm that praised their sacrifice. It is clear that although their mission was doomed, their courage was celebrated. So . . . such actions are clearly not condemned by our faith."

Salvator nodded tightly.

"Whether that is the same answer your primus would give you, I don't know. As you have said, his perspective may be more . . . complex. But for as much as a humble brother may offer you his personal opinion . . . that is mine."

"So now I have two paths before me," Salvator said. "If my highest duty is to God, then which path is the proper one?"

A faint smile flickered across the old monk's face. "Salvator. My son. Why did you set aside your priestly robes when you claimed your father's throne? Remind me."

Startled, he said, "A monk cannot be High King. His vows do not permit it."

"That's not what I asked. You could have remained a priest of our faith, though not a monk. There have been priest-kings before. Why did you give that up, as well?"

"The High Queen required it, as a condition of my elevation."

"And you could have argued with her over the point. Perhaps in time convinced her to change her mind. Yet you didn't even try to do so. Why not?"

Memories stirred in the back of Salvator's mind as he recalled the turmoil of that time. So much uncertainty. So many doubts. "A man cannot serve two causes with equal passion," he said finally.

The abbot reached forward and put a hand on his arm. "Then you did not come here to choose between two paths, Salvator Aurelius. You came to make your peace with what you have already decided."

Salvator shut his eyes for a moment, then nodded.

"The counsel you need now is God's, not mine," the abbot said. "So why don't you join me in the chapel, and unburden your soul to Him? I am sure He can give you more insight into the questions that remain. And perhaps He will quiet the torment in your soul somewhat . . . at least until the next trial begins."

Salvator drew in a deep breath, then nodded.

The abbot walked to the heavy door and opened it. Silently, then, with only the distant patter of rain for accompaniment, the two of them walked side by side toward the chapel.

CHAPTER 3

THE WEATHER was cool when Hedda started toward the river, for which she was grateful. The summer thus far had been a blistering one, which even the thick stands of pine trees surrounding the manor house had been unable to ameliorate. No doubt the Lord and Lady of Valza had scores of servants working to cool them off right now—fanning them with feathers the length of a man's arm, blotting the sweat from their noble brows with silken handkerchiefs, bringing them drinks mixed with ice shavings from the underground storehouse—but for everyone else, work just went on as usual.

She made her way along the twisting path slowly, carefully, not wanting to drop the basket that she carried. Not because her Ladyship would really care if her fine silken garments fell onto the loam—well, she would care if she knew about it, but Hedda wouldn't tell her—but because a far more precious item was bundled on top of the pile, nested deep in the laundry like a rabbit in its burrow.

A baby.

Bands of white linen were wrapped tightly around the tiny

body, so that only his head was visible, and the curious but unfocused eyes danced with patterns of light and shadow as he tried to make sense of what was going on around him. He was Hedda's first child, and while the first few weeks after his birth had been difficult—especially with her Ladyship's rule about new mothers not flagging in their duties—Hedda had now passed beyond the phase when every new morning brought on a fresh wave of panic, and into a euphoric sense of connectedness. It would have seemed unnatural for her to go anywhere without her child now, or to sleep at night without him nestled securely against her side. He was a part of her, as firmly connected as if the blood-filled cord that had once bound them together had not been severed. When he cried, she could feel the sound resonating in her flesh, his distress channeled straight into her heart as if the two of them shared a single body.

She had never known such intense love in all her life.

Humming a child's tune to herself, she finally reached her destination, a place along the riverbank where a flat expanse of rock jutted out over a pool of calm, clear water. Her Ladyship must have her best garments washed in the river, of course. It wasn't good enough that they should be scrubbed in a washbasin along with all the other household linens. No, that water might contain a fragment of dirt from some other garment, that had touched the flesh of another person. Perhaps even (perish the thought!) dirt from a *common* person. One could not allow that to mingle with the sweat of her Ladyship, even in the washwater! Only the pure, running water of the river, cascading down from the distant mountains, was good enough for her linens.

It was rumored that even his Lordship found his wife's excesses a bit odd, but she'd brought him a generous dowry and was attractive enough to make him the envy of other men of his station, so he wasn't about to complain.

Putting down the basket, Hedda worked a few garments out from under the baby, kissed him once on the forehead, and headed toward the water with her washboard. If her Ladyship knew that her fine garments were serving as blankets for a peasant child, she'd no doubt have a fit. Another thing not to tell her.

Hedda had been at work a few minutes and was starting on her second garment when she suddenly became aware that there was someone else present.

Turning back, she scanned the surrounding landscape with a wary eye. This was a safe area, to be sure—his Lordship tolerated no lawlessness in his domain—but you never knew when some local fool might decide to test the boundaries of that governance. Her hand went instinctively to the small knife she wore hanging from her leather belt as she moved closer to the laundry basket, ready to protect her son with all the fierceness of a mother wolf.

And then a child stepped out of the wood. No. She was not a child, though her slight build had caused Hedda to mistake her for such at first. Rather a young girl, somewhere in her early teens, dirty and hollow-eyed. Whoever she was, it appeared to have been some time since she'd had a good meal, for her face was thin and the joints in her bony limbs jutted out like burls. Her long black hair was matted into twisted ropes, in which small bits of forest detritus had become lodged. A wild child, perhaps, lost in the woods at a young age and left to fend for herself. That would explain much about her. It would even account for the one piece of clothing she wore, a relatively clean shift that had clearly been cut for a larger frame. Stolen from someone's laundry basket, no doubt. She'd torn off the bottom of it at knee-length, leaving her dirty feet and legs bare.

But while the rest of her appearance was somewhat odd, it was her eyes that Hedda found most arresting. Almond-shaped, exotic, they stared out at her from under hooded lids with an intensity that was unnerving. Not young eyes, Hedda observed. There was power in that gaze, and also terrible emptiness. The combination was both fascinating and repellant, and she felt drawn to it as one might be drawn to the sight of a mysterious animal lying dead by the roadside, wondering whether it was dead or alive.

"Who are you?" she asked her, trying not to sound as uneasy as she felt.

The girl did not answer. She did not stir. Even the breeze seemed to pass by without touching her, and her flesh might have been carved from stone for all the vitality it possessed.

"Do you want some food?" Hedda offered. Wanting to make the girl speak, or move, or . . . do something. Her left hand remained on her knife as she indicated the small bundle of provisions she'd brought with her, tucked into the basket beside her son. Thank the gods, the little one was sleeping quietly right now, nestled so deeply into the layers of laundry that it was unlikely the strange girl could see him. "I have enough to share."

The visitor did not appear to understand her words, but she watched intently as Hedda crouched down, unwrapping a square of worn linen cloth from the thick heel of bread and slab of hard cheese that it guarded. Breaking off a piece of each, she moved away from the basket and held them out to the girl.

Hunger flashed in her eyes—or so it seemed to Hedda—but still she did not move.

"It's all right. I have enough. Please, take it."

Again she held it out to her. Again the girl did not respond.

Slowly, warily, her hand still upon her knife, she walked a short distance toward the girl. She was close enough to detect her smell now, an odd mix of stale sweat and sweet musk. Like the rest of her, it was both fascinating and repellent. "Here." She lowered herself carefully, never letting down her guard, and placed the bread and cheese on a flat rock nearby. "This is for you."

She backed away.

For a moment she thought the girl was still not going to move. Then the thin limbs stirred, and she began to walk slowly toward the food, her eyes never leaving Hedda's. Her movements were angular and ungraceful, but it seemed more a consequence of habit than of weakness; she picked her way over the rough terrain like a bird might, head jerking with each step. When she reached the food, she glanced down briefly, just long enough to pick it up, and then her eyes fixed on Hedda once more as she bit deeply into the piece of bread, tearing loose a chunk and swallowing it whole, as an animal might gulp down meat.

Heart pounding, Hedda watched her eat. That she was hungry was clear enough. That she was something other than a young girl lost in the woods—for however long—was becoming equally clear. What if this were some sort of supernatural visitation? Hedda had heard tales of spirits who took on human form to work mischief; might not one of them look just like this? Her hand closed instinctively about the hilt of her knife as she watched the girl finish off the last of the offering. Should she give her the rest of the food? Sometimes spirits would leave you alone if you were generous enough. At least that's what her grandmother had told her. Hedda wished she'd paid more attention to the old woman when she was a child, so she might know what sort of spirit this was and how she could get it to go away.

Finally the girl was finished eating. She looked at Hedda for a moment, then started down the slope toward her.

Hedda drew in a sharp breath. There was nothing overtly threatening about her, but every instinct in her maternal heart was crying out for her to keep this strange girl away from the baby. But had the girl even seen him? If Hedda moved the basket away from her now, wouldn't that just reveal how precious its contents were? Frozen with indecision, she settled for positioning herself over the basket, so that the stranger would have to go through her to get to her baby. Much as a mother wolf might position herself over her cub while the shadow of a hawk passed over them both.

The girl came close. Too close. Her sickly sweet smell filled Hedda's nostrils as she picked her way down the hill, closing the distance between them.

Stay back, Hedda thought. Her hand tightened on her knife.

And then the girl was directly in front of her. Those strange hooded eyes locked on her own, transfixing her. Such darkness in those eyes! Such hunger! Their form and color was human, but their substance was something very different. An alien madness, nameless and terrible, seemed to shimmer in their depths.

"Stay back," she whispered. Suddenly very afraid.

The world began to spin about her. She tried to draw her knife from its sheath, but it fell from her hand and clattered to the ground beside the basket. She heard the sound as if from a distance. Too late, it occurred to her that she must have been bewitched. She should have grabbed up the basket and run away while she'd still had the chance, she realized.

It was too late now.

She tried to scream, but her voice would not come. She tried to run, but her body would not obey her. She tried to pray, but the gods did not respond.

Stay back!

The world began to fade around her. Colors seeped out of the landscape like dye bleeding out of a wet garment. A sudden wave of vertigo overcame her, and it took all her strength not to be sick. And then—

The sky overhead was clear and blue.

The girl was gone.

Blinking, Hedda swallowed back on the sour taste in the back of her throat, trying to get her bearings. A breeze gusted briefly across her face, chilling the film of sweat on her skin. Every muscle in her body ached, as though she had just run a long distance.

Weakly, she raised herself up on one elbow. She must have passed out and fallen. Some yards away, the pile of laundry she'd been working on was nearly dry now. Hours must have passed since she had lost consciousness.

The basket was a few feet away from her. Thank the gods she hadn't landed on top of it and crushed the baby! Pushing herself up to a sitting position, she reached out and pulled it toward her. Her hands were shaking as she did so, and she muttered an apology to her poor child for leaving him alone for so long. How hungry he must be!

Then she looked into the basket, and her heart froze in her chest.

Her son was gone.

She could see the hollow place where he had last rested. If she lowered her face to that spot, she could still smell him there, his scent intermingled with that of her Ladyship's sweat. But there was another smell there as well, foreign and foul, that made bile rise in the back of her throat.

She turned away just in time. Waves of sickness wracked her body, and she vomited beside the basket. Horror and loss were expelled in a gush of foul-tasting liquid, again and again, until finally her body—like her soul—was empty. Then she lay on her side on the hard, cold granite, wrapped her arms around her chest, and began to shiver violently, as if winter's cold had descended upon her. She was so lost in spirit now that she no longer knew where she was, or even exactly what had happened . . . only that a part of her soul had been stolen away from her and she did not know how to go on without it.

Later, when her mind could function again, she would think about following the girl's trail. Later her husband would remind her that a skilled woodsman would know what signs to look for, and if an ordinary man couldn't find them, then a witch certainly could. They'd find the money to hire one, somehow. He would promise her that.

For now, she simply wept.

CHAPTER 4

*T*HE LAND *stretches out in all directions as far as the eye can see. Dry earth, cracked and gray, crumbles to dust beneath Colivar's feet. Here and there a tiny sapling has taken root, but only precariously; the narrow leaves, thin and dry, curl defensively beneath the blazing sun.*

Kneeling in the dirt, he struggles to tend to the saplings. Now and then he pours water over one of them from the wooden bucket by his side, but it is never enough. The ground soaks up the precious stuff within seconds, entrapping it too deeply for the saplings' shallow root system to access. And there are so many of them! Even if the water were able to do them any good, he hasn't got enough to supply them all. Some of them are clearly going to have to die so that the rest might live.

A shadow passes overhead. Wiping the sweat from his brow with a dirt-stained sleeve, he looks up at the sky. The southern sun is a cruel thing, and its heat drains the strength from a man's body in a manner that he will never get used to. It takes him a moment to focus his eyes against the blazing light and to see what is up there, silhouetted against the sun.

Wings.

Jeweled panels of living glass filter the sunlight, sending shadows of blue and green and violet shimmering across the parched earth. When they pass over the saplings, the slender plants seem to tremble in response. Then, one by one, the plants wilt and fade, shrinking down into the ground until there is nothing of them but desiccated skeletons, crumbling in the hot wind.

The sweat of utter frustration films Colivar's skin as he watches. His exhaustion is physical, but also spiritual. For he was the one who planted these saplings, so long ago, and each one that dies now takes a part of him with it.

You knew back then that they would probably die, *he tells himself.* You promised yourself you would not come to care about them. Remember?

One of the violet shadows is headed his way. He throws himself down over the nearest sapling, shielding it with his body. But when the shadow has passed and he rises again, he sees that he has crushed it beneath his own body. Killed it.

What a fool he was, to think that a creature such as he could nurture life!

A Souleater has landed on the ground before him. Its long neck undulates like a serpent as its head seeks out the remaining saplings, and it begins to yank them from the earth. It is one indignity too many for Colivar. Rage lends new strength to his aching limbs as he braces himself to confront the creature, to drive it away or die trying.

And then its form shifts. Colors shimmer in the sunlight, blue-black hide and jeweled wings rippling as they transform into . . . something else.

A woman.

Siderea.

"Forget this place," his ex-lover whispers. "Forget all that you have

become since you cheated death so long ago. Let go of your human half, and I will make a place for you by my side. You know that is what you really want. It's the same thing you've always wanted. I can give it to you now."

The human part of his brain recognizes the trap for what it is, but the other half, the forgotten half, does not care. His blood is stirred by the sound of her words, the scent of her flesh. Suddenly the saplings do not matter to him anymore. Memories are taking over now, of a life he has struggled for centuries to forget. The agonizingly beautiful downstroke of jeweled wings. The cold, fierce wind cutting into his skin. The anguish of his rivals as they spiral down into blackness, to be shattered on the rocks far below.

No! *His human self cries out a warning, but he no longer speaks its language.*

Stumbling, he begins to move toward her.

And her body shimmers again.

And changes.

It takes him a minute to recognize what form she is taking now. When he does, the shock of it stops him dead in his tracks.

The red-headed witch smiles at him. "Hello, Colivar." *Hearing her voice, the Souleaters overhead wheel about and begin to head toward her.* "I hear you've been looking for me."

———

Colivar awakened with a start.

For a moment he just lay there in bed, his heart pounding. Then, with a quick gesture of conjuration, he lit the lamps on the far side of the room. Amber warmth filled the space, soft and reassuring. He drew in a deep breath and bound enough athra to quiet his pounding heart. But mere sorcery could not quiet his spirit.

It was a dream, he told himself. *Nothing more.*

Of course, even his dreams were suspect now. If Siderea had found a new source of power, she might well be playing with the minds of her ex-lovers. Courtesy had stayed her hand in the past—or perhaps just the thought of what the Magisters would do to her if they caught her using witchery on them—but there were no limits in her world now. And Colivar knew from examining the emotional traces she had left behind in Sankara just how much she hated the Magisters. True, his dream had contained some references to things Siderea could not possibly know about, so the whole of the dream had not been sent by her, but that didn't mean that some part of it hadn't been, and his own mind had dressed it up with additional details.

And then there was the matter of the red-headed witch.

He remembered how casually Kamala had used her power in Kierdwyn. As if it cost her nothing. And he remembered the chill echoes of sorcery that he had detected in her abandoned room in Gansang. They'd assumed at the time that those had been the mark of some unnamed Magister who was acting as her patron, but now that he'd had a chance to observe her more closely, he was willing to bet that she walked—and worked—alone. Which left only one possible conclusion.

Call her a Magister, he dared himself.

There was so much power in that title! And, of course, one's own identity was revealed in how one applied it. If Ramirus were to name Kamala a Magister, he would merely be stating that she had mastered sorcery and now lived as a parasite, robbing morati of their lives in order to sustain her own. But Colivar understood more about the Magisters' true nature than Ramirus did. For him, the title resonated with myriad forgotten secrets, fears and failures and betrayals that the others of his kind were not even aware of. If he called a witch by that forbidden name, he would be declaring that she was a part of a complex tapestry they did not even know existed . . . and that she carried the seed of Colivar's own personal torment within her-veins.

How strangely arousing that thought was! It stirred his blood in ways he had not felt in some time. And it raised all sorts of questions about his own nature, questions he'd thought were settled long ago. A heady combination for any Magister.

But most important of all, it gave him something to think about other than Siderea's palace and the presence that he had detected there. Which had caused him many a sleepless night already, and would doubtless continue to do so.

Sorcery had yet to find a cure for nightmares.

By the time Colivar arrived at the meeting, the others were already there. He could sense their presence before he entered the room, and for a moment he hesitated, wondering if he really wanted to join them. The presence of other sorcerers was disturbing enough on a good day, and the fact that he had detected the scent of a Souleater queen at Siderea's palace was not helping matters. It was one thing to find a nest full of eggs and speculate that at some point a queen might have passed through the area, but it was another to drink in that intoxicating scent with every breath, to feel the magical traces of a queen's presence vibrate beneath your fingertips, and to know that a former lover might now be bound to her, sharing that ultimate intimacy.

All things considered, he would much rather go home right now and isolate himself with his thoughts than have to face others of his kind. But he needed the information that would be shared in this meeting; there was simply no way around that. And so, drawing in a deep breath, he pushed open the door and entered the chamber, trying to look more composed than he felt.

Lazaroth, Ramirus, and Sulah stood respectfully as he entered. They had positioned themselves on three sides of a heavy trestle table, using the piece of furniture as a shield between them. At one time Colivar might have been amused by that, but these days even the most casual gesture seemed ominous to him. The beast that lay coiled at the heart of each Magister understood what its relationship to its own kind was—even if its host was not consciously aware of it—and was perpetually bracing itself for combat.

"Magisters." Colivar acknowledged Lazaroth's role as host with a brief nod of respect, then took the place that had been prepared for him, at the fourth side of the table. Power rippled between the Magisters in the warm Kierdwyn air, tendrils of sorcery testing, anticipating, exploring. There was a time when so many Magisters could not even have been in the same room together, much less shared any kind of civilized conversation. Colivar glanced at Ramirus, and saw by the furrowing of his brow that he was remembering that time, too. Sometimes it seemed like yesterday. Should they have taught their apprentices more about that part of their past? For Colivar that would have required too much explanation, too much vulnerability. He had secrets that required forgetfulness. And doubtless Ramirus had made a similar choice. So now the younger Magisters were defined by their ignorance, just as the older ones were by their memories. Colivar thought he knew which category Lazaroth fell into, but with sorcerers you could never be sure; a man might change his flesh and play the role of a newcomer just for the novelty of it. Only when you brought a man through First Transition yourself did you know for certain just how old he was.

"Ramirus, Colivar, Sulah . . . I thank you for coming." Lazaroth nodded to each of them in turn. "Back when you all assisted with the Alkali campaign, I promised to keep you informed of what we discovered there. Today I will make good on that promise. Please feel free to ask any questions you like, and if you have information to offer in return, it would certainly be welcome." A corner of his mouth twitched: the fleeting hint of a cold smile. "Admittedly, our kind are generally more disposed to hoarding information than sharing it. But I think you will agree that the return of an ancient enemy calls for new strategies.

"Kierdwyn's Seers have investigated the breach in the Wrath. Independent witches from Alkali were also brought in, to confirm their findings. I would not have chosen to trust the Alkali in this matter had I been the one making that decision, but the breach took place inside that Protectorate, so Lord Kierdwyn felt they could not rightfully be excluded."

No doubt the delicate Seers would have preferred to march straight into Hell itself rather than get within range of the Wrath, Colivar thought. The willingness of the Guardians to sacrifice themselves never ceased to amaze him. Then again, were they not descended from the same witches and warriors who had offered up their lives centuries ago, to save the world from ruin? Sacrifice was in their blood. They sucked it in along with their mothers' milk.

Yet even such a heritage can be corrupted, he thought soberly. *Even a hero may do terrible things, if circumstances drive him to it.*

"Apparently a number of ikati have already crossed into the south," Lazaroth continued. "As we feared might be the case."

"How many?" Sulah asked.

He shook his head. "Unclear. The impressions are hard to detect, for obvious reasons. Very few of the creatures made physical contact with the terrain—at least in the places we have searched—so there are few anchors to focus on. Most of the traces that do exist appear to have been left by a single Souleater, apparently connected with Nyuku."

"Nyuku?" The color drained from Colivar's face so quickly that he could not stop it. The sorcerous tendrils surrounding him began to prick at his mental armor like a thousand tiny spears, seeking insight into his reaction; it took all his skill—and emotional composure—to fend them off. He could not afford to let these Magisters see how much that name stirred his blood, lest they guess at the cause.

Nyuku is here. In my world. The name sent emotions surging through his veins that he thought he'd conquered long ago. Deep inside, where none of the other Magisters could see, he trembled.

But if Lazaroth noticed his guest's discomfort, he showed no sign of it. "Aye. The name was cited several times in Anukyat's records, as that of the Kannoket who negotiated with him. He may have played a leadership role in the invasion or simply been left behind to guard its flank. Either way, he left his mark all over the terrain, as did one particular Souleater. The fact that those two traces were almost always found together would seem to imply there was some kind of working relationship between them, though we haven't yet determined its nature. When Nyuku left Alkali, after Anukyat's death, apparently the Souleater did so as well." He paused. "All in all, my witches estimate that approximately three dozen Souleaters crossed through the breach. A guard has now been established to watch for any new arrivals, but I suspect that plan will amount to . . . " He sighed. "I believe the applicable phrase is, 'shutting the barn door after the horse has left.'"

Most of the colony must have come south, Colivar thought. He was stunned by the revelation. How could they all have managed the crossing? Even with one of the Spears damaged, the Wrath still remained a formidable barrier. Only the strongest individuals should have been able to cross it.

Or the weakest.

Cold. The memories were so cold. Colivar felt an urge to wrap his arms about himself, as if that could somehow ward them off. Cursing silently, he forced himself to relax his body instead. But it was too late. Ramirus had clearly taken note of his fleeting disquiet, and his eyes were fixed on Colivar now, trying to determine its cause. Though direct sorcerous inquiries would net him nothing, human insight alone was a powerful tool. Colivar would rather face a hundred sorcerers on the battlefield than try to keep secrets from this one.

"You know this Nyuku?" Ramirus asked him quietly.

Colivar knew that he would have to choose his lies carefully; he could not afford to make a mistake with this many Magisters present. "Long ago . . . as you know . . . I lived in the north. There were rumors back then of someone who had crossed the Wrath and lived to talk about it. I heard the name Nyuku mentioned. Whether that was the same man I do not know."

"What else did you hear about him?" Lazaroth asked.

You mean, what else that I am willing of speak of? He drew in a deep breath, his mind racing as he tried to decide just how much information to offer up. Too little would just convince them that he was hiding something important. Too much would lead to questions he dared not answer. "It was said that north of the Wrath there were men who had established some sort of partnership with the Souleaters. Each man was allied to a particular ikati in a sort of . . . spiritual union. Supposedly the creatures were willing to carry these men upon their backs. They had to be mutilated in order to make that possible—some of the dorsal spikes had to be removed—but I guess the ikati found that acceptable. Or so legends claimed, back then." He glanced at Ramirus. "The one that Rhys killed had been mutilated thus. That is why I guessed what I did about its origins."

"Aye," Ramirus said thoughtfully. "I remember that."

Sulah's eyes narrowed skeptically. "Tradition says that any man who comes too close to a Souleater will be drained of life. But that can't be the case if men are using them for transport."

Colivar shrugged stiffly. "These were only tales that I heard, many centuries ago." Would his tone sound truthful enough? This was dangerous ground. "I cannot even vouch for their source, much less their accuracy."

"So it may be that this Nyuku and his Souleater were such a pair," Lazaroth said thoughtfully. "That would certainly explain the traces we found."

"And I think possibly we have seen another one," Ramirus said.

"You mean Kostas?" Sulah asked. "That was Danton's Magister Royal, yes?"

"Perhaps," Ramirus said. "Or perhaps he was something else, that simply posed as a Magister. Do not mistake me: He did have real power at his disposal. Enough to convince Danton that he was one of us. But according to my investigations, all his spells were small ones. Showy on occasion, but always limited in scope. So he might have been using some kind of witchery rather than true sorcery." He paused. "Or perhaps there is a third variant of power that we do not yet know about, which these invaders wield. At any rate, the appearance of a Souleater within minutes of Kostas' death certainly suggests they were connected. And if the stories Colivar heard are correct . . . then the mutilation we saw would imply that both of them were from north of the Wrath."

"If Kostas and Nyuku were working together," Lazaroth said, "then I think we can guess at their intentions. Nyuku used Anukyat to manipulate the Alkali Guardians, and through them an entire Protectorate. Kostas sought a position as counselor to one of the most powerful men on the continent. They seek control over morati society."

"Predators with political aspirations," Ramirus mused. "Interesting."

"How many do you think are playing that game?" Sulah asked. "Passing themselves off as locals—or Magisters—as they quietly move into positions of authority?"

Ramirus shook his head sharply. "Not many are likely to be successful at that game. Remember, this Nyuku kept to the shadows for as long as he could. He never tested his disguise at court. And Kostas, who lived more openly, was peculiar enough in his demeanor that even Danton's servants took note of it. Such men are easy to pick out once the full light of day shines upon them."

"Aye," Lazaroth mused, "I remember hearing rumors that Danton's new Magister was not a human being at all, but rather some kind of malevolent spirit. Perhaps even a demon." He shrugged. "Magisters collect rumors about them the way whores collect trinkets, so I didn't bother to investigate. But perhaps these invaders don't play the human game as well as they think they do. If so, that's a factor we can exploit."

"When did the Alkali invasion begin?" Colivar asked him. "Do we have any idea?"

"All the traces we could find appear to be recent," Lazaroth told him. "Our best guess is that the crossing began earlier this year. Master Favias says that the Alkali Guardians stopped visiting the other Protectorates a few months ago, and disturbances in the Wrath were also noted about the same time. We are guessing that is the most likely time frame."

Colivar nodded. "Which means that Kostas was a newcomer to our world when he first appeared at Danton's court. His people had been isolated for centuries, trapped in one of the harshest regions on earth, with beasts as their closest companions. Our entire world was alien to him. Sorcery could have provided him with the raw knowledge he needed to walk among us, to speak our language, and not to make major gaffs, but internalizing all that knowledge would have required time and practice. He might have planned to put more time into training before making his public debut, had Ramirus not forced his hand by leaving Danton's service prematurely. An opportunity that could not be missed. Under the circumstances, it's to his credit that he managed to appear as human as he did.

"But those who follow after him will not necessarily suffer from the same handicaps. The longer these invaders are in our world, the more time they will have to perfect their masquerade. And even if there are still signs that give such men away, how do you propose we seek them out? With Magisters it is easy to say 'all new faces are suspect' and investigate anyone who made his first appearance among us in the past few months, but there are far too many morati in the world to support that kind of strategy. Can you imagine the chaos that would ensue if the human hordes found out that any stranger in their midst might be the vanguard of an invading army? The streets would run red with blood."

Ramirus' deep-set eyes fixed on him. "Do you really believe that a man from such an alien world could adapt himself perfectly enough to this one to become indistinguishable from . . . say . . . you or me?"

Colivar drew in a sharp breath. Did Ramirus mean that question to be the double-edged sword it was? Or was it just an accident of phrasing? He kept his voice carefully neutral as he responded, "Human beings are extraordinarily adaptable. In time . . . with sorcery and sufficient practice . . . yes, I believe such a man might be able to pass as human. A *normal* human, that is." He looked at Ramirus and added, "Well enough to fool even you."

"And such a masquerade may not be necessary for all of them," Lazaroth pointed out. "Not if they have allies in the southern kingdoms."

For a moment there was silence. The name of Siderea Aminestas hung in the air between them, unvoiced but not unacknowledged.

"Ramirus. Sulah." Lazaroth leaned forward, steepling his fingers on the table before him. "You, like myself, never patronized the great whore. Colivar . . . I've heard that she collected tokens from her lovers, to serve as anchors for her witchery. But that she no longer has yours. Is that true?"

"She used it to call me to her in Corialanus," Colivar responded. "And I did not replace it. So yes, that much is true."

"Is there anyone else for whom that is the case?"

Colivar hesitated. "Fadir was summoned the same day that I was, so his token was also destroyed. I don't know if he ever replaced it. Or how many other Magisters she might also have summoned the same day, who chose not to respond. But matters with Siderea went downhill very quickly after that; I would be surprised if any Magister would have been willing to give her a new token once he saw what was happening to her."

Lazaroth nodded. "So five of us know for a fact that we are free of her influence. How many others can say the same?"

Colivar's eyes narrowed slightly. "The tokens you speak of are destroyed by even the most casual use. The owner's trace is tenuous at best, and will not support a spell of any significance. Such items would not have been given to a morati if they had any real power."

"I credit you with believing that," Lazaroth said coldly, "though I am sure you would tell me the same story even if you didn't. That said, I also credit Queen Siderea with being intelligent enough to know how to leverage those bits of power to greatest effect."

"Without doubt," Ramirus muttered.

"A man's purpose can be swayed by a single dream, his plans undermined by a single well-placed doubt. The men who gave her tokens were her lovers, her companions, her advisers—which means that she knows them as well as any morati can. Are you going to tell me now, with absolute certainty, that she would not know how to conjure such a dream, or insert such a doubt? Or that such tokens could not help her target Magisters with an even greater act of witchery, by circumventing their normal defenses?"

For a moment Colivar said nothing. Even the thoughts in his head were still. "No," he said at last. "I can't tell you that."

Lazaroth leaned back in the chair, his expression darkly triumphant. "From what I hear, her ex-lovers are scouring the world to figure out where she has gone. They want their toys back. Yet it seems that no sorcery can find her. Nor can it locate the Souleaters. Three dozen demons may be loose in our world, and the most powerful men in existence cannot conjure up so much as a piddling clue as to where they went. That worries me, Magisters. It worries me a lot." He paused, then suggested quietly, "Perhaps we should be worrying about it together."

Ramirus raised an eyebrow. "You are proposing some kind of cooperative effort?"

"You know as well as I do what will happen if we fail to get this situation under control."

"That was not my question."

Lazaroth nodded. "Then, yes, I am suggesting we four pool our efforts. And we could invite Fadir to join us, if you think he would be an asset. But no others. For the reasons already discussed."

"Others could not be trusted," Colivar said. The irony of the concept amused him.

"Precisely."

Colivar looked at Ramirus. The expression on the Magister's face was neither surprised nor derisive. In fact, Ramirus had told Colivar a while back that some kind of cooperative effort might become necessary in time. Doubtless he was contemplating whether this particular effort was the one he'd been waiting for.

If Ramirus is still working for House Aurelius, Colivar mused, *then we serve rival monarchs once more. Will he commit to becoming my ally in one war while we are still enemies in another?*

But of course he knew the answer to that. Ramirus lived for

this kind of challenge. The fact that it might prove genuinely dangerous only added spice to the game. How many things were there in the world that could threaten a Magister in any meaningful way?

The white-haired Magister nodded slowly, his fingers stroking his long beard as he spoke. "Your argument is a bit unorthodox, Lazaroth, but there is no denying its merit. I am skeptical about how well the details will play out, but it's clear we've come to a crossroads here, and we cannot just stagger blindly forward.

"I for one am old enough to remember the Dark Ages. I do not wish to return to that time. Ever." He nodded shortly. "So yes. I would be willing to share information with this company, as it pertains to the Souleater invasion. To see what our common resources can make of it."

"As would I," Sulah offered.

Lazaroth looked at Colivar. There was a challenge in his eyes.

"I will do the same," Colivar said quietly.

How carefully you crafted that promise, Ramirus! Promising the world but committing to nothing. Was that for my benefit? Did you fear that I would shy away from a commitment to share everything I knew? Or were you just wary of making such a promise yourself?

You have always hungered after my knowledge, and now you have a context in which to lay claim to it. How pleased you must be that Lazaroth's plan serves your agenda so well!

Of course, he mused, that was probably not a coincidence. Ramirus was not the kind of Magister who left things to chance. The only question was whether he had actually conspired with Lazaroth or had relied upon more subtle means to manipulate him into doing what he wanted. Knowing Ramirus as well as he did, Colivar guessed the latter was more likely.

My ancient and esteemed rival, he thought soberly, *you are more dangerous to me than all the Souleaters put together.*

Given his personal history, that was a truly daunting thought.

———

Standing on the walkway that edged the roof of Kierdwyn Castle, observing how the late afternoon sun shimmered on the snow-capped mountains to the north, Colivar waited. Normally he would have left the Protectorate as soon as Lazaroth's meeting was over, but he still had one more piece of business to take care of.

Then the iron-banded door opened, and a Magister stepped through.

Ramirus.

Colivar nodded as the other man came to where he stood and gazed out at the view by his side. Colivar said nothing immediately, just ran his finger along the edge of the parapet, pausing to note where a dark stain marked the coarse stone. "I gather there was a suicide here once," he said in a companionable tone.

Ramirus glanced down at the mark. "Almost. It was interrupted."

Colivar bound enough sorcery to identify the blood's owner. "Rhys."

Ramirus nodded. "The despair of a man who suddenly discovers that he has betrayed someone he cares about can drive him to desperate extremes. It also makes for an interesting study."

"A death wish that strong is never completely overcome," Colivar said quietly, "though it may take on other guises. Sometimes the thing we call 'courage' is simply its public face."

Ramirus raised an eyebrow. "You think Rhys' courage was no more than that? A death wish?"

"No. I researched his history, and I'm satisfied he was a genuine martyr. Rare as that breed may be. But I wonder . . . had he hungered for life in his final hours, the way men naturally do, might it have made a difference? Might he have made different choices at key moments? Leading to different paths, different options, and ultimately a way to accomplish his goal without dying?" He shrugged. "I was not at the battle, so I don't know all the details of what went on there. But it's an interesting question to contemplate."

Ramirus snorted softly. "You wax philosophical tonight."

Colivar shrugged. "Perhaps the current state of the world brings out the philosopher in me." He wiped his finger on his shirt, leaving a streak of dust behind. "The Alkali campaign was interesting, at any rate. With some interesting participants. I was especially intrigued by the witch who helped us out. The red-headed one. What was her name?"

"Kamala?"

"A curious creature. What did you make of her?"

Ramirus shrugged. "She is very skilled. She knows her art. She also knows Magister customs better than outsiders usually do; I would not be surprised to learn that she served as companion to a Magister at one point." He stared out at the mountains once more. "I found it easy to read her emotions, impossible to read her soul. Sorcery slides right off her—but I am sure you know all that."

"She used her power very freely," he suggested.

"A woman in love does foolish things, sometimes. And a man, for that matter. I have seen witches burn up their final athra for less." He looked at Colivar curiously. "You have a special interest in this woman?"

"I have a special interest in any witch willing to expend her life-essence for a cause. If we can find enough of them, the Magisters can keep to the sidelines in this war."

Ramirus chuckled. "The Magisters will keep to the sidelines anyway. You know that. Men cannot fight against a common enemy when they are more interested in fighting each other."

"But now we have an *alliance*," Colivar reminded him. A faint smirk attended the word.

"Ah. Yes." Ramirus smiled dryly. "We shall see how much that accomplishes."

"You think Lazaroth really believes in it?"

"I think Lazaroth wants to know where Siderea Aminestas is, and everything else he said was merely to distract us. Why he would care so much about her is a question for another day. However, even an imperfect alliance can prove useful. War is indisputably on the horizon, and having us each do reconnaissance separately is a waste of time and resources. Now, how *much* information will be shared between us . . . that is another matter." His cold gaze fixed on Colivar. "But you know that, of course."

"I have provided a good deal of information already," he pointed out.

"Yes," Ramirus' blue eyes glittered in the moonlight. "And when I get home I shall work on figuring out which parts of it were true, and which were no more than artful diversions."

Colivar hesitated. For a moment he seemed to be considering how much to say. At last he offered, "Here is a bit of truth for you. I will be severing my ties to Anshasa."

Ramirus' smile faded. Colivar knew him well enough to catch the sudden spark of interest in his eyes and to feel the cold touch of his power as it probed his defenses, seeking even the faintest hint of his true motivation. But Colivar had woven multiple layers of sorcery about himself to ward off just such an inquiry. Some subjects were significant enough that they merited powerful protection. "You think this matters to me. Why?"

"You and I have served warring monarchs for a generation. It's been good sport, Ramirus. But I don't think Salvator hungers for power the way his father did. Which means that King Farah no longer needs to worry about Aurelius aggression . . . or yours. A lesser Magister can take care of his needs now, so I am free to focus on more important things." His black eyes narrowed as he studied Ramirus intently, aggressively casting out nets of sorcery to pick up any stray trace of emotion that might slip past that flawless mask. No doubt his old rival sensed the effort, though his expression revealed nothing. "So you see, one long-standing barrier between us will soon be removed."

For a moment Ramirus just stared at him. No doubt he could sense the sorcerous tendrils Colivar was using to prod at his soul, seeking more information on the subject. "I think you mistake me," he said at last. All emotion had been deliberately stripped from his voice; and his expression was unreadable as stone. "I have no contract with the High King. So your political machinations are . . . irrelevant."

And then, without further word, he turned and walked back the way he had come, commanding the iron-bound door to open for him as he approached, then closing it behind him as he passed into the castle. He spared no parting word for Colivar, or even a parting glance.

Colivar chuckled softly. He was not surprised by his abrupt exit. Clearly Ramirus had been less than certain he could mask his emotions on the level required to fend off Colivar's sorcery. He'd wanted to get out of range before some stray wisp of emotion could be captured and analyzed. That was fine with Colivar. That Ramirus had sensed his inquiry in the first place, and knew how much Colivar wanted information pertaining to his contract with House Aurelius, was really all that mattered. Now Ramirus would deduce that the first part of their conversation had been meaningless small talk, designed to put him off his guard. What Colivar had *really* wanted to know, he would tell himself, was which Magister was allied to the High King; all the rest had been a distraction. Colivar had already given himself away with his protective spells, wrapping them so tightly around his own thoughts when discussing the Aurelius situation that it was clear that was his true interest.

Lies within lies within lies. Ramirus would spend the next few hours teasing the threads of the exchange apart, trying to determine which words had really mattered, versus which ones had been intended just to throw him off the scent. Did Colivar care more about learning who Salvator's Magister Royal really was, or about Anshasa's political standing in general? Colivar had layered his every word with sorcery, suppressing all hints of genuine emotion, so that Ramirus would have to fall back upon the mundane sorts of clues that came from a man's tone of voice, his expression, his posture . . . and of course, the knowledge that a Magister only guarded his privacy that fiercely when there were secrets he needed to protect.

Meanwhile, the one piece of information that Colivar had really cared about—the reason he'd invited Ramirus here to talk to him in the first place—would be categorized as trivial misdirection and disregarded.

Which had been the plan all along, of course.

He does not know what Kamala is.

Ramirus had clearly not made the connection yet between

the woman who'd helped them in Alkali and the one who had killed Magister Raven in Gansang. Which meant that Colivar's earlier speculation that Raven's murderer might have been a Magister was not something Ramirus yet connected to Kamala. He had all the puzzle pieces regarding her, as Colivar did, but he did not yet know how to assemble them.

Which left Colivar free to do as he pleased with Kamala . . . at least for now.

Satisfied, the Magister shapeshifted at last into his preferred form—an oversized red-tailed hawk—and headed off toward the west, to where a particular tree awaited his attention.

CHAPTER 5

*H*IGH, HIGH *over the tower Kamala flies, and she circles overhead anxiously as Rhys and his warriors make a rapid exit from the narrow structure. They are squeezing out through the jagged windows, battered by wind as they cling to the rock surface of the monument, digging their fingers into every crack and crevice available. Each one tries to make way for the next as quickly as possible, so they can all reach a place of safety. But they are not fast enough. Not fast enough! Kamala's bird-heart pounds wildly in her chest as she watches them, knowing that Anukyat's guards are even now coming down the very staircase these men were just ascending, inside the tower. It was her warning that had rippled through their ranks and sent them racing for the exits, with only moments to spare. But would that give them enough time to save themselves?*

Rhys is outside the tower now, his blond hair whipping in the wind as he embraces one of the long vertical columns. Gripping the rock with white-knuckled hands, he struggles to move to the side without losing his balance. Behind him, the remaining guards wait for him to make enough room for them to join him outside. There is so little time left . . .

But they would have had no time at all if not for Kamala's warning. Anukyat's men would have surprised them from above, trapping Rhys and his allies between them and the forces waiting below. This way, thanks to her, at least the men have a chance. If they can all get outside in time and move out of the guards' line of sight, they can wait until Anukyat's men descend the staircase, then reenter. After which they can proceed to their objective in the uppermost chamber as if this interruption never happened.

She looks out over the acres of wilderness surrounding the Citadel, and she sees something coming.

It is far in the distance at first, but moving rapidly closer. A group of black specks silhouetted against the horizon, arrayed like a flock of birds. The sight of them sends raw fear surging through her heart as she realizes what they must be. No! she thinks. Not Souleaters! Not now!

How many of them there are! Numbers beyond counting, their dark jeweled wings sucking in the sunlight as they approach. Already she can feel the first touch of their power upon her mind, and she lets out a shriek of warning to alert Rhys and his men to the danger. Yes, the guards inside the tower might come to the windows to investigate the cause of such commotion, but that can't be helped. Rhys' men are wholly focused upon the rock face they are clinging to, and if she doesn't warn them, they will not look up to see the danger coming until it is too late.

Then, in the blink of an eye, the Souleaters are sweeping overhead, their wings stirring up fierce whirlwinds that batter the men, threatening to shake them loose from their precarious perches. The maleficent power of the creatures begins to dull their minds, making it hard to think clearly. One of Rhys' men loses his grip on the monument. His fingers slide out of their anchoring crevices as his legs begin to fold under him, and then he falls. Another follows. Not because they lack *the strength to hold on but because they lose the will to do so. The horrific power of the Souleaters devours their very sense of self-preservation, and they do not even have the will to panic as they fall to the rocky ground so far below, but plummet silently, their spirits already defeated.*

Kamala watches helplessly as they die, cursing herself for her own insufficiency. She should have known the Souleaters were coming! She would have if she had intercepted Anukyat's message rather than remaining by the tower to watch over these men. It was her fault they were dying now. Her judgment had brought them down.

Her scream of anguish resonates across the landscape, even as Rhys loses his grip upon the tower and begins to fall—

———————

Kamala sat up in bed suddenly, blinking against the darkness as her eyes adapted to the real world once more. The ancient ruin that she had outfitted as a temporary shelter loomed up black against a dilute sky, while insects chirruped restlessly in the distance, heralding the dawn. Morning was coming and with it another restless day . . . and memories.

Gods, how she hated the Souleaters! The feeling was deeply personal, an intimate rage that mere time and distance could not ameliorate. But it was the Guardians' duty to deal with that vile species, not hers. All she had to do was stay out of their way until their task was completed, she told herself. It was the logical thing to do. It satisfied all the survival instincts she had honed during her childhood, that had enabled her to make it to adulthood.

But as much as she knew that cowardice was the only sensible course, it burned her to contemplate it. She hated the jewel-winged creatures with an all-consuming passion, unlike anything she had ever felt before. Hated them not just for killing Rhys but for making her feel *guilty* over his death. She'd thought herself immune to such emotions and it was deeply disturbing to feel it take root within her now, spreading like a gangrenous infection throughout her psyche. It made her want to take the foul creatures in her naked hands and tear them limb from limb, then bathe herself in their blood until the guilt was finally washed away. Scarlet cleansing, hot and comforting.

This isn't your war, she told herself sternly. *Stay out of it.*

But it had been Rhys' war, and try as she might, she could not forget him. Nor could she banish from her mind the bitter-sweet taste of his purpose, a commitment to something so much more important than a single man's life that he had been willing to die for it. What an alien and terrible concept that was. She hungered to understand it better. She feared what might happen to her if she did.

With a muttered curse she rose from her sleeping place, the final cool breeze of the night flowing across her skin, drying her dream-sweat. A casual gesture summoned pale blue flame over her left shoulder, offering just enough light to read by. A few tiny insects rushed over to inspect it, flitting about her head in delight as she pulled a small piece of paper from her pocket.

Holding it up to the light, she read once more the handful of words scribed neatly upon it.

> *I have information you may find useful. Meet me the first day of the coming great month at noon if you are interested.*

There was no signature, of course, but none was needed. The words she had shared with Colivar after Rhys' funeral had been wrapped in sorcery, so that no one else would hear their arrangements. No one else would write a note like this, or know where to leave it so that she would find it.

Give me a way to contact you, he had pressed her, when the lengthy funeral ritual had ended, and the embers of Rhys' pyre were surrendering their final heat.

Maybe she should not have answered him at all. Maybe it would have been safer for her if she had just walked away and faded into the shadows of the evening, hoping to be forgotten. But that had been a strange night, filled with alien and unnerving emotions. So she had suggested a place where he might leave a message for her, a secret drop point that only the two of them would know about. It had seemed a reasonable idea at the time. Later, of course, she realized just how foolish it was. There was no way she could check the drop point for messages without leaving a sorcerous trail that others could trace back to her. But curiosity had proven too much for her in the end, and so she had sent out wary whispers of power to the place now and again, peeking into the hollow of a particular oak tree, searching for any note he might have left her.

And now she had this one in her hand, hinting at secrets, offering to share them. Was it a genuine offer, or just bait for a trap? Not until she met with Colivar would she know for certain.

He knows that I killed a Magister, she thought soberly. A chill ran up her spine as she remembered the scarf he had offered her outside Danton's palace, a relic of her Gansang adventure. The fact that she'd denied ownership of it clearly had not fooled him. If he revealed her identity to the other Magisters, there would be nowhere safe on earth for her to hide. The Law of the Magisters demanded that any sorcerer who killed another be put to death for it.

But that had happened more than a great month ago. And apparently he hadn't told anyone about her yet.

Why?

He is a Magister, she told herself. *He wants the same thing every Magister wants . . . mysteries to explore, games to play, powerful lives to manipulate . . . anything to stave off the ennui of the centuries.*

Was that what this was really all about? Was she merely his current amusement, and when her secrets had been cataloged and her mysteries resolved, he would turn her over to the others of his kind for justice? Or was there something more that he wanted from her?

For a long time she stood still in the darkness, considering. A pale light began to spread upward from the eastern horizon while she did so, backlighting the ruined towers surrounding her. A lone owl made one last circling pass overhead, then headed off toward its diurnal shelter. Songbirds began to stir in its wake.

Finally, silently, she refolded the note and tucked it into her sleeve. Then she took on wings of her own and headed off to their rendezvous point.

———————

The drop point she had suggested was located in the mountain range just east of Ulran, inside a bowl-shaped depression that some natural (or unnatural) force had scooped out of a steep ridge. She had discovered the place while practicing her transformational skills for Ethanus, and she had spent many an afternoon swooping and soaring over the sheltered green fields within it. No one could reach the spot who did not have wings to carry him there—or sorcery to transport him—and so it had seemed an ideal place for clandestine messages to be left, tucked into the cleft of a tree that had been split by lightning long ago.

She approached the place in bird form, weaving back and forth across the crest of the ridge in seemingly random patterns to disguise the purpose of her flight, straining her sorcerous senses to their utmost limits to detect any possible threat. She used her Sight as well. It was something she rarely did these days, as sorcery was far more powerful, but sometimes her rare inborn ability to see supernatural forces at work could slip through the cracks of a Magister's defenses. It was a morati gift, after all, and as such it was beneath their arrogant notice.

But neither sorcery nor Sight uncovered any sign of power being directed at her, and so, encouraged but still wary, she headed toward the drop point itself. Her sharp bird-vision could pick out details as she approached, including a tiny white patch on the meadow grass that was too perfectly square to be natural. She approached cautiously, using her sorcery to bring its details into focus as she flew, and she could make out the form of a person on some kind of white blanket, surrounded by small objects.

She circled the area a few times, then finally came to ground behind a small stand of trees, just out of sight. There she reclaimed her human form and for a moment just stood there, gathering her breath and her courage. Finally, having adopted what she hoped would resemble a confident demeanor, she stepped out from behind her cover as if she were headed to nothing more significant than a noontime rendezvous with a friend.

Colivar reclined upon a white linen cloth, propped up on one elbow as he casually leafed through the pages of a small illuminated book. He was dressed in finely made garments of black silk and leather, elegant but without any hint of power about them. With the sun shining down upon the pages of the book and the breeze softly stirring his long, black hair, he looked for all the world like some prosperous young lord relaxing within the familiar confines of his own estate.

And then he looked up and his eyes met hers, and for a moment—just a moment—she thought she could sense the vast, dark power behind them. Everything she saw before her was merely an illusion, she realized, crafted for her benefit; his true soul was a shadowy and twisted thing that none would ever ever be allowed to see.

He is more dangerous than all the others, Ethanus had warned her. *Not because his power is so great—though it is—but because his soul is obscured by so many shadows that I am not sure even he knows what the truth is any more.*

Upon seeing her approach, he closed his book and sat upright. "Kamala. So glad you could join me. Please." He indicated the open space opposite him. "Make yourself comfortable."

On the cloth were ornate silver trays laid out with fresh fruit, exotic cheeses, and an assortment of candied delicacies. The smell of honey and syrup was strong, and at the edge of the cloth she could see ants milling back and forth, seeking some way to get past the sorcery that was holding them at bay. There was also a covered basket with the neck of a wine bottle peeking out, its amber glass beaded with cold sweat. Colivar removed the bottle from its wrappings with a flourish as she sat down warily, and made a show of presenting it to her. There was some kind of vintner's mark burned into the cork, but she didn't have a clue what it meant. She hesitated, wondering if this was really the sort of game she wanted to be playing right now, but she was far too curious to back out at this point, so she simply nodded.

"I hope this is an acceptable vintage," he said. "If not, please feel free to conjure one of your own."

The subtle arrogance in his tone almost caused her to do just that . . . which, no doubt, was exactly what he had intended. No real witch would waste her athra on such theatrics. So she simply forced herself to smile pleasantly and no more, as though it were the most natural thing in the world to have a Magister set out a picnic for her. "This will be fine."

In truth, the wine was delicious, full-bodied and not too dry for her taste. Had he made a lucky guess or managed to sneak a spell past her defenses to divine what she would like? The latter was certainly possible; she hadn't invested much time or energy in making sure that sorcerers could not detect her food preferences.

She plucked a candied date from the tray but left the rest of the feast untouched. Despite the fact that she'd skipped breakfast and was actually rather hungry, she was not ready to commit herself to this bizarre scene any more than she had to. Not yet. "You said you had information for me?"

He chuckled softly. "Never one for casual social discourse, were you? I do remember that much from Alkali."

She could not help but stiffen slightly, and she saw his dark eyes flicker with interest as he took note of it. Well, what the hells did he expect? He knew she'd lost a lover in that vile place. "We had other things to worry about in Alkali," she reminded him.

"Indeed." He leaned back, his weight supported on one elbow again, a disarmingly languid pose. "Very well, since you prefer to move right on to business . . . tell me, how much do you know about Siderea Aminestas?"

"The one they call the Witch-Queen?" Kamala's mind raced to work out all the implications of his question. Clearly he was testing her, but to what end? "She's said to be a powerful witch. And a skilled seductress. Rumor says she's already lived longer than a single lifetime, though I don't know if that's true or not." And then she dared a test of her own: "I have even heard rumors that she may be a Magister."

A faint smile flickered across his lips. "She is not a Magister. That much I can guarantee."

"Because women cannot be Magisters?" she challenged him.

"Because *she* is not one." He took a date from the tray. "At any rate, you are clearly behind on the news. Aminestas has abdicated. Disappeared, in fact."

Kamala shrugged. At one point she'd had great interest in the Witch-Queen. In fact, she'd been traveling to Sankara to learn more about the woman when she'd first run into Colivar. But her life had shifted course at a later point, and now she was focused on other things. "And you feel this information would be of interest to me . . . why?"

He bit into his date, shutting his eyes for a moment as he savored its sweetness. His silence was maddening. She wanted to shake him.

"It appears," he said at last, his gaze settling on her once more, "that she has run off with a Souleater."

A cold shiver ran down her spine. "What do you mean?"

"Siderea Aminestas appears to have allied herself with one of the creatures. Much as Anukyat did in Alkali. I am sure you remember what came of that relationship."

The memory stirred a hatred in her that was nigh on overwhelming; it took all her self-control not to let him see how much his words unsettled her. Drawing in a deep breath, she counted five beats of her heart before speaking. "So . . . a woman I've never met, from a country I never visited, who ruled over a people that are of no interest to me, has run off somewhere, for reasons I don't know or care about . . . Souleater or not, what makes this my business? It sounds like you should be talking to the Guardians."

"And what if I told you that none of the Magisters have been able to locate her?"

She blinked. "None of them?"

"Many have tried. All have failed."

"Did they have good anchors to work with?"

"I know of one who made the attempt in Siderea's own palace, surrounded by her possessions, atop sheets stained with her sweat. Her essence was anchored to the place a thousand times over. But he could not connect it to its owner. No one can. As far as our sorcery is concerned, she appears to have disappeared from the face of the earth."

That's not possible, she thought. But she dared not betray how much she understood of the Magisters' art. "Maybe she's dead."

"Death has its own special signature. As I am sure you know. The signs are notably absent in this case. So she is still alive, but somehow hidden from us. Which is . . ." He shook his head; his expression had become grim. "Unprecedented."

"Yes," she murmured. It was difficult to focus sorcery on people without having an item that contained their personal essence; that was one reason she was so careful never to leave her own personal possessions behind her when she traveled. But once you got hold of such an anchor, the connection should be there. A fugitive might mask the trail so that his traces could not be read clearly, or add to them such confusing elements that a Magister would misinterpret them, but *some* kind of connection would be there. All the sorcery in the world could not completely erase such a thing.

How was such a thing possible?

This puzzle put to question the very essence of her power, and she ached to ask him more questions. But until she was ready to admit to him what she was and openly claim her place among the Magisters, such honest discourse was out of the question.

You don't even know that any of this is true, she warned herself. *He could just be testing you.*

"What part do you imagine I might play in this?" she asked.

"I believe you may be able to find her."

"Where all the Magisters have failed?"

"Yes."

She recognized the bait for what it was, but it was too compelling to resist. "Why?"

"Because you are a woman."

She drew in a sharp breath. "If what you need is a woman's magic, then there are a thousand and one witches you could ask for help. You don't need me."

"Yes," he agreed. "There are indeed many witches in the world."

He gazed into his glass in silence for a moment, contemplating the deep red wine. "An ikati queen is able to hide herself from the males of her species," he said. "It's similar to the power she uses to guard her nest; that is what makes it so hard for morati to find her eggs. A necessity of survival. A male Souleater will destroy any nest that contains the offspring of his competitors, hence she must be able to hide her eggs—and herself—from him. So if Siderea has truly allied herself with a Souleater queen, then she, too, may be sheltered by such a power. Which means that none of *us* will be able to find her."

"But you think that I can? Why, because of my sex?" She raised an eyebrow skeptically. "I don't remember any talk about a gender advantage when we were being briefed in Kierdwyn."

"A lot of things have been forgotten," he said quietly. "Even in Kierdwyn."

"But the Magisters are human beings, not Souleaters. Why would a power designed to affect one species distinguish between the sexes of another? I would think that as far as the Souleaters are concerned, we are all just food, and our gender distinctions are meaningless."

He shrugged stiffly. "Perhaps my guess is wrong, then. In which case any effort on your part would be wasted." His mouth twitched slightly. "That would of course be a costly failure . . . for a mere witch."

For a moment her heart almost stopped beating. But he had turned his attention to the glass in his hand once more, shutting his eyes briefly as he sipped the blood-red wine. Was that for her sake? The gift of a moment's privacy, in which she might choose her course?

He knows the truth about me already, she told herself. *He is amused by the sport of getting me to admit I'm a Magister, but that's all it is to him. A game. If he hasn't killed me yet to satisfy the Law, it's for reasons of his own, and a handful of words from me will not change his mind.*

"So now we are back to my original question," she said. "Why should I give a damn about all this?"

He raised an eyebrow. "You mean, apart from helping to save the world from certain destruction? Doing your part to safeguard human civilization, and all that?"

"Yes," she said. Knowing that disdain for human welfare was

as much an identifying trait of the Magisters as was sorcery. Daring him to make note of it in her. "Aside from all that."

A faint smile flickered across his lips. She decided that he was enjoying the game too much for her liking.

Heart pounding, she picked up a piece of fruit, then bound enough power to delicately peel back its rind. Perfectly shaped segments of skin parted like lotus petals, revealing the moist fruit inside. It was a subtle but eloquent waste of power that a mere witch would never countenance, and she hoped its message was clear: *I tire of your games. Find someone else to play cat-and-mouse with.* "You promised me information that I would want to hear," she reminded him. "Thus far I've heard only information that you want me to have. Is there something more, or am I wasting my time here?"

The dark eyes gleamed as they took her measure. What emotions were those, flickering in their depths? Most were indecipherable, but one was familiar enough that she could not possibly mistake it. Desire. Her breath quickened, and a sudden rush of confidence surged through her veins. The political machinations of the Magisters might be alien to her at times, but the lust of men was familiar territory. This game was becoming more interesting by the moment.

But his voice remained cool and dispassionate as he said, "Siderea has an item in her possession that would be of great value to you. Find her, and you may be able to get hold of it." He paused. "Or deliver me information on where she is, and if I can get hold of the item myself, I will deliver it to you in return for that service."

"And what is this mystery item?"

He shook his head, making a *tsk-tsk* sound. "Come now,

Kamala. Information has its price. Surely you would not respect me if I gave mine away for free. Commit to my service and I will tell you all you need to know."

"One does not agree to buy merchandise without assessing its value first," she pointed out.

"Unless the merchandise itself is knowledge, in which case *assessment* and *delivery* amount to the same thing."

"Yet even a saffron merchant will part with a pinch of his wares to convince potential buyers that the rest of his stock is worth their coin."

Silently he bound a bit of power to refill his glass. Draining the life from some innocent soul so that he would not have to reach as far as the bottle. "Very well," he said at last. "I will tell you this much: It is an item many Magisters want to get hold of. They want it enough that if you got to it first, you might be able to . . . shall we say . . . bargain with them for favors."

She could feel her heart skip a beat. "That is . . . interesting."

He lifted the glass to his lips, half-masking a smile. "I thought you might feel that way."

"You don't want this item for yourself?"

"Ironically, it has far more value to you than it does to me." He sipped the wine, his eyes watching her intently over the edge of the glass.

"And what if I do find this woman for you? What happens then?" She looked at him closely, trying to read what was in his soul; his nostrils flared slightly in response to her scrutiny, but he offered her no other insight. "You mean to kill her, don't you?"

A brief shadow passed over his countenance. For a moment— just a moment—his perfect mask slipped from place, and she caught a glimpse of what was behind it. *They were lovers,* she realized. *And he still desires her.*

Was that what was driving him in all this? Could it be that this powerful Magister, among the most ancient of his kind, was jealous of a Souleater? The thought of it was almost too bizarre to fathom.

"The ikati queen must be dealt with," he said, without a hint of emotion. "I doubt that Siderea will step aside and allow that to happen. So, yes, she will probably die in the process."

She raised an eyebrow. "And aren't you concerned that if I found her I might wind up having sympathy for her cause? Perhaps even ally with her, against the cabal of heartless men who seek her destruction?"

With a dismissive flick of his wrist he cast the wine glass away from him; it vanished before hitting the ground. "Her only *cause* now is communion with a creature that feeds on human souls. You are a direct competitor to that creature and will not be tolerated in its territory; no other relationship is possible. Even if Siderea were genuinely interested in parleying with you—or seducing you—that would only be a temporary respite. The fact that ikati queens don't attack each other on sight doesn't mean they are capable of anything akin to human friendship. Sooner or later Siderea must submit to her partner's instincts, and when she does, it will not matter what sort of bargain you have made with either of them."

Which might or might not be true, Kamala reflected. But Colivar was not a fool, and he would not be offering her this deal if he thought there was any chance she'd ally with his target. Which raised other questions, equally compelling . . . but she was not going to learn anything more without giving him something in return, that much was clear.

What did she have to lose?

Slowly, warily, she nodded. "All right. I'll make an attempt to find her. I can't promise you results, but I'll do my best." She cocked her head to one side. "Now show me your saffron, Magister Colivar."

If he noted the suggestive element in her tone he gave no sign of it. "Siderea Aminestas has a box of personal tokens in her possession. They have no identifying marks on them, but appear to be simple blank pieces of paper, folded in quarters. There may be other items stored with them as well, in which case those are probably of equal value and should also be retrieved."

"Whose tokens?" she demanded.

A faint, dry smile flickered across his lips. "Each carries the essence of a Magister."

She exhaled sharply in surprise. For a moment words escaped her. "How many?" she managed at last.

"Several dozen, is my guess. The lady was . . . profligate."

The personal tokens of that many Magisters! The concept was almost too much to absorb. "How did she get hold of such things?"

"They were given to her freely, in return for her services. It seemed a safe enough bargain at the time. Now that she is no longer human . . ." He spread his hands, inviting her to finish the thought.

Suspicion flared in Kamala's heart. "And why is it all right for *me* to have them?"

"They bear no identifying marks of any kind, and would be destroyed by any spell you might use to determine what Magister each one belonged to. So they are of little use to you or to any other thief. Siderea knows which sorcerer is associated with each token, of course, and now that she is no longer human, that knowledge has become . . . inconvenient." A thin, cold smile spread across his face. "Of course, if you were to get hold of all those tokens, no Magister could ever be sure that you hadn't obtained her information as well. They would no doubt bargain fiercely to have their gifts returned to them. Just in case."

You do not care if I manipulate the other Magisters, do you? She knew that the sorcerers had no great love for one another, but even by that measure, this offer was remarkable. Magisters did not usually betray their own kind to outsiders.

Only she was not really an outsider, was she? She was an intrinsic part of their game now, a player instead of a pawn. He knew that. He accepted it.

The revelation brought a rush of heat to her face.

"I'll need an anchor to work with," she whispered.

"Of course." With casual grace he waved his hand over the white cloth between them. A small wooden box appeared, carved ebony with a domed lid. "This is a duplicate of the one she kept her tokens in while she lived in Sankara." He opened the catch and pulled back the lid, displaying its contents to her.

Colorful scarves, glittering bracelets, and a long strand of lilac-colored pearls were jumbled together in seemingly random array, a small fortune's worth of goods. And if even one of them held a clear trace of the Witch-Queen's personal resonance, then their true value was beyond price.

For the first time, the magnitude of what Kamala was being asked to do hit home . . . as well as the magnitude of what she stood to gain if she succeeded.

Colivar lifted up a strand of lavender pearls, their luster liquid in the sunlight. "These are all items that she favored. Signature ornaments, if you will. Bear in mind, recent events may have strained her connection to past anchors. She is no longer the creature she once was. How much of a difference that will make, metaphysically speaking, has yet to be seen."

Kamala reached out to caress a length of scarlet silk. It vibrated beneath her fingertips, warm with the vitality of another woman's life. Memories of perfume filled her nostrils, exotic floral notes with a musky undertone. She resisted the temptation to shut her eyes and drink it in, to begin to search for those elements in the Witch-Queen's anchors that her sorcery could fix on. Traces that would speak to the core of the woman's essence, that even her recent communion with a Souleater could not erase.

Maybe that is why the other Magisters can't find her, she thought suddenly. *Maybe they don't understand a woman's soul well enough to know what to look for.*

"These should do," she said, letting the scarf fall back into the box. A breeze blew softly across her face as she closed it once more, scattering the scent-memory. "Do you have any suggestions as to where to start looking?"

"I have a few ideas, but I don't want to share that information with you just yet. You need to attempt this without any preconceptions so that you are equally open to all possibilities, not swayed by the possible errors of others."

Her mouth twitched. "Of men."

"Is there anything else you will need? Other than that?"

"Aye," she nodded. "One thing more."

"Name it."

Her eyes narrowed slightly. "How do I know that when all this is done, you won't simply discard me? I'm sure many Magisters would consider that the wisest course, under the circumstances."

She could see a muscle along his jaw tighten. Clearly he hadn't expected her to be so forward about this.

You tested me, Magister. Now I test you in turn.

"What is it you want, then? A heartfelt guarantee that I won't kill you? I think you know what that would be worth."

She nodded. "But there is one kind of guarantee that would have meaning."

How badly did he want her help? He had already stressed the bounds of the Law just by talking to her; would he take this final step to win her as an ally? She could see his expression darken as he considered the ramifications of what she was asking for. She waited in silence.

"Very well," he said at last. It seemed to her that his voice was hardly louder than the beat of an insect's wings. "You have my Oath."

Triumph rushed through her veins like wildfire. The sensation was so powerful that it left her breathless; for a brief moment she felt connected to him, as one might be connected to a lover. The ultimate intoxication.

You see, Ethanus? This Law is not some mystical compact that Magisters are bound to, but simply a collection of words. If Colivar is willing to set it aside for the moment's convenience, then surely the others will to choose to do the same. It is only a question of learning what their price is and paying it.

She looked away from him as she gathered the ebony box into her arms; she did not want him to see the triumph in her eyes. The foodstuffs vanished one by one as she rose to her feet, along with whatever sorcery had been holding the insects at bay; a dragonfly flitted by, seeking its midday meal.

"I will leave you a note in this place when I find what you seek," she promised him.

Not *if,* but *when.*

Then she gathered her sorcery about her, wielding her power openly, shamelessly. Calling up the stolen athra that was in her soul as only a true Magister could do, setting it alight, bidding it to consume her flesh. A firestorm of transformation blazed about her, molding her skin into feathers, her arms into wings. No witch would ever have summoned her power so wastefully. She knew it. He knew it. She celebrated her sorcery as he watched.

The wind caught her up then, and she could not resist one wild cry of exultation as she took to the air, heading westward toward the sun.

He stared at the sky for a long, long time. Long after the point when she had passed from sight and sorcery would have been required in order to watch her further.

So this is what it feels like to break the Law.

Amazingly, the gods had not arrived in a storm of black thunder to strike him down for his transgression. Nor had the earth opened up beneath his feet to swallow him whole. But those things were still possible, at least in a metaphorical sense. There was no guarantee they would not happen in the future, because of this.

But for now . . . there was only his memory of the moment. Nearly as ominous as the thunder of the gods. Nearly as daunting as the Abyss itself.

The Law of the Magisters dictated that Kamala must die.

He had sworn by the Law that he would not kill her.

He thought he could feel his darker half stirring, as if the paradox had awakened it from long slumber. Had Colivar's long

centuries of civilized existence weakened its grasp upon his soul
enough that he could rise above this moment, or was he putting
himself in genuine danger? The beast within him had nursed
its grievances for a long time now, trapped within its prison of
human intellect, ready and waiting to devour him whole the
moment he showed the slightest sign of weakness. If it rose to
the surface once more, if it took control of him, would he even
remember what it was like to be human?

It does not matter what the Law is, Ramirus had declared, back
in the days of their early negotiations. *It only matters that we
follow it without question.*

But a female Magister existed now. He could think of only
two ways that might be possible, and one of them shook him
to the core of his very soul. If that was the process that had
brought her into being, then her very existence rendered his
Oath—and the Law itself—irrelevant. No Magister would be
able to kill her. The darkness that lay coiled within their souls
simply would not allow it.

That darkness was whispering to him now. Stirring his blood.
He remembered the taste of her sorcery upon his lips, and a
tremor of dread and desire coursed through his flesh.

To deny that darkness was to deny his own history. His very
soul.

To surrender to it was to risk . . . everything.

Which did he fear more? he wondered.

CHAPTER 6

"THIS IS the place."

Hushed by the reminder of her loss, Hedda's voice was hardly louder than a whisper. It was the second time she'd been back here with her husband. The first time had been to point the way out to a skilled tracker. That man had managed to find a human footprint pressed into the loam where the hollow-eyed girl had once stood, which had set Hedda's heart pounding with hope, but in the end he'd lost the trail as it wound up into the mountains. Too much bare granite, he'd told the grieving mother. Too many other animals scuffing over whatever traces had been left behind, in the time that it had taken Hedda to hire him.

One more thing to feel guilty about.

Merely coming back to this place made her feel overwhelmed by guilt. Never mind that her husband had stood by her side through all of this, without a single note of accusation crossing his lips. "We'll find the trail," he assured her, squeezing her tightly against his side. Dura was a stonemason in Lord Cadern's service, and his strong, calloused hands raised prickles along her arms as he rubbed her briskly. It had been hard for him to get a day off from his current project to tend to this matter, she knew, and he'd had to go deep into debt to pay for a witch to come all the way out from Esla to help them. But she knew he would offer up the very blood in his veins to get his son back, if that's what the gods required of him. And thus far he seemed to believe her story about what had happened.

Unlike the rest of the townsfolk.

She'd heard the whispering, of course. How her baby had fallen into the river and drowned. Or he had crawled off a cliff while she wasn't watching. Or he had died of some illness that she'd failed to detect in time. Now she was just covering up the truth by making up a crazy story about some dirt-covered waif stealing him away, so that her husband would not turn her out of the house. Poor Dura, they whispered. How long would his faith in her last? How much evidence would he need to see before he realized he'd been duped? Crazy Hedda, pressing him to hire a witch who could well reveal her little plot! Did she think he would just go along with her little game?

And now they were here again, looking for her baby, and the witch was picking his way through the piles of branches that a recent windstorm had brought down, using his powers to search the ground for any sign of Hedda's mysterious visitor. He was surprisingly young, to her eyes, barely past the age of puberty, and clearly he was not very experienced in this kind of investigation. But witches were few and far between in the region, and most of the good ones restricted their efforts to healing the children of rich lords, where bringing a moderate fever down a few degrees might earn them enough coin to feed their own families for a month or more. Had Dura been able to meet this witch's price, or had the youth agreed to take less than usual out of compassion? Hedda didn't dare ask.

She watched for what seemed like an eternity as the boy scoured the countryside, squinting intently as he turned over nearly every stone and twig in the area, searching for what he called "an anchor." He seemed particularly interested in the place where Hedda had left food for the strange girl, near where the tracker had later found a partial footprint that he said might belong to her. But after contemplating that location in silence for many long minutes, the witch finally shook his head in frustration and moved on. What exactly was he looking for, Hedda did not know. When the tracker had gone over this turf with his hounds, she'd understood the goal. Scent might still cling to the earth. Broken twigs or scuffed earth might mark the flight of a human girl (or something else?) carrying an infant in her arms. But this random-seeming search, this strange dance of ignorance . . . try as she might, she could not decipher it. She could only watch in abject misery, huddled against Dura's side, praying silently to her gods. *Give me back my child,* she begged them, *and I will do whatever you ask of me. You can even have my life, if you want it. Just bring my son back safely.*

By the time the witch finally turned back to them the details of the surrounding landscape were beginning to fade, as day slowly prepared to give way to night. The minute Hedda saw his face she knew what his answer was going to be, and something within her heart that had been clinging to hope since her son's disappearance finally, irrevocably, let go its grip, and plummeted down into the abyss of absolute despair.

"I am sorry," the witch said softly. Only that.

"Nothing?" Dura's voice was desolate, echoing as if in an empty cave. "Nothing at all?"

The witch shook his head. "There's no good anchor. I found a few traces of a female presence that might or might not belong to the girl you told me about, but nothing clear enough to focus witchery on."

"Maybe it's not the traces that are lacking quality," Dura said, "but the witch."

The youth flushed. "If you want to hire someone better, you're welcome to try."

"My husband didn't mean that," Hedda interjected. She knew from the pain in Dura's voice that he was just striking out blindly, venting his despair at the nearest target; later he would regret such cruel words. The young witch had offered up a portion of his own life-essence in order to help them, after all. "We're both half mad with worry. I'm sure you can understand that."

The youth nodded stiffly. His failure to garner useful information would not impact his fee, of course—a witch was paid for the life-essence he sacrificed, not for the quality of his results—but he seemed genuinely distressed that he had been unable to help them.

What was she supposed to do now? Hedda wondered. Put on a black veil and mourn her son as if she knew for a fact that he was dead? Even if he might still be alive, in the hands of some half-mad waif? What on earth did the girl want him for? The fact that she couldn't even begin to imagine an answer to that question made her feel sick inside.

"There are others, you know." The witch spoke quietly.

"Others?" Dura asked.

"Other children that have disappeared."

Hedda blinked. "You mean . . . like this?"

"Don't know the details. They're just witch rumors, mind you. But I heard there've been a number of infants stolen, from towns all around here. Witches were called in a few times to look for 'em—that's how I heard about it—but no one could find any clues worth a damn. What traces they could find led nowhere. Just like here." A wave of his hand encompassed the surrounding woods. "Now that I've seen it for myself, I give more credit to such stories."

"Did the others . . . did the parents . . . was a strange girl involved?"

He shook his head. "As far as I know, you're the only one who's ever seen anything like that. The other children just disappeared when no one was looking at them. One minute there, the next minute not. All outdoors, I think." He wiped a long straggle of dun-colored hair back from his eyes. "That's the rumor, anyway."

Hedda struggled to absorb this new information. Did this mean that her own loss was part of some greater pattern? If so, what on earth was its purpose? Try as she might, she could not come up with any motive that made sense to her. It wasn't unheard of for children to be stolen away by bandits, this close to the wild—one could get good coin from the slavers for a strong, healthy child—and Lord Cadern kept a wary eye on the woods surrounding his lands for that very reason. But it was rare for an infant to be taken, because a child that young would require too much care. Every now and then there were stories about some noblewoman who stole a peasant's baby to replace one that had been stillborn, but even if those tales were true, it was at best a rare occurrence. Nothing like what this witch was suggesting.

If something like this was happening repeatedly, she told herself, then his Lordship might take note of it. The life of a single peasant meant little to him, but the knowledge that someone was persistently offending against the law and order of his domain . . . that might move him to act. And he had the kind of resources that Hedda and Dura could not possibly muster. Perhaps even access to a Magister.

A faint spark of hope took light in her soul. And she knew from the way her husband's touch shifted on her arm that he shared her moment of insight, and his soul now housed a similar spark.

"Can you bring us more information?" Dura asked the witch. "About the other children who were taken? I'll pay for it, of course."

Again the witch flushed. "You don't have to pay me. There's no athra involved. I'm just sorry I couldn't do more for you today. What information are you looking for?"

"Whatever you can gather. The towns that those incidents took place in. Name, dates, the circumstances of any incidents . . ."

Please, Hedda prayed to her gods. *Please let these crimes be within his Lordship's domain, so that he will care about this. Give us that much, I beg you.*

"I'll find out what I can for you," the young man said. "I promise."

He glanced up at the canopy, where dark shadows were beginning to mottle the highest reaches of the treetops, random golden sparks picking out branches on their undersides. The sun would be setting soon. "We should be heading back," he said.

"Aye," Dura agreed, but he did not move.

Hedda watched as the young witch shouldered his travel pack once more, offered them a last parting glance, and then headed back the way they had come. And then, in his absence, the woods were still. So still. Only her breathing and Dura's, the soft thud of their heartbeats, and the distant rustling of nocturnal creatures as they began to stir from their burrows, waiting for night to fall.

"We'll find him," her husband promised her. "I swear it."

CHAPTER 7

DESERT BREEZES stirred the gauze drapes, rippling them like ocean waters ahead of a storm. Now that the blazing summer sun had set, Jezalya was finally cooling, and the crowds of people who had been coursing through the palace all day were finally taking their leave. Priests and counselors, diplomats and elders, all gone at last. Silence had not fallen upon the palace yet, but its approach was inevitable. Thank the gods.

Siderea touched a hand to her hair, binding a bit of power to urge some straggly bits back into place, refreshing the curls she had set that morning. How strangely exhilarating it was to be able to do such a thing! A witch would not have had the luxury of expending soulfire for such casual cosmetic purposes, but a woman who was bound body and soul to an ikati, and might draw upon that creature for power, could expend life-essence without limit. As long as there were humans in the world for her consort to feed upon, there was athra to spare.

What happens next? The thought from her ikati welled from the shadowy recesses of her mind, taking on human language and structure only as it surfaced in her consciousness. Siderea knew that the original thought had not been expressed in human terms, but in the formless animal instincts of its winged source. It was her own mind that translated the thought into more familiar terms, adorning it with the trappings of civilized understanding, until it manifested in her head as a quasi-human voice. The process was still new to her, and was sometimes a bit unnerving, but the moment of direct contact with her other half always brought with it a sense of soul-deep satisfaction. What a miserable, incomplete creature she had been, before the ikati had come into her life!

We will do what must be done, she responded. Letting her sense of satisfaction with the day's events seep through the mental connection, soothing her winged consort.

Moving to the window, she looked out over her new empire. It was a small thing by the measure of her former life, but it was enough to begin with. Beyond Jezalya's walls there was only wasteland as far as the eye could see. To the north and east, flat-topped mountains with wind-scored slopes dominated the landscape, offering some cover from Jezalya's scrutiny; to the west there was only open land, windswept and empty. Somewhere in the distance—many days' march distant—was a great river, its silt-laden waters flanked by narrow bands of rich farmland, its cities protected by Anshasan troops. There were no easy riches at hand in this region, nor cities close to Jezalya that one might wish to claim . . . but that also meant that there were no enemy armies nearby, nor any foreign prince keeping close watch on Jezalya's business.

Soon the desert tribes would begin to flock to Nasaan's banner. How could it be otherwise, once the gods made it clear how much they favored him? Those tribes who swore fealty to Jezalya would remain healthy and prosperous, while the ones who remained independent would be stricken by a strange ennui, in which even the bloodthirsty passions that normally drove them would fail to arouse any interest. Perhaps the Black Sleep would appear in time, that dread disease that drew all of a man's strength from his limbs until he could do nothing more than lie in a mindless state, drifting in and out of a sleep akin to death. The desert folk believed that the only way to contain the terrible Sleep was to burn its victims to ash, along with all those relatives who might carry the disease. Considerable incentive for a tribe to seek the protection of Nasaan—and through him, the favor of the gods—before the Sleep put all its members at risk.

The fact that the Sleep had nothing to do with gods, and everything to do with the male Souleaters who circled restlessly about Jezalya, feeding upon everything outside its borders, was a secret no one but Siderea needed to know. Like dogs on a leash, the great beasts circled restlessly about their mistress, sucking Jezalya's enemies dry. As more tribes flocked to Nasaan's banner, Siderea would expand the border of her little empire, and though the males might beat their wings in fury to be ordered still farther away, they would obey her. Anyone who did not might find himself in disfavor when the new queen began her first flight, and such a fate was unthinkable.

Why do human politics matter to us? Siderea's ikati consort wondered. *We do not answer to their rules.*

Because the First Kings turned against the ikati, she thought. *Because we must have a base of power from which to operate, if we are to keep that from ever happening again.*

But was that the only reason she cared so much about Jezalya's expansion? Or did the dream of carving out a desert empire from scratch, and eventually laying siege to Anshasa itself, speak

to a more primal hunger? There had been a time when she had
not been mistress of her own fate, much less that of other men.
How long ago that had been! She had spent so many years in
Sankara since then, having every need attended to, every whim
indulged, that it was easy to forget she had begun her life in a
very different mode. Easy to forget the desperation of those
early years. Yet it still played into her psyche, and no doubt it
fueled the hunger for power that sang in her veins now. And
the fact that it was desert kingdoms that she was marking for
conquest added a piquant irony to the situation.

You were not a queen back then, thought the ikati, responding
to her thoughts.

How many questions went unvoiced in the wake of those
words! Thus far Siderea had chosen not to reveal all of her
personal history to her winged consort. Would there come a
time when such decisions were no longer a question of volition,
when she would lose all mental privacy, and holding back secrets
would no longer be an option? Perhaps. Until then, there were
some memories the young ikati might not be able to deal with,
and so she had not yet shared them with her.

No, she thought solemnly. Answering all those questions at
once, while not really answering them at all. *I was not a queen
back then.*

Footsteps were approaching. The rhythm was strong and
purposeful, as befitted a newly crowned prince. Nasaan's meeting
with the city elders must have gone well.

She smoothed the fine silk layers of her gown down over the
curves of her body. Such fabrics cost a fortune here, but what
did that matter to her? Even if royal sycophants had not laid
the wealth of nations at Nasaan's feet, including bolts of silk
and cloth-of-gold from empires halfway across the world, she

still would not have to pay the Anshasan merchants a single coin for their overpriced wares. All she needed was a scrap of the most miserable mottled wool to work with, and she could transform it into whatever manner of elegant fabric she desired. Or with a little more effort (and a lot more stolen athra) she could simply conjure whatever she needed, as if from the air itself.

Casual, thoughtless magic. What a heady indulgence it was! No wonder the Magisters were drunk on their own power. It was a wonder they ever appeared sane at all.

The double doors opened for Nasaan's entrance and closed soundlessly behind him, maneuvered by unseen servants. He was a solid man, hard-muscled and confident, with battle scars that stood out whitely against the sun-baked leather of his skin. Not unhandsome, in his own way, but a man whose charisma was wholly dependent upon the fierce warrior persona that he projected. No amount of silk or perfume could ever soften the edge of such a presence.

He had chosen to wear a leather cuirass, perhaps to remind the city's elders that war was sure to follow if they displeased him, and as he entered the chamber, she moved forward to help him remove it. His eyes watched her like a hawk's as she did so, taking in every movement, seeking meaning in every breath. Since the day of the conquest she had served as his companion at public events, and her polished beauty had lent him a kind of social legitimacy that a rough-hewn warrior alone might not have had. The fact that she was rumored to be some kind of desert spirit—or at least a powerful witch—had bolstered his reputation as well. What kind of man did it take to earn the loyalty of such a creature?

In all that time, they'd had little chance to be alone together.

So they had not yet discussed what their real relationship would be, away from the prying eyes of priests and politicians. She had orchestrated that dance with care, making sure that he never suspected she was behind it. Now, as she unbuckled the short straps that held his cuirass in place, she could feel the tension coiled hot within him. Such a man did not deal well with uncertainty.

He was so easy to play, this one. No unexpected elements. Almost no sport at all.

"You are to be Royal Consort," he said, without greeting or preamble.

She looked up at him.

"Some of the elders argued with me about it. The ones that weren't peeing their britches, that is, for fear I'd cut off their heads." He snorted. "They said you were a foreigner, and they didn't know who you were, so you shouldn't be sitting on Jezalya's throne in any capacity. When what they really meant was that they don't know *what* you were . . . and I didn't enlighten them."

She nodded. Enough of Nasaan's men had caught sight of a strange woman on the battlefield, or had sensed her ikati's presence overhead, that some rumors were inevitable. Channeled properly, they could be useful.

"There's no reason for them to know," she said quietly, as she lifted the heavy cuirass away from his body. The thick, battle-scarred leather was heavy in her hands, and her ikati-sharpened senses could pick up the scent of past battles that clung to it: blood and horses and the fear of captives, overlaid by splashes of celebratory ale. The tunic Nasaan wore beneath the leather was soaked with sweat, and it clung damply to the muscular curves of his body. He was a warrior, no doubt accustomed to being in such a state, but there was no mistaking the look of pleasure on his face as a stray evening breeze wafted into the room, chilling the moisture on his skin. Tiny goosebumps rose along his shoulders, and she reached up to smooth them with her fingertips. The casual intimacy of the gesture made his breath catch in his throat.

She was his consort now. Was that role to be a public convenience only, or a private reality as well? She could see that he was considering the question now, could feel the tension rising in his body as she reached up to his neck to untie his tunic, then lifted the garment up over his head, peeling the fabric away from him like the skin of a moist fruit. He wouldn't reach out and touch her without some sort of official permission, she knew that. He thought she was *djira,* so until she declared what the rules of this game were, he would not make the first move. One did not risk angering demons.

The sense of power was intoxicating.

"You understand," he said, "it's a ceremonial title only. You will have no power in your own name."

She dropped the shirt to the floor beside her. Until this moment, she herself had not decided what path their relationship would take. There was advantage to be had in keeping him at arm's length while subtly stoking the embers of his desire; unrequited lust was powerful stuff if one knew how to channel it properly. But consummating the relationship would forge a powerful bond between them, especially if he believed that it was a demon who was serving his pleasure.

Besides, lust and fear and the reckless arrogance of a warrior made for a heady brew, and it was not one Siderea often had the opportunity to taste.

She moved close to him, close enough to feel the damp

heat that was radiating from his body. She put a hand to his cheek, tracing the ridges and valleys of ancient battle scars, savoring the texture of coarse bristle along his cheek and chin.

"I do not need power in my own name," she murmured. "Do I?" Moving close enough to him for their bodies to touch, her intentions unmistakable.

He reached out to her, hesitantly at first, and then, when she made no sign of protest, more deliberately. Strong hands, calloused from the sword, drew her into a rough embrace against his sweat-slicked chest. The scent of his body filled her nostrils as he reached down to caress her thighs, gathering up the silk of her gown beneath his hands, baring her legs. How long the heat must have simmered in him, to reach this intensity! And how long it had simmered in her, as well. She had not had a man since leaving Sankara, and her body ached to break its long fast.

Coarse, strong hands moved up to her breasts, rubbing the damp silk against her skin, agonizingly pleasurable—

No! came the protest from within.

His mouth was hot and tasted of dates and ale.

This one is male, she reassured the ikati. She remembered the disaster that her seduction of Petrana had become. A lifetime in the past. Now that she was more accustomed to this strange symbiosis, she understood why that effort had failed. *He is not competition to us.*

He is not worthy!

Nasaan's rough caress was awakening a hunger too long denied. It was hard to think clearly, much less navigate the issue of her divided consciousness with that hunger raging through her flesh like wildfire. But she knew how dangerous it was to ignore the Souleater's protests. She remembered the night she had tried to seduce Petrana, when she had first learned that lesson.

He is a prince, she thought to the ikati. *Powerful. Strong. I need him bound to me.* And beneath that thought teased another, unvoiced: *I have my needs as well.*

He has not flown for us! The thought was accompanied by a rush of bestial emotion so powerful that it took Siderea's breath away. Sheer indignation. How could she allow a man to possess her body, when he had not yet proven himself by the only measure that mattered? When he had not yet flown in pursuit of her to the point of exhaustion, been bloodied by the claws of his rivals, been maddened by the taste of their blood upon his tongue? What was his courtship worth if he had not yet offered her the bodies of lesser suitors as a nuptial gift, if she did not have the screams of the wounded to seduce her?

The warm masculine scent that had filled her nostrils began to take on a sour edge. The taste of Nasaan's skin turned bitter on her tongue. The caress that had so thrilled her flesh suddenly seemed harsh and repellent—

NO! This time it was she who screamed the word out, deep within the recesses of their shared mind. Sharing the ikati's instincts was one thing, but having them drown out her human consciousness was another. She would not surrender that much of herself to their union.

Somewhere in the distance Nasaan looked up suddenly, as if sensing that something was wrong. Somewhere in the distance her body, so well versed in the art of seduction that barely a thought was required to guide it, encouraged him to overlook it. Drawing his mouth down to meet her own, wrapping her legs around his hips, encouraging him to lose himself inside her. Sensations of what should have been pleasure shuddered through her flesh, but her mind could not connect to them. She was lost in a maelstrom of internal conflict, primitive and compelling, and she struggled to find some way to impose order upon it so that she might regain control of the situation. But the ikati was equally determined. No man should have access to her until he had proved himself, according to the patterns of courtship that ruled her species.

So Siderea cast herself back into memory, remembering the night of Nasaan's conquest, grasping at shadows of confluence.

All about her the battle rages. Warriors with their lances and horses and swords sweep past her, each one fighting for his own life as well as for a cause. The sound of it is deafening: cries of challenge from all directions, weapons crashing against shields, the squealing of horses in pain. The violence surrounds her like an ocean tide, and she holds it at bay with a single thought, allowing the energy of battle to envelope her but not allowing the warriors themselves to come near.

Not far away is Nasaan. How fierce he is, and how fearless! She watches as his sword thrusts into the side of an enemy warrior, releasing a gush of steaming blood. Never mind that her power has weakened the enemy warriors so that they stand no chance against him. He did not know that would be the case when he first charged headlong into their ranks. It is the offering, the intended sacrifice, that matters.

He is fighting for us, *she thinks to her consort. Not that he thinks of it in those terms, of course. To his mind this is just about winning a city, a piddling desert kingdom that could have fit inside Sankara's walls with room to spare. But Siderea has made herself into a greater prize. He is fighting for her. All of these men are fighting for her, allies and enemies alike, and blood will flow in rivers as proof of*

LEGACY OF KINGS 125

their passion, while she looks on. Feeling their energy flow into her
from all sides, heating her blood, stirring instincts the young ikati
mind does not know how to respond to—

Somewhere in the distance the young queen keened in pleasure. The vision that Siderea had summoned clearly resonated within the ikati. Oh, yes, it resonated. Blood was being shed for her. Males were fighting over her. The blood of the weakest would water the earth, while the offspring of the strongest would hatch. It would all begin at her call, and no male would be allowed to touch her who had not felt the madness take root in his flesh, who had not run that terrible gauntlet—

Nasaan has, Siderea thought to her.

The statement hung suspended in the air for a moment, as a wave of sensation that should have been pleasure crested in Siderea's flesh. Her fingers grasped Nasaan's hair, encouraging his ardor, but her mind was elsewhere.

And then the response came, at last.

He is worthy.

And her wings beat in pleasure against the sunlight as she surrendered herself to the moment.

CHAPTER 8

GWYNOFAR ARRIVED just as Karmandi's ambassador was heading out the door of the audience chamber. The High King had ordered a flagon of ale to wash the stale taste of politics out of his mouth, and he was going over the maps his visitor had left behind when a servant announced his mother's entrance.

He could tell immediately from her expression that some weighty issue was on her mind. Or perhaps it was from something other than her expression. He had developed an uncanny ability to read her mood lately, and he suspected that was because of the mystical connection they'd shared the day she sat upon the Throne of Tears, the day she had acted as a metaphysical conduit for all those of *lyr* heritage. That connection had never completely faded.

Which would explain a number of strange things.

"Mother." He nodded a greeting to her and gestured for a servant to collect the maps and then leave the chamber. He had never become completely comfortable with the royal habit of allowing servants to overhear his personal business.

"Are you busy?" she asked. Always polite.

"Never too busy for you." He brushed a stray lock of hair back from his face. "Not that I wouldn't have welcomed a distraction five minutes ago."

"Karmandi?"

He nodded.

"Territorial dispute?"

He chuckled darkly. "Nothing that burning down a forest or two wouldn't solve."

"Your father would have done that in a heartbeat, were it necessary."

"As will I, if it becomes necessary."

"Yes." A strange, guarded smile spread across her face. "I do believe you would."

He picked up his flagon as the servant gathered up the last of the maps. "I am not as soft as you feared, then."

"You are not as soft as anyone feared, my son."

He took a deep drink of the ale, shutting his eyes for a moment as he tried to open himself up to the emanations of power surrounding her. Ever since her return to the palace he had sensed them about her, though they never took concrete enough form for him to give them a name. Sometimes late at night, on the edge of sleep, he thought he could detect them seeping out from her bedchamber, like dreams that had gone astray. Shadows of forgotten memory, hints of half-formed visions. Trying to grasp hold of the ephemeral images was like trying to capture the breeze in one's hand. Was it a significant phenomenon, worth the time and effort that would be required to decipher it? Or was he simply sensing residual impressions from the Throne of Tears, a dying echo of the power she had once channeled to his entire bloodline? He had not yet managed to sort it all out in his mind. And he was not comfortable discussing it with her—or with anyone—until he did.

"I never did thank you for maintaining my shrine," she said.

Her words startled him back to the present moment. *My shrine.* By that she meant the bloodstained monstrosity in the courtyard. Not that it was bloodstained any longer. The first thing he'd done when she left for Kierdwyn was to have the thing scrubbed down, ten times over, until all evidence of her idolatrous offerings had been erased. It was the least he could do to ease his religious conscience. He'd really wanted to remove the thing entirely, but respect for his mother had overridden Penitent tradition. The mere knowledge that such an idolatrous thing existed within his home was a constant thorn in his side . . . but she was family. And besides, the faith of his forefathers was not entirely delusional, as the Penitents had once believed, but had turned out to be anchored in ancient truths. That deserved some kind of respect, didn't it? Never mind that he hadn't yet figured out how much respect was appropriate.

Did the Protectors in the north still make blood-offerings to the Spears, he wondered? Or had the discovery that their sacred spires were no more than ancient torture chambers dealt a death blow to that tradition? He kept intending to ask her that, but the words always caught in his throat.

"For the moment it may remain." His voice betrayed no emotion. "Not because I value it, but because it is yours."

A strange look passed over her face. A kind of fleeting sadness. "Nevertheless, I am grateful."

The servant finished gathering up the maps and writing implements from his Karmandi meeting and eased silently out the door. Salvator waited until he heard the snick of the latch closing before he said, "Clearly you have something on your mind, Mother. Speak freely. You know you have my ear."

She smiled slightly. "It always was hard to hide things from you."

LEGACY OF KINGS 129

He returned the half-smile. "My royal parents trained me well."

For a moment she looked down at her hands. So slender. So delicate. The fingernails she'd broken off during her Alkali climb had grown back, and the bruises from that adventure had long since faded. Since her return from Kierdwyn she had even put aside her mourning dress, and now there was no visible hint about her of the terrible trials she'd endured recently, or the beloved half-brother—and unborn child—that Alkali had stolen from her.

"I want to return to Kierdwyn," she said.

He nodded. "I would prefer you not use sorcery to travel there, but other than that, I have no issue with it."

"I do not mean to visit, Salvator." The gray eyes fixed on him. What sadness there was in their depths! "I've been invited to study with the Guardians."

For a moment he could find no response. All his royal intelligence had not warned him about this move. "To do . . . what? Join their Order?"

"Perhaps. It's not yet decided."

"That is . . ." He had no words to finish the sentence.

"Unexpected?"

"To say the least."

"They need me, Salvator."

"And I don't?"

Again she smiled slightly. "You may have once, but I don't think that's true any longer. I see more of Danton in you each day. Not his temper, not his arrogance, but his insight, his innate authority. The things that made him great. And your vassals can sense it in you, too; I can see that when they leave your audience chamber. Servants no longer whisper questions about how a Penitent monk could possibly have become High King in the first place . . . now they wonder instead how a prince of Danton's blood could ever have wound up a monk." She shook her head; her expression was a strange mix of pride and sadness. "You don't need me any longer, Salvator. Not as you once did."

"You flatter me," he said, because such a response was required. The praise should have pleased him, but its taste was bittersweet. It was best for the kingdom that he nurture his royal instincts— he knew that—but he mourned the sacrifice that it required. Would he wake up one day to find himself so like his father that all those years of Penitent devotion would be only a distant memory to him? That would be a loss for all the kingdom, as well as for his own soul.

"And if it happens that some day you do need my counsel," she added, "the Guardians' witches can send me back here at a moment's notice. You know that."

"And by the same token you could remain here," he countered, "and my witches could send you to the Guardians whenever you liked. So I don't really comprehend the request."

She sighed; the delicate fingers twisted about one another. "Salvator . . . I've become a symbol to the Guardians. Not only for my *lyr* heritage, though that's certainly part of it. They now think that some of their more cryptic prophecies may make reference to the Throne of Tears . . . and to me." She drew in a deep breath. "There's war on the horizon, you know that. A stranger and more terrible war than any living man has seen. If they're right, I will be on the front lines of that war. I need to prepare for that possibility."

The full meaning of what she was suggesting took a minute to sink in. "You intend to train as a warrior?"

"Favias has suggested it."

"That is . . ." He could not finish the thought.

"Inappropriate, for a queen? A mad enterprise, perhaps?" A corner of her mouth twitched. "There were those who said the same thing about my climbing the Sister, Salvator."

"Aye. I cursed that enterprise myself, once I learned about it."

"And probably would have forbidden it, yes?"

He said nothing.

"I have more strength than you know," she told him. And her eyes warned him: *Do not ask after its source. You will not like the answer.*

That was yet one more secret that she thought he did not know. How strange it was that she would liken him to Danton in one breath, and forget in the next moment that Salvator's father had prided himself on knowing everything that was going on around him . . . even the most closely guarded secrets of his kin.

Aye, Mother, I know what Ramirus did to you. I know that your altered muscles can rival the strength of a man's, and that your reflexes can match that of a seasoned warrior. I also know what the process has cost you. I have seen you stumble on level ground, for not being sure of your own stride. Your flesh is like that of a stranger to you, and you must maneuver it consciously, unlike those of us who still inhabit the same bodies the Creator originally gave us. Thus does He take you to task for what you have done in allowing such a vile power to reshape you.

But training as a warrior would help her with that. The repetitive exercises, the disciplined exertion, all of it was ideal for such a task. Was that why she really wanted to go back to Kierdwyn? To help bring her mind and body back into harmony? If so, she would never admit that to him; it would require confessing too much about her true dealings with Ramirus.

Secrets within secrets within secrets. They made his head spin sometimes.

"I am not averse to your training with the Guardians," he said at last.

She let out a deep sigh of relief. "So I have your permission to return to Kierdwyn?"

"No," he said quietly. "You do not."

Her mouth opened for a moment, then closed again, silently.

"There's no need for you to leave the palace," he told her, perversely pleased by the look of surprise on her face. "We can bring teachers here. I'll have Cresel make the arrangements."

"But, Salvator—"

"Do you feel my people are insufficient to the task?"

She shook her head in exasperation. "Do they know how to call the Souleaters to them? To bring the creatures down from the sky so they can be struck by weapons? Can they teach me where the ikati hide is thinnest, where the blood that runs through their body is closest to the surface, or in what light their eyesight is weakest? Do they know what body parts need to be salvaged when one of them is killed, and in what order they must be cut out of its flesh so that armor and weapons can be made from them? Or why that must be done in the first place?"

"No," he said quietly. "My people do not know those things."

"Well." She folded her arms stubbornly across her chest. "That is what I need to learn."

For a long moment he gazed at her in silence. His face betrayed nothing of the maelstrom of thoughts inside his head.

"Send word to Master Favias," he said at last. "Bid him send me a Guardian who can teach you these things. Or more than one, if necessary. He may send a whole company, if he likes. They are welcome here."

She exhaled noisily and seemed about to protest. But there

LEGACY OF KINGS   133

was really nothing more she could say. In theory, he had just given her everything she'd asked for. There was no justification for arguing the point any further, even though it was clear from her expression that his answer fell short of what she really wanted.

But there is a reason you can't go back to Kierdwyn, Mother. I can't tell you what it is just yet, but trust me, there is one.

"There's one more issue to consider, if I am to remain here." she said. A spark of subtle defiance in her voice.

His brow furrowed. "What?"

"Someone whose counsel I value. Whose counsel I *need.* Someone who is not welcome in your house."

He drew in a sharp breath. "Ramirus."

She nodded.

He crossed his arms over his chest and scowled, but said nothing.

"He knows a lot about the ikati," she told him. "Not because he is a sorcerer but simply because he was alive so long ago, when the legends were fresh. And he is gathering information from the other Magisters as well." She stiffened defiantly. "I said I would respect your prejudices while I live in this palace, and I normally keep him at a distance, but if I am going to have to do my training here, then that is no longer a viable arrangement."

He said it quietly, in a voice edged with ice: "You ask to bring a vessel of corruption into my house?"

"Your issue is with his sorcery. That's not what I need him for."

"One cannot channel corruption through one's soul without being tainted by it."

"And no man is so lost to evil that he cannot seek redemption." She cocked her head to one side. "Isn't that what the Penitents teach? I seem to remember reading it in one of your holy books."

His mouth twitched. "You acknowledge him as evil, then?"

Her eyes narrowed. "I acknowledge that *you* see him that way."

"And what is he to you?"

"A *scholar*, Salvator. A teacher. A man whose steady hand guided this kingdom for decades, and who is responsible for much of its greatness." She paused. "A man who helped raise you. Making you the man you are today. Or have you forgotten that?"

No, I have not forgotten. But nor am I the same youth who left this palace four years ago in search of enlightenment.

But what she asked was reasonable. He knew that. It was because of his command that she was unable to leave the palace, to go to a place where she might meet freely with Ramirus. He could not deny her this.

The penance would be his to bear.

"Very well," he said tightly. "But he will not use sorcery when he visits here, or use his power to alter your mind or flesh in any way. If you have need of some magical service, you will ask my witches to provide it. He may transport himself as he pleases—I realize no words of mine can make him do otherwise—but that is all he will use his power for, under my roof. While he is in my palace, he will play the role of a scholar and nothing more." He paused, watching her closely. "Is that acceptable?"

She bit her lip, then nodded. "Yes. Thank you."

"You think you can get him to agree to that?"

She nodded solemnly. "Aye, Salvator. He will agree."

"Then it's settled. Send word to the Guardians of what we've agreed, and have them send their teachers to the palace." He drew in a deep breath. "And when they arrive, I will train by your side. In knowledge, in combat, in all of it. I'll even learn how to chop up the Souleaters and make soup out of them, if that will be useful."

"Seriously?"

He stepped forward and took her hands in his own; his expression was solemn. "I have never been more serious, Mother. There is war coming. You were right in that. And while I can't predict who will or won't be on the front lines . . ."

He stopped. There was no way to say any more to her without revealing too much. He wasn't yet ready to tell her what he suspected.

"We should prepare for the worst," he said quietly. Just that.

Gratefully, she nodded. And she reached up on tiptoe to kiss him in turn, a barely manageable feat given how he towered over her. She might have the strength of a man in her veins, thanks to Ramirus, but she was still a small and fragile creature in aspect.

Though not in spirit, he thought.

As she took her leave, he lifted the flagon to his lips, sighed, and drank deeply.

I'm sorry I can't tell you the truth, Mother. Sorry I can't explain that my visions are stronger when you are near me, their details clearer, their meaning almost within my grasp. Or that when you leave my presence, they fade once more, and I am left with no more than ominous shadows. Only with you nearby do I have any hope of interpreting my dreams, and finding the creature that nests within my kingdom.

Whatever had happened to Gwynofar on the Throne of Tears, she was clearly some kind of catalyst for him now. Would she have the same effect on other members of his family? Perhaps on all the *lyr*? He dared not ask after that possibility directly.

If the Guardians even suspected that such a thing was possible they would steal her away into the northlands, to subsume her into their ranks forever. He could not allow that to happen. Not while there was still a Souleater in his realm, whose location he must discover. And not while he suspected he might have a special immunity to the power of the ikati, which her presence might be enhancing as well.

I need you more than they do right now. He shut his eyes as the warm alcohol seeped into his blood, soothing his spirit. *Once the Souleater in the High Kingdom is dead . . . then we can decide where to go from there. Together.*

———

Ramirus was waiting for her by the river. Out of deference to Salvator, Gwynofar had not allowed him to use sorcery to transport her, and of course she would not waste a witch's life-essence just to save time. So she had simply ridden the distance, with two servants flanking her, and only as she approached the Magister did they fall behind, out of hearing range.

She did not dismount, but sat upon her white mare as it pawed the ground restlessly, looking down at the Magister.

"He said no," Ramirus said.

She nodded tightly. "Yes."

"You knew that he would."

Again she nodded. "Yes."

It was a warm night. The breeze rippled through her mount's mane and through the Magister's long beard. Fine white strands stirred in the wind.

"What else?" he asked her.

"You are welcome in the palace. You may not use sorcery, save for your own transportation, but he will accept your counsel.

Or at least . . . he will allow *me* to accept your counsel. Which is effectively the same thing."

He nodded. "Then you have what you wanted most."

She whispered it: "Yes."

"There are few who would ask me to accept such limitations."

"There are few who would offer you the chance to be part of a *lyr* prophecy in return."

"Yes," he acknowledged. "There is that."

She hesitated. "Do you think that the prophecy is true, Ramirus? That this war can't be waged without me?"

"Prophecies are strange things, Majesty. Always confusing, often misleading. This one speaks of a woman of power sitting upon a throne of tears. I can think of two women who might satisfy that metaphor. Ironically, given the way things are heading, you may both wind up in the center of things." He shrugged. "Even if the prophecy were correct, I would be wary of reading too precise a meaning into any given passage. But as a general warning that you should prepare for the worst, and learn everything you can about the enemy while you still have time to do so . . . yes, Majesty. That part is certainly true."

"Thank you, Ramirus." She sighed. "Will you stay at the palace, then? Your chambers are the same as when you left them. I allowed no man to touch your things."

"I would have thought Danton would have set fire to the contents after our parting. Or at least smashed everything in sight."

"He wanted to." A soft, sad smile—half nostalgia, half mourning—passed over her face. "I would not allow it." Her slender finger stroked the thin leather reins. "I always hoped you would come back to us."

"Well." He huffed. "To turn you down after that statement would be a veritable act of cruelty."

She cocked her head to one side. "That is 'yes,' then?"

"Aye. That is 'yes.' Though I suspect that when Salvator told you I'd be welcome in the palace, he did not think I would actually be moving in. It will be . . ." A faint, dry smile creased his lips. ". . . interesting."

Her eyes narrowed. "Don't bait him, Ramirus."

He chuckled. "Asking that of me is like asking a fish not to swim, Majesty. But don't worry. I'll try not to be the source of too much torment for your Penitent son. Above and beyond what my mere presence mandates, of course."

He stepped back to give her room, bowing his head slightly in leave-taking. Nodding an acknowledgment of the gesture, she kneed the white mare into motion, turning it back toward the palace. Not until she was out of sight would he draw his power to him, she knew. Not until the shadows of the night had wrapped themselves around him would he meld himself into them, making his exit as silent and secret as the breeze.

Urging her mare into a sudden gallop, she left the flustered servants to pull their horses about and race to catch up as she headed back toward the palace.

CHAPTER 9

THE GODS were watching her.

Kamala could sense them all around her as she stared into the smoke. A circle of gods watching her as she strained her Sight to the utmost, trying to manage by purely morati gifts what she had thus far failed to do with sorcery. Their expressions were impassive, revealing nothing of their purpose, but their presence raised a line of cold goosebumps along her skin.

But even when she was able to shut them out of her awareness enough to focus on her Sight, it was to no avail. Just as sorcery had failed her countless times before, her innate gift failed her now.

With a sigh she sat back on her heels, rubbing her head with weary fingers. Inside the offering bowl a perfumed scarf from Siderea Aminestas' collection was slowly burning to ash, releasing pungent smoke along with its metaphysical resonance. Morati mystics often used such tools as a focus for their Sight, staring into the patterns of the smoke as they tried to conjure meaning from nothingness. Had she really thought that a bit of scented smoke might make a difference to a Magister? Or was the ritual aspect of it simply comforting?

Shutting her eyes for a moment, she drew in a deep breath of the scented air and tried to center her spirit. Whispers seemed to surround her, soft sounds, like the murmuring of insects. The voices of gods? She could sense them gather around her every time she made an effort to find the Witch-Queen. A dozen unknown deities, two dozen, sometimes as many as a hundred, clothed in garments that ranged from the finest silk to the coarsest hemp, in styles she did not recognize. Sorcery might net her an identification or two, picking out names and aspects from among the crowd—*Sekmenit the Bloodthirsty* or *Utark, Lord of the Dead*—but it could not tell her why they were there. The mysterious images just stood by in silence while she searched, offering neither help nor hindrance, then dissipated like the wind soon after her efforts were concluded.

If she could somehow get them to assist her—would that help? Did they know where Siderea Aminestas was? Were they trying to tell her that? Or was this about something else entirely?

With a sigh she rose to her feet. Body and soul both ached from the long hours of futile concentration. *There must be a better way,* she thought.

Conjuring an apple, biting deeply into its cool flesh, she gazed about the polished wooden floor and the maps that she had etched into its surface. This was the first time she had ever conjured a shelter for herself rather than claimed a structure that already existed, and if the results were somewhat bare in decor, at least it had the facilities she required. Her meditation chamber was vast, and the maps etched into its polished wooden floor all radiated out from the center of the room, as if that were the actual center of the world. Each section had been copied from some morati map, adjusted in scale and then burned into the wood with sorcery, exactly as it appeared on the original parchment. The overall result was a discordant creation, its style shifting from panel to panel, mountain ranges transforming from the hurried scratch-marks of a traveling scribe to the rich, sweeping strokes of a master cartographer as they crossed over unseen boundaries . . . but in its entirety, it effectively represented the world. Or at least as much of the world as humans had explored.

The arrangement helped her concentrate, but it did little more than that. Thus far Siderea Aminestas had defied all detection. Mere sorcery could not locate the woman. Not even hers.

But she was not willing to accept failure. It had nothing to do with the box of tokens that Colivar had hinted at, though that was certainly enticing. It had to do with pride.

Think, Kamala. Think. There must be a way.

For the hundredth time, she reviewed what she had learned about the power of the ikati, when they'd all been briefed in Kierdwyn. *Their power can draw human attention toward them, or turn it away. Few ikati can manage the trick well enough to be truly invisible, but when men are distracted, they might as well be. Legends speak of human wars in which the ikati appeared suddenly, seemingly out of nowhere, to feast upon the dying. It is hard to know how much that reflects their mesmeric power, since generally in the midst of battle no one stops to study the sky.*

A new thought flickered briefly in the back of her head but was gone too quickly for her to attach a name to it.

If this queen can hide herself from others of her kind, she thought, *then that's probably the kind of power she's using. Not true invisibility,*

but rather, an ability to make her subject look somewhere else, at
something else instead.

A shiver of excitement ran through Kamala. And also dread.
The thought that was taking shape in her mind had potential,
but the amount of work that would be required to test it was
almost too vast to imagine. A morati lifetime might not be
enough for it.

Looking down at the floor surrounding her, she contemplated
its scale. Tiny lines represented wide, raging rivers. A line of
loosely drawn mountain peaks might represent an entire range.
The whole of the territory that she had explored in her years
with Ethanus took up no more space than the palm of her hand
. . . if that much.

Somewhere in that vast world there would be a place she
could not investigate. A place she *would* not investigate.

It would likely be very small. Maybe only the size of a nesting
site. Invisible from a distance, just as the actual nest would be.
If one were close enough to be affected by its power, could one
somehow detect that effect? That would be a much larger range.

If one's viewpoint were close enough, would that suffice?

With a shaky breath, she considered the world map laid out
before her.

I cannot search every inch of it, she thought.

But the ikati did not live everywhere. They preferred stark
mountains for their nesting sites. They required a source of water
somewhere near open ground, so that their vast wingstroke
would not be impeded when they came to drink. And since
they now fed exclusively on human beings, they would want to
be near a population center of some kind. During the First Age
of Kings they had been drawn to the great human cities like
flies to honey.

She ran her eyes down the edges of the mountain ranges, pausing at each lake, each river coursing through an open plain. (But at this scale, how many smaller ones might she miss?) She used her sorcery to determine where human habitations were clustered. (But how many morati must be in one place for a Souleater's hunger to be satisfied?) She tried to figure out what kind of climate the creatures would prefer. (Would they flee as far south as they could, to escape the curse that once bound them, or would they stay in the north right now, where the summer days were longest? If the latter, then how far from the Wrath would they need to be to feel safe?)

Slowly, inch by inch, she edited the map with her sorcery. Erasing any locations that could not possibly meet her criteria. Sometimes that meant a whole mountain range had to go. Sometimes just a single canyon.

When she was done, she stared down at the map in silence, contemplating her results.

Well. That leaves only half the world to search. Much better.

But daunting though the undertaking was, she knew she had to try. There simply was no better option. And besides, what else was she going to do with her time? Twiddle her thumbs creating palaces on mountaintops, like some of the Magisters apparently did? This task at least had real meaning.

—And for one heart-wrenching moment she was back at Rhys' funeral, looking down at his body. Remembering the emptiness of that moment, and the cold kiss of envy she had felt then.

Now I, too, have purpose.

She wrote to Colivar before she began. A simple note, which sorcery deposited at their secret drop point. *Tell me all that you know of the sort of terrain that Souleaters prefer,* she wrote. *Do not try to guess at what details will be relevant, but tell me everything.* Favias had briefed them in Kierdwyn, but she doubted that he knew as much as Colivar did about the ikati's true habits. She was beginning to doubt that anyone knew as much about the Souleaters as Colivar did.

But his response might take days to come, if it came at all. There was no point in wasting all that time. Settling herself down in the center of the vast map, conjuring a pillow to rest her head on and a small bit of food and water to have by her side, she shut her eyes, sighed deeply, and extended her sorcerous senses out into the world, to begin the impossible search.

CHAPTER 10

THE DESERT region on the room-sized map was represented by a gleaming field of diamonds, each one faceted to perfection. To the east of the desert, past a wide ridge of black onyx mountains, a narrow band of emeralds appeared, the fertile shoreline of the great southern River of Life. Smooth chrysocolla tiles represented its waters. To the north of the desert, diamond sands gave way to a city sculpted out of gold and silver, whose soaring monuments were now edged in fire from the late afternoon sunlight trickling into the room. The chrysocolla river wound through the vast map, progressing in tight serpentine loops, with gleaming cities at every turn. And then there was the lapis Sea of Tears, beyond which every northern nation had been assigned its own semiprecious stone. Amethyst for Sankara, topaz for Sendal, blue chalcedony for Corialanus. The High Kingdom was laid out in jasper, each vassal state a different variety of the stone. An observant spectator might note that the surface of that particular nation was smooth, its mountains represented by bands of flat black stone, the whole of it polished to a slippery gloss. A savvy spectator might make note of the fact that such a surface was much easier to move military markers across.

Right now the crystal markers of Anshasa's armies were clustered about that nation's capital city or ranged along the shoreline nearby just to the north: small faceted obelisks to represent hundreds of men, large ones to represent thousands. There was a cluster of troop crystals up north as well, across the base of the isthmus of Tathys . . . the one land route that gave access to the High Kingdom's territories. Was that a defensive formation, or did it indicate an aggressive campaign in the planning stages? As Colivar looked down at it, he could not tell from the positioning.

In a world without Magisters, such a map would have been priceless. But in a world where powerful sorcery was regularly harnessed to serve the whims of kings, it was merely indulgent.

His Most Merciful Majesty Hasim Farah, Scourge of the Tethys, Guardian of the River of Life, Custodian of the Sacred City, looked up from his musings when he heard his Magister enter. A faint, dry smile spread across his face as he blinked. "Colivar, isn't it? I knew someone by that name once. I think. Over time one forgets."

Colivar chuckled. "I beg your indulgence for my long absence." He bowed his head respectfully. "Of, course, his Majesty always has the means to summon me should he require my service. Unless he has forgotten that as well."

"Yes, yes." Farah waved a ringed hand absently. "You are free to go about as you please, of course. I merely jest." He clapped his hands loudly, and a eunuch in white silk appeared, seemingly from nowhere. "Refreshment for my Magister Royal." The man bowed and hurried off.

Colivar was too distracted to be hungry, but he had learned long ago that there was no point in turning down Farah's hospitality. The king was a son of the desert, and his native culture made such gestures obligatory. It was easier to break bread and eat a handful of olives than it was to argue about whether such things were necessary.

"Come." Farah walked over to Colivar, patting him on the back as he gestured for him to walk alongside him. Colivar had known very few men who would touch a Magister so casually. "You keep the rains falling, so that my storehouses are full of grain. My wives are fecund, my slaves are eager for pleasure, and the Green Vomit—or whatever that miserable plague is called— has never crossed my borders. What more could a king ask for?"

Colivar glanced back at the map. "It looks to me like you have a few new projects planned."

"Ah." Farah followed his gaze to the military markers in Tethys, and to the jasper expanses beyond them. "Tempting, isn't it? A new High King, young and untested. Mistrustful of Magisters, I'm told, and shackled by a religion of guilt and self-denial. Thus far I've restricted myself to gathering intelligence on him, and perhaps a few subtle political jabs managed through proxies, but I admit that the prospect of all-out war is appealing. We haven't fought the High Kingdom in an honest and open manner for many years."

"Don't underestimate Salvator Aurelius," Colivar warned. "There's more to him than meets the eye."

"Of course. His mother would not have summoned him to the throne were it otherwise." He shook his head. "Imagine that. A woman determining who would be High King! I'm torn between being amazed that such a thing could happen and wanting to see such a woman for myself."

Colivar smiled. "Only *see* her, Majesty?"

The Anshasan king laughed long and hard. The sound was rich with energy and power, and it reverberated off the stone walls like the pealing of a great bell. "You know me too well, my Magister. Come. Break bread with me."

He led Colivar to a lavish chamber, where servants were already laying out the ritual repast. Richly woven rugs and cushions lay scattered about the floor, and the heavy drapes that covered the smooth stone walls suggested the folds of a tent. Colivar was never quite sure if Farah actually preferred that style, or merely understood the value of nurturing a desert mystique among his subjects. The fierce tribes of the south were the stuff of legend, all the more so because few Anshasans had ever actually seen one of their warriors in the flesh. By playing up his desert heritage, Farah became part of that legend. The result lent him strength in diplomatic circles and discouraged aggressive posturing by his rivals; one did not pick a fight with a desert chieftain unless one had a sword in hand and was ready to fight to the death.

As Farah settled down onto a pile of richly embroidered cushions, his long robe billowing out around him, he was joined by half a dozen women in various stages of dishabille. Each was from a different province of his empire, and they ranged in color from a young beauty with the bronze finish of the sun-kissed delta to a leggy seductress with skin as black as charcoal. All of them were exquisitely beautiful, of course, and dressed in a combination of glittering jewels and filmy silks that left little to the imagination. That, too, was desert custom, a statement of power that no Anshasan would mistake: *Covet what is mine, but know that you may not touch it, save by my command.*

Not that Farah would deny Colivar any woman he wanted,

of course. In fact, as the Magister settled himself onto his own
pile of cushions, the southern king waved over Safya, one of his
favorites, to attend him. Lending one's wife or servant to a
valued servitor was a desert custom as casual as breaking bread,
and Safya had pleased the Magister in the past. On this day,
however, he had little interest in such pastimes.

The eunuch arrived and set out a tray of bread and olives
between them; the dense loaf was freshly baked, still warm from
the oven, and its scent filled the chamber like a fine perfume.
Farah broke off a piece of it for himself and then passed the
loaf to Colivar, who did the same. Not until they had both eaten
a token mouthful of the stuff and washed it down with a ritual
swallow of ale did Farah speak again.

"You're got some weighty business on your mind, or else I've
forgotten how to read you."

Colivar bowed his head solemnly. "Your Majesty is insightful,
as always."

"Something to do with these Souleaters you've been hunting?"

Colivar's expression darkened. "Aye," he said quietly.
"Something to do with them."

For a moment the Magister just stared into his cup and said
nothing. Then, in a low voice, he said, "I regret that I must
leave your service."

Farah drew in a sharp breath. "Have I not treated you well?
Do the size and scope of my kingdom not bestow status upon
you, such as benefits you in the rivalries among your own kind?
You said once that such things mattered to you."

"Indeed, our contract has been a satisfying one. I am sorry
to leave you."

Farah sat back, a perplexed scowl upon his face. Losing the
service of a Magister of Colivar's repute was no small thing,

especially with possible warfare looming in the north. "Anything that you desire, if I can give it to you, you know that I will. Even the best of my wives." He waved a hand about the room, a gesture that encompassed the women by his side, the rich trappings that surrounded them, and the whole of the vast kingdom that lay beyond. "Have I ever denied you anything?"

"You've been most generous," Colivar agreed. "Believe me when I say this, I regret this move with all my heart."

Farah exhaled noisily in frustration. "Then what's the problem? Does it have something to do with this investigation of yours?"

Lips tight, Colivar nodded.

"You know you're free to come and go as you please. That was our arrangement from the start. I've never placed limits upon you. If you need more time to yourself, well then, take it."

Colivar nodded. "It's been a good arrangement. And up to this point, it was sufficient for my needs. But now . . ." He sighed heavily. "The Souleaters have invaded in force, and we don't know where they are. They have to be found—and dealt with—before they have a chance to establish new nests. Otherwise, the war will be lost before it has even begun."

Farah frowned. "And my kingdom can't serve you as a base of operations? There are few nations that could offer you better facilities, I think. If you need a staging ground for war . . ."

"Majesty." Colivar's expression was tight. "Forgive me. It has come to the point where I must focus all my attention on one task, and I need to make sure nothing is going to distract me. Not even a contract as pleasant as this one." He glanced at Safya with a half-smile; she blushed prettily.

With a heavy sigh, Farah settled back into his cushions. A copper-skinned beauty raised an olive to his lips and he accepted it absently, chewing without pleasure as he contemplated the situation.

"I will need to replace you," he said at last. "That is no easy thing."

Colivar nodded. He'd been with Farah since the man's first days on the throne, drawn to the challenge of helping a young prince build an empire. Farah had never experienced the need to search for a Magister Royal, or lived through an interim period without one.

There would be no danger to him during such an interim, of course. The kingdoms of the world would not last long if sorcerous vultures moved in the minute a Magister walked away from his job. All of the sorcerers understood that, and they would give Farah a reasonable period of time to seek a new contract, just as they had done with Danton. A powerful nation like Anshasa would have applicants appearing out of the woodwork the instant Colivar's resignation became public knowledge, so there would be no lack of options for him.

But the secrecy with which the Magisters habitually shrouded their business meant that a morati king had little ability to evaluate candidates. Most morati knew less about the predilections of individual Magisters than they did about clouds in the sky. Farah had been fortunate in his deal with Colivar, and he knew it; he might not be so fortunate again.

This has been a good situation for me, too. Colivar thought solemnly. *I will miss it.* "If you will permit me, Majesty, I have a suggestion."

Farah raised an eyebrow.

"I know of a Magister who is without a contract right now. I believe he might be interested in serving Anshasa. If you like, I will let him know that you have a contract to offer."

Farah's eyes narrowed suspiciously. "Didn't you tell me once that Magisters were sworn enemies to one another? I seem to recall a comment about how your average sorcerer would rather have his eyes gouged out by a red-hot poker than help another of his own kind. Yet you would help this one?"

"We are rivals, not enemies," he said quietly. *And such injury means little, when we can steal the athra required to build new eyes in the time it would take you to blink your own.* "And my relations with this particular Magister are . . . uniquely civilized."

"I see."

"You need someone with knowledge of the Souleaters. Sulah has been following their progress along with me. He will know what signs to look for."

The implication of his words took a moment to sink in. When they did, one of the women drew back from Farah and wrapped her arms protectively about herself; goosebumps prickled her charcoal skin.

"You expect there will be *signs* in Anshasa?"

Colivar shrugged stiffly. "Your kingdom is vast. The Souleaters must seek shelter somewhere. Better to be watchful, don't you think, than to risk being taken by surprise? Sulah knows what to look for. And he has connections with other Magisters who are sworn to cooperate in this matter. If he calls for help, they— *we*—will come."

Farah's eyes narrowed. "Magisters swearing to aid one another. Why does that worry me more than Souleaters?"

"It is a bad sign," Colivar agreed, smiling faintly. "Normally no enemy could have brought that about. But these are not normal times."

Farah frowned as he considered the matter. The reasons Colivar had given for leaving his service were weak, and clearly he knew that. Farah would have given the Magister all the time and space that he required for his business, and they could have made it work. But the truth was, Colivar feared that if he remained bound to a particular domain and then the Souleaters moved into it, it might awaken territorial instincts in him that were better off forgotten. Instincts he might not be able to control. And that was a truth he could not share with any morati . . . or even with his own kind.

Some of the Magisters thought that their curse had been weakening over time. New recruits certainly didn't seem to suffer through First Transition the way earlier generations had. If that were indeed the case, then Sulah's youth meant he might have better resistance to the ancient drives than the ones who had come before him. Certainly better than Colivar, who was among the oldest of his kind, and uniquely weak in that area.

Youth was needed here. Human instincts were needed here. Colivar could offer neither.

"Very well," Farah said at last. He was clearly not pleased by what was happening, but he was wise enough to know that arguing with a Magister was a pointless exercise. "Bring me this Sulah. If he suits my needs, and I think I can work with him, he may take over your contract."

A knot inside Colivar's chest loosened a bit. It was only one knot of many, but the change in pressure was noticeable. "I thank you, Majesty."

With a gentle touch to Safya's cheek, genuine in its regret, he rose to his feet. Farah had a taste for interesting women, and Colivar would miss having access to them. "I think it is best that I leave now, Majesty. I have much to do."

Farah nodded regally. "I am sorry to see you go, Magister

Colivar, but I understand. Know that you have both my gratitude and blessing."

With a final nod of leave-taking, Colivar began to walk away. He could have done one of a hundred other things instead, things involving wings or shadows or flashes of light or quivering portals hanging in midair . . . but he simply walked. It seemed a respectful gesture to mark the end of their contract. The end of this part of his life.

"Magister Colivar."

He turned back to look at the king.

"You will always be welcome here. I know that's not the usual custom, but it is *my* custom, and I will see that your successor honors it. Whoever that turns out to be."

Colivar had nothing to say to that. Magisters were fiercely territorial creatures, and no matter what courtesies a king like Hasim Farah might offer, he would never show up in the court of a rival without proper clearance. Doing so might stress the beasts within them both to the breaking point.

So many customs, so many constraints, all to keep us human. What happens if those tools ever fail us?

"I understand," he said at last. And he added—because it was expected of him—"Thank you."

From the corner of his eye he could see Safya returning to her master's side as he finally left the chamber.

CHAPTER 11

*M*OUNTAINS.

Stark granite cliffs, bleached white by the cool morning sunlight.

Jagged ravines, shadow-rivers coursing down their length.

Stark granite cliffs, blazing gold in the noontime sun.

Snow-clad peaks, desolate and irrelevant, despised by the ikati.

Stark granite cliffs, crowned with sunset's orange fire, darkness licking about their lower flanks . . .

Night fell again. How many times now? Kamala had lost count. The concentration required by her search shut out all other things, including any sense of time. The rhythm of the world was marked only by those things that might aid or hinder her search; nothing else had any meaning.

When evening fell, the bats would leave their caverns, streamers of black wings stretching miles across the face of a blood red sunset. When their flight was low enough, she could use them to focus on, following the twisting fractal patterns of their flight as they swooped down low over the earth, seeking sustenance. Any power obscuring things on the ground below, she reasoned, would interfere with her ability to focus on such details. She could cover many miles that way, scanning her gaze along the shifting column, alert to any place where the details of its formation seemed unclear. Much easier—and more interesting—than studying the earth below.

But all too soon the vast black streamers were gone, and only individual bats remained, moving too quickly for her to focus on. So she adjusted her vision to see the heat of living things and continued onward into the night, scanning the ground for detail. Any detail. It did not matter what she focused on, exactly, only whether she could see it clearly.

It had been days now. Her mind ached from the effort. Her soul ached from boredom. A million trees. Ten million rocks. All were meaningless, save that she had to look at them. How many were there in this vast wilderness? A tiny bird could move a mountain of sand grain by grain, but that did not mean he would not go crazy from boredom halfway through the job.

She'd intended to do her search in stages, returning to her body each night to mark out the day's route on her great map, but instead she'd just kept going, ignoring the hunger pangs that resonated through her abandoned flesh. Sorcery would keep her body alive well enough, though her body clearly wasn't happy about the exercise. Was it determination that kept her going, or did she just not have the heart to return to her maps and see how little ground she had really covered?

At dawn the bats would return to their haven, aiding her search once more. As the cool, blue light of morning spread out across the land in their wake, she envisioned herself with broad wings sweeping out from her shoulders. Souleater wings, flickering crystal in the sunlight. It helped her figure out how much space was required for their flight, so that she did not have to bother searching areas they could not enter. And it was, in a strange way, a pleasing exercise. She passed the time by imagining she could feel how the wings would beat against the air, in that strange, sweeping stroke, so unlike that of any bird. She couldn't quite work out the mechanics of it. Perhaps when she returned home she would make herself a Souleater's body and test its capacity in some secret place—

Damn.

She'd gotten so caught up in the imagined sensations of her flight that she'd lost sight of what she was doing. It wasn't the first time that had happened—boredom had its cost—but this was the longest lapse yet. Looking back, she saw that the last landmark she'd really paid attention to—an odd spire of wind-carved rock—was miles behind her now. Almost out of sight. She was going to have to refocus her sorcerous vision back on that spot and pick up where she'd left off.

With a sigh, she gathered the athra she needed to shift her focus. At least it would be easier going in that direction; without the need to study the ground as she moved, she could reclaim all that distance with a single thought. It was the one advantage of not actually having her body with her.

But she felt an odd twinge as she made the adjustment. If her real body had been in this place, she would have said that her heart had just skipped a beat, but of course it wasn't, so it couldn't. How very strange. The feeling was gone an instant later, but its physical echo was disconcerting. She should probably return to her body and feed it some real food. Sorcery could keep one's flesh alive as long as fresh athra was available, but it wasn't a natural state even for a Magister, and one wasn't supposed to remain like that for too long. Could that be what was wrong? Was her survival instinct telling her that she needed to go back and tend to her physical shell?

Just finish this stretch of ground first, she told herself. It would be all too confusing to come back to this spot later, given that she had passed over it without studying it closely. Too easy to forget later just where her inattention had begun . . . or ended.

Taking a deep mental breath, she focused her senses upon the earth beneath her and began to move forward once more.

But what if it was her soulfire that was the problem? Was it possible she was nearing transition, and was somehow sensing its onset? That wasn't supposed to be possible, according to what Ethanus had taught her. But then, female Magisters weren't supposed to be possible either. And she'd had the Sight in her morati years, which the rest of the Magisters didn't. Maybe this was how that gift was supposed to manifest after First Transition. Maybe in time she would learn to sense when her consorts were about to die, so that she could choose the time and place of her next transition.

If that was what was going on, then she really needed to go back to her body. She remembered her last transition—

Shit.

The ground beneath her was unfamiliar. She'd been daydreaming again. How far had she gone this time, lost in her private reverie? She looked back behind her and saw the narrow spire again, about the same distance away as the last time. Strange. She hadn't thought her mind had been wandering that long.

A strange, cold shiver coursed through her metaphysical substance. If she'd had a spine present, she'd have felt it there.

Slowly, carefully, she headed back toward her starting point. This time she watched the ground as she did so. Or, rather, she tried to watch it. But a flock of birds suddenly rose up, banking into perfect formation as they headed south, and she wondered if she could use them as she had used the bats earlier—

Concentrate.

These mountains had no snow on them, but other ranges did. She had assumed that Souleaters would hate the snow, but maybe that assumption was wrong. Maybe they'd gotten used to it after all their centuries in the north, and now it felt like home to them. Maybe she shouldn't be searching this range at all, she thought. Off to the northwest there was a line of peaks that were all capped in white; maybe she should go explore there instead—

Concentrate!

Gods, she was tired. She could feel her body's hunger coursing through her, now, could smell the sharp tang of the olives that she had conjured by the side of her body—

NO!

Shaking, she reached the spire at last. She had no trouble bringing its details into clear focus, but as soon as she tried to look back the way she had just come, her attention faltered. Sorcery only made the matter worse. Only when she gave up on magical tricks entirely and tried to bring her senses under control by sheer force of will did she get anywhere, and even then her vision wavered. Is this what the other Magisters saw when they were in the vicinity of a Souleater queen's power? Or were they not even able to do this much?

She knew she should go home, then and there. She knew she should return her consciousness to her body, figure out where this place was on her map, and deliver that information to Colivar. He and his people could then hunt the Witch-Queen down, and he could retrieve the box of tokens and deliver it to

Kamala. That was the intelligent plan. The prudent, self-preserving thing to do.

Assuming he actually would deliver it to her, of course. Which was by no means certain.

She should have demanded an Oath for that too, she thought. She should have left nothing to chance.

Too late now.

Just confirm this is the right place, she told herself. *Nothing more. Make sure it is what it seems to be, and then you can go back home and figure out what to do next.*

Slowly, warily, she edged her way forward. Power seemed to ripple in the air ahead of her, visible to her Sight but almost completely invisible to her sorcery. It was a bizarre phenomenon, and she had no clue about how to interpret it.

My body is safe, she reminded herself. *A single thought can return me to it. A second thought can sever any trace that an enemy might use to follow me back home. So nothing can hurt me here.*

And then she came to the place where the strange effect seemed to begin. She braced herself for some kind of resistance at the boundary, but there was none. For a brief moment the desire to return to her body was nearly overwhelming, but she pushed that thought out of her mind. Years of practicing mental discipline under Ethanus' tutelage paid off; the power that guarded this place loosened its stranglehold upon her mind, and she was able to move forward once more.

And then she was inside.

The land itself seemed utterly mundane in its physical aspect, but something about it made her very uneasy. Things were all wrong here. *She* was all wrong here. That awareness was not born of intellectual knowledge but of instinct, a sudden certainty that welled up from the center of her being, a desire to turn and flee this place for her own safety. But that same instinct also urged her to keep moving forward, to claim this place for her own. If there was some other creature who felt she had rights to this place, then let her challenge Kamala for it. She would make this territory her own, and then its resonance would bear her mark. Then it would be the others who felt it beating at their brain like some terrible drumbeat, scattering all rational thought, driving home the fact of her sovereignty. Who would dare to oppose her then?

Steady, Kamala. Steady.

Shaken, she tried to focus on her physical surroundings as a means of disciplining her mind. Thus far in her search she had relied solely upon sight, but now she conjured a full array of sorcerous senses to complement her vision. An odd, musky sweetness wafted past her, alien and familiar at the same time; something inside her found it powerfully repellent, so much so that she instinctively moved away from it. Then the breeze shifted slightly, and she caught another scent, coming from the southwest. Corruption. Death. Something had died there, whose corpse was slowly surrendering the last scraps of its flesh to scavengers and rot. But there was something else in that direction, too. A subtle note that she could not identify, mixed in with the message of decay. Carefully she moved in that direction, scanning the landscape around her for any sign of threat as she did so. Repeating over and over again the single reminder, as if it were a spell of protection: *I can return home any time I want to.*

If she'd had a heart present, it would surely have been pounding now.

She passed over a steep ridge, then eased herself down into a rocky valley on the other side. The smell was becoming stronger, but not in the manner of natural odors. It was more like a memory of odor that clung to the landscape as a whole, rather than drifting along in the air. After a moment she realized what was causing the strangeness . . . and it sent a chill through her very spirit.

The smell was not real.

All her life, she had been able to sense supernatural forces. It was a gift that morati called the Sight, since its manifestation was usually visual in nature. With her Sight she had seen the power of Ethanus' magical repairs glowing in the corner of his house and had watched his sorcery flicker about her during their lessons, like a swarm of mad fireflies. But the gift was not limited to sight alone, and sometimes it manifested in other ways.

Like now.

What she was smelling was power . . . and the death of power. Some creature had met its end here, violently enough that its spiritual essence had been splattered across the landscape. That was the trace that she was sensing now, that her mind was interpreting as *scent*: psychic bloodstains.

Fascinated now, she began to follow the strange trail back to its source. Each mountain and ravine that she crossed took her farther and farther away from the other strange scent, which was an added benefit of the task. Whatever the musky-sweet odor signified, she sensed that she didn't want to be anywhere near its source.

And then she came around a bend and saw the skeletons.

There were two of them. One was that of a vast creature, its ribcage cavernous, its tail a long, sinuous python of sun-bleached bone. The other, lying some distance away from it, was a smaller thing, maybe half its size, but it was clearly of the same species.

Their wings were missing, but even so, there was no mistaking what the creatures were. Or, rather, what they once had been.

Souleaters.

They had no flesh upon their bones, nor did any sign of the jeweled wings remain. The bones themselves were strangely white, as were the long, curved spikes that rose from each vertebra, but, she did not get the sense they had actually been around long enough to be bleached so thoroughly by natural forces. Indeed, the skeletons of smaller animals could be seen nearby, and those all had the appearance one would expect from natural corpses: bones stained dark with dried blood, scraps of desiccated skin and flesh hanging like ragged pennants from ossiferous masts, maggot casings littered between and about the ribs. Those creatures had died naturally, it seemed. So what had befallen these two ikati?

Kamala drew her power to her in order to investigate that question. It was a difficult task, since she had to reach back to her body to establish a conduit; sorcery this complex required body and soul to be working in harmony. But she was determined to figure out what had happened here, and so she focused all her will upon that distant connection, straining her stolen athra to the utmost to strengthen the channel between body and mind.

And darkness closed in about her suddenly, severing her from the living world in an instant. Death whipped about her, frigid cold piercing her like a thousand razor-edged knives. Maybe a century from now she would come to take transition for granted, but for now it was like suddenly being submerged in a black and icy lake, with no sense of where the surface was. For a moment she panicked and lost her focus, but then sheer survival instinct kicked in. A Magister could not last for more than a handful of seconds without a living soul to draw strength from, so she knew she must find a new one, and quickly. Those who floundered during this process did not survive.

Reaching out with all the force of her will, she searched for a suitable consort. Who could say what factors directed a Magister to one morati as opposed to another? No sorcerer had yet succeeded in controlling the process, or even understanding it. A sorcerer's soul simply reached out in its moment of need and somewhere, somehow, a living soul responded, offering it the proper channel. Why did lightning strike one tree as opposed to another?

She could feel the connection when it was made, and she imagined that she could sense the nature of the soul that her sorcery had chosen. A young and vibrant life, full of vital energy. Though it should not have been possible for her to sense its location, it seemed to her that it was somewhere nearby. Molten hot power began to flow into her, the kind of athra that only a living soul could manufacture; she could feel it being absorbed into her own parasitic core, banishing the ice and the fear, flooding her spirit with fresh life.

And then suddenly she was being dragged out of herself, into a darkness that was more absolute and terrible than transition itself. A mindless emptiness seemed to suck all the strength out of her soul in an instant, leaving nothing but a void in its wake. Her thoughts swirled down into a bottomless abyss, and she could not recover them. It was impossible to think, in that moment. Impossible to protect herself. The very substance of the darkness surrounding her ripped at the substance of her spirit like some terrible predator, and her strength of will bled out into it.

She struggled against the tide of destruction, but its grip was too powerful. Like an animal caught in the jaws of some great beast, her mind lurched madly in whatever direction it could, trying desperately to break loose. But she could feel her strength leaving her even as she did so. Somewhere in that darkness was a terrible Hunger, and she could feel it closing in on her now, threatening to draw her down into a vast, saber-toothed maw from which there was no escape.

With a mental scream—half anguish, half defiance—she made one last desperate attempt to break away from it. She had not spent a lifetime pursuing forbidden knowledge and dodging murderous Magisters only to give up now; anything that tried to devour her soul was going to have to fight for every mouthful. Summoning the final tattered remnants of her strength, she pitted the last of her will against that of the Hunger, struggling to sever whatever supernatural tie was binding her to it—

And the connection snapped. The force of it was stunning. Rent and bleeding, her soul staggered backward, trying to remain oriented enough to find an escape route. From somewhere in the distance came memories of a body that was waiting for her, a body that she was intimately connected to, a body she might return to with a single thought—

She summoned that thought. Set fire to it and let it blaze in the face of the Hunger, like a torch in the face of a ravenous wolf. The grip of the darkness loosened suddenly and she could feel herself breaking free of it, metaphysical blood splattering across the landscape as the maw of the Hunger closed behind her—but too late, too late, this prey had escaped it . . .

Gasping, she opened her eyes. Waves of sickness rose up from her gut, and for a minute she thought she would vomit. Was she really back in her own body now? Hundreds of miles away from the source of the Hunger, where it could not possibly follow her? Hot bile rose up in the back of her throat, and she swallowed it back gratefully, relieved by the unmistakable sign that she had in fact reconnected to her flesh.

What the hell had just happened to her? In all the lessons Ethanus had given her about transition and its dangers, he had never even hinted at something like this. Was she the first Magister to encounter such a threat, or was this one of the many things that her kind didn't talk about?

It was then that she realized that she was not alone.

Colivar.

He stood over her, his expression unreadable. Or maybe there was a hint of amusement in his eyes. In one hand he held a piece of paper, and she recognized the note that she had sent him. In her haste to begin her search she must have been careless about preparing it, and he'd used it as an anchor to locate her.

There was nothing more dangerous than falling into the black abyss of transition while a rival sorcerer was nearby. A Magister wanted nothing more than to grasp that rare moment of opportunity when another Magister was helpless, for whatever purpose amused him. Had he done something to her while she was trapped in that inner darkness? Inserted some suggestion into her brain, perhaps, wrapped a spell around her spirit, adhered some sorcerous sign to her that he would be able to use later, to track her? The list of possibilities was endless.

But she was exhausted from her struggle in the mountains, and right now she just didn't care.

His mouth twitched into a dry smile. "Our usual arrangements seemed a bit slow, given the urgency of the situation. I took the liberty of coming to deliver this in person."

It took her a minute to realize that he was holding out the piece of paper to her. Hand trembling with weakness, she took it from him. Below her original note he had scribed a list of geographical attributes. She let the paper flutter from her hand, onto the floor by her side. And she met his eyes with her own, noting with satisfaction just how startled he was when he realized what was in them.

"I found something," she whispered.

How black his eyes were, in that moment. How hungry. For an instant they offered her a window into that part of his soul where his most precious secrets were guarded. Colivar *needed* Siderea to be found, she realized, the way morati men need food and water.

And then the moment was gone. She blinked, wondering if it had even been real.

"Tell me," he said.

She shut her eyes, trying to remember. "I saw Souleater skeletons. At least that's what I think they were. There were other bones, too, all around them. Some of them might have been wolves. I don't know."

"How many Souleaters?"

"Two. Close by each other. One was smaller than the other. Maybe half the size of the one I fought in the High Kingdom."

His indrawn breath was a soft hiss.

"That's bad?"

He did not answer her, but looked down at the vast map with narrow eyes. Black fire burned in their depths. "Where?"

It took her a minute to realize she did not have that information. The shock of her transition had scrambled her memory of the place, and try as she might she could not put the pieces back together. Her head ached from trying.

Slowly, she rolled over on her side, raising herself up on one elbow. Her head spun as she tried to get her bearings, tracing out her search route in her head even as she drew it out with her finger on the floor. There: She had followed that mountain ridge. Swung around that lake. Crossed that river. Gods, it looked like such a short distance now . . .

And then her knowledge ended. Just ended. It was as if the enchantment that clung to the place had somehow affixed itself to her very mind, and she could not think past it. Shutting her eyes, she struggled to force her way through . . . and the memory of her transition came back to her in a rush, and with it a flood tide of sickness and fear, as though that black void were once more swallowing her whole. She doubled over and vomited onto the map, spasm after spasm, as if her body thought it could expel the source of her fear along with all her internal fluids.

Strong hands grasped her by the shoulders, steadying her from behind. The shock of having another Magister lay hands on her when she was helpless was almost as powerful as the original wave of sickness, and she tried to jerk away from him. But she didn't have enough strength left in her, and his grip was too strong. Then sickness took control again, and for a short eternity it was all she could think about.

When the last of the spasms had finally subsided, Colivar drew her gently backward. "Here. Take this." He was holding a cup of water before her. Every instinct in her soul cried out for her to break free of his grasp, not to let another Magister control her movements like this . . . but he hadn't hurt her yet, had he? Certainly he'd had enough opportunity to do so by this point. So, swallowing thickly, she nodded, and allowed him to bring the cup up to her lips, easing a bit of water into her mouth. It was clear and cool as fresh mountain water, which was not the state her own supply would have been in by now. As she drank, Colivar waved his hand over the floor surrounding them, banishing the mess she had just made into some other less hygienic dimension.

The mountain range she had been tracing curled about like a serpent's tail, she saw. She stared at it numbly, trying to retrieve her voice. "I can't focus in on the exact location," she gasped, when her throat and tongue finally agreed to acknowledge her commands. "I'm sorry."

"It's all right." His nod stirred her hair; her neck prickled to feel his nearness like that. It was a strange and uncomfortable intimacy. "I know the area. It suits all the parameters I gave you." He nodded toward the list that was lying on the floor beside her. "And more importantly . . ." He hesitated. "I detected nothing there myself. Which confirms my suspicion about the role you might be able to play in all this."

For a moment she hesitated. How much should she trust him? There was no denying that he had more knowledge about these matters than she did. And she needed that knowledge. She needed to understand what had happened to her.

He would not give information to her without some kind of trade, she knew that.

"Colivar, I . . . I went into transition there." She trembled slightly as she spoke, despite her best attempt not to. "Something . . . attacked me. I think. It was as if all my strength were being sucked out of me. I felt as if I were being . . . devoured." She shivered, trying to tamp down the memory. Describing the incident brought all those feelings rushing back into her head, and she was in no hurry to relive the experience.

For a long time he said nothing. She felt him move back from her, then rise to his feet. His footsteps resonated on the hardwood floor as he walked a few paces away from her, and she turned around to look at him. For a few long seconds he just stood there with his back to her, and she wondered whether he was going to leave her without saying a word. Wondered how she might possibly have offended him.

But then he spoke again, and when she heard how strained his voice was she understood. He did not want her to know what he was feeling. He needed the distance between them, as emotional armor.

"It would appear you found a Souleater," he said quietly. "And it appears, as well, that you may have answered one very important question about our own relationship to that species . . . though I think not an answer any Magister wants to hear." He paused, then muttered, "I know I didn't want to hear it."

A portal appeared before him so suddenly that it startled Kamala; by the time she realized what it was, he was gone. The list he had given her fluttered briefly behind him, then slowly came to rest on the wooden floor just south of where she had drawn the Wrath.

He will come back, she thought, mystified. *He'll want all the details I have to offer. He's just not ready to deal with all that yet.*

And a whisper came, rising up from the depths of her soul: *I'm not ready to deal with it either.*

CHAPTER 12

STEEL CLASHES against steel, metal ringing as blades strike—scrape—withdraw. Again. Again. Gleaming arcs of silver cutting through the warm air of the armory, shimmering as they pass one another. Graceful curves of feint and parry interwoven in a polished metal tapestry. Steel blades shimmering like lakewater before a storm as the force of each blow ripples down their length.

"Enough."

Gwynofar let her sword arm drop down by her side, grateful for the reprieve. Sweat was dripping down her face, and her shoulders felt as if molten lead had been poured into her joints. "Remind me why we're doing this?"

"Because you felt you needed more time in training than Salvator did, given that he was trained in combat from his youth. You asked me for private lessons, remember?"

"No, I meant the swordplay."

Favias raised an eyebrow. "You wanted to train as a Guardian."

Gwynofar raised an eyebrow back at him. "I somehow doubt that a Souleater is going to attack me with a short sword."

Favias dropped his practice weapon onto the rough-hewn

table and began to unbuckle his protective gear. Layer upon layer of shallow cuts and abrasions bore witness to the many students he had instructed in the past. "Ramirus said that your reflexes need extra work. That because of his sorcery your mind and body are no longer perfectly meshed, and I should drill you in as many different exercises as I can, to encourage their union."

She blinked. "Really? He said that?"

"Indeed, Majesty. Which part of it surprises you?"

"I thought we had moved past that point already." She began to work her way out of her own armor. It was her least favorite part of these practice sessions. The stiff leather was sweat-drenched and uncomfortable, especially for a woman who had rarely worn anything harsher than lamb's wool against her skin. Then again, compared to the biting winds of the Alkali mountains, it was a veritable caress. "I don't feel uncomfortable with my own body any more, though I did at first. And I would have thought that climbing the Sister had proven my capacity."

"In that one task you did well enough, Majesty. But there's no telling when other weaknesses may surface." He shrugged his shoulders; his joints cracked audibly. "There are reasons why we don't use witchery to enhance the bodies of our warriors. The process can backfire in any one of a hundred ways. I imagine Ramirus would rather have you test for any problems now, in the safety of your own home, than risk an unhappy surprise in the midst of battle."

"Such as?"

Favias twisted his head to one side and then the other. He was in good shape, thanks to a warrior's regimen of diet and exercise, but he was no longer young, and sometimes it showed. "The Guardians' archives are full of tales of those warriors who used witchery to enhance their martial capacity, only to discover later that such tricks aren't as simple as they seem."

"You really think there is danger in my case?"

He stepped toward her suddenly, swinging his fist sideways toward her head. Startled, she blocked the blow. For a moment they stood locked in position, strength against strength, as he tried to press forward, and she tried to push him away. Her shoulder burned with pain from the exertion, but she refused to give in.

Finally his hand fell away. "Gwynofar Aurelius . . . you are smaller and more delicate in frame than my youngest daughter. Yet right now you can match the strength of my best men. What happens to a human body when those two qualities are combined? Nature doesn't normally allow such a combination to occur, but we have forced her to accommodate our needs. What price will she demand in compensation?"

"You said that others tried it in the past. What happened to them?"

He took up the lances they had been practicing with earlier and began to put them back in their rack. "One man had his bones shatter in battle; apparently they were too slender to support the kind of force his altered muscles were exerting upon them. One woman had her heart fail; it was too small to support the kind of creature she had become. And it is said that one man who survived the process in body later lost his mind; he would no longer accept the altered limbs as part of his own person, but believed they belonged to someone else, who was trying to take control of him. They found him face down in the barracks, in a pool of blood, after he had attempted to saw his own legs off.

"Now, I am sure that Ramirus knew of those particular episodes and took them into account when he bolstered your strength, so your heart and your bones and key internal organs were no doubt strengthened along with your muscular capacity. But the warning is still a valid one. How many elements of the human body must be in perfect harmony in order for it to operate at peak efficiency? And then there is the religious element. If you believe that some god created man in his current form, wouldn't it be the ultimate hubris to assume we could improve upon his design? Might he not strike us down for our efforts, just to prove that point?"

She smiled slightly. "I believe it is only the god of the Penitents who lays claim to infallibility."

"Yes." He chuckled. "Egotistical bastard, isn't he?"

As he put the last weapon in its rack, he caught sight of a liveried youth standing in the doorway, waiting for one of them to notice him. "Yes? What is it?"

The page bowed toward Gwynofar. "Magister Ramirus requests that the Queen Mother and Master Guardian come speak with him. As soon as possible, if you please."

For Ramirus to ask for both of them was uncharacteristic; usually his counsel was channeled through Gwynofar. Favias looked at her. "Any idea what's going on?"

"Not a clue." A shadow passed over her face as she put the last of her equipment aside. "But given the nature of the message, it's not likely to be good news, is it?"

"That depends on what you call *good news*," he reminded her. "In wartime the distinction is not always so clear."

She set the last pieces of practice equipment aside, leaving them for servants to clean and store, and they headed back toward the keep.

———

The High King was in his study when Gwynofar came to see him. Danton's study. There was no longer blood on the floor, but he could sense where it had once been splattered across the wooden planks, and where it had pooled beneath his father's body. And his brothers' bodies. So much death that day, due to one man's treachery. It tested his Penitent spirit to the utmost, trying not to imagine what he might do to Kostas if he had him in his hands right now. What it would feel like to wring that lizard's neck with his own bare hands, to slowly choke the life out of that unholy creature.

Hatred corrupts the soul, he reminded himself.

But vengeance heals the spirit, his father would have countered. *Embrace your rage. Give it outlet. Self-denial is a vampire that bleeds a man of strength.*

And there was the reason his father could never have become a Penitent, in a nutshell.

"Excuse me, Sire."

Salvator looked up from his papers to acknowledge his servant's presence.

"The High Queen Gwynofar wishes to speak to you."

Surprised, Salvator nodded, and he gestured with the quill in his hand for her to be brought to him. This early in the day he would have expected her to be training with Favias. Was that not the schedule they had set? What news could not wait until later?

It was clear from her appearance that she had indeed been practicing with Favias. Thin strands of blond hair were plastered to her face, and her coarse soldier's clothing had long creases in it from where the practice armor crushed it against her body. But the sweat on her face was dry now, and she was not breathing heavily, as she was wont to do when her lessons had just ended. So she had not come straight to Salvator. Stranger and stranger. His brow furrowed in concern as he put the quill down atop his work, and stood to greet her.

She drew in a deep breath, trying to settle her spirit. Clearly something had shaken her badly.

At last she said, "There is a Souleater in the High Kingdom."

He could feel his heart skip a beat. Suspecting such a thing was one matter; having it finally confirmed was another. "How do you know?"

"Ramirus brought us word." There was a shadow of defiance in her tone, as if she were daring him to question her source. "Another Magister picked up the trail. They think it may be a queen. A female of the species." Her clear eyes fixed on him, and he could sense her trying to read his expression, but he made sure that his face was composed, controlled, and offered her no clues. "They think the Witch-Queen herself may be involved."

"We knew she was somewhere," he said quietly. Trying to keep all that emotion out of his voice.

"You are not surprised." It was a question.

"I have . . . suspected."

"You didn't tell me that."

"Tell you what? That I had dreams the enemy was in my realm? That sometimes late at night I imagine I can smell the creature herself—"

He stopped himself, but not in time.

"How would you know her scent?" she demanded. "The one that served Kostas was long gone by the time you returned home. There haven't been any other Souleaters around for you to smell." She paused. "Have there?"

"Not that I know of."

"Then how . . . ?"

What was he to tell her? That their scent came to him in dreams? That Siderea had appeared to him once, soaked in some strange, disturbing perfume, and he had sensed without knowing how he did so that the source of that smell was not human?

"Dreams, Mother. I've had dreams. Nothing more." He waved away the question. "Where is this Souleater hiding?"

"North in the Spinas Mountains."

He drew in a sharp breath.

"What is it, my son?"

He did not answer her, but turned back to his desk. Leafing through the pile of correspondence on top of it, he sought a particular letter, from one of his Penitent informants. He scanned it once more, his eyes narrowing as he did so, then began to read aloud.

> . . . *as you have commanded us to report to you any oddities we observe, I must report a series of events for which no one here has any explanation. Children have been disappearing from this area, and no human cause can be found. Most often it is babies that disappear, but a few older ones have gone missing as well. They are stolen from different locations, at different times of day or night, with no clear pattern. One infant was stolen out from under the watchful eye of his mother. No man can say how or why it is happening, but they are sure it is not the work of common slavers. One witness described a dirty and disheveled young girl who appeared just before her child disappeared, but her identity is unknown, and even the most powerful witches cannot seem to establish a link to her. As far as their spells are concerned, it is as if she does not exist.*
>
> *Families have taken to keeping their children locked up inside the house, but even that is no sure protection;*

*one man returned home to find his wife in a coma-like
sleep and his infant daughter missing.*

*There is some speculation that the child thieves are
operating out of the Spinas, for all the towns that suffered
losses are clustered about the northern branch of that range,
the so-called "dragon's tail." But expeditions into the
mountains have turned up no sign of human activity, or
anything else that would explain the attacks . . .*

He stopped reading. His expression was grave.

"You think these two things are connected somehow," she
said.

"The coincidence would be remarkable if it were otherwise,
don't you think?" He put the letters back in place. "Is she gathering food, do you suppose? But no, why bother doing that?
The Souleaters don't require physical proximity to drain men of
life, and if a queen wanted human flesh . . . there are surely
easier ways to get hold of it."

Memories flickered faintly in his brain. He shut his eyes,
trying to bring them into focus. "There was some trouble in
that region during my father's reign. Cresel told me about them
when I first returned. Something about a town where all the
people disappeared, or died . . . I don't remember exactly . . .
I'm pretty sure that was in the same region. So whatever is out
there, it may have been there for a while."

"Favias says that they think the Souleater invasion began
some time ago. Early spring, at least."

"Just after the skies turned red," he mused. "Do you recall
that? The clouds to the north turned deep crimson when the
sun was setting, as if the sky itself were bleeding. Our priests
declared it to be a sign from God, but they could not come to

any agreement on what it meant. So now you say that these creatures may have arrived in the human kingdoms about the same time. Souleaters would certainly fit the omen." He shook his head in frustration, unable to make the puzzle pieces fit together. "But why? Why *children*? Nothing in the ancient legends even hints at something like this."

Gwynofar drew in a deep breath. "Ramirus might know."

Salvator stiffened. "A Magister? No, thank you."

"He knows a lot about these creatures. And there are others of his kind who know even more. He is ancient, Salvator, he was alive when men still told stories from the time of the Great War—"

"*No*, Mother." His tone was firm. "I agreed to be polite to him for your sake, even to allow him in my house, but please don't mistake that for true acceptance."

"It's foolish to turn away a source of useful information because of religious prejudice."

Anger stirred within him. "It's more than *prejudice*, Mother. His power is corrupt, and a man who wields such power is doubly corrupt. All that he touches is unclean."

"That's your belief."

"It is fact."

She glared. "Like the 'fact' that the *lyr* gift is nothing more than idolatrous fantasy? Your Church was wrong about that. Perhaps it is wrong about this."

His jaw clenched tightly. He said nothing.

"Salvator, please." She walked up to him and took both his hands in her own. How tiny her fingers were, how delicate! Yet he knew they were possessed of a strength that could crush men's bones. The abomination of it made him sick to his stomach. "I know you're a rational man, deep inside. I know that you don't accept anything blindly, even in matters of faith. Our world is threatened now, and these Magisters are offering to help us. Explain to me why it's so important that we shut them out. Help me to understand."

He sighed heavily, squeezed her hands, and then pulled free of her. Steepling his hands before his face, he shut his eyes for a moment, struggling to find the right words for what he needed to say. She had never asked this of him before. She might never ask again. He had to do this right.

Help me, oh, God, to open her eyes, that she might see the truth and accept it.

"Witchery is God's most sacred gift to mankind," he said at last, "not only because of what it can do for us, but because of what we must become in order to wield it. A selfish man is not able to access such power directly, because he will not sacrifice his own life to do so. Thus are the ambitions of tyrants held in check, and men of greed forced to bargain with men of conscience. This was all part of God's plan for us, which He wove into the very fabric of our nature upon the day of Creation.

"Sorcery defies that plan. Not only because of what it is, but because of who can use it. It places unlimited power into the hands of the cruelest of men and rewards human callousness. Witchery ennobles us; sorcery corrupts. And where men are corrupted, society is corrupted.

"Do you understand now, Mother? This isn't about any individual Magister. It's about how their power defies God's will and threatens to alter the balance of human society."

He drew in a deep breath. "So where does this power come from, that spits upon the natural order? There were no Magisters during the First Age of Kings, we know that. Nor do we have records of any that existed during the Great War. It was only later that they first appeared, during that barbaric period we now call the Dark Ages. Creatures of darkness, spawned in an era of ignorance and violence. *Their power is not a human thing,* one early Penitent wrote, *but rather a bestial corruption, that revels in bloodshed.* I believe—"

He stopped suddenly.

"Salvator?"

Go on. Tell her. It is time she knew the truth.

It is time the world knew the truth.

"I believe—my Church believes—that mankind would have recovered from the Great War much sooner if not for the Magisters. Not only because of the power they wielded, but because of the influence they had upon human society. The earliest Penitent writings attest to this. In fact, my Church . . ."

He hesitated. Wondering how much he dared say to her and how she would receive it. The air in the room suddenly seemed charged with energy, which the wrong words might spark to conflagration.

Or perhaps the right ones.

"My Church was founded because of the Magisters," he told her. "Because of the burden of sin that they brought into the world. Do you understand, Mother? When a Penitent fasts, or denies himself sexual concourse, or scourges his flesh with leather straps . . . he is not doing that just to offer penance for the sins of mankind. He is doing that because of the *Magisters.* God decreed that penance must be offered for all earthly power, so since they will not offer it themselves, we do so for them. Without such penance the world cannot remain in balance."

"You do penance for Magisters?" She blinked. "Truly?"

"Yes, Mother. I do penance for Ramirus being in this house and for any corruption he manifests while he is here. I do penance for every act of sorcery he performs at my behest." *And at yours*, he thought.

"What a cruel god you serve," she whispered.

His expression was cold. "He is harsh with us as a father is harsh with his children when they stray. Not because He wants to see us in pain, but because He wants us to become stronger." He paused. "Do you doubt my strength, Mother?"

"No." She said it softly. "Never."

"I will lead an expedition into the Spinas Mountains to find this Souleater. Ramirus may come along because he knows the way. This other one that you speak of, the one who discovered the Souleater's lair, he may come as well if you feel it's necessary. For his information alone. But no Magister will use any sorcery on my behalf. That condition is not open to negotiation. If any Magister wishes to be part of this, he must give me his oath on that."

"You will go yourself?" she asked, startled. "Is that wise?"

He hesitated. Was it time to tell her what he suspected, that he might be unusually resistant to this creature's power? That his people might not be able to find the ikati without him? But no, he would rather test that theory first, before sharing it with others. Even her.

This was the perfect testing ground.

"My father rode to battle at the head of his army," he said brusquely. "Should I do less?"

"Your father had a Magister to protect him," she pointed out.

"And I have witches who are just as powerful. Never forget that, Mother. There is nothing sorcery can do that witchery can't, if someone is willing to pay the price. So my condition stands. If it is acceptable to your Magisters, then they may come with us."

"With *us*?"

He raised an eyebrow. "Weren't you going to ask to come along, Mother? Weren't you going to demand it of me, if I said no? Would you not argue that your *lyr* blood has special significance, that your *lyr* rank has special responsibilities, and besides, I had already given you permission to play a Guardian's role? Not to mention that perhaps there is a power in you that we don't yet know about, which might prove useful in such an endeavor? All of which is perfectly true." The corner of his mouth twitched. "I thought I would save us both some time and just cut to the chase."

And I need to test your part in this, as well, he thought grimly. *Though I will not speak of that either until the testing is done.*

The lines of tension across her brow eased a bit. "You are truly your father's son, Salvator." She shook her head. "In more ways than you will ever know."

He leaned down to kiss her on the forehead. "Have Ramirus come to me at noon, if he accepts my terms, and we can discuss the parameters of the expedition. Favias as well. Cresel can oversee matters here and spread whatever rumors are needed to keep noses out of our business. I'm sure he did it often enough for Danton. For now, if you will excuse me . . ." His expression darkened somewhat. "I have prayers to offer."

She did not ask what those prayers would be about. Which was a good thing for both of them, he thought. There were some things a mother did not want to know.

CHAPTER 13

TAKING A deep breath, Salvator stepped through the portal. It was as if he had suddenly been immersed in a turbulent ice-cold river. Frigid black currents closed over his head, and he had to fight the instinctive panic that overcame a man when his environment was suddenly out of his control. Attending that was a rush of guilt, for he knew the cost of this witch's trick. Every current of power that swirled about him represented a moment of someone's life, sacrificed just in order to save him travel time. The fact that such a service had been offered up voluntarily, by Penitents who believed that in serving him they were serving the will of the Creator, was of little comfort. It should not have been necessary in the first place.

An instant later—an eternity later—he stepped through to the other side. Blinking, he looked around, trying to get oriented. He was standing on a small plateau surrounded by steep and forbidding mountains, their tips highlighted by the cool, dim light of morning. At the far end of the plateau a small retinue was waiting, some local lordling and his cadre of personal guards. They wore the colors of Lord Cadern, but Salvator didn't know the local rank markings well enough to evaluate the status of any individual. Off to the side were two dozen horses, saddled and ready, attended by liveried grooms. Salvator wondered if Lord Cadern himself was present. Normally it would have been an insult for the local lord to fail to receive the High King himself, but Salvator hadn't told Cadern he'd be coming in person, only that he was sending out a small expedition. So there had been no reason for any special ceremony. Looking about now, Salvator could see that Cadern had supplied all the things the High King had asked for, and that was what mattered.

The men who were present recognized Salvator the minute he stepped through the portal, and the guards bowed their heads low in obeisance. Their leader's face went white, which answered any question about whether or not Lord Cadern was present. Clearly he wasn't. The man glanced sharply at one of his retainers, who shut her eyes briefly in concentration. A witch, most likely. Salvator imagined he could hear her spell crackle in the air as an invisible message was launched: *The High King is here!* How much panic would follow in the wake of that message? he wondered. Was Cadern even now scrambling to find a witch to transport him to this field so that he could offer proper obeisance in person? Or was it too early for that, and he was still asleep? If so, he was likely to have a few bad dreams before rising.

Flanking the field where the portal spell had manifested, two Magisters stood like vultures on opposing hillsides. On the right was Ramirus, stiff-backed and regal, his long black robes devouring the newborn sunlight. Salvator nodded to him briefly, coldly, acknowledging his presence without any sign of approval. The fact that the High King had agreed to let Ramirus accompany them on this mission didn't mean he had to be happy about it. Opposite Ramirus was a less formal vulture, a thin man, tall and sharp-featured, with long black hair caught up in a queue at the nape of his neck. That must be Colivar, Ramirus' rival. This one's garments were black, but it was a mundane color, dull and imperfect, and they were cut in the manner of simple morati clothing. A curious affectation. Did he think that such a show of unpretentious attire would lead men to mistake him for something less than he was? Colivar affected a casual pose as he waited, leaning against a tree, a half-eaten apple in his hand. But the intensity of his gaze belied any suggestion of casual purpose. Much was on the line today, not only in the coming war between men and Souleaters, but also in that cold, knife-edged rivalry that was the Magisters' favorite sport. Salvator might not understand all the details of that game—or care to—but he knew that nothing else, not even the business of saving the world, would be allowed to interfere with it.

Colivar knows more about the Souleaters than any man alive, Ramirus had told Salvator. Secrets within secrets. Ask a Magister to shed light on one of them and you put yourself in his power. Salvator had refused to take the bait.

At least Ramirus had given his oath not to use his sorcery on Salvator's behalf. Supposedly Colivar had agreed as well.

And what if your life is endangered by this Souleater? Ramirus had demanded. *Shall I stay my hand even then?*

Yes, Salvator had responded. Staring into the eyes of that ancient unclean soul without hesitation or doubt. *I would rather be torn to pieces by a Souleater than submit to your sorcery.*

No doubt both Magisters thought him a fool for that. A shortsighted religious fool who would put his own life at risk for the sake of a whimsical and outdated prejudice. But if so, then they did not understand the nature of his faith, or the spiritual value of religious martyrdom. If he, the High King, chose death over corruption, might not others come to question their casual acceptance of sorcery? If his death inspired men to throw off the shackles of the Magisters and turn their eyes to their Creator instead, would not his duty on earth have been well served? Would not his life have been well lived and properly ended?

Gwynofar seemed to understand that much. She mourned his dedication to such a path, but she understood the passion that drove him, and seemed to respect it.

A gentle but respectful touch on his arm urged the High King to move forward; others needed room to follow him. Salvator nodded and moved off to one side. Half a dozen Guardians emerged from the shimmering portal behind him, led by Favias himself. Then came a small contingent of royal bodyguards—God forbid the High King should ever go anywhere without them!—and behind them, flanked by two of her personal guards, the Queen Mother.

How like some barbarian goddess she appeared in that moment, as she stepped through the witch's portal! The royal armorer had crafted a fitted steel breastplate especially for her, investing the best of his art into the effort. The upraised wings of the Aurelius hawk curled gracefully about Gwynofar's breasts in damascened glory; and her golden hair flowed down over her shoulders like a brilliant waterfall, spilling out from beneath the matching half-helm. All her years seemed to fall away from her in that moment, along with all her ties to the mortal world. She seemed the living embodiment of the Maiden Warrior: pure, eternal, unconquerable. The embodiment of myth, sent to earth to inspire men. Was this how Danton had seen her?

Then the witches who had conjured the portal stepped through it themselves, and the spell collapsed behind them.

Penitent custom required that he kneel before the witches and thank them for the sacrifice they had just made. Royal custom required that he avoid any act of submission while in the presence of . . . well, anyone. He settled for a solemn nod of respect, and he knew from their expression that they understood what it represented. Never before had there been a Penitent king, so there were no precedents to guide them.

"Your Majesty."

The leader of the local delegation stepped forward; the look of guarded embarrassment on his face confirmed Salvator's guess that Lord Cadern was not going to be showing up anytime soon. The man bowed deeply. "We are humbled and honored by your visit. If his Lordship had realized you would be coming in person . . ."

Salvator waved off the apology. "Too much ceremony would only have delayed our business." He looked toward the horses, now made restless by the sudden arrival of so many strangers. "These are for my people?"

"Yes, Majesty." The man bowed again. "His Lordship has provided a local guide as well, as requested." He waved forward a man who had been standing to the side of the local retinue, a tall, wiry northerner dressed in the coarse woolen garments of a trapper. "This is Herzog. He knows the region better than anyone else."

"Your Majesty." Herzog knelt ungracefully before Salvator, clearly uncomfortable with all the fuss. Judging from his personal hygiene, he was rarely in the presence of civilized men, much less men of rank. "I am at your service." For a moment he looked as if he expected to be given a ring to kiss, but of course Salvator offered none. Acts of reverence should be reserved for the Creator.

"We are glad for your service, Herzog. You know the place we're looking for?"

"Aye." He rose to his feet. "It's near one of the landmarks trappers use, though lately no one seems much interested in that stretch of woods."

Salvator felt his gut tighten at what was surely a confirmation of their worst fears. If a female Souleater was in the area, then humans would naturally turn away from the place and come up with their own reasons for doing so. At least that's how it had been explained to him.

It seemed to Salvator that he could sense her in the distance. She was too far away for him to detect with his human senses, but on some deep, visceral level, he simply *knew* she was there. And he sensed, with chill certainty, that she was aware of his presence.

Trying to still the pounding of his heart, Salvator waved his people toward the waiting horses. One particularly fine animal, a pure white mare, broke free of the herd and went galloping across the plateau to where Ramirus stood. The Magister's robe transformed itself as he mounted, dividing neatly up the center so that its two halves could settle smoothly over the animal's flanks. By contrast, Colivar simply walked over to where the horses stood, separated out a dappled gray mount by hand, and vaulted up into the saddle. That such a prosaic action was probably meant as a gesture of respect to Salvator was not lost on the High King. Nor was the fact that the primary purpose of the gesture was probably to show up Ramirus.

By the Creator's mercy, I am glad I do not have to deal with these vile creatures on a daily basis.

Two servants were ready to help Gwynofar up to her saddle, but she waved them back and mounted the high-shouldered animal without assistance, bearing the weight of the steel armor as effortlessly as if it were a length of gossamer silk. The Guardians were not surprised to witness such strength in her, but Salvator's guards were apparently behind on their gossip, and several stood there with their mouths hanging open. *Of such moments are legends born,* the High King thought dryly, as he waved away a guard whose hands were cupped low to receive the royal foot. Even if Salvator had needed help gaining his saddle, he would not treat another man like a footstool to do it.

But no help was needed. He was tall and agile, and four years of hard labor in the fields of the monastery had toughened his flesh; these soldiers might be more skilled in swordplay than he was, but he doubted that any of them could beat him in a direct contest of strength.

A Souleater might be another matter.

Before mounting his own horse Favias made his rounds of the company, giving out the special weapons the Guardians had brought with them. Arrows with glassy cobalt tips, lances with long, curved cobalt heads, and swords with strips of the same blue substance set into the cutting edges. Most of the items were clearly ancient, made from the blades of Souleaters killed in the Great War centuries ago, but four long spears had been newly crafted. He presented one of them to Salvator.

"This was made from a tail blade of Kostas' Souleater," he told him. "It's said such a weapon will cut through the hide of an ikati as if it were butter, and it leaves behind a poison that destroys the creature's flesh from the inside out." A faint, dry smile flickered across his face. "Don't nick your finger on it."

Salvator's expression was solemn as he took the weapon from him. *This is the Souleater who caused my father's death,* he thought.

And my brothers'. He felt a cold satisfaction in knowing that the vile creature had been cut into pieces and would now be forced to serve his family in a war against its own kind.

Favias gave one of the other spears to Gwynofar. It towered well over her head, disproportionate to her delicate frame, but no one questioned that. They knew that all her strength and determination would mean little if she did not have a long enough reach to protect herself from the enemy. If a Souleater surprised them while they were on horseback, every inch would count.

Favias kept a spear for himself and gave the last to his second-in-command. Then, Salvator turned to Cadern's men. "Tell his Lordship we are grateful for his assistance. We will return when our business is done and let him know the results."

The man bowed his head respectfully. "May the gods—" he began. And then he stopped himself.

For a moment there was silence. Salvator's lips tightened.

"May your journey be a safe one," the man muttered. A red flush of embarrassment brightened his cheeks. He bowed deeply, no doubt to hide his face.

Salvator nodded stiffly. "The Creator willing, it shall be so."

And then the High King turned his horse around, to face the Spinas Mountains, and signaled for the company to begin its journey.

————

I should not be here, Colivar thought.

She was close. So very close. He imagined he could smell her now, though of course they were still too far away for that. But memories were coming back to him, of other times and places when he had known that smell. Sweet musk intoxicant, mixed with the blood scent of a fresh kill . . . soaked into the Witch-Queen's silken sheets along with her perfume . . . filling the sky.

I should not have come here.

He remembered the spiritual paralysis that had overcome him at Danton's castle, when the Souleater had risen. Centuries of resolve melting away in an instant, leaving him helpless. He had thought it would be easy to attack an ikati. He had more reason than any other man to want to do so. And yet he had frozen.

—icy wind rushing past his cheek, frozen blood shattering into a thousand crystals—

He shook his head to banish the unwelcome images and took his place at the rear of the party, letting the trapper lead the way to the landmark that Kamala had told him about.

Kamala.

For a moment he flashed back to the sensation of her body pressed against his, her skin warm and damp with sweat as she trembled in the aftermath of her vision. Why had that affected him so deeply? Did he find her attractive as a woman, as a sorcerer, or . . . as something else? The question was not one he was prepared—or equipped—to answer.

The terrain was dismal for riding, dominated by steep and rocky inclines; periodically the horses had to wend their way single file through passes so narrow their riders' legs scraped against the rock walls as they rode. At times it seemed as though it would have been easier to walk. But the distance was simply too great to cover on foot in a day, and even though Colivar had assured them that the Souleaters were creatures of sunlight, unlikely to assault anyone after darkness fell, none of the morati wanted to be camped in the mountains after sunset.

As the morning wore on, the company climbed higher and

higher into the treacherous range, following trails that only Herzog could see. The farther north they rode, the more uneasy their guide seemed to become. Clearly the man knew how to get them where they wanted to go, but the farther they went, the more reluctant he became to lead them. Which confirmed Colivar's belief that a queen was indeed nearby. How would her power affect the *lyr* in the party? What about the young High King? Ramirus had suggested that Salvator might have some kind of special immunity to the ikati's power. It was an interesting suggestion, which would no doubt be tested soon enough.

Finally the company broke out of a wooded stretch and onto a stark plateau. Steep granite escarpments dominated the landscape on all sides of them, and to the north a cliff's edge had eroded away, leaving a line of jagged columns behind. In one place a narrow column stood alone, jutting up from the ground as if it had grown there organically, a sight eerily reminiscent of the sacred spires in the north. The wind had carved its edges into odd twisted shapes, out of keeping with the landscape surrounding it.

Herzog waved toward the spire and turned back to the High King. "Is this what you were looking for?"

Salvator turned to look at Ramirus, who in turn looked over at Colivar. The black-haired Magister studied the spire for a long moment, remembering the sorcerous images Kamala had shared with him. Finally he nodded. "Yes. That's it." He looked out across the landscape. "I thought the queen would be southwest of this spot, but now I see the place, I think that instead we should look to the north . . ."

He stopped himself. A muscle in his jaw twitched. The Souleater's power was beating at all their brains, altering the very channels of thought. He had to wrestle with his own mind just to think clearly.

"Southwest," he said at last. It took effort for him to force the words out. "That is the proper direction. As we planned."

"It'd be better to circle north a bit," Herzog cautioned. "There's better terrain up there." He pointed. "We can come around—"

"*Southwest*," Salvator said firmly.

For a moment they all just sat there, staring at him. Then, snorting in exasperation, Salvator kneed his horse into motion, claimed the point position, and began to ride southwest. His guards scurried to keep up with him, and one by one the others followed obediently behind. Even Colivar had to concentrate with all his might just to do so, when every instinct was telling him that this was the wrong way to go. But Salvator led them with regal confidence, and in time the territorial magic that had been numbing their minds let up. It took no sorcery to sense the smug pride radiating from him then. He, the Penitent King, had led his men safely through a land where even Magisters faltered.

Colivar moved into the point position to guide them after that, moving from landmark to landmark as he recognized them from the images that Kamala had shared with him. If only he could have brought her along, they might have progressed much more quickly! But he was not yet ready to reveal the woman's full role in this affair, and so they would have to make do with second-hand knowledge.

Are you more afraid that Ramirus will hurt her if he learns the truth, he asked himself, *or that he will claim her for himself?*

Another question he was not ready to answer.

Then the party came around a bend, and they saw the Souleater skeleton.

In life it must have been an impressive creature, and its long, sinuous armature stretched snake-like across the rocky ground for many yards. There was a sense of coiled energy about it, as if it might start to move again at any moment. Perhaps that was what made the horses unwilling to approach it. Or perhaps it was the scent of death, which seemed to cling to the bones, faded enough that human senses could barely detect it. Horses were more alert to such things.

For a moment the whole company just sat there, staring at it. A flock of Souleaters could have passed overhead at that moment, and none of them would have noticed. This was the creature that had once destroyed all the works of mankind . . . and would do so again, if given a chance. Doom clung to its bones like a shroud.

Colivar finally tore his gaze away from the dead ikati and sought the other one that he had been told would be present. "Over there," he said, spotting it at last.

As Kamala had reported to him, the second Souleater was smaller than the first. Much smaller. Probably a juvenile, Colivar thought. Which raised all sorts of questions he couldn't begin to answer.

"They killed each other," Salvator observed.

But Colivar shook his head. "No. That one's too young. It wouldn't have challenged a fully grown male. And if the latter had been hunting newborns, then only one of them would be dead."

"They do that?" Gwynofar asked. "Hunt their own young?"

Colivar nodded. "The young one of today is the rival of tomorrow. Easier to kill them when they're small. A Souleater's deadliest enemy is his own kind."

Ramirus kneed his horse into motion and approached the

larger skeleton. Its ribcage vaulted high enough that he could touch it without dismounting. He reached out a hand to place it on the bone.

"No!" Colivar cried.

Ramirus froze in midmotion. Colivar could sense the others holding their breath, and he cursed himself for having spoken.

Ramirus looked back at him.

"Don't touch it with sorcery," Colivar said quietly.

It was clear from the look on Ramirus' face that he wanted an explanation. But Colivar wasn't about to tell the man about Kamala's experience with the Souleater queen, or the fact that any sorcery that connected a Magister to an ikati was likely to have dire consequences.

But was a skeleton like this really likely to have the same effect? Deep in his heart he knew such a fear was ridiculous. Then why had he stopped Ramirus? Was he really afraid that the Magister might get sucked into oblivion if he touched the thing with his power? Or was he afraid that if he used his sorcery on the skeleton, he might learn too much of the truth?

One of Favias' Seers dismounted and approached the larger skeleton on foot, ending the conversation. He looked up at Colivar for approval; the Magister made no move to stop him. It was unlikely that a witch would be endangered merely by using his power on a dead Souleater the way that a sorcerer might be. And besides . . . witches were expendable.

The man studied the skeleton for a moment, then put his hands upon two of the vast, arching ribs, curling his fingers about them as he began to concentrate. He lowered his head and shut his eyes, muttering some occult formula under his breath. Out of the corner of one eye Colivar saw Salvator bow his head in prayer, along with a few of the guards attending him. For Penitents, this simple act of witchery was a sacred religious sacrifice.

At last the witch raised his head. Staring into the sky, he addressed the others without turning back to them, as if narrating a vision that was unfolding before his eyes as he spoke.

"They died in combat. Not against each other. I see a third one, that killed them both. First the small one was attacked, and this one was drawn to the noise of combat." He paused, his brow furrowing tightly from the intensity of his concentration. "I sense . . . victory without joy . . . terrible emptiness . . . an awareness that this is but the last in a long, long line of deaths. It's finally over now. No more killing is needed. The offenders are gone." He rubbed his head. "That's all I can get, I'm sorry. The trace is very old."

"Did the third one look like these two?" Colivar asked quietly.

The Seer shut his eyes for a moment, trying to remember details. "No. No. It was . . . thinner than the others. Sleeker. It had broader wings, with trailing bits . . . and no spikes. These two had spikes running down their spines, but not the killer."

Colivar drew in a sharp breath.

Ramirus looked at him. "A female?"

Colivar hesitated, then nodded stiffly. He didn't dare respond aloud, lest his tone of voice reveal too much. Fragments of memory were beginning to take form in his brain now: jeweled wings, noxious orange clouds, and blue-black spines slicked with poison. He shook his head, trying to banish them. Hating himself, for letting Ramirus see how much this moment was affecting him.

He shouldn't have come here.

"There is more." The Seer paused, then pointed toward the west. "That way."

"More ikati?" Favias asked.

The Seer hesitated. "I'm not sure. I sense more death. But it isn't clear what the source is."

All eyes turned to Salvator. After a moment the High King nodded. "Lead us," he ordered Herzog.

With a tense nod, the trapper obeyed. Salvator's guards clustered closely around the High King as the party fell into line once more, eager to protect him. Foolish effort! As if mounted soldiers could protect Salvator from the kind of predator that could freeze men's souls with a glance! Likely they would simply stand there paralyzed if their master was attacked, frozen in helpless horror as they watched him die.

At least that would give them something substantial to repent, Colivar thought dryly.

Herzog led the way as ordered, but he did not look nearly as confident about his path as he had been earlier. Periodically he stopped to consult with the Seer who had touched the skeleton. The latter seemed to be having a hard time translating his mystical visions into practical directions.

And then they found the bodies.

They had been traveling along a dried river bed flanked by steep granite walls on both sides. Frequent rock falls had strewn obstacles all along the path, which made for slow going. They were just coming around a bend in the valley, skirting a particularly bad stretch of turf, when Herzog pulled up his horse suddenly and cursed under his breath. Immediately all the guards reached for their weapons, but there was no attack forthcoming. With a trembling hand Herzog pointed to the path ahead of them, which only he could see. Finally Favias waved for the Guardians to follow him and urged his horse forward, past the trapper's position. When he could finally see what was around the bend, he, too, pulled up short, and Colivar heard him beseech the gods for mercy under his breath.

One by one the rest of the party followed them, and Colivar could hear several men whispering prayers as they did so. He had taken up the rear himself so as to have a bit of privacy with his thoughts, thus he was the last to come around the bend and see what awaited them.

Bones.

Hundreds of bones. Thousands of them. Skeletons had been shattered on the rocks on all sides, and the river bed was littered with broken shards. The arrangement suggested scavengers tearing bodies to pieces, fighting over scraps, carrying choice bits off to gnaw them in privacy . . . which suggested in turn that the skeletons had still had flesh on them when they were first cast down here.

The men were dismounting now to take a closer look. Only the Seer remained on horseback, using his higher vantage point to keep a watchful eye over the site, alert to incoming danger. He was shaking, Colivar noted. That was another difference between sorcerers and witches. It was unlikely any Magister would be so unnerved by the mere sight of death.

Yet even Colivar could feel the eerie quality of the place raise goosebumps along his flesh as he dismounted. How many people had died here? How many miles away were the nearest centers of human population from which they must have been brought? Was there some reason that people had come here of their own accord, then wreaked such destruction upon themselves? Or had someone gathered up all these bodies, brought them here, and left them for animals to tear apart? Colivar's soul was callous enough that the mere existence of the graveyard did not horrify him as it did the morati, yet the questions it raised were . . . disturbing.

He walked to where Ramirus stood, near a particularly precarious rock pile where several whole skeletons were located, and for a moment they both just stared at the scene in silence.

The skeletons were all those of children. Infants, mostly, whose tiny skulls had been crushed. A few larger skulls could be seen here and there, and one or two long bones that might have belonged to older children were wedged in between the rocks, but the overall purpose of this place was clear. Babies had been cast down onto these rocks like refuse.

Why?

Colivar hesitated, then reached down and picked up one of the smaller bones. A tiny phalange, fragment of a forgotten finger. He knew that there was risk in using any sorcery here, as the queen might be able to sense it, but he could not resist the temptation. Turning the small bone over in his hand, he let his sorcery seep into it, seeking its history. *Lost lost lost lost fear hunger cold cold COLD! . . . Mama! Mama!* He saw a baby hurtling down from out of the sky, then another. Dead. They were both dead, even before they fell. This was a garbage heap, nothing more. The actual killing had taken place elsewhere.

For some strange reason that comforted him.

"Hunger," Ramirus muttered. He had a bone in his own hand, a long femur scored with the tooth marks of some hungry beast. "These bones cry out with hunger . . . and with fear."

Colivar closed his fist about his own specimen, exploring that concept. "This one was offered food, but not in a form he could digest." He could feel the spasms of an infant vomiting resonate in his own body as he absorbed that information, and he quickly dropped the bone, severing the sorcerous connection. The hot bile that had risen suddenly in his throat settled down again. He picked up another bone, that of an older child. "This one was too afraid to eat," he observed.

The crunch of boots on gravel was approaching them from behind. Several pairs, at least. Neither of the Magisters turned around.

"What is this place?" Favias asked from behind them.

"A graveyard for children," Ramirus said quietly. "Apparently cast down here after their deaths."

"Cast down how?"

It took Colivar a moment to realize what the man was asking. Shutting his eyes for a moment, he brought back to mind the vision that the tiny bone had granted him. Seeking the information that mattered most.

"Dropped from overhead," he said at last. "From *directly* overhead."

A hawk might lift an infant in its talons and smash it down onto the rocks, like a gull cracking abalone, but there was only one species that had the size and the strength to carry larger children aloft. But why? Ikati did not require physical contact with their prey in order to feed on their life-essence; that was what made them so very dangerous. And if one of them had wanted meat, then why would it have cast its own meal down onto the rocks? The vision that Colivar had conjured showed a whole infant hurtling down from the sky, its flesh unbroken. It simply made no sense.

From behind them, Herzog coughed. "Begging your Magisters' pardon, but the children that have been reported missing in this region . . . might these be them? If a Souleater brought them here, that would explain why there was no trail for witches to find."

"But would a Souleater steal children?" Salvator wondered aloud. "And only to kill them? It makes no sense."

Colivar opened his mouth to respond—to tell the High King that this place was a mystery to him as well—when suddenly he felt it. A sound just beyond the threshold of hearing that resonated silently in his flesh. A tremor in the fabric of the universe that set all of reality to vibrating like a plucked harp string. Glancing at Ramirus, he could see from the expression on the other Magister's face that he had felt it, too. None of the others had. Not even the witches.

Which could mean only one thing.

"She's coming," he whispered.

Favias turned and shouted an order to his people. Dismounting quickly, the Guardians took up their bows and nocked blue-tipped arrows in readiness. The other members of the party followed their lead and dismounted also, looking about nervously for cover as they did so. The Guardians didn't bother with that. They understood that physical barriers were meaningless at this point. Either they could draw the Souleater down to them, within range of their weapons, or they were all dead men.

A growing heat suffused Colivar's flesh as he watched them make their preparations. Strange instincts warred within him. He wanted to run. He wanted to meld himself into the shadows, so he could not be seen. He wanted to stand atop the tallest pile of bones, spread out his arms, and welcome the ikati queen. Was all that the result of her power playing upon his mind, or was memory playing tricks on his soul?

Careful, Colivar, careful. This is the real test now, by which all Magisters will judge you. Ramirus seemed unaffected, he noted. Outside of the man's commitment to protect Gwynofar, he had little emotional investment in this campaign, and he could watch the battle with impunity, shielded by his sorcery, until it became necessary to conjure a portal and flee. Or so he no doubt thought. But who was to say that any sorcery would work properly in a queen's presence? Unlike male ikati, she had the ability to direct her mesmeric power against her own species, and that had especially dark implications for the Magisters. Should Colivar warn Ramirus about that? He couldn't think clearly enough to decide.

"There!" a voice cried out suddenly. One of the Guardians was pointing upward.

She was no more than a black spot against the sun at this point, but a hot thrill ran up Colivar's spine as he caught sight of her. Several of the guards looked up briefly, then shrugged and looked away. That was the result of her power, convincing them that what they had seen was of no consequence. The fact that she could influence their minds from such a distance was truly daunting; Colivar had not known that such a thing was possible. Or perhaps he had just forgotten that it was possible.

He could feel her mesmerism lapping at his brain now, but he knew all the tricks of seeing past it. Staring at the open sky to one side of her, he let his peripheral awareness gather information for him. The more you focused directly on a queen, the more power she had over you. He remembered that now. He was remembering so much now. The illusions he had woven about his life were beginning to give way as she approached, like slivers of fine vellum curling away from a flame. False memories, adopted over time to protect him from the real ones, fell to pieces around him. He felt strangely naked, stripped of that self-deception. And for perhaps the first time in centuries, a flicker of genuine fear took root in his soul.

As the distant black shape moved away from the sun, allowing men to stare directly at it, Colivar could pick out the people whose resistance was strongest. Gwynofar, of course. She was struggling to stay focused, but at least she was looking in the right direction. Salvator was by her side, and he did not seem to be straining at all. The gift of the *lyr* was strong in him. What was this creature in the eyes of his faith? Some kind of terrible demon? An emissary from his destroyer-god, sent to earth to punish mankind for his many iniquities? Beast or demon, it was clear from the way Salvator gripped his weapon that he was ready and willing to do combat with it.

But the queen did not come down toward them. She remained circling high above, frustratingly out of range of their weapons. A simple ikati would not have known to do that. It would have wanted a closer look, and closed some of that distance. Which meant that this creature was something more than a mere ikati.

She is from the northern colony, Colivar thought. He had known that all along, of course—there was no other possible explanation for her presence here—but a chill ran down his spine nonetheless, to have it finally confirmed. As for what that meant to him . . .

"What is the issue with sorcery?" Ramirus' voice carried just enough power to guarantee that the morati would not hear him. "Your warning about the Souleater skeleton. What was that about?"

Colivar hesitated. He knew just how much an honest answer would reveal. Too much. Yet the need was undeniable. And they were allies now, weren't they? At least when it came to these creatures.

If you knew where my knowledge came from, Ramirus, this battle would be the least of your concerns.

Finally he said, "If you connect to a Souleater directly, you may die. I'm not sure about that. It's never been tested. But the risk is there."

A white eyebrow arched delicately upward. "And you think this . . . why?"

Colivar did not answer. He could feel Ramirus' power lapping at the edges of his brain, trying to pry loose some shard of useful information, but it was only a token effort. They both knew his mental shields were too strong to be breached so casually.

Then one of the Guardians lifted up his hands, as if to channel a cry toward the heavens. He was going to try the same trick that Rhys had used outside Danton's castle, to draw the Souleater to him. *That will not help you with a female,* Colivar thought. But he held his tongue as the man let loose the sharp, piercing cry. Yet another thing he could not admit to knowing.

This time, he could feel the cry resound in his flesh. This time, it was meant for him.

High overhead the ikati queen did not so much as pause in her wingstroke, but her power began to lap down over the party with increasing intensity. Two of the horses tried to pull back against their reins, and Colivar saw that the warrior who reached out to steady them stumbled slightly as he did so. One of the archers put out his hand to a nearby boulder to steady himself, as the strength in his legs began to fail him. Salvator's witch seemed about to perform some kind of spell when he lost his concentration, swayed, and then went down heavily on one knee. Colivar saw Ramirus glance over at Salvator, who seemed startled by his witch's fall; clearly whatever strategy the High King had prepared for that day had depended upon this man's talents. The High King moved over to where the man knelt and helped him to his feet, refusing to meet the Magisters' eyes as he did so. Even in the face of death he would accept no help from one of their kind. Colivar was both amazed and appalled. Did he think that stubbornness alone would save him?

You damned fool, Salvator! You will die here along with all your people, in the name of that idiotic faith of yours. Who will benefit from that, other than our enemy?

And then suddenly Gwynofar thrust her spear into the ground, ran the largest rock heap, and began to climb. Startled, Salvator called her back, but she ignored him. One of the royal guards ran up to her, but he hesitated an instant before grappling with the Queen Mother . . . and then she was out of reach. He struggled to catch up with her but in doing so dislodged several large rocks and lost his footing; he hit the ground hard and then lay still.

Colivar watched in fascination as Gwynofar worked her way up the rock pile. The climb was treacherous, but her altered muscles had been designed for just such a task, and compared to the monument in Alkali, this was practically a promenade on the garden path. Even with the steel cuirass she wore and the heavy sword sheathed across her back, she seemed to have little difficulty making the climb. Within several minutes she had gained the top of the mound, and she moved across it with an almost animal alacrity. Colivar conjured an overhead view to watch her, and he saw that in one place there was a pile of sun-bleached bones. She was moving steadily toward that now, tiny skeletons crunching underfoot with each step. When she reached the center of it, she stood up straight and tall, defying the waves of debilitating power that were beating down from above. Was she immune to the queen's power, as her son appeared to be, or simply determined enough to overcome it? The elevation she had gained was minimal when measured against the ikati's own position, but from his conjured perspective Colivar could see that her new placement set her apart from the rest of the morati, and the macabre nest of bones that lay at her feet would draw the Souleater's eye directly to her.

She was offering herself as bait.

For a moment she stood there, just catching her breath. Colivar himself was hardly breathing. Did she understand what she was doing, in any conscious sense? Or was blind *lyr* instinct driving her now, and she was simply going along with it? A Souleater queen had no reason to answer a mating challenge such as the one the Guardian had performed; that was meant for the males of the species. But a female invading her territory was another matter. Would she recognize Gwynofar as a legitimate rival? Enough to be consumed by rage at the sight of her? Nothing else was likely to bring her down now that the witches were immobilized.

Drawing in a deep breath, Gwynofar spread her arms wide. And then she began to speak. Crying out to the Souleater with all her strength, willing her voice to be carried upward by the wind, clear and true. And there was more than mere volume to her words. Colivar could see power shimmering about her skin, but not a structured spellcasting. Something more organic, more innate. *Lyr* magic? Was that of her own conjuring, or had some Seer in the party prepared her for this? If the Guardians had arranged for such a strategy in advance, then they had more knowledge of the Souleaters than Colivar had given them credit for.

"This is my land!" Gwynofar yelled to the skies. "*My* land! These are my trees, this is my water, this is my sky! The earth here is mine, the food here is mine, the people here are mine to do with as I please. Do you hear me, soulsucker? You have no rights here. The very earth rejects you. It vomits you up and casts you out. The very sky reviles you. It knows who is queen here, who belongs here, who *owns* this land . . . and whose children will feed here."

It seemed to Colivar that the steady beat of wings faltered for a moment. The creature could not possibly understand Gwynofar's words—could she?—but the tone of the Queen Mother's voice left no doubt about her meaning. The flight pattern of the great creature changed suddenly. The ikati pulled in her wings and began to descend swiftly, jeweled patterns streaming across her flanks as she approached. Mesmeric, seductive. Even though he knew the danger of looking directly at the creature, Colivar found that he could not look away. His soul was hungry for what those colors represented, for something that had been out of his reach for centuries. He'd thought he had forgotten it. He'd thought it no longer mattered.

The knowledge of the truth shamed him, even as it stirred his blood.

The men in the company should have been scrambling to take up positions near the rocky mound, to ready themselves for the Souleater's descent. But most of them seemed to be frozen in place, or at least slowed in their actions; only the Guardians moved with anything akin to normal efficiency, though they were clearly affected as well. Salvator alone seemed to be functioning normally. He grabbed his witch, shook him out of his stupor, and dragged him over to where Gwynofar's spear protruded from the ground. From the expression on the High King's face, Colivar guessed that Gwynofar's dramatic self-sacrifice had taken him by surprise, and he was not at all pleased that she had put herself out of reach like this.

"Now!" he commanded, turning the witch to face Gwynofar. And he stepped forward, yanked the spear out of its rocky sheath, and cast it in a high arc toward where his mother stood. But it had not been designed for such use, and its balance was not right; the tip began to drop too soon, and it did not look as though it was going to clear the top of the mound.

—But then the witch's power grabbed hold of it, steadied its flight, and lent it added height to its arc. Clearing the rocky heap by inches, the weapon skidded to a halt right by Gwynofar's feet. She picked it up gratefully. Her longsword was in her hand, but the Souleater would have to be right on top of her before she could use it. With a spear in hand she had better options.

The few archers who were capable of moving were in place now, flanking Gwynofar's position. No doubt some of them would have tried to climb up beside her if there had been time, but the queen was descending too quickly; any man who tried to make that precarious climb would not be in a position to fire when she came within range. Standing at the base of the mound, the archers struggled to be able to look at their target as they waited for the great winged beast to come within range.

Now the Souleater's musky-sweet scent enveloped them, a thousand times more powerful than the faint scent Colivar had detected at the Witch-Queen's palace. Enticing. Unbearable. His human soul wanted to vomit it up, while his other soul, his darker soul, hungered to wallow in it. Colivar glanced over at Ramirus to see how he was responding. The other Magister's expression was grim. It was clearly taking all of Ramirus' self-control to watch Gwynofar set herself up as bait and do nothing about it. She must have ordered him to stay his hand; he would never have accepted such a restriction from Salvator alone. Even so, Colivar suspected that if it came to the point when Ramirus felt that her life was truly threatened, he would probably act anyway. Penitent sensitivities be damned.

Oathbreaker, Colivar thought derisively. Hatred welled up inside him suddenly, for Ramirus and all the other Magisters. But mostly for Ramirus. What an arrogant fool he was, to think he was Colivar's equal! Century after century he nurtured his plans for defeating Colivar, and century after century they were frustrated. But he never accepted it. He never stopped dreaming of victory. When would the idiot learn? He was not Colivar's master. He would *never* be Colivar's master.

It was time Colivar drove that lesson home once and for all.

In a distant part of his brain he knew what was happening to him. But that part had surrendered its sovereignty now, and something darker had taken its place. Fury raged like wildfire in his veins as he gathered his power to him, knowing just how much strength and skill it would take to break through Ramirus' defenses. He also knew what the real source of his fury was, and he knew that he had to resist it, but he lacked the resources. All the connections that had previously bound him to the human world, which he might have drawn on for strength, had been severed. His human lover had disappeared, and she was probably no longer human anyway. His royal contract with Farah had been severed by his own hand. He no longer had a human agenda to serve, a human leader to protect, or even a meaningful human order to follow, outside of that ludicrous deal with Salvator.

A Magister without human ties was a truly terrifying thing. Few understood that as intimately as he did.

And he had broken the Law. The minute he'd recognized Kamala for what she was and had chosen to do nothing about it he had severed his tie to that ancient agreement, cutting himself off from the sorcerous construct that had raised his kind up out of barbarism. True, centuries had passed since the beast within him had last surfaced, and maybe he'd believed that time and self-discipline had weakened it. But he'd been wrong. The darkness within him might have been beaten into submission centuries ago, when the shackles of the Law were first imposed on it, but it had never been fully vanquished. And now those shackles had been struck off, and the ikati queen was calling to him, and Colivar knew with utter certainty that if he gave in to the animal rage that was surging through his veins right now and struck out at Ramirus, he would be lost forever.

But the rage was too powerful to contain, and it surged out of Colivar, a raw and angry force, hungry for violence. The ground surrounding him trembled as he struggled to redirect the terrible power to something other than his rival, and rocks exploded in a shower of sparks between the two Magisters. Spirals of crimson flame began to swirl wildly around him, searing his own flesh when they came too close. He could see alarm in Ramirus' eyes, but not surprise. Ramirus had been affected by the queen's presence as well, and deep inside, where the instincts of their kind lurked secretly, he knew what was happening. But he still had the Law to bolster his humanity, and he was bound by contract to the Aurelius. More importantly, he did not have Colivar's memories. He did not have Colivar's needs. He might feel that he was staring down into the abyss of madness at that moment, but he did not know the name of the horror that lay coiled in its depths, nor had he once embraced it.

No one knew the truth but Colivar.

The shadow of the queen fell over them suddenly, and Colivar was able to look away from Ramirus at last. Her long serpentine tail flexed like a whip as she hovered above Gwynofar, taking stock of her human challenger; the great jeweled wings sent stained-glass sparks skipping madly across the earth. Colivar could see a jeweled cocoon on her back, where the lesser wings had been folded back to protect some precious cargo. His heart lurched in his chest when he realized what it was—what it must be—and for a moment the sheer force of memory was so strong that it almost drove him to his knees. Heat rushed to his groin with searing intensity, as all the power he had been directing outward began to collapse in upon him. If he did not focus it somehow, and release it to do *something*, it would surely consume him.

The archers were waiting. They were not sure of their range yet. Their faces were white with strain from the effort required to focus on the queen's motion without looking at her directly. It was crucial they launch their attack at precisely the right moment. Too soon, and their efforts would fall short. Too late, and the creature might be upon Gwynofar before they could bring her down. Every man knew that when the moment came, he would have no more than a single instant in which to look directly at the queen and locate his target before her power overwhelmed him. If the special tips on their arrows did what legend promised they would, they might be enough to bring her down, but only if they struck in the places where the creature was vulnerable. In theory the men knew what those were. In theory. But their knowledge was derived from arcane prophecies and thousand-year old anatomical charts, and no man knew how much use any of it would really be.

With a cry of defiance and challenge, the queen began to descend upon her rival

—and the archers let loose their first volley.

—and Colivar's power whipped toward the arrows, hot red flames of sorcery exploding outwards, filling the air between them. Spirals of fire formed about each shaft, blazing so brightly that the archers themselves had to look away. Thus no morati saw the arrows shuddering as Colivar's sorcery took hold of them in their flight, altering the course of some, steadying the course of others. Sending them straight into their target.

They struck home.

All of them.

Cobalt arrowheads pierced through the ikati's armor where it was weakest, driving deep into the Souleater's flesh. Some struck soft points that the Guardians knew about and had been aiming for; others had been redirected to weak spots that only Colivar recognized. His sorcery drove them forward with ten times their normal velocity, thrusting them deep in the creature's flesh, so that the barbed heads would tear the queen's muscles to pieces every time she moved. Whatever mysterious poison the arrowheads carried was lodged deep in her flesh now and could begin to do its work.

The Souleater screamed.

A second volley was loosed. This time Colivar did not assist. The sudden release of all that sorcery had left him feeling unsteady, and he feared that if he tried to conjure a second wave of power he might not be able to control it. Dimly he was aware of Ramirus beside him, and he knew that if the other Magister turned on him at that moment he could do little to defend himself.

But Ramirus' attention was on Gwynofar.

She stood atop a granite boulder in the midst of the sea of bones, blond hair whipping about her face as she braced herself to meet the creature head-on, with nothing but a spear for protection. Fear flickered in the backs of her eyes, but there was neither weakness nor hesitation in her stance. For forty generations her bloodline had been trained for this moment—*bred* for this moment—and she would not fail. Proudly she stood atop her precarious perch, alone and vulnerable, and when the air to one side of her began to shimmer, she did not move toward it. One of the witches was offering her a portal, so that she might save herself, but using it would betray her purpose. Bait had no value if it was not in plain sight.

It was clear to all that the poisonous arrows were having their effect upon the ikati. The queen's layered wings were losing their coordination now and her flight was becoming unsteady; the long tail whipped about wildly, destabilizing her even further. Spasms rippled through her body as she screamed once more, this time a cry of raw hatred. Her black faceted eyes turned toward the Guardians, the source of her anguish; several of the archers collapsed as her gaze swept over them, struck down by the sheer force of her fury. Colivar could see that those few who remained were unsteady on their feet, and they struggled to let loose one more volley before their limbs failed them utterly. But they had used up all their special arrows now, and the next round, steel-headed, skittered across the creature's hide like blunt rocks skimming across a pond.

Hovering unsteadily over the field of bones, the ikati turned her attention back to Gwynofar. For a moment Colivar thought that the creature would actually dive down toward her—or perhaps collapse upon her—but evidently pain and rage had not dulled her intelligence quite that much. Suddenly her long tail whipped about from behind, cracking through the air with audible force as it swept toward Gwynofar. Salvator's mother did not flinch. She stood her ground until the last possible moment and then, when the deadly blow was nearly upon her, dropped down to the ground beside the boulder she'd been standing on and used the massive rock as a shield. The deadly blow whistled inches past her head without making contact.

So Gwynofar's seemingly vulnerable position had in fact been a strategically sound one, Colivar noted. He was beginning to appreciate why Ramirus had such interest in her.

A long, dark shape hurtled toward the queen from somewhere beside the mount. The spear struck the queen in her right shoulder, driving deep into her flesh. Her upper wing set spasmed, and she began to lose control of her flight. Desperately she threw herself toward the mount, clawed feet grasping at its flanks as she landed. For a moment it seemed as if the crumbling slope would not support her, but then she got a grip on a solid outcropping and was able to lurch up to the summit.

Colivar felt an ancient thrill course through his blood, to see her grounded thus. The ancient witch-warriors had understood that the first and foremost goal in fighting a Souleater was to bring it down to a warrior's level. Denied the power of flight, a Souleater was a bulky and awkward creature, deadly for the power that it had to suck the strength from men's souls, but as physically vulnerable as any large beast.

Which was not to say that this one could not kill many men before she expired. Possibly the entire war party.

The portal still shimmered to one side of Gwynofar; whatever witch had conjured it was expending obscene amounts of energy to keep it open. If the Souleater's power had drained him at all, that might prove a fatal offering. *Take the portal,* Colivar urged Gwynofar mentally. *Your job is done. Leave the rest of this fight to stronger men.*

But even as he thought those words he was remembering other women, armor-clad and desperate, who had stood before these creatures and refused to give ground. Wives, avenging their fallen husbands. Mothers, avenging their children. Witches, protecting their world. They were the first *lyr*, founders of the northern bloodlines, whose courage now burned in Gwynofar's blood . . . along with their stubbornness.

She did not move.

The serpentine head shot out at her. She stood her ground and met it with her spear braced, ready to strike as soon as she had a proper target. She would probably only have one shot and she had to make it count. The ikati seemed to know this, and she pulled up short at the last moment, hissing in frustration. Colivar could see that the Souleater poison was beginning to slow her down, stiffening the muscles in her neck so that each new motion was painful and unwieldy. But that did not make her any less dangerous.

And then the queen struck. The move was lightning-fast, and Colivar realized grimly that the moment of seeming weakness had been a feint. Taken off her guard, Gwynofar thrust outward with her lance as the creature lunged at her. The cobalt spear tip pierced the thick muscle of the queen's neck and was driven in deeply by the creature's own momentum. Razor-toothed jaws snapped shut mere inches from Gwynofar's head, and the spear was torn from her grasp. Her blow had been all but wasted. The Souleater poison might do its work over time, but Gwynofar had failed to strike any organ or artery that would keep the queen from attacking her again . . . and now she had only a sword with which to protect herself.

Colivar glanced at Ramirus; the Magister's jaw was clenched tight, his hands balled into fists by his side. The minute Ramirus disobeyed Gwynofar, breaking their contract, the human connection that was enabling him to maintain self-control would be severed. Surely he was old enough to understand that. Surely it was the only reason that he stayed his hand now, though his knuckles were white from the force of self-denial.

The queen lunged at Gwynofar again. The Queen Mother held her sword at the ready, but it was merely a token gesture; by the time the ikati got within range of her blade, it would be too late to halt the momentum of that great body, and the sheer force of impact would surely crush her.

And then a figure stepped through the portal.

He moved so quickly that at first Colivar did not realize who it was. One moment he was emerging from the shimmering spell, and the next he was thrusting his spear forward into the creature's side. Deep, deep into the queen's torso, cobalt blade slicing through the iron hide like butter, parting flesh, seeking the vital organs deep within.

Turning on her new attacker, the ikati tried to knock him loose with one of her forelegs, and she managed to score his face with her razor-sharp talons, leaving deep gouges running from forehead to chin. But the man held his ground, and he brought his full weight to bear upon the spear, driving it deeper and deeper into her body.

Salvator.

Twisting her head about, the queen met his eyes. All the terrible power of her species was focused in that gaze: the power to freeze a man in his tracks, to drain him of strength, to leave him a soulless shell. The female ikati could focus her power as the males could not, and she did so now, pitting all of her dying strength against this one single target. In all the fights that Colivar had witnessed, he had never seen a man stand up to such an assault.

Salvator ignored her.

Gritting his teeth in determination, he gave one last thrust to the deeply imbedded spear. A shudder ran through her body as the great wings suddenly spasmed—not only the main flight wings, but the forward wings as well. The delicate membranes that had been folded across her back jerked open, and something that was not quite the size of a man fell from her back, hitting the rocky slope hard enough to send gravel flying, and then tumbling end over end, scattering bones along the way.

A rider.

Colivar moved forward quickly, and he reached the base of the slope just as the body landed with a thud upon a bed of jagged rocks. It was that of a small girl, barely past the age of puberty, with a dirt-streaked face and a torn, filthy shift. One of her arms was twisted behind her at an angle no unbroken limb could manage, and her body was bruised and bleeding in half a dozen places. As Colivar approached, the girl raised her head and hissed at him. There was fury in her eyes, and pain, and a thousand other bestial emotions . . . but not one drop of humanity, he noted. That had been devoured by the Souleater long ago.

For a moment the two of them just stared at one another. High above them the thrashing of the dying ikati loosed an avalanche of small rocks, which rained down upon them both. Colivar felt one strike his temple, drawing blood. He did not move.

And then the thrashing ceased. Somewhere in the distance a final blow was struck . . . and the ikati was dead at last.

The girl shrieked.

It was not a human sound, nor even a bestial one. It was a bloodcurdling amalgam of terror and madness and agony such as never should have issued from any living throat. The fact that it came from so young a girl made the sound doubly horrifying. Colivar could sense the men surrounding him freeze in their tracks, unable to comprehend such a sound. But Colivar understood it. He had heard it before. And in the depths of his soul, where his own darkest secrets lay buried, he understood the pain behind it, and he could feel his own heart bleed for her.

Moving wildly now, she tried to draw back from him. A shard of bone broke through the skin of her upper arm, and she howled in pain as another bone snapped, but still she scrambled backward. Pure animal instinct. She must have been joined to the ikati for a very long time, to have so completely lost touch with her humanity. Her age was probably just an illusion. Sometimes that happened. Sometimes they wanted to retain the appearance they'd had the night they were joined to the ikati, so they drew upon the power of their consorts to keep looking young.

Colivar could have used sorcery to help heal her wounds, or at least ease her pain. But that would have been a violation in her eyes, and he could not bring himself to do it.

"*Kossut!*" she hissed. "*Kossut tal getu!*"

In another universe Guardians were climbing the rock mount, trying to get to the Souleater before the poison in its flesh dissolved the body parts they needed to harvest. More spear tips must be crafted. More arrowheads must be made. If the ancient formulas that the Archivist had researched did what they were supposed to do, then the creature's hide could be crafted into new armor, tougher to pierce than the finest steel plate.

Slowly, Colivar knelt down before the girl. She was sputtering broken phrases in a foreign tongue, fragments of a language that he had not heard for so many years he had to struggle to remember its meaning.

"What is she saying?" Ramirus asked him. Sometime in the last few minutes he had come up beside Colivar, and now he gazed down at the girl with naked curiosity.

"That her children are gone," Colivar answered. "Someone took them from her. She thinks that is what we are here for, to steal her children. But she says they have already taken them all, so there is nothing left for us." He furrowed his brow as he listened to the broken words, trying to make sense of them. "*Queen of sand, queen of ice, there must be two . . .*" He shook his head. "I can't make sense of it all. The dialect has changed since . . ." He hesitated. "It is a dialect I do not know."

"What language?"

Favias' voice came from behind them. "Kannoket."

Colivar nodded.

Ramirus reached out toward the girl. Colivar's first instinct was to stop him, but he did not interfere. She was not his to protect.

A misty image began to take shape above her head. It started as a mass of swirling gray clouds, with hints of orange light playing about the edges. As Ramirus teased the image into finer focus, the clouds parted, revealing a bird's-eye view of a mountainous land. In the distance, on all sides, were vast expanses of ice and snow, lifeless but beautiful. In the middle of that frozen wasteland was a narrow island of green earth, set in a valley between several rugged ice-bound peaks. There were houses in the valley, constructed of sod and manure, and herds of sheep had gathered to graze near the banks of a clear black river. It might have seemed a peaceful scene, under other circumstances. But the animals were clearly agitated, and as Colivar watched, they looked about nervously, as if expecting that at any moment some danger might come rushing at them.

The earth rumbled.

The herd began to move . . . and then began to run, scattering terrified across the landscape. People came out of the sod houses to see what was going on, and one of them pointed to the mountain directly to the north of them. It was a tall peak, with footpaths winding up its rocky flanks and a wide caldera at its summit. Hot pools steamed about its base, and smoke was rising from the caldera itself, as a bulging dome began to push upward through the rock.

And the mountain exploded.

The girl who had fallen off the Souleater shivered violently, and she wrapped her good arm about her knees as she rocked back and forth, keening in terror. Colivar watched in horrified fascination as Ramirus' vision was filled with roiling clouds of gray ash, backlit with the orange light of molten lava. One particularly thick cloud began to move down the volcano's flank, heading toward the pristine valley below: a wall of ash and fire roaring down the mountainside, searing everything in its path. Crops were incinerated, houses charred and blackened, animals seared like cooked meat. The people turned to run, but even if they could have run fast enough to get away, there was nowhere to go. A few tried to make it to the river, but they could not get there in time . . . nor was it likely that the boiling steam rising up from the river's surface would have provided a useful shelter.

It was all over in moments. Where once there had been an expanse of rich and verdant life, now there was only death and ruin. There was no movement left, save for the clouds roiling overhead. No noise, save for the mountain's rumbling.

The image faded.

It was a moment before Colivar could bring himself to speak. "Their food source was destroyed," he whispered. "That's why they came south. The Wrath wasn't strong enough to hold them against the force of certain starvation. Perhaps it had never been strong enough, but no one had ever tested it on that scale before . . ."

"The sunsets," Favias said quietly.

Colivar knew what he meant. There had been a few months in the winter when the northern sky had turned the color of blood, especially at sunset, and men had wondered at the cause. Various religions had come up with explanations that had to do with warring gods, ancient omens, or even the end of the earth. Now they knew the truth.

That was when the invasion had begun.

That was *why* it had begun.

Overhead the sound of knives hacking at flesh could be heard, and occasional curses in northern dialects. Other men moved silently among the fallen warriors, seeking those who were still alive. There were many bodies that would never stir again, including that of the Penitent witch, who had expended the last of his life-essence to keep the portal open. A sacred cause, for which his intolerant god would surely reward him.

Kneeling down by the girl's side, Colivar whispered hoarsely to her in her own language. The Kannoket words tasted strange on his tongue. At first it seemed she did not hear him, but then she began to respond. Tears ran down her face as broken sounds poured out of her. They made little sense to him, but he could use his sorcery to draw meaning from them in the privacy of his own head. All he needed was an anchor to work with.

She was quite mad, of course. She would never be anything

but mad, ever again. That was the price a human being paid for such an unnatural union.

And a Souleater, also.

When he had gathered all the information he needed, he took her dirt-streaked face in his hands—gently, oh so gently!—and gazed steadily into her eyes. She trembled in his grasp but did not pull away. Perhaps she could sense what he truly was . . . or what he had once been. In all the centuries since his First Transition he had rarely felt anything akin to human compassion, but he felt it now. What a strange and alien feeling it was.

Carefully, gently, he severed the vital connection between her heart and her brain. He eased his sorcery into her flesh as delicately as he could, not wanting her to be aware of what he was doing. *Go to sleep, little sister. Find your peace in the next world. There is none for you here.*

Slowly, the girl relaxed. The rhythm of her breathing slowed, and her trembling began to subside. He released her from his hands, and she lowered her head to the rocky earth, dazed and exhausted. Her eyelids fluttered shut. The heart that had been pounding so wildly managed a few final beats, then subsided into silence.

Gently, Colivar brushed the tangled hair back from her face. He did it respectfully, reverently, as befit the queen mother of an entire species. It amazed him how human his emotions felt, in that moment. Which was, of course, the ultimate irony, given that the cause of it was anything but human.

Standing up, he saw that Salvator now stood beside him, along with Ramirus, Gwynofar, and Favias. The other Guardians were still up on the mound, cutting apart the dead Souleater, and Salvator's men were tending to the fallen. Death was in the air.

Three parallel gashes now ran diagonally across one side of the High King's face, barely missing his eye. It gave his expression a strangely predatory aspect as he glared at Colivar. For one mad moment the Magister thought Salvator might actually have the audacity to berate him for using his sorcery to help bring the Souleater down. His own eyes narrowed, and the warning in them was clear: *Don't start with me now, Salvator. I'm not in the mood.*

But the High King said only, "What have you learned?"

He drew in a deep breath, trying to settle his thoughts. "The men of the colony took her eggs. That's why the nests we found were all wrong. She hadn't made them. They wanted to raise another queen that they could bind to a southern woman, so they took her eggs away from her . . . a new queen will not hatch if another one is too close by . . ." His words trailed off. Further explanation was unnecessary. The consequences of that effort were all around them, the desperate attempts of a raging beast to replace what had been stolen from her. How many clutches had they taken? How many times had her maternal instinct been awakened, only to have it violated? How many human children had she kidnapped from their mothers in turn, trying to fill the terrible void inside her, only to find that she lacked the capacity to keep them alive? Casting each one down upon the rocks as it died, weeping over its fallen body before setting out to try again.

"They left some of the males to guard her. That is . . . an offense among their kind. So she killed them all. The ones we found . . . they were the last ones to die." He shook his head solemnly. "She says that only one of her daughters is alive. They took her down south, to what she calls *a place of sand and sun.* They wanted to be as far from the ice as possible, so that no man could ever trap them in the cold and the dark again."

"Anshasa," Ramirus said quietly.

Colivar shut his eyes for a moment. "There are several nations surrounding the Great Desert. And several smaller deserts, besides that one. But yes, Anshasa is a possibility."

"If there is only one female left . . ." Favias began.

Colivar nodded. "If the last queen dies, the entire species can be destroyed. It may take years to destroy them all. But those who are killed will not be replaced."

"Then we must find this other queen and deal with her," Salvator said firmly. "Before she lays a clutch of her own."

Easier said than done, Colivar mused. *Especially when that one is bound to a woman of the Witch-Queen's formidable intelligence.*

One of the guards was walking toward them. The expression on his face was grim.

"What is the count?" Salvator asked him.

"Three dead, for certain. Three more in some kind of coma. We can't wake them up."

"Szandor?" Salvator asked, naming the witch.

Lips tight, the man shook his head.

Salvator sighed, and he made some kind of religious sign over his heart. "May the Creator have mercy upon their souls."

The Guardians were climbing down from the mount now, passing Gwynofar from hand to hand to help her descend. Salvator watched for a moment, then headed toward where the horses were being held. "We'll ride south, to the Danovar monastery. The brothers will see to our wounded, and we can arrange for transportation home from there."

"Are we Magisters welcome to accompany you?" Colivar asked, a faint edge to his voice.

The High King turned to him. The bloody cuts on his face made his expression of displeasure all the more marked. For a moment he just stared at Colivar, and the Magister could only imagine what was going through his mind. But he simply nodded slowly, coldly, and responded, "You may follow us if you wish. But I make no promise about your reception at the monastery." He glanced up at the dead ikati perched high above them, its long tail dripping blood down the side of the rock mound. "You are but one step removed from such creatures, in the eyes of my Church."

"And in your eyes?"

Salvator's gaze was dark and cold. There was no answer in them.

As the morati began to gather up their things, Colivar turned back to the girl's body. How peaceful she looked now! There was a time when he had wanted nothing more than to know such peace, at any cost.

"It's time, Colivar."

He did not turn around when Ramirus spoke, or otherwise acknowledge him.

"War is no longer looming on the horizon," the Magister said quietly. "It has engulfed us. We need all our weapons at hand."

He said nothing.

"You need to tell us what you know about these creatures. All of it."

Still he said nothing.

Finally he heard Ramirus walk away. He heard Gwynofar expressing her gratitude to him for his service to the expedition. Doubtless she would have thanked Colivar as well, had he shown any sign of being approachable. But his mood had chilled the very air around him, and no one dared come near.

He listened quietly for a few minutes more, then let his flesh melt into a winged form—black-feathered, in mourning for the dead queen—and took to the sky, where no one would be able to ask him questions.

QUICKENING

CHAPTER 14

THE VISITOR arrived in the depths of night, which said much for the strength and confidence of his Souleater; few ikati flew long distances without the kiss of sunlight upon their wings. It was a dark night, with only a single crescent moon to guide the pair's passage, so little effort was required to mask their flight from the prying eyes of Jezalya's sentries. No one would see the great creature approach the city as long as it stayed behind the mounts that flanked Jezalya; no one would see its dark bulk silhouetted against the gleaming sand when it landed.

The ikati queen observed the pair approaching the city and relayed that knowledge to Siderea. Through their connection Siderea felt as if she could sense the pair's presence, and even get a sense of the man's state of mind. Was that possible? Her recent transformation sometimes affected her witchery in strange ways, and at this point nothing would surprise her. The presence she was sensing was a patient one, if her impressions were true. Calculating. It was a curious mindset for one of the riders. Usually when such men came into her presence they were highly agitated, and she could literally taste the effort that it took for them to maintain a human demeanor. But for this one, she sensed, the subterfuge came more naturally.

The gates of the city would not open until morning. So her visitor would probably wait until then and arrive on foot, pretending he was nothing more than a common traveler. Anything else would be a waste of power, not to mention an offense against Siderea's territorial rights. Souleaters other than the queen were not allowed in her city.

So she had time to prepare.

Dawn's light was just beginning to creep into her bedchamber when Siderea called her maidservants to her. Sleepy young girls rushed to her side, bringing paint and powder and the brushes needed to apply them. Blinking the sleep from their eyes, they helped her apply delicate layers of color to her cheeks, then curled her long dark hair into sinuous ringlets. And of course they applied perfume. Always perfume. The fact that Souleaters were unusually sensitive to smell lent added power to that facet of her feminine armory in dealing with their human consorts. Though of course any artificial scent had to be compatible with the natural perfume of her own ikati, that musky-sweet smell which clung to her skin these days no matter how often she bathed. But that, too, affected the riders in interesting ways, and among mortals it added yet another layer to her mystique. *The scent of demons*, some called it. They whispered that descriptor in the shadows, when they thought she was not listening.

But she was always listening.

She dressed in layers of silk gauze the colors of Souleater wings. The delicate arrangement of fabric was almost but not entirely opaque, and hinted at the curves beneath without actually revealing them. Such garments had always been useful to her in manipulating men, and the ones who were bound to ikati were especially susceptible to such visual tricks. Which was as it should be. The rider who claimed her as his mate would become first among his own kind, until such time as a rival managed to displace him. Rarely was the tie between sex and power so overt among humans.

How different things might be now if her ikati were fully grown and ready to mate! The queen's sexual instincts were still abstract and unfocused. It was a good thing as far as the males were concerned, as it allowed them time to sort out their alliances with minimal bloodshed; they did not yet have a fertile queen to fight over. But once that changed, so would the dynamics of the colony. Siderea remembered her visions of combat from the night she had seduced Nasaan. If the young queen had responded so powerfully to those images while she was still a juvenile, what would it be like when the full force of sexual maturity came into play? It was a thought that was both unnerving and exhilarating to Siderea. Some days she felt as if she had dived off a high cliff in joining herself to the creature, and was now in midair, falling free, with no knowledge of what lay below.

A black-skinned servant entered and waited silently for Siderea to notice him. She did not look away from her mirror. Giving one last pat to her hair, running a finger along the inner curve of one breast to part the silk layers above it in the most alluring manner possible, she murmured, "Have my guest brought to the garden," and she heard him scurry to obey.

The palace that Dervasti had built was a grand thing by desert standards, though few princes of the north would have deemed it so. Still, there was no denying the sheer cost of its marble, imported from distant quarries, or the opulence of its gold-chased décor. Nasaan had brought statues of the gods into the main hall, richly carved idols draped in jewels and silk, to guarantee the favor of the deities. And the favor of the priests, of course. One could have an interesting argument over which mattered more to him.

But the garden was hers, an opulent indulgence in this water-starved region. The lush, green plants that filled the palace courtyard to overflowing were a more powerful symbol of princely wealth than if the whole of the palace had been stuffed to its ceilings with gold bullion. Never mind that Siderea could conjure water with less than a moment's thought. Visitors did not have to know that.

She would have preferred to receive her guest while reclining on a gilt-edged couch, as she knew it would set off her physical charms to best advantage, but her consort bridled at the thought. *No show of submission!* It was pointless to try to explain to the ikati that among humans such a pose could mean the very opposite of submission—that it was a sign of power to have a guest attend upon her as though he were a servant. Not to mention that driving a man to desire a woman he could not possess was a staple of desert protocol. But human logic alone could not override the powerful ikati instinct, and Siderea had learned that there were times it was simply not worth the effort of arguing with her. And so she moved to a particularly lush portion of the garden, stood beneath an arch of tangled vines and hanging fuchsia blossoms, draped the gossamer layers of violet and blue silk about her to best advantage, and waited.

The servant finally returned. "Lady,' he said, bowing deeply. "A man named Nyuku begs leave to attend upon you."

The name startled her. *Nyuku* was here? Well, that would certainly explain why the other Souleaters had not challenged him on his way in. Nyuku had been dominant among the riders for so long that none of the others could remember a time when it had been otherwise. Or so they told her, on those few occasions when she allowed them to speak to her. In the fierce world of the ikati, where leadership must be earned anew each season and death could be the price of failed ambition, such a record was no small thing. Half of the Souleaters here probably bore scars from the claws and spikes of Nyuku's consort.

She had expected him to come to her, but not so soon. No doubt the situation up north had forced his hand.

"Bring him to me," she commanded. Feeling the young queen's heartbeat quicken in anticipation, echoed by her own.

The servant bowed again and left her. Two guards entered silently, and took up discreet positions behind some flowering bushes. A necessary protocol, now that she was Royal Consort. No man could be allowed to meet with her alone.

She wove a subtle spell that would keep them from overhearing her conversation, and waited.

The servant returned, a black-haired man following behind him. Like the other riders Nyuku was spare of flesh, his skin coarsened by a lifetime of exposure to the harsh arctic winds. Unlike the others, he was freshly bathed, with no more smell about him than the ubiquitous musky scent of a Souleater. It was a pleasant surprise. His gleaming black hair was pulled back into a neat queue at the back of his neck, and it looked as if he had dressed it with oil to keep it in place. A remarkably human affectation. His clothes were simple but finely made, and of woven fabric; if he wore any garments made of Souleater skin, they were not visible to her. His long-lashed eyes were almondine in shape, and a sharp intelligence flashed in their depths as he took in the room, the guards . . . and her. Thoroughly human in aspect and expression, she noted. No one who saw him standing there would suspect he was anything else.

The servant bowed respectfully. "Madame Consort, I present to you Nyuku of the northlands." It was clear from his tone that he was disappointed not to have a longer name to offer her, or a string of formal titles. Few visitors appeared before her or Nasaan without an impressive array of family names and titles to lay before the city's rulers as offerings, even if they'd had to make some of them up in the antechamber. For a man to ignore such customs and just give one name spoke of great self-confidence . . . or great arrogance.

The line between the two could sometimes be quite thin.

"Nyuku," she purred. She held out her hand to him. "I do believe the others have mentioned you."

She was pleased to see that the gesture startled him; it was always good policy to put these riders off their guard. As he stepped forward to take her hand, she noted that his body language was also remarkably human. *This one has made a study of us,* she assessed. As he came up to her, he bowed his head slightly, and then, after a moment's hesitation, reached out for her hand. She allowed him to take it. In the back of her mind the ikati queen grew agitated. *Shh,* Siderea soothed her. *I know what I'm doing.* But there was very real danger in inviting any of the riders to touch her, she knew that. If his Souleater believed it to be a more significant invitation, things could turn bad very quickly.

She watched as he raised the hand to his lips in a thoroughly civilized gesture and kissed it gently, his eyes never leaving hers. For a moment she thought she could sense his consort through those eyes, a dark and terrible creature beating his wings in fury, raging at what he considered a deliberate sexual provocation. If the creature managed to take control of Nyuku right now, she had no doubt he would vent that fury on her. She was playing a dangerous game, to be sure.

But it was a game she had always enjoyed, and the fact that she now had a Souleater for a partner only made it more interesting.

When Nyuku released her hand, he took a step back from her, establishing the proper distance between them once more. Siderea could feel her queen settle down a bit, though she was still clearly wary of the situation.

"You know who I am?" he asked.

"I know what the others have told me about you."

A corner of his mouth twitched. "Good things, no doubt."

She smiled graciously, with only the faintest hint of irony in her voice. "Of course."

This man would be her mate someday. The mechanics of that were not something she had fully accepted yet; she was accustomed to choosing her own lovers. But apparently when the proper time came, she would desire him, whether or not he had won over her human heart. Human concerns would not matter once the mating flight began.

Or so the others had told her. They had their own agenda, of course.

It may not be this one who dominates the flight, the queen thought to her. Trying to comfort her. *Another may bring him down.*

He ruled the colony for a long time, Siderea responded. *That means he is hard to defeat.*

In frozen skies, where the sunlight is pale. Who is to say what will happen over hot desert sands, with the sun beating down on their wings?

Now *that* was an interesting question. Was Nyuku concerned that his hard-won status might be threatened in this new environment? The suggestion of vulnerability in him seemed to restore the proper balance of power between them, and it awakened her fiercest predatory instincts.

"So, to what do I owe the pleasure of this visit?" she asked. Razor-edged questions danced just beneath the surface of her smile: *Why are you in my territory? How long do you mean to stay? What advantage do you hope to gain from being here?*

"To present myself to our new queen, of course."

"And to see what manner of woman has joined your ranks." He smiled slightly. "Of course."

"And perhaps to show the others that the new queen will receive you, while she still holds them at arm's length. Which might affect their confidence in the next flight, giving you advantage."

His smile took on a faintly predatory edge. "We are what we are, Madame Consort."

Indeed we are, she thought with satisfaction. "So, then." She spread her hands wide, inviting his inspection of her. "What do you see in me?"

His gaze was frank and sexual; men who were bound to Souleaters did not apologize for their base instincts. "A woman of beauty and power. A ruler of consequence, who has already begun to establish a new empire for our people, away from the prying eyes of our enemies."

"I take it you approve."

He smiled slightly. "What man would not approve of such a woman?"

She chuckled softly. "I did not expect such a courtier in you, Nyuku. Few of your men even know how to bathe, much less how to flatter a woman."

"The human world has its rules. If we mean to be safe here, then we must learn them. It is what the Souleaters failed to do the first time, and why the First Kings were able to drive them into exile." His eyes were so dark in color that they seemed nearly black, iris and pupil bleeding into one another as if they had no boundaries. If one could facet such eyes, they might almost look like those of an ikati. "This time, of course, the ikati have allies. So I expect things will go more smoothly."

"Allies such as you and I."

The dark eyes glittered. "Yes."

"And the northern queen? What of her? How does she figure into all this?"

The words were a test, and he clearly knew it. She could see the hesitation in his eyes. How much did she know already? He clearly did not want to be the one to bring her bad news. Finally, in a solemn tone, he pronounced, "The northern queen is dead, Madame Consort."

She was not so dishonest as to feign surprise; her expression was artfully impassive. "And the ones that guarded her?"

"All gone. I could find nothing but skeletons remaining."

"Then my queen is the last one remaining."

He nodded grimly. "Aye."

A smile of cold satisfaction spread across her face. A true human might have found such an expression distasteful. But an altered human, bound to an ikati, would have no issue with her celebrating the death of a rival.

"So," she said. "The survival of our species . . . " She let the words trail off, inviting him to finish the sentence.

"Depends upon you, Madame Consort."

What power there was in those words! What responsibility! It boggled the mind just to think about it.

"How did she die?" Siderea asked. Also a test.

"The High King Salvator Aurelius led a retinue into her territory. It is said that he struck the deathblow himself."

His spy network was flawed, she noted. Or else he was testing her. Did these men play that kind of game? "No," she corrected him. "It was not the High King who struck the death blow. Though your story is the one being put out for public consumption . . . for obvious reasons."

She caught the flicker of surprise in his eyes. Fool! Had he thought that she was completely isolated here, without spies of her own? Dependent upon him and his kind for knowledge of the outside world? Well, that was only to be expected. He and his kind were accustomed to dealing with children, young girls who were bound to equally young ikati, so that the two of them could grow to adulthood side-by-side in blissful ignorance. But Siderea was a different sort of creature. Seasoned witch, ruler of men, seducer of kings and Magisters . . . Little wonder that Nyuku and his kind were unprepared to deal with her.

I have allies in places you would never suspect, she thought.

"Who, then?" he demanded. "Who struck the blow?"

Had he loved her northern counterpart? Were any of these men—half-human, half-ikati—truly capable of love? The northern queen's rider would have been Nyuku's mate, a child bride bound to him by ties of ikati passion. Now she was dead, and he had nothing left. Oh, he might still be the strongest and fiercest of his kind, and his ikati could probably take on any challenger with two wings tied behind its back, but it was his connection to the ikati queen that had given him true authority. Now that queen was dead, and he was just one more individual in a brawling colony of bad-tempered predators, blooding themselves over pecking-order politics while waiting for the new queen to declare her flight.

Such power, all vested in a female! It was a heady elixir.

"A Magister killed her," she told him. Savoring the anger that came into his eyes as she spoke the words.

"Which one?"

She opened her mouth to speak the name, but for a moment could not form the sounds. Hatred welled up inside her with such force that it left her breathless. *You have his hair*, she told herself. Remembering those few precious strands that she had stolen from Colivar, with all their sorcerous potential. They were tucked away in her treasure box now, along with less powerful tokens from less powerful Magisters. Waiting for the day she would use them all to strike at their owners. So her hatred was not an impotent thing. Someday, somehow, she would have her vengeance on those who had betrayed her, this one first and foremost.

"Colivar struck the deathblow," she said.

She could see that the name had some personal meaning to him, though he tried to hide that fact. She kept her own expression neutral, but inside her mind was racing. Something new and very interesting had just entered the picture, and she was not sure how she wished to address it.

"Colivar?" he demanded. "You're sure that was the name?"

"Yes. Why?" She asked, as casually as she could, "Do you know him?"

He released his breath in a long reptilian hiss. "I knew someone by that name once. Long ago. But it can't possibly be the same man."

She shrugged. "The name is unusual, but I'm sure it's not unique. Doubtless other men have borne similar names."

"Describe him to me."

The ikati queen bridled at the sudden imperiousness of his tone, but Siderea soothed her with a thought. *Quiet. This is important.* She was watching Nyuku now as a hawk might watch its prey, alert to the subtlest movement that might enable her to read him. "His coloring is similar to yours. His features are angular, with dark eyes canted upward at the corners. Clean-shaven, with long, straight hair, midnight black in color. I would say he looks about thirty years of age . . . but that has little meaning with a Magister, of course. A few inches taller than you, perhaps." And in what she hoped was a suitably nonchalant tone, she asked, "Does that sound like the man you once knew?"

A nameless black emotion flickered in the depths of Nyuku's eyes. For a moment Siderea felt as if she were not looking at a man at all, but gazing directly into the eyes of his ikati. And what she saw revealed in those eyes made the hairs on the back of her neck rise.

"I know of him," Nyuku said. An obvious evasion.

"Not a friend of yours, I take it."

"I have no friends among the Magisters." His expression was controlled, unreadable. Whatever it was about Colivar that mattered to him, he clearly did not intend to share it with her.

At least not of his own free will.

Carefully she drew a bit of power from her consort and bound it to her purpose. Delicate power, meticulously focused: a surgeon's scalpel of spellcasting. The riders she had met thus far had not shown any sign of true witchery. For all that they had the power to claim athra from their winged consorts, they seemed to do little with it except forage for food and fight with one another. But it would be foolish for her to assume that Nyuku was subject to the same restriction. He was, after all, the leader of his kind, and he seemed to be a lot more savvy than the others.

She reached out a tendril of her power toward him. There was no resistance. Was he just unaccustomed to having other people attempt to probe his thoughts, or was he truly lacking in the most basic defensive skills of a witch? Even an untrained child could manage better protection than this. And here he was with a lifetime's worth of power being channeled through his soul each passing moment, his to claim for spellcasting whenever he wanted to. Incredible!

Carefully, oh so carefully, she reached out to touch his mind, to learn the truth about him and Colivar—

—And a roaring filled her brain as magma-hot power suddenly rushed through her. Not pouring inward, as she had intended, bearing his secret knowledge to her on a tide of witchery. Outward, outward, the power flowed, from the center of her own soul outward, directly toward him. Lava streams of energy gushing out through her every pore, soulfire tearing her skin as it burst forth, searing her soul in its passage. Some vast hunger in him was drawing it out of her. Dragging it out. A cold blackness wrapped itself around her, sucking the very strength out of her soul. In the distance her ikati keened in panic, and the creature's raw, preternatural terror poured into Siderea's head, drowning out all other thoughts than the desperate need to survive.

Somehow, she managed to break free. To sever the connection. When she did so—when she managed to pull herself together enough to focus on her immediate surroundings once more—she realized that she had fallen. Nyuku had stepped forward to catch her, and had possibly kept her from hurting herself. But he was still holding on to her, and that was unacceptable to Siderea's ikati. Rage welled up inside their conjoined soul, and Siderea might have struck out at him with her talons (fingernails?) if the guards had not gotten to them first and pulled Nyuku roughly away from her. For a moment the whole tableau was frozen, the four of them staring at one another, no one moving. In Nyuku's eyes she could see a Souleater clearly now, rage and indignation blazing. How *dare* these humans get between him and a queen! In that instant she could see how much effort it took for the human part of him to maintain a civilized façade, and not strike out at these men, as his Souleater half hungered to.

Slowly she rose to her feet, gathering her dignity about her. What in all the hells had just happened? She had used her witchery on Amalik once for much the same purpose, and that had not been a problem. Was Nyuku somehow different? Or had the fact that she was now bound to a Souleater herself somehow altered her witchery, so that using it against these men would now be a dangerous undertaking?

"Let him go," she ordered.

The guards released Nyuku's arms. He did not move. Anger radiated from him like heat from desert sand.

"You meant well," she said coldly. "But do not ever touch me again without invitation."

For a long moment he stared at her. Then, stiffly, he bowed his head, acknowledging the order.

She gestured to the guards. As they withdrew to their former posts, she wrapped her power around them once more, to guard whatever secrets her next words might reveal. But she could see that they were doubly wary now, and it was hard to control their senses.

"Colivar is an enemy," she said bluntly. "I mean to destroy him. If that's an agenda you also serve, then we have business in common. If not . . ." She shrugged.

It was powerful bait. Most of the riders would kill for a chance to serve as her ally, desperate to win her favor in the hopes that somehow it might benefit them when the queen made her first flight. They were pitiful creatures, for the most

part. But this one . . . this one was different. This one was
something more.

"Magisters are hard to kill," he said evenly.

"I am well aware of that."

"You believe you have the means to do so?"

There was no more powerful anchor in all the world than
part of a man's own body. The fact that she had removed Colivar's
hair from him while it was still a vital part of his identity, rather
than scavenging it from the bed or the floor after his body had
spontaneously discarded it, gave it phenomenal power.

"I have the means," she said with a smile. Watching him
closely.

He licked his lips, considering the situation. It was not the
response she had expected from him. Either she had misjudged
the intensity of his interest in Colivar, or something more complicated was playing out. Some new mystery of considerable significance, which he must weigh before he could answer her. She
cursed the fact that she could not use her power to steal that
secret from him.

Have patience, she told herself. *He will deliver his knowledge
to you in time. They always do.*

There were always the traditional methods, she reminded
herself.

"Perhaps I misread you," she mused aloud, "and you do not
want him dead after all."

Nyuku's eyes narrowed. "I want him dead. But his death must
be by my hand."

She raised an eyebrow. "Why?"

"Personal reasons, Madame Consort."

Could this be an issue of sexual rivalry? It was no secret
that Colivar had once been Siderea's lover; surely Nyuku knew

that. Which meant that his Souleater might consider Colivar a rival. If so, all the force of that species' primitive competitive instinct would be pouring into Nyuku's head right now. Not only the desire to rend this new rival to pieces in a metaphorical sense, but to do so physically, by tooth and claw. To taste the blood of the arrogant Magister who would stand between him and the queen.

It was a pleasing prospect.

"He may die by your hand," she allowed, "but it is my hand that will bring him down. My hand that will isolate him, destroy the things he values most, and crush his spirit. When I am done with him, you may have him. Only when I am done with him. Do you accept those terms?"

He bowed his head. "I do, Madame Consort."

"Can you order the others to assist me in this?"

The question was at once a compliment and a challenge. If Nyuku's Souleater became mate to a queen again, then he would have authority over the other riders. Right now he had nothing.

The question was a reminder of his own insufficiency, of the fact that he needed *her* to restore his power.

"If I tell them our queen needs something," he told her, "they will obey."

She smiled, pleased. This one was proving easy to manipulate. Through him the others could be controlled. A man was still a man, she reflected, whether he toiled in the fields, sat upon an ivory throne, or shared his soul with a legendary monster.

"Then we will speak more on this later," she said. "In the meantime, you will stay near the palace so that I know where to find you."

The command was a boon of considerable power, as the riders measured such things; a sign of favor from the new queen would increase Nyuku's status measurably. But it was also clearly a dismissal. He had gained much from this interview, but he must not mistake the nature of their relationship; her favor must be earned continually, and never taken for granted.

He bowed his head respectfully and turned to leave. Siderea could almost hear his Souleater whispering feverishly to him in the background. Then he paused, and looked back at her. It seemed she could sense the two minds conferring inside his head. Trying to decide what to say? Or perhaps, what not to say?

"You will not need a trap for Colivar," he informed her. "He will come to you. He *must* come to you. His true nature leaves him no other option."

He bowed one last time, then took his leave without waiting for response.

Which was, she observed, a power play in its own right. *You may ask me to play the role of a servant,* it said, *but do not mistake me for someone with a servant's weakness.* Siderea was intrigued by the move. Did he think such a show of independence would please her? Or was it meant as an act of defiance?

Either way, she appreciated the spirit behind it, and did not challenge his exit.

CHAPTER 15

T HE SPIRE in the royal garden was awash in moonlight, cool highlights rippling along its surface as the clouds passed overhead. Disturbingly beautiful. Salvator stared at the thing in silence, noting the dark streaks where his mother had offered up her blood in sacrifice, yet again. To a god of rocks. He wanted to despise the practice as passionately as a Penitent should, but now that he understood its true purpose, it was hard to summon up the same kind of loathing he used to feel. True, it was still an idolatrous faith, but it had served to keep the *lyr* focused and united for forty generations, so that their natural immunity to the Souleater's power could be preserved. The same immunity he apparently enjoyed. And now he knew just how important that might turn out to be.

Tolerance is the first step toward damnation, he reminded himself.

Footsteps approached, but he did not turn around. They were light footsteps, hardly weighty enough to break the pine needles that carpeted the ground. Then they were still, and for a moment there was silence. He wondered if his mother was keeping her distance to respect his meditative mood, or if she was afraid that his willingness to stand in front of the sacred spire would shatter like glass the minute she interrupted his contemplation.

At last he said aloud, "That was a reckless thing you did, with the Souleater."

"It needed to be done."

"You should have let me know what you had planned. I didn't like being taken by surprise."

"If I had told you, would you not have told me my plan was too reckless? Forbidden me from even attempting it?"

A muscle along the line of his jaw tightened. "Very likely."

She came up beside him. There was a deep purple bruise on her cheek, just starting to turn yellow about the edges, from where the dying Souleater had struck her. He knew that his own face looked even worse, with its three deep claw-gouges running from forehead to chin. Back when his witches had staunched the flow of blood and cleansed the wounds of infection, they had offered to erase the marks entirely, but he had told them not to. God had chosen to scourge him, and he would bear the marks of it with pride.

"Did you feel the Souleater's power at all?" he asked her.

For a moment she was silent, her eyes flickering downward as she replayed the battle in her mind. Finally she nodded. "Yes. I believe I did. Not enough to keep me from looking at the queen directly, but there was a kind of . . . inertia. It took effort to do anything other than stand there frozen. When she first struck at me with her tail, I almost didn't get out of the way in time."

"But then you did."

"Yes. But it took all the strength of will that I possessed." She cocked her head to one side. "And what of you, my son? Did her power touch your soul as well?"

He turned back to face the spire. For a moment he did not speak.

"No," he said at last. "I felt the territorial effect at first, but once I realized what it was and focused my mind accordingly, I felt . . . nothing."

He could hear her draw in a sharp breath. "Truly?"

"Truly, mother. This species appears to have no power over me."

But its human allies do, he thought darkly. Siderea had sent him a dream a while back, so he was clearly not immune to *her* power. But even that dream had been an imperfect creation, and in the end he had banished it. How much did this strange gift matter when dealing with the Souleaters' human allies?

Gwynofar put a hand on his arm. "You have *lyr* blood in your veins. Whatever immunity our ancestors possessed, that allowed them to fight the Great War, is now vested in you."

"But I'm only half-*lyr*," he reminded her. "So why should my immunity be any greater than yours? That makes no sense at all. You inherited the gift from both sides of your family. I am half . . . something else."

She chuckled softly. "Exactly. You inherited the *lyr* blood from me and sheer Aurelius stubbornness from your father. Clearly the combination is more than a Souleater queen can handle."

Despite himself he smiled. "Do you really think that's the answer?"

"One of many, perhaps."

"And my faith? What about that?" He attempted to keep his tone light. "Do you believe that Penitent beliefs played a part in this?"

She hesitated. That alone spoke volumes. Before the battle she would have discounted the concept immediately. The events of the last few days must have shaken her badly.

"You were a monk for four years," she said finally. "In that time you focused yourself on spiritual matters and isolated yourself from all outside distractions. It is not impossible that such a lifestyle might have had an impact on . . . mental capacity."

Is that all? he wanted to press her. But the concession was already a great one, and he did not want to make her feel sorry she had offered it.

Maybe it was your attachment to Ramirus, and the fact that you allowed him to reshape your body, that compromised your gift. Maybe the fact that I was willing to surrender my life to a Souleater rather than submit to sorcery was what gave me the power to resist her.

If that was true, then he would be hard pressed to find another like himself. True *lyr* rarely joined the Penitents, nor did they often marry into families where Penitents might be found. If Ramirus had not arranged to bring Gwynofar south so that she could marry Danton . . .

He stopped. Just stopped. Opened his mouth and then shut it again, wordlessly; no sound would come.

"Salvator?"

His thoughts hung in midair, suspended. He could not get hold of them.

"What's wrong?"

He knew, Salvator realized. A strange mix of emotions came over him, half anger and half awe. Ramirus couldn't possibly have understood what the *lyr* truly were, back when he had arranged Danton's marriage—no one knew, back then—but he had known that Gwynofar's bloodline had some special magical heritage, and he must have known the history of the Aurelius line as well. Maybe there was some secret bit of history in the Aurelius line that Danton himself had not been aware of, which Ramirus had thought might cause the *lyr* gift to manifest more powerfully if the two families were joined.

That is why he arranged Danton's marriage, he thought, stunned. *It was a breeding experiment.*

He sat down heavily on one of the stone benches that faced the spire. His hands were shaking.

"Salvator." Gwynofar sat down beside him and put a hand on his arm, "Tell me what's wrong."

He looked at his mother and blinked. He did not know what to say. Should he tell her that she had been crossbred like some prize mare, in hopes that new and interesting traits might surface in her colts? And that even while Ramirus had been watching over the Aurelius children, guiding them through the trials and tribulations of royal childhood, he had been putting them through tests of his own devising? This was what her marriage to Danton had really been about, he realized. Seeing what happened when the two bloodlines merged. That was why Salvator and his siblings had been created.

Experiments. They were all nothing more than a Magister's experiments.

"I was worried," he managed. Forcing meaningless words out, because he had to say something. The storm of indignation inside his head was deafening.

"About what?"

He shut his eyes, trying to restore his focus. What had they been talking about before this? "Apparently I have the ability to face down a Souleater as if it were nothing more than a simple beast. Possibly I am the only man alive who has that capacity. Which means . . . what? Do I strap on a sword now and go gallivanting about the kingdom, searching for monsters to kill?"

"Is it what you want to do?" she asked quietly.

"It would make it damn hard to run the kingdom."

"Then forget about looking for Souleaters. That's the Guardians' job."

"And after they find them? What then? Do I leave them to battle the creatures alone, without my gift, or abandon my throne to help them?" He reached up a hand to rub his forehead, where a sharp pain was slowly taking root. "If only I could have had a few years to consolidate my rule, before all this began! My reign is too fresh and untested for this, the High Kingdom too unsettled. I can't simply walk away and expect things to be the same when I come back."

"Why not?"

He exhaled noisily. "Because there are enemies at our borders. Restless nobles within it. Judgments that need to be made, territories negotiated, disputes resolved. An empire this vast can't run itself."

"But none of those things require *you*, my son. At least not in the short term. I can handle some of them. I did that for Danton when he went off to war. And you have officers who can handle the rest. If you need more than that . . . then call in Valemar. Have him take charge when you're absent. He can do that well enough if you instruct him properly."

"And what if my brother decides that he likes the feel of a crown upon his head? And doesn't want to give it up when I come home? What then?"

"Salvator." She reached up and put her hands on the sides of his face. "You came home because I asked you to take the throne, not because you wanted it. How many times have you told me that? The crown sits uncomfortably on your head, you said, and you wish your duty did not require you to wear it. So if Valemar took the crown from you—if he proved he had the strength and the savvy to unseat you, which would be a sure sign of his political capacity—would that be such a terrible thing?"

The suggestion made him angry, but he didn't know why. Every word she was saying was true. How many nights had he lain awake, wishing that God would remove this burden from his life? And yet . . . it was *his* burden. No man should be taking it from him.

And Valemar was not a Penitent. If he took over, the power of the High Kingdom would no longer be in the hands of the true faith. An idolater would control it. That mattered far more than his personal fate.

She chuckled as her hands fell to her sides once more. "I see Danton's pride in your eyes."

He smiled faintly. "I am my father's son."

"And what would he have done, in your shoes?"

He did not hesitate. "Taken his place at the head of an elite group of Guardians. Bathed in the blood of Souleaters and exulted in their destruction, until the last of the creatures were gone from the earth forever. And so fierce would his reputation be that no man would have the courage to touch anything that had his name on it, while he was gone. The throne would still be empty and waiting for him when he returned."

"You have that same spark in you," she said. "I've seen it. You channel it into faith instead of warfare, but it is no less a driving passion."

"I do not have his reputation."

"Perhaps not. But war gives man a chance to establish a reputation of his own. Unless you shy away from that kind of bloodshed."

"Penitents are not pacifists, Mother. Even the monks train at arms, as an exercise in self-discipline. And many were the times in the past when persecutions required us to use such skills. Our God is both Creator and Destroyer, remember that."

"And now the Destroyer has come to your doorstep."

"To the world's doorstep, I think."

"The High Kingdom *is* the world." A faint smile flickered across her face. "Or so your father always told me."

He sighed and shook his head. "I can't tell you what I would not give to have his counsel now."

"I think . . ." She hesitated. "I think he would not comprehend your misgivings. He was a simple man, in many ways. If he believed that someone had to die, then he killed him, without hesitation or remorse. Now there are Souleaters who need to die, so he would tell you to do whatever was necessary to see that they met their Creator." A faint smile flickered across her face. "Or their Destroyer, if you prefer."

And you, Mother? If I asked you to share the burden of war with me, would you be so quick to celebrate this conflict?

"Valemar may have the same gift that I do," he said. "My sisters as well. Though they are hardly well suited to a monster-killing expedition."

"Valemar is not a warrior," she said bluntly. "I love him dearly, but he is not made of the same stuff that you are. And your sisters are content with women's lives and have no place on the battlefield."

She ran a featherlight finger down his cheek, tracing one of the crimson gashes. Because Salvator's witches had closed the wound properly, there was no pain, but the touch felt odd, as if the scarred cheek were not truly his own. "Besides, their gods are concerned with things like crops and rainfall and human fecundity. Not with saving the world. Your faith is your armor, my son."

For a moment he was taken aback. Was she praising his religion? If so, this was new ground; he did not know how to negotiate it. "And you, Mother? Do you fear bloodshed?"

Her hand fell away from his cheek; her expression grew somber. "I do believe I've already answered that question. The dead Souleater queen, remember?"

He shook his head. "It's one thing to defend your home territory from a threat. To know that your family may die if you do not act. It's another thing to spill blood in a foreign land, where the people are not your own, and where you cannot count on any support save that which you bring with you."

She gazed into his eyes for a long moment. "What are you asking me, Salvator?"

He drew in a deep breath. All the words he had prepared for this moment fled from his mind. Who knew if they had even been the right words to begin with? "I believe . . . you have a special power, Mother. I believe that the gift that was granted you on the Throne of Tears, your ability to connect the *lyr* to one another, and to awaken the ancient power in their blood . . . has not left you."

"What do you mean?"

"This immunity I seem to have . . . it appears to be stronger when you are nearby. I think that was part of the reason I was unaffected by the queen's power. What if you have the same effect on all the *lyr*, Mother? Most of the Guardians have some tie to the *lyr*, if only a distant one. What if you are a catalyst for *all* of them?"

She stared at him. Just that, for a small eternity. Unnamed emotions flickered in the depths of her eyes.

"The prophecy that led us to the Throne," she said at last, "had a passage at the end of it that Favias thought might refer to me. I was not so sure. But if what you say is true . . ." Her voice trailed off into silence.

"What did it say?"

She shut her eyes, concentrating, and recited:

The mother of men will raise up her sword against the mother
*   of madness*
The queen who sits upon the throne of tears will bring demons
*   to weep*
The masters of the earth will sip from her blood, to bolster their
*   courage*
As they gird themselves for battle with the glory of her faith

"There was more," she said, opening her eyes. "But Kierdwyn's Archivist thought the rest referred to events that had already come to pass, so those verses were no longer meaningful. Of course, it's all quite cryptic." She smiled faintly. "I do think that is required in writing prophecies."

"Why did you not share this with me before?"

"Because of the reference to my faith. If this passage does in fact refer to me ... and if you are among those it calls *the masters of the earth* ... then the last line suggests you will fight in the name of my gods."

He drew in a sharp breath. "Not likely."

"Thus the reason we have not had this conversation before, my son. But if what you are saying now is true, then another meaning is possible. If the *blood of the lyr* refers to our inheritance—"

"—Then the 'glory of your faith' might refer to that heritage. To our immunity."

"Perhaps. Of course," she shrugged, "it is possible the passage doesn't even refer to me at all. Siderea Aminestas satisfies the same description, at least in a metaphorical sense.

While the reference to drinking blood might well turn out to be literal. Though whether that would signify a magical act, or some sort of ritual, one can only speculate. We simply don't know enough to interpret the passage with any certainty." She smiled dryly. "Yet another reason I didn't bother you with it."

"You need to be at the front lines with me," he said.

The smile fled. A shadow passed over her eyes.

"Yes," she whispered. "I understand that now."

"I will call Valemar to court. We can find some excuse for it that sounds reasonable. No one must know the truth. The less warning our enemies have that I may be absent from my throne, the less quickly they will be able to take advantage of that absence." He looked sharply at her. "You think Valemar can handle all this?"

"If he fails, he will have his mother to answer to."

Despite himself, Salvator smiled. "Do you know what my father once said about you, Mother? *More fierce in spirit than all the armies of Anshasa, and more stubborn than the gods themselves.* I thought he was exaggerating at the time."

A corner of her mouth twitched. "And now?"

"As you said. A Souleater queen is dead. I would not like to get between you and the next one."

"It is a mother's destiny to protect her children." Again the half-smile. "And their world."

Her words stirred new thoughts. Disturbing thoughts. "Siderea Aminestas did not have any children," he recalled.

She raised an eyebrow. "And this is significant . . . why?"

"What was the first line of that prophecy? *The mother of men will raise up her sword against the mother of madness.* So the first reference cannot possibly be to her."

"Which means that the second might be?"

"You are the one who puts stock in such things. But if she

were to go insane . . . then, as I understand things, her Souleater would go mad as well." He was remembering the wild Witch-Queen of his dreams, with her faceted eyes and erratic demeanor. So close to madness even then. He had sensed it in her. Now, if what Colivar had suggested was true, one of the world's most fearsome creatures might be wedded to that madness. And along with it Siderea's intelligence, her political acumen, and her seductive gifts. What an adversary that joint creature might become!

This is what the Creator has been preparing me for all my life. This is why the Penitents exist.

Never mind that the very gift that enabled him to stand up to the ikati was the result of a Magister's political machinations. He himself was untouched by sorcery, and that was what mattered.

There were no Magisters among the *lyr*, he remembered suddenly. Did that mean that the Creator was protecting those bloodlines? Or was there some more mundane explanation? Some reason that *lyr* blood was incompatible with sorcery?

Too many mysteries, he thought. At the heart of each one was a weapon they needed, if they were to keep the Second Age of Kings from ending in tragedy like the First. But such secrets had to be ferreted out and identified before they could be put to use. So what was at the heart of this one?

CHAPTER 16

THE WINDSWEPT peak was surrounded by a sea of clouds, which frothed against the flanks of nearby mountaintops like an angry ocean. Here and there, when the clouds parted briefly, one could catch a glimpse of the earth far below, but the distance made it seem unreal, like something out of a dream. Then the clouds would shift and the opening would close, and there were only granite peaks rising up from an ocean of white once more, a chain of jagged islands extending as far as the eye could see.

Fadir was the last to arrive. His sorcery shimmered in the thin mountain air, allowing him to step through onto the bare granite surface as smoothly as if he were taking a stroll through the royal gardens. The surprise on his face as he looked around, however, was unmistakable. With a quick nod to the others present—Ramirus, Lazaroth, and Sulah had arrived some time ago—he looked out over the stark landscape, seeking some clue as to where he was or why he had been summoned here. There were no clues visible.

"What's this all about?" he demanded.

Lazaroth shrugged. "Your guess is as good as ours."

The air on the mountaintop was thin and cold, which normally would have been a welcome change from the oppressive summer heat, but Fadir wasn't dressed for it, and a cold breeze raised rows of goosebumps down his arms. With a muttered curse he bound enough power to conjure more appropriate dress, and his clothing reshaped itself into a long woolen gown that matched Ramirus' own. For once, the ancient Magister was setting the fashion for them all.

"So where's Colivar?" Fadir demanded.

Lazaroth shot him a derisive look, which made it clear the answer to that question was the same as the first, and he was not going to bother repeating himself.

With a snort Fadir settled himself down on a knee-high ridge near the others, to wait.

Colivar watched them from the shadows for a long while, sorcery guarding him from their sight. Earlier in the day his thoughts had been in turmoil, and he had come very close to canceling this meeting altogether. But now that he was here, a strange calm had come over him. What an alien emotion it seemed, at that moment! Calm had been a rare indulgence in his early days as a Magister, a state nearly beyond his comprehension. How much he had changed since then! And yet, the things that mattered most in him had not changed at all.

Ramirus is right, he thought solemnly. *The time has come for them to know the truth about what they are.*

But that didn't make the task at hand any easier.

The sun was beginning to sink beneath the clouds, edging them in golden fire, when he finally stepped out of the shadows. He had chosen a traditional robe for this meeting, which was such a marked contrast to his usual attire that the others were clearly taken by surprise. He could see Ramirus looking him over, eyes narrow as he tried to read meaning into Colivar's sartorial choice. *Maybe I did it just to distract you*, Colivar thought. *Maybe I do not want you looking too closely at other things.*

He walked to the circle of rocks where they sat, but he remained standing. For a moment he just studied them all. Allies. Was that what he was supposed to call them now? As if such a thing were truly possible.

A thin, chill wind gusted briefly across the circle, and Colivar raised a hand absently and summoned sorcery to banish it. Warmer air took its place at his command, more comfortable for the lungs. But the mountaintop was still a barren and forbidding place, which is why he had chosen it for this meeting. It suited his current mood.

"Fellow Magisters," he said, "I've asked you here in order to pass on some information my mentor gave me, back when I was still a student. In those days it was customary for a teacher to pass on not only his knowledge to his student, but some of his memories as well. So please understand, much of what I am about to tell you, I witnessed through his eyes, as he did through the eyes of his teacher before him. So we know these things as if we had seen them ourselves." He paused. "A custom that was wisely abandoned.

"I've never spoken of these things to any living man before today, and I will never do so again. So whatever knowledge you don't get out of my words today you will have to seek out on your own." He paused. "Are those terms acceptable?"

He looked at the Magisters one by one, his dark gaze moving around the circle. There was nothing of his usual arrogance in that gaze, or cynicism, or humor, or any other recognizably human emotion. Only a blackness so empty, so haunting, that it seemed to fill the circle they had established, silencing all sound, swallowing all sentiment.

One by one, the Magisters nodded.

For a moment Colivar shut his eyes, and his brow tensed slightly as he braced himself for what was to come. But when he finally spoke, it was in a quiet tone, devoid of any emotion. He had practiced this speech so many times it was almost as if he were reading from a script. Performing.

That was the safest way.

"First, understand that the ikati are lone predators by nature, utterly intolerant of their own kind. No two males will ever enter the same territory unless forced to, and if that happens, they're more likely to fight to the death than accept the situation, even for an hour. The females are marginally gentler, as they prefer to drive their rivals away rather than fight them. And they have the ability to turn their mesmeric power against their own kind, which helps protect them from unwanted attention. But if territory is an issue, then they too will kill without hesitation.

"This antagonism is not by choice," he stressed. "It is innate. Instinctive. To a wild ikati, every other member of its species is a mortal enemy. Only under the most extreme circumstances can they ever bring themselves to share territory, or work toward a common goal."

"What about the armies of ikati?" Sulah asked. "The ones that supposedly filled the skies during the First Age of Kings?"

Colivar shook his head. "Legends, nothing more. If there had ever been two ikati in the same territory back then, they would have fought for dominance until one of them surrendered and fled . . . or was killed. It was the only way they knew."

"*Back then*," Ramirus said sharply. It was obviously meant as a question, but Colivar did not respond to it.

Ah, my old enemy, you are sharper than all the rest of them put together. And older than most of them, as well. I wonder how much of the story you have already figured out.

"You know that their strength comes from stolen life," Colivar continued, "and from sunlight. They need open spaces—cloudless skies—the heat of the sun upon their wings. So our ancestors used fire to drive them north. First the illusion of fire and then, when they ran short of witches to conjure such images, the real thing. They filled the heavens with smoke, so thick that the Souleaters were driven north in order to avoid it." He paused. "That is not to say such tactics would work again. Their weakness is not what it once was."

Ramirus nodded. "Kostas set fire to Danton's forest himself."

Colivar nodded. "I doubt he considered the forest a real threat, since any Magister could conjure images of smoke and fire without need for material fuel. I imagine he meant the fire as a gesture of triumph. Or perhaps as a message that the ikati could no longer be controlled by such primitive methods.

"You all know that when the Wrath was conjured, a small band of witches volunteered to be trapped on the northern side. Isolated in that frozen wasteland, they meant to hunt down and kill the last of the Souleaters, even if it cost them the last of their life-essence to do so."

He could hear emotion edging its way into his tone, and he paused for a moment to settle his spirit. Ramirus' eyes were fixed on him with a rare intensity, and they seemed to be drilling into his very soul. But that was just an illusion, Colivar knew. He had enough sorcerous defenses in place right now to ward off an army of Magisters. As long as he did not provide them with simple physical clues as to his state of mind, his mental privacy was assured.

"That was their dream," he continued, in a more guarded tone.

"Their passion. To ransom the world with their own deaths."
How could these Magisters possibly understand such a passion?
he wondered. Men who were willing to sacrifice themselves for
others did not ever become Magisters. Everyone knew that.

Focus, Colivar. Focus.

"North of the Wrath was a land of utter desolation. The ikati
could simply fly over it, of course, but the witches had to struggle
along on foot, or else expend their final reserves of soulfire to ease
the journey. Many died along the way, but those who survived were
relentless. Determined to save the world." No doubt they would
read the edge in his tone as disdain, he thought. That was fine.
"Had they not already been exhausted by months of battle, they
might have thought to question why the ikati were fleeing from
them at all. For if there really were no other living creatures in that
wasteland, then the witches themselves were their only possible
food source. The Souleaters *should* have turned on them, desperately
trying to get close enough to sap them of their last living energy.
But they didn't. Because they had sensed what the witches could
not . . . that there were other humans in the wasteland."

He looked at Ramirus and said, "Show them what you
conjured after the battle."

Ramirus nodded; he did not seem surprised by the request.
With a short gesture of his hand he summoned up a wave of
power, bound it to his purpose, and cast it into the center of
their circle. All without looking that way himself. His eyes never
left Colivar.

An image began to take shape in the center of their circle.
It was the same one that Ramirus had conjured from the memories of the Souleater's rider, of a land warmed by volcanoes, and
the tribal people who lived there. Ramirus let them study it just
long enough to grasp its full meaning, then banished it.

"The habitable territory was small," Colivar said. "Not nearly sufficient for so many ikati. So terrible battles took place in the skies as the creatures fought with one another. The exhausted witches watched it all, praying to their gods that the cursed creatures would just tear each other to pieces and save them the effort. They were too weak and exhausted after their long journey to take on so many.

"But the ikati didn't all die. A few survived. One queen. A handful of males, more adaptable than most, who proved able to share the same hunting grounds without attacking each other on sight. And then the witches . . ."

He shut his eyes. And he poured all his strength into his sorcerous shields, not only the ones that guarded his thoughts, but the ones that would keep other men from reading his facial expression. Even as he did so, he knew that Ramirus was taking note of the effort, and that the mere fact that he had conjured that level of defense told his rival more than he would have wanted him to know.

"It could have ended then," he whispered. "If they had given up their lives as they had promised to do, if they had expended the last of their athra destroying those last few survivors . . . it could all have ended. And the world would have been safe.

"But the temptation was too great. And they . . . they were weak. So they decided to delay the final destruction of the creatures. Maybe they could figure out a way to tap into their athra and claim the life-energy that the creatures had stolen from others, to replenish their own failing stores. After that they would be stronger, and could complete their mission more easily. Or so they told themselves. Maybe they could even find a way to go home after that. Breach the Wrath, somehow. It was a distant dream, but a compelling one."

"That is why the ikati survived?" Sulah asked. Clearly incredulous. "The hunters chose to spare them?"

Colivar's expression was grave as he nodded. "Temptation is an insidious beast, that devours a man by stages. He doesn't wake up one morning and think to himself, *Today I will betray the world*. His soul is corrupted bit by bit, a thousand featherweights of hope and fear and doubt settling onto him one by one . . . until the combined weight of them is more than his conscience can bear. And then, one day, that conscience finds that it no longer has a voice, and only the temptation remains.

"So it was with these witches.

"Eventually they did learn how to tap into the ikati's athra, but at a terrible price. For when a man opens himself up to a Souleater's life-essence, he absorbs something of its soul as well. By the time they realized that, it was too late to turn back. The sheer animal force of the ikati spirit, replete with an array of primitive and terrifying passions, was . . . intoxicating. Addictive. Once a man tasted it, he must have more. And the more he indulged in it, the more power the beast had over him."

He gazed down at his hands for a moment, then shrugged stiffly. "As I said, they were weak.

"Pairs began to form, men and ikati bound together in a strange and unnatural symbiosis. Human thought and bestial instinct merged, making the Souleater more than it had been before, even as it made the human less." He looked up at them. "That is what these pairs are, you see. No longer two individuals, nor a single creature either. Something in between. Capable of human reasoning, but driven by the darkest of animal instincts. And centuries of necessity have now taught the ikati how to deal with an ash-filled sky and how to hibernate in times of darkness. The things they once feared most no longer have any power over them. Our ancestors' greatest weapons have all been neutralized." His expression was grim. "We have nothing."

"The girl whose memories I conjured," Ramirus said. "Who screamed when the Souleater died. She was bound to it thus?"

Colivar nodded. "The death of one partner can destroy the mind of the survivor, if they've been connected long enough. The communal soul is literally ripped in two by the experience. For a human it is bad enough, but for a Souleater . . ." He shook his head. "Severance reduces it from a creature capable of intelligent thought to a mindless beast in an instant." He looked at Ramirus. "You have seen that happen."

"Outside Danton's palace."

"Yes."

Fadir folded his arms over his chest. "If killing one can destroy the other . . . that may prove useful."

Colivar stiffened. *Be wary of what knowledge you give them,* he warned himself. But Ramirus was right. They needed to understand what the ikati were. They need to know what *they* were. The time had come.

"There was one witch whose ikati consort was destroyed," Colivar continued. "The sudden loss of half his soul was more than he could bear, more than any man could bear. He went mad. And in his madness, he managed to do what no one had thought possible. He crossed the Wrath and reentered the southlands. Maddened by his loss, starving for athra, he struggled to find a way to feed on the life-essence of others without a Souleater to help him"

He could see comprehension dawn in their eyes now, as one by one they realized just where this tale was heading. A black and terrible revelation, to be sure. It pleased him perversely to see how much it surprised them.

"He was the first Magister," he pronounced. "The source of our kind, the seed of all our power. He believed that his Souleater had been fully excised from his mind, but in truth it had not been. Once merged, man and ikati are never wholly separate again. A spark of the ikati essence still remained within this man, and in time he learned how to draw upon it, to feed as the Souleaters did. It was the only way to stay alive.

"In time his mind became stable enough that he could interact with other human beings, and he passed that spark on to another witch. Along with all his memories." Colivar paused. "That is what we pass on to each new Magister, when we guide him through First Transition. Without that spark, no man can manage the transformation. Oh, there have been witches down through the ages who guessed at the truth in their dying moments, and who tried to reach out and steal the life-essence of others so that they might survive. But such independent efforts always fail. Because knowledge is not enough. Power is not enough. *Humans* are incapable of feeding on their own kind."

He gave that statement a moment to sink in, along with its chilling emphasis. Then he turned to Ramirus. "You're old enough to remember what it was like in the beginning. The constant wailing of the beast in the back of your head. The fire of its rage coursing through your veins. The hatred for your own kind, so intense that at times it threatened to overwhelm all human thought. You remember the fear we lived with back then, of what would happen if we let our guard down, even for a minute. The constant struggle we faced, to find a way to deny the beast outlet so that we could continue our pretense of being human."

Ramirus said nothing, but he nodded.

"That was the Souleater in us. Our second nature, struggling to manifest. Even now we still feel its hunger, we are still driven by its instincts . . . but we've learned to call those things by other names. We make excuses for them, inventing mantras of comfort. *Powerful men naturally distrust one another. Sorcery requires a callous and ruthless soul. Longevity dulls the conscience.* We want there to be *human* reasons for what we do. We don't want to believe that something less than human is driving us. That we are, ourselves, something less than human."

"I remember," Ramirus said quietly.

"That is why our Law has the power that it does. Because it is an expression of human intellect, not ikati instinct. That is why we're driven to bind ourselves to morati. Serving those who are fully human helps shackle the beast within us. Every human lover we take, every royal contract we establish, every restriction we observe that helps keep the morati world safe . . . they are all investments in our own humanity. Without them . . ."

His voice threatened to break. He shut his eyes for a moment. A cold wind stirred his long black hair.

"Without them we are lost," he said at last. Emotionless once more.

Silence fell upon the circle. Colivar kept his eyes shut, not trusting himself to look at the others. *I have borne this secret alone for centuries,* he thought. *Now it is your burden as well. May you handle it better than I did.*

"So we are Souleaters," Lazarus said. Testing the words as he voiced them.

No confirmation was required.

"Is that why we can't locate them?" Sulah asked.

Colivar nodded. "Most likely. As far as your sorcery is concerned, they're not a separate species, but kin to us. You may even be seeing them, and simply mistaking them for Magisters. Search with that in mind, and you may have better success."

That is, if their queen—and Siderea—allows you to find them.

"So the Penitents were right after all," Ramirus mused.

Despite his mood, a dry smile flickered briefly across Colivar's face. "Yes. Ironic, isn't it? Salvator and his mad faith. All those tales of damnation and corruption, that seem so ridiculous on the surface . . . his people are the only ones who see us for what we really are. Corrupted souls, no longer human, whose very life-essence is now monstrous in nature. And, yes, our corruption is contagious. They're right in that as well. If First Transition is some kind of grand supernatural infection, might there not be lesser infections, whose nature we don't yet recognize? Far better for a man to live without benefit of sorcery at all than to invite an ikati into his soul. All things considered . . . perhaps his is not so foolish a faith as we make it out to be."

He shut his eyes for a moment. There were other things he could say to them, other truths to reveal, but he did not want them to learn too much. Some secrets should never be shared.

And how clear was his memory of those secrets, anyway? Down through the centuries he had woven false memories for himself, so that if others used sorcery to investigate his past, they would garner nothing but lies. But such a practice had its price. With so many false identities layered over his own, it was possible to forget which parts were real. Now fate was demanding that he peel all those false memories away, like the layers of an onion. If he did that, would he even recognize what was at their core?

Too many questions. Too many emotions, rooted in things he did not want to talk about. He could not afford to let other Magisters see him in this state.

"Now you know the truth," he said shortly. "Share it with the others, as you see fit. Or spare them such a terrible revelation, and let them live on in ignorance. Which path is preferable?" He spread his hands. "The choice is yours. I have played my part."

He turned to leave.

"Colivar." It was Ramirus.

Colivar turned back halfway, just far enough to meet his eye.

"The traitor. The first Magister. How was he able to cross the Wrath?"

Colivar drew in a sharp breath, and almost refused to answer. But he knew that if he didn't do so now, the question would surely come up again. Better to get it over with.

"The essence of the Wrath is death," he explained. "It inspires mortal fear in all living things that approach it, on that visceral level where survival instinct reigns supreme. The ikati are creatures of instinct, and so they have no defense against it. Human intellect is more resilient, but we, too, are subject to instinct, and approaching the Wrath is as difficult for us as walking off the edge of a cliff would be. The mind may accept the necessity of such an act, but the spirit rebels.

"But if a man *wants* to die . . . if he is ready to embrace death with every fiber of his being, to invite it to devour him body and soul, exulting in the thought of his own destruction . . . then the Wrath has no power over him. None at all."

A corner of his mouth twitched slightly. "Not a path I recommend, Ramirus. But do let me know if you decide to try it."

And then he turned from the circle of Magisters and walked quickly to where the shadows were waiting for him, before any more questions could be asked.

———

The mountainside was cold and windy, even by northern standards. But Colivar was not in the mood to change it.

He climbed down to a place where the rock face leveled out into a sizeable shelf and stood there, the wind whipping his long robe about his legs. The stinging bite of the frigid air against his face suited his mood, and he did nothing to blunt its edge.

Several yards above him, something stirred in the shadows. A snow lynx moved out from its hiding place amidst the rocks, then worked its way down to the ledge where he was standing. No sooner had it reached the granite shelf than sorcery began to ripple through its flesh, transforming it. The skeleton became upright, paws became hands, fur became skin. Soon Kamala stood before him, her red hair blowing wild in the wind. The dying rays of the sun lent her a golden halo, making her seem more like some strange mountain spirit than a woman of flesh and blood. Strangely appropriate.

"You heard it all?" he asked her.

"Yes." She nodded solemnly. "Thank you for inviting me."

He shrugged. "You have as much right to know the truth as any of us."

There were other things he could have said to her, but he did not. He didn't trust his own words, or even his feelings. The fact that he had invited her here would have to be enough.

Wordlessly he turned from her, meaning to take on wings and depart. But she put a hand on his arm, stopping him. The moment was jarring; he was not used to other people touching him uninvited.

He turned back to her.

"What am I?" she whispered.

He hesitated. How wide her eyes were, how hungry! She was as starved for understanding as he had been, many years ago. He wished that he had more to offer her than shadows and mysteries.

"I don't know," he said. "That spark of supernatural contagion that makes us Magisters, which we've passed down from generation to generation, was originally derived from a male ikati. Clearly it imbues us with all the instincts and passions of that sex. Which is perhaps why women have found it so hard to adapt." He saw the look of surprise on her face, and a faint, dry smile flickered across his lips. "Yes, my dear. That's the real reason all the Magisters are male. The question of a nurturing spirit—or lack thereof, in your case—is secondary. The ikati can only bind themselves to humans of the same gender. So the spark of the ikati that we carry within us simply follows the same rules. That's my theory, at least."

He put a hand out to touch her face; she did not move away, but allowed his cold fingers to caress the warmth of her cheek. "But now you are here," he murmured. "And I don't have a clue why. The Magisters themselves have changed over time, so perhaps our darker half is changing as well, and the spark that we pass on to our students has simply lost its edge. So that whatever qualities were once so incompatible with a female host have faded over time, until the remaining soul-shards can be absorbed by anyone. If so, then you will not be the only woman to join our ranks . . . you are merely the first. Or perhaps . . ."

He hesitated.

She put her hand over his. Her fingers were soft and warm, and they stirred feelings in him that he was not ready to confront. Not yet.

"Tell me," she murmured. There was a faint air of seductiveness to her tone, as if she sensed the energy between them and wished to harness it. It affected him more deeply than he would have expected.

"What if the spark that set all this in motion was not merely the essence of a male ikati, but rather . . . what if each Magister carries within him the imprint of the entire species? So that the spark you absorbed from your mentor was not merely the watered-down essence of a single male, weakened by so many centuries of transmission that a woman could finally absorb it, but something more significant. What if that seed contained within it the essence of the *entire* species, in every variety that it might manifest . . . including the one variant that would prefer a female host."

"The soul of a queen," she whispered.

He nodded. "It's possible that has manifested in you. If so . . . your powers may be different from ours. As well as the instincts you absorbed."

"That is why you wanted me to search for the Witch-Queen. Why you thought I might be able to find her, when the rest of you could not."

He nodded. "And you still may be able to, especially now that you understand more about the powers involved. Only be forewarned: If a Magister's ikati instincts gain enough influence over him, he may instinctively recognize you for what you are. And if that happens . . ." He drew in a sharp breath. "There is great power in such things, Kamala. But also great danger."

"They will desire me."

Despite the gravity of the moment, he almost smiled. *What man would not desire you?* "That's a rather tame word, given the nature of ikati passion. These are creatures who will rip each other to pieces in courtship. Even the call of a Guardian, which mimics their mating challenge, can be enough to drive a male into a frenzy. So I strongly suggest you avoid awakening those instincts in us. And in yourself."

He gazed at her for a moment in silence, then moved a step toward her. Close enough to feel her warmth radiating against

him and to catch her scent upon the wind. As if from a great
distance, he watched himself raise up a hand to her cheek again.
Her eyes were wary, but she did not back away. The touch of
her flesh was warm, despite the frigid air surrounding them,
and it awakened memories of another heat, all-consuming, that
he had struggled for too long to forget. The beast within him
stirred in its confinement, sensing weakness; he withdrew his
hand quickly, as though her flesh had burned him.

"No man can teach you your own nature," he said quietly.
"You must discover that for yourself. As I did, in my time."

*The part of us that is human will fear you. The part of us that
is ikati will desire you. Wielding those two elements, you will have
the power to destroy us all.*

He did not trust himself to say any more, but stepped back
from her silently, and summoned the power needed to reshape
his flesh. A moment later his broad wings caught hold of the
wind, and he soared outward from the mountain, heading down
toward the sea of clouds. Molding the currents of air with his
sorcery as he went, so that they would be strong enough to
support him.

If she said anything to him as he left, he did not hear it.

CHAPTER 17

SULAH STOOD alone in the desert, waves of heat rippling all around him. Now and then the wind stirred up a plume of sand, twisting it into a long streamer that would scurry across the landscape like a drunken dancer. Fleeting beauty in the midst of utter desolation: the paradox of his new home. The sharply angled late afternoon sunlight picked out features along the landscape, underscoring them with ink-black shadows. One shadow in particular seemed more symmetrical than most, and he headed toward it, wondering what sort of man-made structure might exist in such a place.

As he came closer, he could see that a large tent had been pitched on the shifting sand, in the fashion of desert nomads. The shadowy space inside seemed cool and inviting, and as he entered, he felt as if he were diving headfirst into a mountain pool. There was incense burning within, or perhaps some other source of perfume; a sweet smell that he could not name filled the shadowy space, exotic and pleasing. He blinked as his eyes slowly adjusted to the darkness, picking out details of the interior.

Richly woven rugs were layered underfoot, their patterns intricate and their pile lush. Cushions decorated with mirrored embroidery glittered as he walked by, teasing him with captured sparks of sunlight. A low table inlaid with ivory vines supported a decorative wine service, sterling silver with cabochon stones set about the lips of a pair of goblets. An ornately decorated water pipe sat by its side. Whoever owned this tent, he was no common tribesman.

"Welcome, Sulah."

Startled, he turned around to find the Witch-Queen reclining on a couch at the far end of the tent. She was dressed in a sleeveless white gown that made the copper tone of her skin seem to glow. Bronze ornaments worked with tribal patterns adorned her neck, her bare arms, and her hair. She was, as always, exquisitely beautiful, and at one time he'd found her attractive, but now that he knew her for what she was—what she had become—it put a damper on any attraction he might have felt for her.

He took a step backward, looking around the tent for hidden dangers as he readied his power in case of possible assault.

"Hush, my love." Her voice was liquid silver in the darkness. "It's only a dream. I wanted to talk to you, and this seemed the best way to do it. Safest for both of us, yes?"

She rose from the couch, the fine silken layers of her gown flowing like water over the smooth curves of her body. Sulah remembered the night she first seduced him—the unexpected smoothness of her flesh, the warmth of her tongue against his skin—and it took effort to turn his thoughts away from those memories, even as they heated his flesh. But whatever her purpose had been in creating this dreamscape, he needed his wits about him to deal with it. "What is it you want?"

She tsk-tsked. "Such cruelty, Sulah. Such suspicion. You were nicer to me in Sankara."

You were human in Sankara, he wanted to say. But he bit his lip and did not respond.

She walked over to the table and leaned down to fill the two goblets with wine. The loose neck of her gown fell partway open as she did so, revealing breasts that were full and firm. It took effort not to look at them.

"Here." She walked to where he stood and offered him one of the goblets. When he hesitated, she smiled. "It's just a dream, Sulah. I can't poison you here."

No, but if you have the power to draw me into your dream, then who is to say where that power ends?

Slowly he took the goblet from her, lifted it to his lips, and sipped from the contents. It was wine. Good wine, but simply wine. What else had he expected?

"You really are far too suspicious," she said. She was close to him now. The human scent beneath that strange perfume stirred memories that made his flesh tighten. "Have the others been telling you stories about me?"

"What is it you want?" he repeated. Fighting the urge to take a step backward.

"You mean that for all your power you can't guess?"

"I prefer to be told."

She shrugged lightly. "Perhaps I need a Magister's assistance."

"You know many Magisters. Some are used to doing you favors." *Do you think me weaker than they are?* he wanted to demand. *Easier to manipulate?* "Why me?"

He had shared her bed once. Only once. It had been a strange whim, motivated as much by the pleasure of keeping secrets from the other Magisters as by any physical desire. She had proven skilled and passionate, and he did not regret that night, but the scent of too many sorcerers clung to her bed for his liking.

"That is why, Sulah." She ran a featherlight finger down his chest, more a suggestion than a caress. "The others have taken me into their confidence, they have shared their secrets with me, some have even given me tokens of their personal essence. You have not. If I were to approach one of the others, he would have to question whether or not I had done something to sway his mind in my favor. But you . . . you have no need to be suspicious. Because you know that I have no power over you." She chuckled softly. "No more than any woman does."

A cool breeze moved through the tent's interior, stirring Sulah's hair. No witch would waste athra on such a superfluous effect in the real world, but in a dream it cost her nothing.

"So what is it you need help with?" he asked.

Her smile faded; a more sober expression took its place. "You know what has happened to me. You know the power I now have at my disposal."

"I have heard rumors," he said carefully.

"I won't defend the Souleaters. They're a brutal species, and the men who control them are little better. Mortal kings are wise to fear them. But it doesn't have to be that way, Sulah. Their fury can be tempered, their passions controlled. Their power can be harnessed. Such power! You cannot even imagine the raw potential of it. And all that would be required to make that happen is the right leadership."

"Which is you?"

She shook her head. "A woman can't lead them. Not directly. But a woman can be the one who decides which man wears the crown." She cocked her head to one side. "Which offers some interesting possibilities, don't you think? Perhaps even . . . interesting alliances."

Sulah drew in a sharp breath. Was she suggesting what he thought she was?

Careful, Sulah. You know her reputation. No woman wields the kind of political power she once did without an arsenal of manipulative skills that would put the First Kings to shame.

But there was no denying that her suggestion stirred his blood. And now that Colivar had explained what the Magisters were really about, he understood just where that sensation was coming from. Deep within him, the seed of something that was not human wanted what she was offering. Wanted it badly. And for a brief moment, the force of that desire seemed to take on a life of its own. In that moment it seemed to Sulah that he could feel the Souleater inside him, hungering for power over its own kind in a way that no mere human could understand. The sensation of it was sickening, but it was also strangely exhilarating. He did not know whether to run from the feeling or embrace it.

Did she know the truth about the Magisters? he wondered suddenly. Given this woman's reputation for collecting secrets he wouldn't put anything past her.

"There are other Magisters who owe you no debt," he pointed out. "They would be better suited to such an arrangement. Why not send your dreams to them?"

She chuckled softly. "Because you're young, Sulah. Still very human, as Magisters measure such things. Capable of a kind of passion the others lack. And passion is needed for this." She paused. "The Souleaters don't respond to intellect. I can't rule over them by the side of a man who understands nothing else."

He drew in a long, slow breath. For a moment, no words would come.

"You are surprised," she murmured.

"It was . . . not what I expected."

"That I would seek a man to share my throne with?" A hint of dark amusement flickered in her eyes. "Or that it would be you?"

"Yes."

She brought her goblet up to her lips, not quite masking her smile, and sipped from it. He could see her nostrils flare delicately as she did so, like a predator on the trail of its quarry. For some reason that image disturbed him more than all the rest put together.

"The Souleaters can't be controlled by a woman," she said. "Not by a woman *alone*. A couple is required." She put a hand on his cheek. Warm, so warm. The scent of past indulgences rose from her fingertips. "Lovers," she whispered.

He wanted to push her hand away, but that would be giving her a kind of victory. "You're asking a lot of me."

"I offer a lot in return."

"Why seek out a Magister for this at all? Aren't there men who ride the Souleaters? Don't they have enough passion for you? Why bring in an outsider to rule over them, when you know they are sure to reject him?"

"Because those men are not my equals," she said quietly.

She let her hand fall away from his face; her touch left fire in its wake. "Centuries of isolation in the north have shaped them into something less than men. Life for them has been reduced to fighting bloody battles with tooth and claw until someone comes out on top; nothing else matters in their world. True, they speak our language, they wear our clothing—a few even bathe—but at heart they are simpleminded barbarians, so drunk on the bestial passions of their consorts that they can barely think straight. Is that who I should take as my mate, and entrust half my new empire to? I think not."

Do you know that sorcerers are hunting you? he thought. *Do you know that you are feared now, as much as you once were loved? That the Magisters would rather work cooperatively—against all tradition and instinct—than let you expand the territory of these creatures one more inch?*

Of course she knew that. That's why she had created this dreamscape.

"So you offer me a throne among beasts," he said, "at the cost of a world's destruction."

"Ah. So is it saving the world you want now? Is that the new goal of the Magisters?" Again she chuckled. "Well, then, what's the best way to do that? Not with a war you're destined to lose, against an enemy that can suck the life out of your very soul— yes, even out of a sorcerer's soul—but by more subtle means. Political means.

"You can't destroy the Souleaters, Sulah. Not with all the Magisters of the world allied against them . . . which you don't have. But you can, perhaps, control them. I've set the stage for that already. I need a man by my side whom I can rely on to help me. That man will gain access to a kind of power no Magister has ever known before." She paused, giving those words a chance to sink in. "The kind of power any Magister would covet."

Did she know just how tempting those words were? As one of the youngest of the Magisters, he had lived in the shadow of ancients like Colivar and Ramirus since the night of his First Transition. What would it be like to reverse that situation, so that the ancients envied him instead? Perhaps even feared him?

Gods, this woman was dangerous! He had been right to be wary of her. Yet could anyone less dangerous hope to take control of these creatures? Was there not a terrible kind of logic to her plan, and did it not offer a better chance of success than his current precarious alliance, which the touch of a feather might shatter?

It is right that one of us should rule over the Souleaters. The words came welling up from the depths of his soul as if from some outside source. Seductive and chilling. How much could he trust his own thoughts right now?

The Witch-Queen was silent. Watching him. Waiting.

"I need time to think about this," he said at last.

"There's not a lot of time left, Sulah. Events are moving quickly now. The longer the Souleaters go without proper leadership, the harder it will be to bring them under control in the end."

"I understand that."

She considered, then nodded. "A few days, then. After that I'll be approaching other candidates. You understand."

"I understand." *Another will rule over the Souleaters. Another will become the envy of the Magisters.* He shook his head, trying to banish the thought. "How will I reach you with my answer?"

"I will reach you. Like this. If we seal a deal . . . then we will meet on more solid ground. Agreed?"

He nodded.

She put her goblet aside, then took his face in both her hands and drew him down to her lips. He did not resist. Her kiss was warm and moist and tasted of wine. The perfume of her skin filled his nostrils, and it seemed to him that the dark presence within him stirred, aroused by the scent. Heat stirred in his loins, but it was a strangely distant heat, without urgency; his mind was focused on other things.

"Think well, my Magister," she murmured.

And then one by one the elements of the dream faded away, until there remained only sand and sun . . . and then darkness.

CHAPTER 18

I T WAS a strange feeling for Colivar, entering Farah's palace
as a guest. Stranger still for Farah's servants, who didn't know
quite what to make of his sudden arrival. How deeply did one
bow to a visiting Magister? Weren't the sorcerers at war with
one another? Should they be worrying about that? Colivar had
never been visited by Magisters while he had lived in the palace,
so Farah's servants had no experience with this kind of thing.

He should have warned them he was coming. Or Sulah should
have warned them he was coming. Oh, well.

Finally one flustered guard offered to bring Colivar to the
king. Then he became even more flustered when Colivar said
it was not the king he had come to talk to. Finally they got it
all sorted out, and with a pair of guards flanking him—presumably to do him honor, since it would have taken an army of
guards to do anything more meaningful—he made his way to
Sulah's apartments.

Farah had set aside one wing of the palace for the use of his
Magister Royal. Since Colivar had rarely made use of it, and
accordingly had never invested any time or energy in its

appearance, he was curious to see what Sulah had done with the place. It was certainly not what he'd expected. The border between Farah's realm and that of his sorcerer was all but indiscernible; even the gauze curtains were of the same cut and color in both parts of the building. Sulah's main chamber was appointed with classic Anshasan furniture and art, and Sulah himself was dressed in the long flowing robes of a desert chieftain. It was a strange juxtaposition with his pale northern features. The robes were black, in deference to Magister custom, but bands of different textures suggested the broad stripes of tribal fashion: a subtle homage to his new homeland.

"Colivar!" He rose from his chair as Colivar entered; the book he had been reading vanished from his hand. "Thank you for coming so quickly."

"No request of yours has ever wasted my time, Sulah." He studied the younger man's attire with a bemused expression. "I see you are going native."

Sulah shrugged. "I thought if I was going to do the Magister Royal thing I should get into the full spirit of it." His tone was light, but his expression was solemn. "Wine?"

Colivar nodded. He wasn't thirsty, and he might have turned down the offer if it had been voiced anywhere else. But Anshasans took their hospitality seriously, and some of the locals would view a refusal to drink as an insult. He didn't want to try to second-guess just how native Sulah had gone.

And, in truth, he mused, it was genuinely refreshing to fall back into his old patterns of behavior. He had served in Anshasa for a very long time, and there was a curious kind of comfort in the familiar rituals of southern life.

He waited until the wine had been poured, tasted, and praised, with all the appropriate social trappings, then said, "I'm sure you didn't call me here just for a wine tasting. What's on your mind?"

Sulah sighed and put his cup aside. For a moment he just stared at it, running his finger around the rim. Then he said, "Siderea came to me."

Whatever Colivar had expected from him, that certainly wasn't it. "When? Where? Do the others know?"

"She came in a dream. And no, no one else knows. You are the first I've told."

To say that such a confession startled Colivar would be an understatement. The fact that Sulah was offering him this kind of information was nothing short of remarkable. Of course, Sulah had always valued Colivar's counsel—perhaps more than he should—and now that the four Magisters had their "alliance," it was not inconceivable they would share information with one another. But rivalry and mistrust still ran strong in their blood, rooted as it was in their ikati heritage. If Sulah was revealing something like this to Colivar, it suggested that the situation was so disturbing to him that he felt he could not resolve it on his own. But that would hardly be something he'd admit to, and Colivar knew that if he pressed him for details he didn't want to reveal, the man's defensive instincts might kick in, and he'd close up like a clamshell.

"What did she want?" he asked, trying to sound as if they were discussing nothing more significant than the weather.

Sulah drew in a deep breath. "She wanted me to share her throne," he said. "To join her circle of Souleater vassals and help her rule the world."

Colivar opened his mouth, but no sound would come. He was dimly aware that his own attempt not to show any emotion had just failed miserably, but he was not sure exactly what his expression revealed. Whatever he had expected to hear from Sulah, this was certainly not it. "I take it you said no?"

"I haven't said anything yet. As soon as I turn her down, she'll make the same offer to someone else. Yes? So my silence buys us time." He sat down heavily in an upholstered chair and rubbed his temple wearily. There was an air of physical tension about him that was unlike anything Colivar had ever seen in his student before . . . but he had seen it in other Magisters, long ago, and he recognized its source.

She spoke to the Souleater in him. And awakened its hunger. Does that mean she knows what we are? Has she guessed the truth? The thought of Siderea teasing Sulah's nonhuman instincts to the surface and then playing them like a finely tuned instrument was disturbing on more levels than he could count. And the sudden surge of jealousy that attended the thought was surprising to him. Unnerving. Clearly the presence of a Souleater queen in their world was starting to break down the mechanisms Colivar normally used to hold his more primitive instincts at bay. The other Magisters might suffer a similar fate in time, but they were not vulnerable in quite the same way that he was; the breakdown would not come as quickly for them, nor was it likely to hit as hard when it did.

Dark times were coming, to be sure.

"Someone will say yes," Colivar agreed.

"Probably one of her past lovers. And when that happens, the Magisters may turn against one another, not in petty squabbling but as prelude to some greater conflict."

"Which is no doubt what she wants. Morati would be hard pressed to destroy us. Even Souleaters would have a hard time of it. Magister against Magister, on the other hand . . ."

Sulah looked up sharply "You think she wants us all dead?"

"Whatever she felt about us before, we are rivals to her now, and a threat to the empire she apparently means to establish."

Sulah nodded. He had never been the most guarded of sorcerers, and Colivar had been his teacher for long enough that he could normally read him like a book, but there were depths right now that were veiled from his scrutiny. That worried him.

"The one who accepts her offer will not be viewed as a threat," Sulah pointed out.

Only if she means what she says, Colivar thought. *Only if this offer is legitimate, and not some sort of trick.* Sulah was equally suspicious, of course. Why else would he share this with Colivar? He asked quietly, "Were you tempted?"

Sulah exhaled sharply. "Of course I was tempted. What Magister wouldn't be tempted? Forget about the power. Forget about the woman herself. We stand upon the cusp of an age in which the very nature of the world may be altered, and she offers the chance to ride the crest of that transformation rather than be drowned by it." He looked sharply at Colivar. "Were you not the one who taught me that novelty is the ultimate temptation to a Magister? I didn't really understand you back then. I was too young. Now that I have a bit more time under my belt, I do."

But Siderea does not, Colivar thought. *If she did, she would have approached one of the older Magisters first. Those who would be happy to see the entire world destroyed if it bought them five minutes of novelty.*

Which did beg the question: Why Sulah?

"Would you be willing to show me the dream?" Colivar asked. "Its setting, at least?" He knew Siderea well enough to know that her dreams were meticulously crafted, and it was rare they did not communicate on multiple levels. Sulah probably did not know her well enough to know what to look for. Colivar did.

Sulah hesitated. The request was a highly intimate one, and not one a Magister would normally indulge. But these were not normal times. Nodding, he began to concentrate. The room itself seemed to shimmer as images from his dreamscape began to form in front of him, detail by detail. Desert, tent, rugs, furnishings, and finally the Witch-Queen herself. The vision was not wholly opaque; it was possible to see the shadow of an Anshasan sideboard behind one wall of the tent, and Siderea's left leg co-existed with the ghost of a chair leg. But it was a detailed and realistic conjuring, and Colivar's eyes narrowed as he studied every detail, leaving Siderea herself for last.

How familiar she looked, yet how changed! Even in this static vision he could see the alien energy that now blazed in her eyes, a force that was simultaneously more and less than human. The rugs she was standing on looked familiar, but he could not remember where he had seen them before. And the jewelry. That looked familiar as well.

And then it came to him.

"Tefilat," he muttered.

"What?" Sulah asked.

"Tefilat. A city in the southwestern desert, near the border of Anshasa. Abandoned long ago. The Great War all but destroyed it." He indicated Siderea's necklace, the rugs, the goblets. "These designs are all based on tribal patterns of the Hom'ra, a tribe that makes its home in that region. The original designs were meant to ward off evil spirits. Tefilat is supposed to be full of them." He paused. "Which is not without some grounding in truth."

"Meaning?"

"The landscape there is ideal for Souleaters. Wide sandstone canyons scoured by the wind, with deep natural alcoves for shelter. Tefilat was built into the walls of one particularly large canyon, originally by constructing homes inside the natural alcoves, later by carving buildings out of the rock itself. It is . . . remarkable.

"It's also a region the Souleaters favored, to feast upon the tribes that lived there. One of the greatest battles of the south was waged in and around Tefilat. It's said that hundreds of witches converged upon the city in its final hours. Their spells still resonate in the sandstone." He nodded. "I've been there. You can feel it.

"Such power plays strange games with the mind. The Hom'ra speak of a city of wraiths, and of fearsome demons who emerge from the canyon at sunset. They believe the place is cursed." He paused. "There were no demons there when last I visited, but the 'cursed' label may not be that far off the mark. I would certainly hesitate to use sorcery in Tefilat without first testing to see how reliable it was. Especially as we are kin to the very creatures those witches were trying to destroy."

He gazed down at the illusionary carpet. "She is there now," he muttered. "Or she has passed through there recently. Or her people are there now, and are bringing back artifacts to her. Any way you look at it . . ."

"There will be clues in Tefilat," Sulah said.

He nodded. "Exactly."

"I assume we need to go there, then. Just Magisters, do you think, or bring along some morati as well? I'm sure Farah would support an expedition if needed."

"Farah would provide an army if it was needed," Colivar agreed. "But first we need to know exactly what's out there."

"Our sorcery's of limited value in such a place, according to what you just told me. Can we rely upon it for reconnaissance?"

For a long moment Colivar was silent. Long enough that Sulah shifted his weight impatiently and coughed softly, as if to remind him that someone else was still in the room. But he would not interrupt Colivar's contemplations. The habits of a long apprenticeship were too deeply ingrained in him. Some portion of his soul would always recognize Colivar as his Master . . . no matter how much Colivar urged him to do otherwise.

"I have a means to determine if *she* is there," Colivar said at last. "Once we know that, the rest can be decided."

"I thought you said she could hide herself from us. That our sorcery was incapable of piercing a queen's cover. Didn't you?"

"Yes," he said quietly. Solemnly. "I did."

"You have other methods, then?"

He said nothing. Just reached out to put a hand on the other man's shoulder for a moment. It was a strangely amicable gesture, which stirred memories of another life, lived long, long ago. When men were merely men, and the souls of terrible beasts did not claw at their souls from the inside.

"I will let you know when I have answers," he promised him.

———

Kamala circled her target area several times before deciding to approach. She could pick out a spell that Colivar had established to detect any incoming Magister, and she stayed well outside its boundaries. True, it looked as if it were merely a token effort, not meant to defend the place so much as to make sure that Colivar knew when visitors were arriving. But old habits were hard to break.

Finally, when she was satisfied that all was as it should be, she landed and reclaimed her human form. For a moment she just stood there, the hot summer breeze ruffling her hair as she took in the alien landscape. Red stone and red sand, washed in sunset's orange sunlight. It was both barren and beautiful, a vision from another world.

There was a small building atop a nearby rise, built in the style of a temple. Gleaming white columns held up a roof of the same color, from which panels of white gauze depended, taking the place of walls. As the breeze passed by, it rippled the gauze like water, making the whole structure seem insubstantial. Magical.

Which it well might be, she mused. It was much easier to create the illusion of such a place than to conjure that much mass. But its appearance was pleasing to her, and since she sensed that Colivar had created it just for this meeting, she decided to take it at face value and simply appreciate his work.

She walked up the white stone staircase and felt the shade of the building's interior envelop her as she passed between its pillars. Inside, she could see that carved alabaster couches with white silk cushions had been arranged in a perfect square. Colivar's presence on one of them, in his black attire, was visually dramatic.

But she was dressed in the same color now, and provided an equally arresting contrast.

"Kamala." He stood as she approached. There was a subtle tension about him that she could taste, and instinctively she knew that whatever was bothering him had some kind of sexual undertone. She had serviced enough men in her youth to read those signs loud and clear. "Thank you for coming," he said.

"Your note made it sound urgent."

"Events move quickly these days."

He nodded toward a glass decanter set on a small table between two of the couches; the red wine in it gleamed like fresh blood in the ruddy sunlight. She waved aside the offer and entered the seating area instead, choosing a couch opposite his own and settling herself on it. Jet black on pristine white. She could feel the room settle into perfect symmetry as he sat down directly opposite her, and she knew that the furniture had been positioned so that the light of the setting sun would set her red hair ablaze.

"I need your help," he said.

She nodded. "I assumed as much."

"I have a lead on where Siderea Aminestas might be. Or else a trail that may lead to her. I need to know which it is."

She raised an eyebrow curiously. "So I'm your queen-tracker, now?"

He chuckled softly. "Do you know someone better suited to the task?"

"No," she said. A faint smile flickered across her own lips. "I do not."

"There's a city to the south called Tefilat. I need to know what's out there."

"You mean, you need to know if *she* is there."

He nodded. "Can you do that?"

She remembered how hard it had been to enter the territory of the northern queen, even in a vision. If Siderea possessed that same power, then she could lose herself in the vastness of the desert, and no one would ever be able to find her; there weren't enough clear landmarks in such terrain for Kamala to focus on. But in a more structured environment it was possible. Not likely, but possible. "Perhaps," she said. "Do you have a map for me? I don't know this region."

"Something better than a map."

He reached out to hand her something; when she opened her hand beneath his to receive it, he poured a thin stream of reddish sand into her upturned palm. "This is from Tefilat."

She closed her fingers over the sand, feeling its fine gritty texture. Then she extended her senses into it, where the hidden traces of its past history might be found. Its locational energy was strong and clear, and she knew she would have no trouble using it as an anchor to connect to its point of origin.

Briefly she thought of retiring to some private place to begin, but then she remembered how he had come to her while she'd been searching the Spinas. The memory brought a strange rush of warmth to her cheeks. He hadn't hurt her then, when she had lain helpless before him. It would make no sense for him to do so now.

"One thing," he warned her, as she sat back on the couch and prepared herself for the mental journey. "Sorcery may not work properly there."

Again the faint smile appeared. "Have you ever asked me to go to a place where sorcery *did* work properly?"

She shut her eyes without waiting for his response. Apparently Tefilat was not far away; she required no more than a few seconds to establish a clear focus for her sorcery. Then it was a simple act to send her senses outward, as she had done in the Spinas, to explore the place. It was a safe enough procedure, providing one did not mind leaving one's insensate body in the hands of another Magister.

A strange ruddy landscape took shape around her. In some places the earth was molded into sweeping shapes, patterned with stripes in orange and rust, as if a layer of cloth had been draped over the terrain. In other places there were wind-carved monuments that were both beautiful and strange, with shapes that played tricks upon the mind's eye, seeming to shift from one form to another as her mind moved past them.

Guided by the traces in the sand, her sorcerous viewpoint shifted to a vast canyon with a dry riverbed coursing down its center. The walls on both sides were high, with shadowed alcoves large enough to contain a house. Some of them had actually had houses in them, which had been abandoned long ago. Their walls were crumbling as time and wind reclaimed them, and in some places it was hard to tell where a house ended and the natural debris of the canyon began.

Then she came around a turn and saw Tefilat itself.

It would have been a breathtaking sight for anyone. For Kamala, raised in the slums of Gansang, it was nigh on overwhelming. Here there were not simply dwellings tucked into the natural shelves and alcoves of the canyon walls, but tall and elegant buildings, in some cases several stories high. Across their intricate façades sandstone stripes rippled and eddied, as if the buildings had somehow grown there organically rather than having been carved by the hand of man.

It was beautiful in its grandeur. Eerie in its emptiness.

And it was tainted.

She could feel the warped power that resonated from the ancient stone, could see it shimmering darkly about the richly carved walls, could taste its *wrongness* in her very soul. Fragments of shattered spells clung to this place, along with memories of human fear and echoes of terrible bloodshed. No, she would not want to stand here in her real body, subject to these dark, fragmented energies. It was little wonder people now avoided this place.

But someone had been here recently; she could sense that clearly. She struggled to get some sense of identity. At first she could conjure only hazy images, echoes from the distant past. Armies gathering. Spells being cast. The shadows of vast wings coursing along the valley's floor. Bodies left behind in the wake of those shadows, living flesh from which the human consciousness had been sucked dry.

Then she began to pick up clearer impressions, from more recent events. She saw desert tribesmen passing through the place, and her power provided the proper label: *Hom'ra*. Then others appeared. Witches. She narrowed her eyes instinctively as she struggled to make out details, even though her physical eyes were not required for this search.

Just then a wing-shadow passed overhead. She saw a few of the Hom'ra look nervously upward, but most of them seemed to be unaware of the Souleater's presence. She could sense the creature's power licking at their souls, sipping from the essence of their lives to feed upon as it passed overhead. Then, as quickly as it had come, it was gone. The tribesmen continued their work of bringing supplies into the city as if nothing untoward had happened, until a woman approached them. She was dressed in a white sleeveless gown and shrouded in so many layers of protective sorcery that Kamala could not see through them to determine her identity. The Hom'ra bowed to the woman as she passed, not as one did to an earthly ruler, but with a sense of fearful reverence.

Focusing her concentration to the utmost, Kamala tried to break through the power that surrounded the woman, to get a clearer view of her. But she could not focus directly on her, no matter how hard she tried. The sensation was a familiar one, and it sent a shiver coursing through her soul. This had to be Siderea; there was no other explanation. Thank the gods the Witch-Queen herself was not present, and all Kamala had to contend with were conjured images, crafted from the residual energies of past events. Those had no consciousness of their own.

But something here did, she realized suddenly. *Something* was watching her. She could sense its scrutiny like a chill breath on the back of her neck, and she whipped about suddenly, using her sorcery to take in the entire panorama, all at once. Yet she could not identify any focus for the strange sensation. Was this some trick of local metaphysics, like Colivar had warned her about? The sensation grew more intense even as she searched for the source. It seemed to be coming from all directions, as though there were not one source point, but many. A circle of source points, gradually taking shape around her . . .

As they slowly resolved themselves, she realized what they were.

There were dozens of figures surrounding her now. Ghostly images, human and half human, and a few that were something else entirely. They emerged one by one from the air, as if drawing their substance from the very landscape. And one by one they took up position around her, forming a perfect circle with her at the center. There were three ranks of them visible and more were forming behind those, circle after circle of impassive figures, their expressions unreadable, their bodies motionless—

She broke contact and fled the scene. Her mind slammed back into her body with such force that it left her breathless. For a moment it was all she could do to breathe steadily, and she struggled to maintain sufficient composure that Colivar would not realize what had happened.

Gods. Those were the same gods who had been watching her when she began her search for the northern queen. She hadn't actually seen them back then, but she had sensed their presence. And these felt like the same entities.

But who were they? What did they want with her? She could not begin to fathom an answer.

It could just be the power of Tefilat playing with her mind, she told herself. Maybe the sorcerous effort of this search had triggered memories of the other one, and the city's strange resonance had caused the two efforts to get all mixed up in her mind. But that still begged the question of why gods had been watching her the first time. Did they have a vested interest in this Souleater war? Or did they consider a female Magister an unnatural creature, perhaps, whose sorcery disturbed the natural order of things? Their stoic expressions had offered no clue.

When she thought she had enough control of herself to handle human conversation again, she opened her eyes.

Night had fallen during her search, and a series of torches had been lit. Colivar was watching her closely, tiny reflected flames dancing in his eyes.

"Well?" he demanded. "What did you see?"

Did he know that something had gone wrong? She would operate on the assumption that he did not until he indicated otherwise. "She's not there now," Kamala rasped. The startling vision had caused her throat to seize up She coughed lightly, trying to get the muscles to relax. "But she was there previously, along with the Hom'ra. Not very long ago. And her Souleater was there also."

"One will not travel far without the other," he said. Then: "Tell me everything."

So she described her vision in as much detail as she could, conjuring images when words failed her. Only when it came to the final vision, that of the gods themselves, did she keep her silence. The message of that part might be personal, and she had no reason to share it.

When she had finished her recitation, Colivar was silent for a moment, digesting all the information she had given him. "Clearly they're using the city as a staging ground of sorts," he said finally. "But for what? Tefilat is out in the middle of nowhere. It's too far from any potential target to be of use in morati affairs, and distance has little meaning to a sorcerer, so there'd be no point in going out there."

"There's a point," Kamala said.

Colivar raised an eyebrow.

"You said it yourself," she told him. "Sorcery isn't reliable there. Magisters don't like to go to places where they can't trust their power. Like with the Wrath. Remember? Nyuku took shelter right by it, because he knew no Magister was likely to come calling." It seemed to her that Colivar stiffened slightly when she mentioned Nyuku's name, but she couldn't be sure. "And any spell that detected his presence would have been taken with a grain of salt, because sorcery couldn't be relied upon there."

It had been a brilliant plan, she thought. If Ethanus had not suggested she go there herself to escape the other Magisters, Rhys would likely have died in that secret prison, and the invasion of the Souleaters might never have been detected. Until it was too late.

Colivar walked over to the small table where the wine glasses sat and picked one up. "It's not impossible," he muttered. The crimson wine glowed like fresh blood in the torchlight.

"But Tefilat isn't the Wrath," she said. "I didn't sense any disruption on that scale. There's no reason a Magister couldn't function there, if he was careful enough."

"No," he agreed. His expression was thoughtful. "I visited there when I first became Farah's Magister Royal. It's an eerie place, and sorcery doesn't always work quite right, but it's not a major threat to anyone." He nodded. "But you're right. Magisters generally avoid such locations. If I wanted to hide something from sorcerers, I would definitely seek a place like that to do it in."

He took a deep drink from the glass. A slow drink. She could see the muscles in his throat ripple as he swallowed. Then he lowered the glass, gazing thoughtfully into its depths. "Whoever your Master was," he said, "he taught you well."

A flush rose to her cheeks. Did he really think that, or was he just trying to ferret out some clue about her origins? Knowing his great age and the breadth of his experience, even the second question was a compliment.

"Clearly we need to learn what's out there," he said, when she did not respond to him. Then he chuckled softly. "*We*. What a strange concept that is! I suppose now I must deliver this information to my *allies*. How the world has changed." He sighed melodramatically, then sipped from the glass once more.

She drew in a deep breath, gathering her courage. "And what about me?"

"What about you?"

"I'm part of this now, Colivar. You know that. So how long do you think you can hide me from the others without someone catching on? Sooner or later the others will ask where your information is coming from. If they haven't already. They know that a *man's* sorcery can't find Siderea. So if you don't tell them about me, they may start asking questions about *you.*" She thought she saw a muscle twitch along the line of his jaw. "Is that what you want?" she pressed.

The dark eyes were unreadable, as always. "Kamala . . . you know the risk."

"I passed for a witch in Kierdwyn."

"By the skin of your teeth, my dear. *I* guessed the truth."

"But you're not like the others," she dared.

He turned away from her so that she could not see the expression on his face.

"The gift of the female Souleater is obfuscation," she persisted. "If she doesn't want to be found, then the males of the species can't find her. Yes?" She walked up behind him, close enough that he could feel the heat of her body radiating against his own. As she could feel his. "What if I possess that same gift?" she whispered. "What if that's the reason that no one but you has ever asked the right questions about me? What if the others can't focus their suspicions on me the way they normally would because of that gift? Because instinctively I know how to turn their attention aside, without even being aware I'm doing it?"

He said nothing. The tension in his body was palpable. She had to hold herself back from placing her hand on his arm, knowing what a shock it would be to him. How much power it would give her over him.

"Is it possible?" she pressed.

He was silent for a moment. And then nodded. "Aye. If you are what I said you might be, that day on the mountain . . . it's possible."

He turned back to her. The expression in his eyes was strangely haunted; looking into them made her breath catch in her throat. "You're playing a dangerous game," he whispered.

She whispered back, "Is there any other game worth playing?"

He almost reached out to touch her. His body didn't actually move, but she could sense the movement within him, muscles balanced on the knife edge of commitment. She held her breath, waiting.

And then the moment passed.

He chuckled softly. "Whoever your Master was, do give him my regards."

"Does that mean 'yes,' Colivar?"

"There's a lot to think about, my dear. Let me talk to the others. See where things stand. The moment for this must be perfectly right."

"I could meet with them on my own," she said. A faint note of defiance entering her voice.

He smiled slightly. "No, Kamala. You won't do that. Because I know these men well enough to guide you along that road with some hope of safety, whereas without me you would not know where to begin. Trust me on that."

"Is that what you mean to do?" The words left her lips before she could stop them. "Guide me to safety?"

A strange, unnamed emotion flickered in the depths of his eyes. He put his glass down on the table and moved closer to her. Tension shivered in the air between them, a strange admixture of desire and defiance. Of all the ways this moment might end, she did not know what resolution she wanted.

And then he stepped away from her.

"When we're done with Tefilat," he said quietly, "we'll talk about it."

He walked to the western boundary of the room, not looking back at her. A breeze lifted the gauze curtains out of his way. For a moment he paused at the head of the staircase, and then he stepped over the edge. His flesh transformed so quickly, so perfectly, that his wings captured the breeze before that first step was completed. White wings. Framed by the white marble archway, curtains rippling to both sides of him, he set off into the night sky, moonlight gleaming along his feathers.

Not until he was out of sight did Kamala begin to breathe steadily again.

CHAPTER 19

ETHANUS WAS working on deciphering a Bursan codex when the knock came on his door. At first he didn't hear it. Daylight was fading, and the effort it took to make out the figures on the well-worn parchment required all his concentration. He could have used his power to refresh them, of course, drawing upon the memory inherent in the ancient fragments to restore them to their original condition. But where was the challenge in that? And so he didn't hear the knocking at first. Only when it was repeated with increasing volume did he realize that it was a signal meant for him, and not just the rapping of a hungry woodpecker in the forest outside.

Carefully putting his work aside, brushing a bit of dust from his woolen gown, he headed toward the door, wondering who on earth would be bothering him at this hour. Or at any hour. He doubted that more than one person even knew where he lived, and she would surely have better sense than to come here. The Law was not a thing to be taken lightly.

But when he opened the door, he saw that she was indeed

standing there. The dying sun backlit her bright red hair, lending it a fiery aura, like that of an angel. Or a demon.

Or both, he thought.

"You fled my custody," he admonished her. Not because he was really angry, but because dealing with the murderer of a Magister had certain requirements. "It was my duty to see that you were punished for your crime. Failing to do that, I've been dishonored in the eyes of all sorcerers. And now you've come back? For what purpose? To compromise me further? What possible reason would I have to welcome you into my home?"

"Your desire to learn the true history of the Magisters," she said. Green eyes burning with a quiet defiance that was achingly familiar. "The name of the secret darkness that lurks within our blood. The reason that we must play a role in the war to come, or watch the entire world go up in flames. The part you must play in that war, in order for us to be successful."

For a moment he just stared at her. Digesting her words, as though they were some foreign and unfamiliar food. Finally he decided he had done it long enough to satisfy propriety . . . or at least his own conscience.

"That'll do it," he said at last, nodding gruffly as he stepped aside to let her enter. "Come in."

———

Night had fallen by the time Kamala came to the end of her report, but Ethanus had not yet lit the lamps. Darkness licked at the single candle flame he had set on the table between them, as if struggling to consume its light.

When she was finally done, Ethanus was silent for a long while. The candle sputtered, drowning in its own wax.

"Colivar told you all this?" he asked at last.

"He told Ramirus, Fadir, and Sulah. And invited me to overhear."

"Did they know you were there?"

"No," she said, tipping over the candle to drain off some of its excess wax. She felt strangely tired, as if she had just undergone some great physical exertion. "Not that I know of, anyway."

The Magisters were really Souleaters. Or if not Souleaters themselves, then something that was not wholly human either. For some reason the revelation had seemed more reasonable to Kamala on the frozen, wind-scoured mountaintop than it did here, in these quiet surroundings. She could see her former teacher struggling to absorb it all. Finally he asked, "This information comes from . . . where?"

"Colivar said that the first Magisters used to share memories with their students, and that his teacher had given him these. I guess they originally came from the traitor who first crossed the Wrath."

His brow furrowed. "That seems . . . odd."

He rose from his seat, taking up what was left of the candle, and began to walk around the room, lighting the lamps. "You know that I am old," he told her. "Not as old as Colivar, perhaps, but old enough to have heard tales of the early days from my own teacher. Stories of the days before the Law. And he never mentioned anything like that. Memory sharing? We trusted each other even less in the early days than we do now." He shook his head. "Colivar has always been an odd one, and his relationship with his mentor may well have differed from the norm. But even so."

"You don't act like the part about our being Souleaters surprises you."

He sighed heavily, then blew out the candle and put it aside.

"The first Magisters believed that there was more to First Transition than learning how to steal the life-essence of others. My own teacher hinted at us being something other than human. I discounted that as part of his madness. The earliest generations of our kind were all quite mad, you know. Though in some it was more evident than in others." He reclaimed his seat and stared down at his hands thoughtfully, as if some kind of answer could be found there. "That madness is what I came here to escape, Kamala. The madness that I saw in the eyes of my fellow Magisters when they hung over me like vultures, my final night in Ulran. It wasn't that I feared the insanity in them, you understand, but I didn't want to surrender to it myself. Though I never guessed what lay at the heart of it . . ."

"You never told me all that," she said quietly.

He shrugged "There are some things a man prefers not to speak of."

"Isolation can no longer protect you," she said.

He did not respond.

"If what Colivar says is true, the return of the Souleaters may awaken the monster in each of us. Distance may not matter."

"So you've become a crusader now." He chuckled darkly. "That's quite a transformation, from what you were before."

She could feel a flush come to her face. A half dozen edged retorts rose to her lips . . . and remained unvoiced. Was it so unreasonable for her to fear these creatures? To fear what the earth might become if they returned in force? Surely that was enough to legitimately frighten anyone.

She remembered Rhys' funeral and the strange sense of longing she had felt, gazing down at her lover's still form. She had never known the kind of purpose that drove him and his people, that might drive a man to risk his life for a cause. But she had felt its power at that moment, and she envied him such passion.

"Be wary in your crusade," Ethanus warned her. "A Magister can choose to play the odds if it amuses him—even risk his life if the prize is great enough—but he doesn't have the power to sacrifice it outright. Mortal men can cast themselves onto a funeral pyre for the sake of a greater cause, but we cannot. The moment we accept certain death, we extinguish that supernatural spark that makes it possible for us to steal the lives of others."

"Are you sure?" she asked. A hint of defiance in her voice.

It was rare to see him startled. Rarer still that she was the one who startled him.

"Has that ever actually happened?" she pressed, leaning forward on the table. "Or is it just something we all assume is true? Like we once assumed that no woman could ever become a Magister. Do we really *know* that the willingness to sacrifice one's life for a cause would sever the link with one's consort, or are we only guessing that?"

For a moment the room was silent. So silent. You could hear the crickets chirping outside.

"No," he said solemnly. "I know of no case where that has ever been confirmed. That doesn't mean it hasn't happened, mind you. But there is no record of it that I know of."

"So it might not even be true."

"Yes." He licked his lips briefly, as if tasting the strange thought. "It might not even be true. But do you want to take that chance?"

She did not answer him. A pair of pewter cups were standing on the mantle, and she summoned them to the table with a short gesture, conjuring brandy to fill them. Ethanus stared at the one in front of him for a long moment, then raised it to his lips and took a deep drink. And another. Not until the cup was empty did he put it down.

"I suppose I should be afraid of what part you're going to ask me to play in all this," he said.

She smiled slightly. "Nothing overtly sacrificial."

He refilled the cup with his own sorcery. It was an uncharacteristic gesture, and an eloquent statement of just how much the night's revelations had disconcerted him. "Speak, then."

"I need your assistance as a scholar."

He raised an eyebrow.

"I remember you had a penchant for religious codices. Yes?"

"I have an interest in mankind's ancient religions. And in some of the modern ones, insofar as they evolved from ancient roots. Why? Are you planning to join some god's priesthood?"

"No. But I've been having strange visions, and I'm hoping you can help me interpret them. The first time was when I tried to find the Souleater queen for Colivar. And then it happened again when I searched Tefilat for him. They also come to me at night sometimes, just when I'm falling asleep. I thought that if any man alive could help me interpret them, it would be you."

"Religious visions?"

She nodded. "I see gods. Many gods. A vast circle of them, surrounding me. I can't see them all clearly enough to try to count them—the ones in the outer ranks are hazy, as if in fog—but the last time there were dozens that I could pick out clearly. Perhaps several hundred, all told."

His eyes narrowed thoughtfully. "What are they doing in these visions?"

"Watching me. I get the sense they're actively interested in what I'm doing, that it matters to them what choices I make. They never make any indication of that, mind you, but I just seem to know it, as certainly as I know my own name." She shook her head. "They never say a word to me. Or move. It's like they are . . . statues. All around me. A circle of statues, channeling some sort of spiritual energy." She blinked. "I don't know what to make of it. I thought you might."

"Show me," he said quietly.

Closing her eyes for a moment, she summoned up sufficient power to craft a vision for him. He moved their cups out of the way as it took shape over the table.

One by one her gods appeared. Tall gods. Short gods. Gods of rock, gods of wood, gods of wax with feathers stuck in them. She had never seen them this clearly in her visions, but the act of conjuring their images for Ethanus seemed to bring them into sharper focus. Fascinated, she studied them even as he did.

What a strange amalgamation of deities! She had never been a religious creature and had paid no more than token homage to the gods of Gansang. Nevertheless, she recognized just how odd some of these figures were, not only in design but in substance. The air about them seemed to resonate with all kinds of discordant power; she wondered if Ethanus could feel it.

In the end she was able to conjure images of nearly a hundred of them, with misty images crowding behind them and bleeding into the shadows of the room. Ethanus studied them for a while, then got up and began to walk around the table. She pushed her chair back to get out of his way while he walked a full circuit of her vision. He used his own power on several occasions to bring some feature into finer focus.

"Do you know what they are?" she asked him.

"I know what some of them are." He pointed to a tall figure with a crown of green and orange feathers. "That one is Duat, Lord of Death. From the Zoav jungle. And that one"—he pointed to a golden figure encrusted with gems—"that looks like an Anshasan deity. With a Skandir war god standing next to him. And that odd-shaped rock, that represents Jaasa, a water god revered by the desert nomads. How very curious."

"So are they really gods, or just . . . images of gods?"

"Well, what you are showing me are clearly idols, that is, physical representations of gods. But the line can be very thin between the two, Kamala. Some idols have centuries of prayer invested in them, which can transform them into more than mere statues. Others may have been used as the focal point for spirit conjuring and may even retain the essence of the beings who once possessed them. And witchery can turn such things into spiritual conduits, although that's a costly endeavor. Windows into other realms. So, in answer to your question . . . yes."

She wrapped her arms around herself, somewhat frustrated; she'd hoped for a simple answer, and this was not it.

"The question," he mused aloud, "is *why?*"

"Why are they watching me?"

"Why are they all standing together?"

She shrugged. "The world is about to end, apparently. Maybe the gods are worried about it."

He shook his head. "These are statues you're seeing. Whatever power they might have absorbed down through the centuries, whatever supernatural creatures might inhabit them now, they are still just statues. Physical objects, which can only exist in one location at a time." He looked up at her. "Such things matter in a vision, Kamala. They wouldn't have manifested in such a form if it weren't significant."

She drew in a sharp breath. "I see them whenever I search for the Witch-Queen's location."

He nodded. "Perhaps there is a connection, then. You say she has the power to hide from those who are hunting her. Perhaps these idols channel more energy than she can mask. Perhaps their essence is . . . bleeding through somehow? I don't know."

"So, then, what's the location?" She tried not to let frustration creep into her voice, but it was hard to be so close to the answers she sought and not know how to access them. "You've named gods from the four corners of the world. Where would they all come together like that?"

He did not answer her right away. His expression thoughtful, he got up from the table and walked over to his map chest. The cabinet of shallow drawers contained the most precious and delicate documents that he had gathered during his centuries of scholarship. There was strange and touching irony in how gently he handled them, taking care not to damage the fragile parchment sheets. In the house of any other Magister such things would have been reinforced with sorcery so that nothing short of a hurricane could damage them. But Kamala knew him well enough to know that he took pleasure in their fragility. *One should never take knowledge for granted*, he had told her. Their fragility forced him to handle them with appropriate reverence.

He chose one particular document from the collection, brought it to the table, and laid it out before her. A map. She banished her cups from the table so that the two of them would have room to look at it without risking a spill.

The map was an odd creation, reversed from the vantage point that cartographers usually preferred. With south at the top and north at the bottom, it defied her immediate recognition, and it took her a minute to get her bearings. Once she realized the trick, the various land masses and waterways began to take on recognizable form. Cities to the north, flanking a great delta. Mountains to the west, and a series of long ridges to the east. A vast expanse in the middle with dark, irregular lines running across it. It was all meticulously labeled, but the script was one she did not recognize, and the map was so old that the ink had faded, making it hard to see the letters. Any sorcerer other than Ethanus would have fixed the thing long ago.

"Do you recognize it?" he asked her. Always the teacher. But she didn't have to think long to answer him; the map that Colivar had showed her earlier had covered much of the same territory.

"This is Anshasa," she said, sketching out the borders of Farah's kingdom with her finger. And there," She pointed, "Tefilat."

"Look south," Ethanus prompted.

South were the strange lines, labeled in an unknown script. Where a number of them crossed there was a crude picture of a walled city, larger than anything else in the area. A circular wall surrounded it. A title of some sort was written above it, and there was smaller writing beneath it.

"These are caravan routes," he told her, indicating the lines. "They connect the markets of the south with Anshasa. Any man who controls a source of water along that route stands to make a fortune. Wars are fought over such locations." He pointed to the city. "Can you read the markings?"

She couldn't, but that was what sorcery was for. Binding enough athra to gather the knowledge she needed, she gave her eyes a moment to adjust to the foreign script. When the strange shapes began to resolve into more familiar letters she began to read. "City of the Gods . . ."

Her voice left her suddenly. Her heart skipped a beat.

"Read on," he prompted her.

She reached out to touch the faded script; her hand was trembling. "Let no man storm these gates, lest the gods of Jezalya strike him down."

"I'd heard tales of the place long ago," Ethanus said. "Legends, really. Some powerful spirit who was crossing the desert supposedly grew thirsty and commanded the earth to bring forth water, which it did in such copious quantity that the gods themselves were impressed. They all came to visit the place, not only those who were native to the desert, but deities from all over the world. A great palace was built so that those who wished to live there might do so. I know little about it, except for those legends. But it will be easy enough to gather information now that we know where to look."

She nodded. Normally it would be hard for her to focus her sorcery on such a place; the desert was so featureless there were no easy landmarks to follow. But if Jezalya's gods had truly been appearing in her dreams, there might be some residual energies to work with. Shutting her eyes, she tried to focus on the figures that had appeared to her. Now that Ethanus had identified them, she could see that they were indeed statues, but she could also feel the power that emanated from them. A true sacred presence, or simply the residue of morati devotions? It mattered little to her sorcery. Centuries of religious focus could transform a sculpture of stone and wood into something that had power in its own right. She could sense that power now as she imagined herself inside their circle, surrounded by Jezalya's gods. *Help me*, she thought. *Show me the way.*

She could feel her consciousness expanding as she extended tendrils of sorcerous inquiry southward, using that connection as her anchor. Forest and ocean and alabaster cities passed beneath her viewpoint—and then she came to a land that blazed with heat, set beneath a merciless sun. Since the real Jezalya would be shrouded in night's darkness right now, that meant she was not merely seeing features of the landscape but was tapping into the very essence of the land, revealing its spiritual signature.

A hunger for water enveloped her, not something born in the minds of men, or even animals, but arising from the land itself. That was a recent thing. This place had once been green, she saw. Images from ancient history flashed in and out of existence too quickly for her to focus on any one of them. Lush grasslands. Vast lakes. Herds of animals roaming as far as the eye could see. Had the Great War destroyed this place too, or was there some more natural cause for the devastation? It was hard not to stop and study such images, but she had work to do. Focusing with all her strength on her objective, she willed the distractions to fade, until only the desert remained.

She located a trade route. It would not have been discernable to a human eye, for the restless sands had buried any signs of human passage, but her Sight could pick out the spiritual traces left behind by the hundreds of caravans who had passed that way over the centuries. This was her path to the city. She followed it with her mind's eye, ignoring the ghostly echoes of merchants and soldiers and beasts of burden that had traveled this path before her. Sometimes when the echoes grew quiet, she thought she could hear Jezalya's gods whispering in the distance, though whether they were trying to tell her something, or were just passing the time in sacred gossip, she could not tell.

Something moved in the corner of her vision. In another time and place she might have focused on it, but she needed to stay focused on finding the city. But then there were more shadows, flitting about the edge of her awareness like angry flies. She tried to ignore them, but they grew larger with each passing minute, until one swooped down low over her vantage point, its vast black wings blotting out the sun. Kamala had to remind herself that she was not actually present where they were flying and that there was nothing in this vision that could hurt her, save perhaps the Witch-Queen herself; nonetheless, every fiber of her being cried out for her to flee, as more and more of the monstrous shadows filled the skies above her. Souleaters.

And then she saw the city.

It was still many miles in the distance, but it gleamed in the sunlight like a precious stone, drawing her eye directly toward it. Most of it was shielded behind a wall many times the height of a man, but a single tower rose up from the heart of the city, with a great golden finial at its summit. The precious metal caught the light of the sun and reflected it outward, providing a beacon that could be seen from many miles away. A lighthouse in the desert.

This, she knew, was Jezalya.

Gazing at the city, she suddenly realized that her whole search was pointless. Obviously the woman wasn't here. There was no point in wasting any more time searching the desert for her. Jezalya was of no interest to Siderea Aminestas. Colivar was looking in the right place after all. The clues were all in Tefilat, and he would find them there.

If not for what she had experienced in the Spinas, she might not have recognized the power for what it was: a masterpiece of obfuscation. Siderea Aminestas was not here; she had never been here; she would never be here; that message was as clear as the sun in the sky and the camel tracks leading up to the city's main gate. Kamala knew enough by now of how a queen's power worked to recognize the signs of it here, but though she admired the artistry of it, shaking it off was another thing. The person who had woven the spells surrounding this city was no simple beast, instinctively throwing up barriers in the wilderness, but a woman renowned for her skill at human manipulation. Kamala knew that it would take all the strength of her will to pierce through such a defense. And she also knew that if she succeeded in doing so, the Witch-Queen would sense her interference and know that her enemies had found her.

Now was not the time.

Dark shapes flitted hungrily about her as she withdrew her awareness from the desert, returning to the cool confines of Ethanus' study. For a moment she just sat there, trying to focus on the night and the silence in order to still the pounding of her heart. Ethanus, ever patient, waited.

"She's there," she whispered. "In Jezalya. I think the other Souleaters are there as well, but she keeps them far away from the city." She shuddered, remembering the hungry, restless shadows. So many of them. What were they all feeding on? "I have to tell Colivar."

Would the other Magisters be able to see through Siderea's power as Kamala had? Or would they need her to go back there, to gather more information for them? She felt a cold chill run down her spine at the thought of confronting the Witch-Queen directly, but also a strange sense of excitement. It was right that they should test their power against each other this way. Waging a war not with armies and siege engines, but with the gift of the ikati, that could turn a man's attention away from his target. She remembered how Siderea's power had tried to turn her thoughts to Tefilat, insisting that she must go there instead—

She stiffened suddenly. All color drained from her face. "Kamala?"

"It's a trap," she whispered. "Tefilat. It's a trap! She wants him to look for her there. That's what Sulah's dream was all about." She shook her head, as if trying to clear it. Was Siderea's power still affecting her brain, or were her thoughts her own now? "I have to warn him!"

She got up from the table so hurriedly that her chair fell back, clattering noisily to the floor behind her. "Ethanus, I—"

"Go," he said. "Do what you have to."

She began to draw her power to her. Normally she would never do so inside the house of another Magister, but there was no time to waste. Ethanus watched her mold a portal for herself, his expression calm. Unflappable. The world could come crashing down around them all and Ethanus' heart would not miss a beat. What opposites they were!

She leaned across the table and kissed him on the forehead. At least that surprised him.

And then she wrapped the portal spell around her and disappeared into the darkness.

CHAPTER 20

COLIVAR CIRCLED Tefilat several times before finally moving in. In wide, sweeping circles he flew over the desert surrounding the abandoned city, scrutinizing every grain of sand with his sorcery. Seeking . . . what? Some kind of trap? A sign that *she* was currently here, despite Kamala's assurances to the contrary?

Even while he did his reconnaissance, he knew how futile such an effort was. Tefilat resonated with so many residual energies that it was all but impossible to pick out the one or two that might be meaningful. It was as if a hundred witches were there right now, casting all their spells at once . . . and doing it badly. Fragments of ancient power hung in the air like a dust cloud, making it hard to see anything clearly. Broken spells, failed summonings, frustrated conjurations: the detritus of an ancient war. Looking for signs of trouble here was like looking for signs of shark activity in a storm-tossed, churning sea.

When he finally landed, it took him a few seconds longer to reclaim his human form than it should have. The last of his feathers did not want to recede, and his skin felt rough where they were finally absorbed. It seemed to him that Tefilat's effect had worsened since the last time he had visited, many years ago. Or maybe that was just his nerves speaking. At any rate, there seemed to be no one around right now. He scanned the area once more, just to make certain, and then headed toward the city proper. He wrapped sorcery about himself as he went, to discourage prying eyes. Though gods alone knew if such a spell would have any power in this place.

The canyon was ancient, carved out by a river the earth had swallowed up long ago, leaving only ghostly memories of water clinging to the narrow bed at its center. Its walls were colorful, with bands of rust, orange, and in one place an odd shade of pink, layered as neatly as masonry in some places, buckling into strange curvilinear patterns in others. He knew from earlier explorations that each stripe had been formed in a previous age, and contained both relics of that age and faint resonances of the things that had lived here then. The concept had fascinated him once, but now his only concern was to make sure that nothing was hidden within the shadowy caves and crevices of the place, besides the inevitable snakes and lizards.

But all was as it should be, and there was no sign of any fresh magic that he could discern.

Finally he came to Tefilat itself. Though he had been there several times before and theoretically knew what to expect, still the sight of the place awed him. Not simply because of its grandeur, but because it had been created in an age before sorcery, when every magical task had been measured in human life.

Or, more to the point, human life with a name attached.

The main buildings had been carved directly out of the cliff face and, amazingly enough, had stood the test of time. Had any new witchery been embedded in the stone by recent visitors? Too much faded power clung to the façade for him to be sure.

When he reached the widest part of the canyon—the town square, as it were—he stood still for a moment, listening. Just listening. But only silence greeted his ears, broken by the faint susurration of wind in the distance. Kneeling down, he bound a bit of sorcery, molding it twice over just to make sure that he had it right, then he let it sink into the ground around his feet, shutting his eyes as he absorbed the images it was gathering for him.

Nomads had passed through here recently. He could see them in their desert robes, richly striped and edged in plaited cord: Hom'ra. He watched as they brought in supplies on the backs of asses and then unpacked them. Heavy amphorae sealed with wax comprised the bulk of the delivery, and baskets of what Colivar guessed to be foodstuffs. There was a sigil on several of the amphora seals that he did not recognize.

Interesting.

Letting the vision fade, he headed toward the largest building in the complex. It was a two-story structure with columns flanking the main entrance and a frieze depicting a mythological battle scene overhead. He paused for a moment to take in the carved images, his mind applying names to gods and events that the morati world had long forgotten. Then he bound a bit of power to test the entrance for wards—there were none—and to establish one of his own that would be triggered by anyone else entering the building behind him. The place seemed utterly deserted, but one could never be too careful.

The temperature dropped as soon as he entered the shadowy interior, becoming almost tolerable by desert standards. He blinked as his eyes adjusted to the relative darkness, resisting the impulse to cool the air further. He didn't want to use any more sorcery in this place than he had to.

The main chamber was empty, but a layer of sand and dust had accumulated underfoot, and footprints had recently scuffed a path across the room, heading toward an interior chamber. Many footprints, he noted. Whatever was happening here had been going on for some time.

He followed the path to a rear chamber. Only a trickle of sunlight could reach this far, but it was enough for him to see what was inside.

Furniture was stacked along the rearmost wall. The items were rough-hewn and simply made, such as a common laborer might own. Along another wall were the supplies he had seen in his vision. He walked over to one of the amphorae and briefly considered using sorcery to determine its contents and purpose. But the sigil impressed into its seal might well be an anchor for witchery, or even sorcery, so he left it untouched. Anywhere else he would have trusted in his ability to summon knowledge from the thing without triggering a ward, but in Tefilat it was best not to take chances.

Someone was clearly preparing this place for habitation. But why? There wasn't enough human life in this blighted region to support Souleaters, and the local tribes preferred to keep far away from Tefilat's polluted resonance. There must be something here that someone wanted.

Something Siderea wanted.

Moving warily, Colivar progressed from the sunlit rooms near the cliff face to a network of chambers and passages that extended deep into the earth. Tefilat's creators had followed the twists and turns of a natural cavern system, carving out chambers wherever space permitted. The layout was strange to a sorcerer's eye, as a Magister could simply have created rooms wherever he wanted them. But the witches who had built this place had not been free to waste energy on that scale, and so the complex was random in its arrangement, a veritable labyrinth of twisting corridors and irregular chambers. Colivar had explored the entire system when he had first taken up his post in Anshasa, and it took but a whisper of sorcery to call those memories back to him, so that he had a mental map of the place. By the light of a small sorcerous flame he followed the faint scuffmarks of Tefilat's recent visitors as he traced their path through the twisting complex, searching for whatever anomaly might explain their interest.

And in a small chamber, deep within the earth, he found it at last.

A far wall had been broken open, giving access to some kind of space beyond. A secret room? He summoned more light, and he could see that the second chamber was richly decorated, with relief carvings of some sort covering the walls.

With one last spell to make sure he was still alone in Tefilat—he was—and another to check for wards at the entrance to the hidden chamber—there were none—he stepped over the rubble at the base of the opening and entered the mysterious room.

Every wall was covered with carvings. They seemed to be historical images, mostly battle scenes from the Great War; he recognized many of the references. He had seen other rooms like this, tucked away in various strongholds throughout the world, though few had been this carefully hidden. They represented the last desperate attempt of the First Kings to record the history of mankind in a form that might weather the fall of human civilization.

One particular set of images drew his eye, and he walked across the room to get a closer look at them.

Souleaters.

He shouldn't have been surprised to find the ikati depicted in Tefilat. One of the key campaigns of the Great War had been fought here. And yet . . . something seemed wrong about the images. It took him a moment to realize what it was. When he finally did, his heart skipped a beat in his chest.

The carvings depicted a swarm of Souleaters descending upon a town and warriors rising up to fight them. But the Souleaters had been solitary predators during the Great War. It was rare that two would ever have been seen in the sky together, and for them to gather in a swarm like this would simply be unheard of. They would have been too busy killing each other to bother with anything else. Not until their merger with the witches in the arctic had they developed enough tolerance of their own species to come together like this.

So this place must have been created long after the Great War, by someone who knew how the species had changed. But how was that possible, when all the remaining Souleaters had been trapped in the far north? Was it possible that some had remained down here as well? He reached out a hand to touch one of the carved Souleaters, binding a whisper of power to investigate its origin.

Even as he did so, he realized his mistake.

Too late.

A spell that had been hidden deep within the rock sprang to life at his touch, subsuming his own sorcery for strength. A strange shimmering webwork of power appeared along the walls and ceiling of the chamber and began to close in on him; he struggled to hold it at bay, but his sorcery had no effect upon it. The alien power seemed to have his own resonance, as if he himself had summoned it into being; how was that possible? It was closing in around him now, but he could not do anything to stop it, because that would have required protecting himself from . . . himself. Then the light about him began to fade, and he felt himself choking on darkness as the chill of transition began to envelope him. *No!* he despaired. *Not now!* He struggled against the cold and the darkness, trying to find a new consort quickly enough to save himself, but he couldn't break through the spell that was strangling him. His soul was suffocating, its last cold sparks of stolen athra sputtering out, and he could do nothing to save it.

And then the world outside flickered out like a dying candle, and there was only fear.

CHAPTER 21

MIST. THAT was all Gwynofar could see at first. Damp mist covering the ground about her feet. Tendrils of mist curling about her ankles. Clouds of mist overhead where the sky should be, a few hints of pale blue seeping through here and there, quickly swallowed by whiteness.

Where was she?

Squinting against the haze, she thought she could make out some vague shapes ahead of her, and she headed toward them. The ground seemed solid enough beneath its foggy blanket, and her shoes made soft squelching sounds as they pressed into the damp earth, disquieting in an otherwise eerie silence. Now and then she felt something small crunch underfoot, and memories from her childhood provided a name: *pine cone.*

What was this place?

Slowly the mist began to fade, trees becoming visible one by one as she continued walking, emerging from the fog like soldiers in a pine-clad army. Silent. So silent. Then the last of the mist withdrew from the tree-trunks, and she could see where human faces had been carved into them long ago, now glistening from a coating of dew.

Ancestor trees.

She could see now that she was walking along a narrow path that wound its way between several thick stands of the carved trees. This place was both familiar and unfamiliar to her, and though she had the distinct feeling she had been here before, she did not recognize the faces that surrounded her. But their identities did not really matter right now; that was not what she had come for.

She wrapped her arms about herself as she walked, sensing that she was here for an important reason but having no clue what it was.

At last she came to a place where shadowy pine groves gave way to an open field. Here, where more sunlight could reach the ground, a single young sapling had taken root. Gwynofar approached it, then stopped. She felt as if she should recognize this place, but she was unable to put a name to it.

And then the sapling began to transform. Drawing added substance from the air surrounding it, painting itself in colors that could not have arisen from mere bark, it slowly took on the form of a child. A very young child, whose features were hauntingly familiar to her. After a moment she realized why, and a terrible sorrow filled her heart.

"Anrhys," she whispered. Part of her brain now understood this was a dream, but another part—the larger part—did not care. She fell to her knees as the apparition of her dead child approached her, tears of sorrow and pain running down her cheeks. The real Anrhys had never known the touch of forest air upon his face or the soft crunch of pine needles beneath his feet. She had killed him while he was still in her womb, sacrificing him for a cause he never knew anything about. Even the tree that had been planted over his ashes—the tree that now stood before her—would never bear his true features, only a witch's estimate of what he might have looked like had he lived long enough to reach manhood. The guilt that welled up inside her seemed vast enough to consume an army of souls. She wanted to reach out and embrace him, to bury her face in his pale blond hair—so like her own!—and weep and weep and weep, until all the terrible guilt in her soul was washed away. Telling him she was sorry—so sorry!—and praying to hear some response from him that hinted at forgiveness. Something in which she might discover even a shadow of absolution.

But she could not approach him. She dared not approach him. She was spellbound by his presence, terrified that if she made contact with him—if she tried to make him real in any way—the dream would fade, and he would be lost to her again.

It was he who held out his hands to her. It took her a moment to realize that he was offering her something, and he expected her to come forward and take it. Nestled in each palm, she saw, was a small natural black crystal, whose irregular facets reflected the sunlight in glints of color as he moved. They were of a like size and shape, though not perfectly identical, and it seemed to her that somehow they belonged together. And they belonged to her.

Take them. He did not speak the words aloud, but she could hear them nonetheless. *You will need them.*

Slowly, hesitantly, she rose to her feet and approached him. How hard it was to be this close to her lost child and not draw him into her arms! But she dared not touch him, lest the flood tide of emotion that was nearly overwhelming her right now drown her. She reached out her own arms toward him, instead, and rather than take the crystals from him directly, cupped her hands beneath his own, waiting to receive them. After a moment he nodded and turned his hands over, dropping one small stone into the center of each hand. Where they touched her palms she could feel that they were radiating a strange warmth, as if they were living things, and they pulsed as if from the beat of an unseen heart.

The centuries are entrusted to you, came the unvoiced words. *Guard them well.*

Then the crystals in her hands began to change shape. Their columnar spines melted back into the base rock, until there were only smooth black stones in her hands, roughly hemispherical in shape. And then those, too, began to melt. Soon her cupped palms held not rock, but pools of thick red liquid. Blood. She trembled as it began to drip down between her fingers, pattering to the ground like crimson rain. The earth itself seemed to shudder as the first drops struck, as if some sleeping creature buried deep beneath her feet had suddenly stirred to life . . . or perhaps the earth itself was awakening.

Transfixed, she watched as the blood at her feet began to spread out across the earth, finally reaching the base of a nearby tree. The roots seemed to shudder as they drew in the precious liquid, and the slender needles began to transform in color, one after the other, until the entire tree had turned crimson. Other trees were following suit now, as the blood reached them; in a few minutes' time the entire clearing was filled with transformed foliage: a forest of blood. Then the first tree began to transform in shape. Its branches curled in upon themselves, and the knots in its trunk vanished. The bark that had covered the carved ancestral face grew smooth and pale, like human skin, and the eyes glistened wetly, as though they were somehow conscious.

And a man stood before her. His clothing was ancient in style and gashed in several places. A deep cut across his face glistened with fresh blood, and his tunic was splattered with mud. Another man appeared beside him. Then another. The fourth to take shape was a woman; she was dressed in a man's garments, her long hair tangled and wild and streaked with blood from a wound in her skull. More and more figures appeared as Gwynofar watched, until there was a veritable army of blood-stained warriors surrounding her. She had seen enough illustrations of the Great War to recognize the style of their armor, and her breath caught in her throat as she realized just who the figures were supposed to be.

These were the men and women who had fought the Souleaters the first time. The martyrs of the *lyr*. Her ancestors.

She opened her mouth to ask them why they had called her here, what it was they wanted from her . . . but even as the words formed on her lips, the whole of the scene suddenly began to dissolve. Mist rose up around the warriors' feet as their flesh gave way to less solid substance, and the colors of their clothing dissipated into the air in ripples and eddies, until all of it was gone. Gwynofar looked about desperately for her child, but he had disappeared long ago. She had lost him again! A short moan of anguish escaped her, even as the last details of the dreamscape faded from sight.

And in the end there was only featureless mist, as there had been at the beginning: a vast white silence broken only by the pattering of blood as it dripped from her hands, and by the broken, mournful beating of her heart.

———

Gwynofar lay upon a bed of silken sheets, her thin linen shift slicked to her skin by a layer of cold sweat, struggling to get her bearings. Moonlight coming in through the narrow windows picked out embroidered details on the canopy overhead but left the fabric itself in shadow, resulting in a ghostly display of feathery patterns that seemed to hang in midair, dreamlike. For a moment she just stared at them, trying to get her mind to focus. Was she awake yet? If so, then she knew she must do her best to interpret the strange dream she'd had while its memory was still fresh in her mind. Once she slept again, many details would be forgotten.

The centuries are entrusted to you, Anrhys had said.

What did that mean? And what were the crystals that he had given to her supposed to represent?

The eyes of the Souleaters look like black crystal, she recalled. She remembered when the northern queen had locked eyes with her, and her soul had almost been sucked into those terrible orbs. But she did not think this dream was meant to refer to Souleaters. No, this was about something more personal, something that would provide strength and healing for the *lyr* armies. Not something that would harm them.

Her hands curled instinctively at her sides, and it seemed to her for a moment she could see Anrhys standing before her again. Not moving. Not saying anything. She remembered the feel of warm, sticky blood beneath her fingers, and a wave of fresh mourning came over her, as intense as the moment in which she had realized what the cost of her Alkali mission would be, the nature of the sacrifice that would be required to bring the Throne of Tears to life. For a moment she was back in the tower, experiencing the fear of that terrible day, feeling the cold bite of despair in her soul.

And then it came to her. She understood.

And for a moment she just lay still on the bed, her heart pounding so hard the heavy frame seemed to tremble. Unable to move. Barely able to think. Anrhys was gone now—again!—but she knew why he had come to her.

With sudden determination she rose up, reached for the robe that had been laid out across the foot of her bed, and headed toward the door. The moons had set long ago. but the first dim light of dawn was seeping through the windows, just enough to see by as she exited her bedchamber, struggling to get her arms into her sleeves as she walked. Outside her door two startled maidservants stumbled to their feet, trying to look as if they had not just been sleeping, and the pair of guards stationed outside the entrance to her apartment chamber snapped to attention as soon as they saw her. Gwynofar did not acknowledge them. She did not see anyone or anything. The person who she needed would come to her, she knew that. His wards would sense her agitation and alert him to her need, and he would wake up and come to her.

Never mind that he had promised not to work sorcery in Salvator's palace. She knew him well enough by now to understand when and why that vow might be broken. Besides, Salvator had said that he was allowed to use sorcery for transportation, and that was what she wanted him for, wasn't it?

He was there as she turned a corner, waiting for her. His black robes were nearly invisible in the pre-dawn darkness, but his white hair and beard glowed as if they contained their own source of light. As it had been on so many occasions when she had been a child: a familiar and comforting sight.

"Majesty?" His eyes were narrow with concern.

"Kierdwyn," she said breathlessly. Her heart was pounding so hard it was difficult to speak. "I must go to Kierdwyn, Ramirus."

He hesitated only for a moment, then nodded. He shut his eyes for a moment, and it seemed to Gwynofar that he was concentrating on something. She understood sorcerous protocol well enough to know that he must send word ahead to Kierdwyn's Magister Royal—was it Lazaroth now?—before entering the man's territory, but it was difficult for her to accept such a delay. Any delay. She paced anxiously in front of him, fearful that her precious moment of revelation would fade before she had a chance to test it.

At last his eyes opened. His expression was calm and serene, and she tried to draw strength from that serenity. He looked her over, shook his head slightly, and with a wave of his hand banished her nightwear, replacing it with a simple day gown of summer-weight wool. Her sleep-tangled hair was smoothed and separated by the same power, and a golden circlet bearing the Aurelius arms took its accustomed place above her brow.

"Now you are fit for your father's house." The air before her began to shimmer and ripple like water. "Come," he said, offering her his hand. She took it, and together they stepped through the portal.

Behind them a note appeared in midair, then slowly began to flutter toward the ground. *Salvator,* it said. *Have gone to Kierdwyn with Ramirus. Will return soon. G.*

By the time it reached the floor, the portal had vanished.

———

"Lord Alkali wanted to keep it, of course." Lord Kierdwyn's tone was distracted as he sought the proper key on the ring. "He all but threatened to go to war over it. But in the end he had no real choice. We told him that since a member of House Kierdwyn had unlocked its secret, and might still have some sort of magical connection to it, it belonged in Kierdwyn's care." Settling at last on a large brass key, he inserted it into the lock on the ironbound door and turned it clockwise. The mechanism of the lock fell into place with a loud metallic thunk. "Truth be told, it had less to do with you than with the fact that a Souleater invasion had just taken place right under his nose and he hadn't even known about it. Priceless artifacts should not be guarded by idiots."

He took hold of the heavy door and pulled; Gwynofar and Ramirus stepped back to give him room to swing it open. Beyond the threshold was a dark chamber, windowless; the shadow of a single large object could be seen in its center, but no details were visible.

Lord Kierdwyn opened wide the hood on the lantern he had brought with him and handed it to Gwynofar. "Why is it that you need to see this so urgently?"

She shook her head. "I don't know, Father."

Despite how frantic she had been to come here, she suddenly found herself hesitant to approach the thing. No one knew better than she did just how powerful the Throne of Tears was, or how destructive it could be. For a moment she shut her eyes, remembering the day she had channeled its power to all her people, linking together every man, woman and child of *lyr* descent and pouring fearsome images into their heads.

And killing her unborn child.

Her hand trembled as she entered the room, sending the lantern's light dancing about its walls. The Throne seemed even larger and more ghastly than she had remembered it. In this setting it appeared almost alive, its vast sculpted wings poised as if to take flight, its blue-black surface—made from a Souleater's skin—organic and expectant. Her skin crawled as she looked at it, and her hand moved over her belly instinctively, as if trying to protect her unborn child from its influence. But that child was gone now; the Throne had already claimed him.

Forcing herself to move closer, she knelt before the great seat, searching out one feature in particular. Had she remembered it right? Deep carvings trapped the lantern's light, casting shadows that made it hard to distinguish any fine details. She angled the lantern upward, trying to focus the light where she needed it—and suddenly a circle of candles appeared, surrounding both her and the throne. Hundred of candles, some resting on the floor itself, some raised high on stands, offering light from every angle. She nodded her appreciation to Ramirus without looking back at him, then leaned in closer to study the arms of the chair. Now she could see where her blood had dripped down its arms as she had prayed for the gods to accept her sacrifice, and where her nails had gouged deeply into the ancient wood as images of past wars had surged through her. And there was the place where she had first made her blood-offering, tearing open the flesh of her arm on the sharp talons that jutted out from the arms of the throne, smearing her blood on the fist-sized spheres they guarded.

Spheres of black crystal.

With a trembling hand she touched one of them. There was nothing mystical about the feel of it, but there hadn't been that first day, either, until her sacrifice had awakened the Throne's power. Rubbing off a layer of crusted blood that had dulled the crystal's surface, she saw its sharp facets catch the light, reflecting back Ramirus' candle flames in a thousand broken bits. At first glance it reminded her of a Souleater's eye—an eerie confluence—but looking more closely, she could see that the facets were random in size and shape, as if a thousand shattered fragments of black glass had been glued together and attached to a spherical base. Her fingers explored the upper edge of the thing, as far as the design of the chair allowed. Only half of the sphere was visible, she realized; the upper half was obscured by the sculpted claw.

If it was there at all.

With sudden determination she dug her nails under one of the claws and tried to break it off. But she couldn't get a good enough purchase on the polished surface, and her fingers slid off with no more than a broken nail to show for the effort. Behind her she could hear one of the men moving toward her, alarmed by her assault on the artifact. But she knew that the gods had brought her this far for a reason, and they would not let anyone stop her now.

Reaching up to her head, she removed the circlet that Ramirus had conjured for her. It was thin and flat, and it slid easily under one of the claws. Grasping it tightly with both hands, she twisted it with all the strength that her altered muscles possessed, trying to force the thing from its mooring. The circlet bent but did not break, and after a moment the claw snapped free; she could hear it skittering across the floor as she attacked the next one. And the next. Four claws had to be removed before the crystal could be loosened in its mooring, and two more before she could pull it free.

When she did so, she sat back on her heels, breathless, and stared at the thing in her hands. It was hemispherical, just as the crystals in her dreams had been. The flat portion was irregular, and bore the scars of some sharp instrument having been driven through it.

"What is it?" her father asked, moving to her side so he could see it more clearly.

"I don't know," she whispered. The crystal was warm in her hand and seemed to thrum with unnamed energies, but she lacked the skill to interpret them. "We need a Seer. Someone with *lyr* blood, if possible."

He nodded sharply and went to summon one. Gwynofar turned her attention to freeing the other crystal. This time Ramirus helped, bracing the chair so that it did not move as she attempted to yank the claws free. She noted that he hadn't questioned why she had asked for a Seer rather than accepting his aid. Which was good, because she couldn't have answered him. She was running on instinct now, trusting to the gods to direct her.

By the time Kierdwyn returned with a Seer, Gwynofar had released the second crystal from its setting. Like the first, it showed signs of having been struck from some larger piece. Breath held, she put the two pieces together, and found that they fit perfectly together. Two halves of a whole. But what was its purpose?

She turned to the Seer—a young woman who had clearly

been dragged out of bed for this meeting—and held the crystal globe out to her. The Seer took it into her hands, keeping the two halves pressed together as she turned it over, studying it. Except for the place where a long, thin chip was missing—presumably where some sort of chisel had been applied—it was perfectly spherical. Sparks of candlelight danced along its facets as it moved, giving it a strangely animated aspect.

When the Seer seemed satisfied that she had gleaned all the information she could by physical inspection, she closed her hands over it, shut her eyes, and began to incant softly. Gwynofar muttered a prayer of thanksgiving under her breath for the sacrifice of life that was being offered, and she could see that her father was doing the same. Ramirus alone watched impassively, immune to such sentiments. The concept of sacrifice meant little to a Magister.

"So many souls," the Seer murmured, her eyes still closed. "Each one an offering. So much death! Blood and ash and tears pour in the offering bowl, overflowing. Never alone. Never alone. Give our prayers to the others. Bind our souls to the others. Anchor us to the earth, until the final battle has been fought . . ."

The Seer fell silent. It seemed to Gwynofar that she shuddered slightly, and her hands tightened about the crystal sphere. Then, slowly, she looked up at them. Her eyes, which had been cool and clear only a few minutes before, were now bloodshot from the strain of her spellcasting. Whatever secrets this thing contained, it had not surrendered them easily.

"It's an anchor." Her voice dropped to a whisper, tinged with awe. "The people who were bound to it are long gone, and their spirits have expired, but their resonance remains affixed to it." She shook her head in amazement. "So many people! It would be impossible to give names to them all. This sphere . . ." She turned it over in her hand; the pieces shifted as she did so, the two halves separating slightly. "It was conjured from their flesh. Their blood. Collected from men and women who fell in battle, offered up by those who knew they were about to die . . . each drop of blood was an anchor to its owner . . . so many of them . . ." Her voice trailed off into awestruck silence.

"This is the essence of our people," Lord Kierdwyn said reverently, "preserved against the ravages of time."

"And no doubt why the Throne had the effect it did," Ramirus provided. He was staring at the grotesque chair, his eyes narrow; unlike the Seer, he did not require incantations to focus his power. "The spells that were woven into it were simply meant to link the messenger to the message. It must have been the traces contained in this funeral crystal that allowed her Majesty to connect to its ancestral memories, providing a means whereby all the *lyr* might be connected . . ." There was a strange tone to his voice that Gwynofar had never heard from him before. Awe?

The Seer looked at Gwynofar. "Do you wish me to repair it?"

Another sacrifice, offered freely. Not for power's sake but to honor the dead. Gwynofar thought about what elements of this matter were important enough to merit such a sacrifice and finally said, "Fasten the two halves together again. Don't repair the other damage."

The woman nodded and muttered a soft incantation, summoning her power. When she handed the sphere to Gwynofar, it still bore the chips and chisel-marks of its fracturing, but it was whole once more.

This was the flesh and blood of a lost generation, she thought. And a fulcrum point for the current generation. It was impossible to hold such a thing in one's hand and not feel a sense of reverence, as one did on holy ground.

The centuries are entrusted to you, Anrhys had said. Now she held them in her hand. But for what purpose?

"I need to take this with me," she said softly.

She half expected her father to object, but he did not. He just stared at the Throne for a moment and then asked, "Why?"

She shook her head. "I don't know. The vision that brought me here said that I was meant to guard it. I don't know if that means it needs to be kept safe or . . . or used for something."

"You are connected to it," Ramirus told her. "Ever since the day you awakened the Throne. You are as much a part of it now as the martyrs for whom it was crafted."

"We're all part of it," she whispered.

Slowly Lord Kierdwyn crouched down before her. He took her hands in his, folded her fingers over the sphere, and waited until she met his eyes before speaking. "Gwynofar, I don't know where this path will lead you, but clearly it's your destiny to follow it. And anything the gods have so clearly ordained, it is our duty to facilitate. So take this anchor with you, if you feel you need to. Guard it as you see fit. And remember, if it is true that our enemies have no dominion over the blood of the *lyr*, then this may be the one thing on earth that cannot be corrupted by their power."

Gwynofar nodded solemnly. Her father stood, then offered her a hand to help her to her feet. "Do you need to return home immediately? I can summon Lazaroth to provide transportation, though I'm not sure where he is right now. He said he had some personal business he needed to attend to. I have the means to contact him, but it may take some time."

"I will see to her transportation," Ramirus said.

"No," Gwynofar said abruptly.

She held up the crystal. Its strange, irregular facets burned with reflected firelight. Did the number and shape of the facets have any meaning? Or had the thing just been sculpted with mad abandon, reflecting the chaos of its age? "Sorcery must never touch this," she whispered. She didn't know why that was important, but something inside told her that it was. Very important.

Ramirus' white brow furrowed. "It will be a good week's journey without a portal."

"The weather is good," she said stubbornly. "I'll enjoy the ride."

"Pardon, your Majesty." It was Kierdwyn's Seer. "There's no need for that. I'm sure my fellow Seers will be willing to offer up a spellsong for you."

Gwynofar nodded regally, accepting the offer. Transportation was costly magic, and the etiquette of the Protectorates required that she not ask her father's witches to make such a sacrifice unless it was absolutely necessary. But it didn't surprise her that they would volunteer their efforts. The spellsongs of the Guardians allowed a group of witches to pool their power so that the cost in life-essence was divided among them. Spread out among a dozen souls, the sacrifice was minimal, and there was great honor in offering such a service. Especially to Gwynofar, who had sacrificed her own child in the name of their cause.

"It will take time to gather them," Lord Kierdwyn said. "Will you have breakfast with us, in the meantime?" A corner of his mouth twitched. "Your mother will never forgive me if I let her sleep through your visit."

Gwynofar smiled faintly. The expression felt strange to her. "Well," she said. "I certainly wouldn't want to get you in trouble.

So I suppose we'll have to stay." She turned to Ramirus. "I do need to get word to Salvator. If he wakes up to discover that I disappeared from the palace with no explanation . . . he will not be pleased."

A corner of the Magister's mouth twitched. "I have already seen to that, Majesty."

She smiled faintly. "You care for me well, as always."

The ice-blue eyes glittered. "It is my duty."

But he was not even curious about why she had forbidden the use of sorcery on the crystal, she noted. Was there meaning in that?

Curiosity is second nature to a Magister, Danton had once told her. *He can no more resist its summons than a man can resist the urge to breathe.*

Disquieted, she waited in silence for her father to shut and lock the heavy door, then she turned to follow him back to the heart of the keep. While Ramirus banished the candles he had conjured, leaving the Throne of Tears in darkness once more.

CHAPTER 22

To SAY that the royal palace of Anshasa was visible from miles away would be an understatement. Its vast, gold-plated dome reflected the light of the sun with blinding brilliance, providing a beacon so powerful that even at midday it was visible from well across the city. As one drew closer, it was possible to see that the pillars of the building were richly carved and painted, their designs celebrating various sacred events. Over the main doors, a colorful frieze depicted the sigil of Hasim Farah's family line as the central point of Creation, from which all other royal houses descended.

Compared to the stark beauty of Colivar's white temple this place was . . . well, no one would accuse King Hasim Farah of being too tasteful. Yet Colivar himself might have built the place, Kamala mused. It wasn't the kind of project Magisters usually got involved with, but no doubt there were dozens of Magisters who had conjured monuments on this scale for one monarch or another. What was the life of another unknown peasant, when measured against the pride of a monarch?

But Colivar's white temple no longer existed. She had gone

to the place where it once had stood and had found only impressions of it, without any traces of the man himself. She had gone to all the other places where he had said she might search for him, and he had not been there, either. She had even returned to the tree they had once used as a meeting point, and found no note, nor any recent trace that might offer insight into his whereabouts.

She even tried to find him with sorcery, which would have been a risky venture on a good day. But she had no anchor to work with, and either his defenses were too strong for her, or . . .

Or what?

Gazing at the royal palace, she was aware of a knot of fear forming in the pit of her stomach. Maybe all of this meant nothing. She was hardly a trusted confidant of Colivar's, after all. He was under no obligation to report to her.

But now she had to find him. And she had tried all possible options save one.

She walked toward the palace with what she hoped was a show of confidence. Power was wrapped so tightly about her that not a whisper of soulfire could possibly peep through, but that did not mean that her nature would go undetected. The defensive spells surrounding the palace would detect any use of magic, even if they could not identify its exact nature. Sulah would know that someone of power had entered his domain.

Unless the power of an ikati queen could shield her from his scrutiny.

How did one conjure a power like that? she wondered. Was it something she could tap into consciously? Or would she need to join her mind to a Souleater's to do that?

And an even bigger question: Would such an attempt

strengthen the Souleater essence that hid in the dark recesses of her soul?

The guards at the palace gate received her as they would any unknown visitor. She was wearing robes in the local style, flowing layers of striped linen, and while it might have raised a few eyebrows when she lifted the hems up above her knees to climb the stairs, apparently she looked mundane enough to pass muster.

"Tell the Magister Royal that Kamala requests audience," she told them, hoping that was the correct phrasing to use. This was not a game she was used to.

Did Sulah even know her name? Part of her hoped not; the fewer Magisters who took notice of her, the better. But given how important the campaign in Alkali had turned out to be, she was willing to bet that someone had mentioned her to him. Hopefully it would be enough to pique his curiosity now.

She was allowed to wait inside the entrance while a servant ran off to deliver her message. Shortly afterward, he returned, bowed deeply, and said, "He will see you."

The inside of the building was as opulent as the outside, but she barely saw it as she followed the man through a series of richly furnished chambers. Her mind was busy running over the words she would say, while she tried to prepare enough defensive sorcery that those words would reveal nothing more than she wished them to.

Sulah was in the west wing, in a high-ceilinged chamber that looked like some kind of private study. He was a young man—in appearance at least—with the pale blond hair and fair skin she had come to associate with the northern bloodlines. Was it possible he had some *lyr* blood in him? Supposedly that wasn't possible, but these days she took nothing for granted.

"Kamala." He stood as she entered. "You're the witch who accompanied Rhys into Alkali, aren't you?"

She was surprised to feel the knot in her gut loosen up a bit when he referred to her as a witch. Apparently her battered subterfuge was holding. "I am."

"The tales I heard of your adventures were quite remarkable. A pleasure to meet you at last." He offered his hand. "Though I do admit to some surprise at seeing you this far from home."

I have no home, she thought, accepting the gesture as a woman should, with the fleeting touch of her fingertips. His demeanor surprised her, not only because she had not expected such a friendly welcome, but because his manner was so . . . well, so morati. Perhaps he was still young enough that habits of morati life came naturally to him. It was certainly not that way with Colivar. No matter how friendly that one seemed, no matter how casual his manner was, she never forgot for a moment that he was a predator at heart, and one of the most ancient and powerful of his kind.

As this one may be as well, she told herself. *Don't be swayed by appearances.*

"I have some business in the south," she answered him. She didn't want to give him any real information about herself, but she knew that she would not be able to get what she wanted without offering something in return.

"And you wish me to be part of that business. Is that it?"

His bluntness startled her. "I need your help finding someone," she said.

"Ah. I see." He steepled his fingers before him. "And what reason would I have to help you, instead of simply telling you to seek out a witch instead? Though"—the lips curled in a half-smile—"if the stories I hear are true, you are more skilled than most others of your kind."

"Because the one I seek is Colivar," she said.

The smile faded. The energy in the room seemed to shift palpably, taking on a strangely edged quality. Was that just because she was asking one Magister to help her find another— an odd request at the best of times—or was something more going on? She wished she knew him well enough to read him.

"Indeed."

"I have a message for him." She could sense Sulah's power pricking at her mental defenses, searching for additional data, but keeping Magisters out of her brain had become second nature for her by this point.

"And you think that I would know how to contact him . . . why, exactly?"

Because I know you are his ally. Because I heard his words to you on the mountaintop. Because I believe that he trusts you, as much as any Magister can ever trust another. "It was said in Kierdwyn that the two of you had worked together in the past." There had been enough Magisters in Kierdwyn after the Alkali campaign to make that a safe lie. "So I thought I would take a chance and see if you could help."

"Interesting," he mused. "And in return for my playing the part of delivery boy, what do you offer?"

She drew in a deep breath. She'd expected the question, of course. It was actually a very good sign; if he had no interest in helping her he wouldn't be sounding her out on price. But this was dangerous ground. The only thing she really had to offer him was the information she'd gathered for Colivar, and Sulah probably had that already. Or if he didn't, it was because Colivar had chosen not to share it with him, which meant that she shouldn't do so either. She couldn't tell him about Siderea's location because she had a vested interest in Colivar being the first Magister to get there. And she certainly couldn't tell him that she suspected a trap had been set for Colivar in Tefilat. No alliance of Magisters was ever on such solid ground that the temptation to send an ally directly into an enemy's clutches might not outweigh all other interests.

"I have information for Colivar," she said. "Obviously I can't give it to anyone else until I've delivered it. But once that's done, I wouldn't be averse to sharing it with others."

She could sense his mind churning as he considered the offer. "That might not please him."

"Then he does not have to know," she said quietly.

Learn the secrets of another Magister, Sulah. Keep secrets from him in turn. It was powerful bait, and she watched as he considered it.

"You will give me the same report you give to him," he said finally.

She bowed her head. "Of course, Magister Sulah."

They both knew she would not do that. But they also both knew that she must come close to the mark, for fear of being caught in a lie. Sulah might not get every single bit of information she had gathered for Colivar, but he'd get enough of it to make it worth his while.

"Very well." He nodded sharply. "I accept your offer."

He walked over to where a map was laid out on a nearby table. From where she stood she could see that it depicted Anshasa and the lands immediately surrounding it. It was considerably more detailed than the map Ethanus had shown her, and it was labeled in languages familiar to her; she quickly bound a bit of power to fix the image of it in her memory, against future need.

"Colivar isn't here now," Sulah said, "But I expect him to return shortly. I can arrange for you to wait here for him, or I can contact you when he returns."

She bit her lip, wondering how to get more information out of him without giving away too much. "Have you seen him recently?" she dared.

His blue eyes narrowed. For a moment she thought he might try to steal her information directly from her mind, and she braced herself to parry his effort. But it never came. No doubt he was guessing that she was Colivar's servant and was weighing the risk of interfering with another man's property. That might have bothered her once. There was a time when she might even have made some rash statement of independence, just to make it clear that no man owned her. But if recent affairs had not tempered her spirit, they had at least taught her the value of subtlety. If it served her purpose for Sulah to think she was Colivar's servant, then she would not correct him.

"He was here a few days ago," Sulah said. "He went out to gather some information and was going to return after that."

Information on the Souleater queen, Kamala guessed *But then I gave that to him. So he should have returned to you by now.*

Unless the news that there was no queen in Tefilat had made him feel that he could visit there safely, to seek more information on his own.

A cold shiver ran up her spine.

I am too late.

"Then let him know when you see him that I have news for him. Something he'll wish to hear before taking any further action. He'll know how to reach me." It took all of her self control to keep her expression from revealing the depths of her dismay. If Colivar had already gone to Tefilat, then he was exactly where Siderea Aminestas wanted him to be. And Kamala had failed to warn him in time. She wanted to put her fist through the stone wall in frustration, venting her rage at the gods. Maybe if Sulah had not been standing there, she would have done so. As it was, she just took a deep breath, fixed a mask of utter impassivity upon her face, and politely took her leave.

The servant who had brought her to Sulah was waiting outside the chamber door. When he saw her come out, he bowed his head briefly, then turned to lead her back to the main gate. She started to follow him . . . and then realized that there was one more piece of information she needed to have. And she would not get a better opportunity to gather it than this.

It took little effort to warp the servant's mind so that he remembered having led her out of the palace already. The man shook his head in confusion for a moment, then took off in pursuit of his next task. No other morati would be able to see her; her sorcery could see to that. Only a Magister was resistant to such tricks.

Perhaps.

Heart pounding, she tried to still her spirit so that she could focus her mind inward. If Colivar's theory was right, then somewhere deep inside her was the seed of a Souleater's power. Perhaps even a queen's power. Could she awaken it somehow? And what would the cost to her be, if she did?

I may have been drawing upon it unconsciously all along, she reminded herself. *If so, it should be possible to wield it consciously as well. Yes?*

Shutting her eyes, she tried to bring to mind the strange essence of the power that had surrounded the northern queen. Tried to taste once more that armor of invisibility that had shielded the ikati's territory, turning Kamala's attention aside any time she tried to look in the wrong direction. The same kind of power that now guarded the Witch-Queen in Jezalya, albeit less dramatically. It had not proven an insurmountable obstacle to Kamala, but such a power might have a much greater effect upon the males of her kind.

Or so she hoped.

Unexpectedly, memories began to flash through her mind. Disjointed fragments of recall, divorced from context. Her assault on Magister Raven. Her battle with the Souleater. Her midnight passage through the halls of Anukyat's castle, past guards who should have seen her, past wards that should have detected her.

A cold shiver ran down her spine as something dark stirred within her, a sense of alien power that was both terrifying and invigorating. No, she thought defiantly, it was not an alien power. It was her birthright.

Come to me, she whispered mentally, trying to coax the source of that power out of its hiding place. *Lend me your strength. Shield me with your gift.* Then she corrected herself: *Our gift.*

It seemed to her that the sorcerous cocoon she had woven around herself grew warmer then, as if something new had been added to its substance. Or was that only her imagination? Did she want to claim this new power so badly that she was fantasizing changes where none existed?

There was only one way to find out.

Breath held, heart pounding, she reentered Sulah's chamber. He was sitting at his desk, studying the great map, adding notes to it now and then. An inkwell hovered a few inches over the desk, and when he reached out with his quill it positioned itself perfectly beneath his point, so that not a drop of ink was spilled.

He did not appear to notice her return.

She watched him for a while, then took a step into the room. Then another.

He still did not acknowledge her presence.

Step by step she moved closer to him, until she was squarely within his line of vision. All he had to do was look up, and he would see her. She found herself trembling as she waited for that to happen. Imagining how terrible his rage would be, once he detected the invasion.

But he detected nothing. Time and time again he dipped his pen in the ink and added notes to the map as if there were no one else in the room.

You can't sneak up on a Magister, Ethanus had taught her. *The very spell that makes you invisible to morati eyes reveals your presence to us, and no trick of sorcery can make it otherwise. A Magister may not be able to see your face, or even know exactly where you're standing, but if you get close enough to him he'll sense the nearness of your sorcery. Such a thing cannot be hidden.*

A sudden noise from somewhere outside the chamber startled Kamala. Before she could move out of the way Sulah looked up. Panic surged in her gut as she realized she was standing directly between him and the doorway, but it was too late to correct the situation.

The clear blue eyes turned her way, and for a moment it seemed he was looking directly at her. Then the spell supporting his inkwell seemed to falter, and he turned his attention to reinforcing it. By the time he was done with that, the disturbance outside the door had ceased, and he went back to his work as if nothing untoward had happened.

He had not seen her.

He had not seen her!

Legs trembling, she backed away, then turned and hurriedly

left the chamber. Servants in the hall beyond moved out of her way without even realizing they were doing so, in response to the spell that now protected her. Magisters would do so as well, she realized. Colivar had been right about what she was, which meant that Siderea's own arsenal was now at her fingertips. She just had to figure out how to use it.

Colivar.

He had gone to Tefilat. Alone. She knew that with utter certainty, as surely as she knew that the sun would rise in the morning. He had walked straight into Siderea's trap. And she, Kamala, had played a part in sending him there. As had Sulah. They all had danced to the Witch-Queen's tune without even knowing it.

Anger welled up inside her, along with a terrible guilt. The latter was an alien, sickening emotion, even more powerful than the remorse she had felt at Rhys' funeral. What had happened to the fierce young whore who once made no apologies to anyone, offered no regrets for anything, and accepted the consequences of her actions as the necessary price of independence? The closer she got to other people, the more she seemed to lose sight of her.

Colivar.

There were reasons to want him alive, she told herself. He was ancient enough that his word was respected, and powerful enough that he did not need to fear the displeasure of any other Magister. And he had hinted that he might help her untangle herself from the mess she had gotten herself into with Raven's murder. Losing that kind of assistance was no small thing. So if she wanted to keep him alive, it was for purely practical reasons. Guilt had nothing to do with it.

No one noticed her leaving the palace. Why should they? A

single bird, rising up from an empty balcony into the morning sky, was of no interest to anyone. Eyes turned away from her without knowing why. Sorcerous defenses let her pass without a ripple of awareness. Sulah remained focused on his map, and all the things that normally took place in a royal palace continued to take place, as normal.

Sunlight warming her wings, heart cold with dread, Kamala turned toward Tefilat.

CHAPTER 23

TEFILAT WAS dry. Dry in a way that sucked all the moisture out of one's flesh, making every cell in one's body scream out for water. It seemed to Kamala that she could feel her skin aging as she stood there, and though she had dressed lightly for the trip, allowing for the desert heat, she now added a long, loose robe to her ensemble, to protect her from the worst of the blazing sun.

Surely only madmen would choose to live in such a place.

She scouted the ancient city in the form of a bird at first, then as a lizard, scuttling over the red earth, freezing whenever she caught sight of any motion. Despite her experiment with Sulah she was loath to trust too much to the strange power of the ikati queen, lest she make careless assumptions about its parameters.

But when a bird of prey passed overhead and did not even glance down at her lizardlike body, she felt a tingle of triumph. Was it possible that no creature could see her at all? Not Magisters, not morati? It was a heady concept.

Stay focused, she told herself. *You have a job to do here.*

She could just barely make out Colivar's trail across the canyon floor. It was a faint trail, as befitted a Magister who habitually took great care to erase all signs of his passage. But one could never erase such traces completely. By now she had interacted with him often enough (intimately enough?) that she was able to pick out the faint traces of his resonance, untangling them from all the other traces that clung to the place, and from the random sparks of power that buzzed about the place like frenzied horseflies.

She could see where he had entered the central plaza, where he had stood for a while, no doubt studying his surroundings. And she could see where his trail led up a short flight of stairs, into the most opulent structure facing the plaza. There were traces of sorcery hanging about the building's façade that appeared to be his, perhaps a ward of some kind. She considered for a moment whether or not she wanted to disturb it—a spell that was primed to deliver information to him might be the fastest way to locate him—but she decided upon a more cautious approach. This whole place made her skin crawl as it was; she didn't want to disturb it any more than she had to.

Of Colivar himself there was no sign. None. The traces of his passage were cold, dead things, that seemed to have no living source. If he had been taken somewhere far away, would they look like that? She had never attempted to track a Magister in this manner before, so she did not know. Ethanus' lessons had not included such things.

He is not dead, she thought stubbornly. *I need him too much for him to be dead.*

Wary of disturbing the main entrance, she changed back into lizard form and scuttled up the wall. It took considerable effort, and her skin itched when the change was done, as if she had not done it quite right. But it was worth the effort. Anyone watching for a Magister's arrival at the upper level would probably be watching for winged creatures, as that was the form sorcerers habitually used for travel. A sandstone-colored lizard would hardly be noticed. And then there was Kamala's unique sorcery. If the power of the ikati queen could turn living eyes away from her, could it cause sorcery to look past her presence as well? There were so many questions she needed answers for, but she had no one to help her answer them. She was a brand new creature with unknown, unnamed powers, and only by trial and error would she learn what her limits were.

She clung to the wall of the canyon for a good while, looking the place over with her sorcery. From up here it was easier to get a fix on things, and at last she felt satisfied that she was genuinely alone.

Which was not a good thing, since there was someone she wanted to find.

With a brief check for wards at the upper windows (there were none), she slipped inside the building and reclaimed her human form. The room she was in was dusty, with a fine reddish grit that had drifted into dunes along the walls. No footprints were visible, nor any other sign of recent passage. But that meant very little, she knew. She was using sorcery to smooth the dust behind her own passage, so that she left no footprints of her own; someone else could have done the same.

Carefully she made her way through the upper chambers, room by room, searching for . . . what? What kind of clue did you look for when a Magister had disappeared? There was nothing of interest on the upper level. On the lower level she picked up Colivar's trace once more. He had walked through this place under his own power, it seemed. That was a good sign, at least. She followed his trail into a room filled with furniture and supplies, but it did not appear that he had touched anything, nor was there a residue of his sorcery anywhere that she could detect. None of these objects had mattered to him.

They did not matter to her.

Deeper she went into the complex, scratching marks into the walls as she went so she could find her way back later, not wanting to use any more sorcery than she had to in this place. She did have to conjure light for herself once she left the front chambers, but she kept it to a minimum, and she bound it to her own body so that no traces of it would be left behind. She wanted to leave as little of her own resonance in this place as possible.

You won't find him here, she told herself. *At best, maybe you'll find some clue that tells you where to look for him next. If that.*

At last she came to what looked like a dead end. The tunnel she had been following terminated in a small chamber whose far wall had collapsed, leaving a steep slope of rubble blocking the way. Colivar's trail headed straight toward the slope and then seemed to pass underneath it. Had the way been open when Colivar came through here? Might he have gotten trapped in a surprise rockfall? That would be an ignominious end for a Magister, she thought soberly. It was also a humbling reminder that for all their power, sorcerers could be as fragile as the morati if they were surprised. Sorcery took time and concentration to muster, and if you did not have enough time, or failed to concentrate properly, then the most complex and powerful of defenses were meaningless. You would die just as Kostas had died, the night that Gwynofar cut his head off.

She stared in frustration at the rubble, trying to decide what to do next. Obviously the obstruction was too massive for her to clear out by purely physical means. But shifting or banishing that much mass would require considerable sorcery, and she was loath to throw power around on that scale until she knew exactly what had happened here. Perhaps if she reached into the rubble with her senses and simply looked for a dead body, she could at least determine if Colivar had met his end here. That at least would be something.

She had just began to gather her sorcery in preparation for the effort when she caught sight of something glinting amidst the rocks. Reaching down, she pulled loose a small metal object.

A silver ring.

She brushed the dirt from it so that she could make it out more clearly. And a shudder ran up her spine as she recognized it. Colivar had worn this ring the day they'd had their picnic. She closed her hand over it, pressing it into her palm, and trembled slightly. What would she do if he were really gone? she asked herself. Who would guide her through the maze of Magister politics then?

"So many guests." The voice came from behind her. "I should have put out refreshments."

Kamala whipped about, summoning power even as she did so. Or trying to. But her legs seemed strangely numb, and they would not obey her; she fell heavily to her knees, banging them painfully against rough stone floor. Her power slipped from her grasp even as she struggled to control it. Her head and heart pounded wildly. The room began to spin about her. The ring dropped from her hand.

"I did not expect a woman," the voice mused.

Before her stood a figure dressed in black. Magister black. His face was shadowed by a deep hood, but his voice sounded strangely familiar. She tried to focus her mind enough to identify it but could not. The whole of her past history was becoming a blur now, and trying to summon specific memories was impossible. All she knew was that her hand burned where Colivar's ring had been pressed into it, and it seemed to her she could feel the venom it had carried seeping through her skin and into her bloodstream.

How could she have been so foolish?

She looked up at the figure and tried to mouth words. A question, perhaps. Or a curse. But she had forgotten how to speak, and the only sound that came out was a muffled cry. Then a thick, choking fog began to wrap itself around her, layer by layer, and try as she might she could not banish it.

"Don't fight the effect," the Magister told her. "It will only make it hurt more."

It was the last thing she heard.

Chapter 24

"SALVATOR AURELIUS, son of Danton Aurelius, High King, Priest Emeritus, Scion of the One True Church."

The words echoed from the vaulted ceiling high overhead, resonating along the sweeping stone arches of the sanctuary. Tall, narrow windows capped with stained glass sent shafts of light streaming across the polished stone floor, alternating with bands of knife-edged shadow. Nine throne-like chairs on a raised platform were arranged in a U shape facing the entrance, four on each side and one at the far end. Each man seated along the sides wore a long robe and a stiffened cap of deep crimson wool, with the narrow bands of a priest's stola flanking the medallion of the Primus Council on his chest. The one woman among them was dressed identically, her small frame the only overt indication of her sex. Beyond the question of clothing, the variance among them was striking. Salvator recognized the black-skinned Primus Naga, broadshouldered and solid as a rock; milk-pale Primus Argentus, his hair like spun gold; and ruddy-faced Primus Pisaro, slit-eyed and pockmarked. Salvator did not recognize the others, but it was clear from their appearance that they had come from every corner of the earth. A rare and impressive gathering, indeed.

The man who was speaking stood at the end of the room. Primus Soltan was a tall man, physically impressive even without his formal robes, doubly intimidating with them. His voice was strong and solemn, and authority echoed in its depths. Salvator had met him twice before, once when he had first been anointed as Priest, later at his coronation. The man had impressed him, and that was saying a lot; the son of Danton Aurelius was not easily impressed.

In front of Soltan a young woman knelt, her head bowed, hands covering her face. A witch no doubt, who had offered to sacrifice a portion of her life to serve the Council in this meeting. Most likely she was maintaining a channel of mental communication among the primi, so they could confer secretly while Salvator stood in front of them. But that was only a guess.

"You have called us from the four corners of the earth," Soltan pronounced. His tone was solemn, with just a hint of challenge in its depths. "A long journey for some, and in several cases a costly one. Now we are here, to attend upon the words of the Penitent High King. What business do you have for us that merits such a meeting?"

The formality of the challenge made Salvator glad that he had worn his most impressive costume to the meeting. He had toyed with the idea of coming here in a simple gown, unadorned, a statement of his continuing humility before God. But Gwynofar had quashed that idea as soon as she'd heard it, and he trusted her instincts in this sort of thing. Danton would have been proud of him now, standing there in his royal gown of black-and-gold damask, the double-headed Aurelius eagle resplendent upon his chest. The fact that the silken grandeur of his outfit was in stark contrast to the three ragged Souleater scars running across his face lent those wounds additional power.

Look like a High King, his mother had said, *and they will treat you like a High King.* She was right, as always. Gwynofar Aurelius, costumier to kings.

"Esteemed Primi." He bowed his head respectfully, but not too deeply. There was no established protocol for determining the balance of authority between a High King and his primus, and therefore no precedent to guide them. He must give this man the respect he was due without offering undue submission. It was a delicate dance.

The fact that these foreign primi had answered his summons at all was a vast concession to his power. Somewhere down the line he knew that he was going to have to pay for that.

Once we were brothers in faith, he thought. *Now we are rivals in politics.*

"Fellow servants of the Creator," he said, "I thank you for receiving me. On this day, the Church and the High Kingdom are bound together in the spirit of faith and common purpose. May the Creator look favorably upon my words, offered in humble service to His will." He could see the lips of several primi moving silently, and he could almost hear the unvoiced benediction: *Amen.*

"Earlier this summer, as your Eminences know, the ancient barrier in the northlands was breached, and a colony of Souleaters entered the human kingdoms. Though Penitents and pagans alike were braced for battle with them, ready to die if necessary in defense of the human kingdoms, the creatures did not attack immediately. Rather, they disappeared into the mists, to gather their strength in solitude, preparing for a greater campaign.

"The Church has now given its blessing to our battle against these creatures." He nodded briefly to the primi, acknowledging their spiritual authority. "I have been at the forefront of the effort to locate them and to gather the information needed to cast them into the Destroyer's Pit forever. For as God has sent these creatures forth to test mankind, so shall He receive them when that test is completed, that they may roast in the fires of eternal torment until the universe itself expires.

"You all know of the recent battle in my lands, which destroyed the northern queen, and I have delivered to you the information that we gathered on that day. Today I bring you more information . . . and a request."

He could see one of Soltan's eyebrows rise slightly. How many thought-whispers were buzzing about him now, carried on the wings of witchery? Each one was costing a precious second of that witch's life. Secrecy through sacrifice.

"Those who know the creatures best have been convinced to share their knowledge," Salvator continued. "Those with access to artifacts of power have opened their gates to us. Those with the power to find these creatures will surely do so soon, and we must be prepared to act as soon as they succeed.

"There is but one Souleater queen remaining. If she is killed, the entire species can be eradicated. But as soon as she lays eggs and creates more queens, that opportunity will be gone forever. Then a second Dark Ages will truly be upon us. We cannot allow that to happen.

"Our timetable is short, as war is measured. My sources estimate that in half a year the new queen will be mature and ready to mate. Possibly earlier. The season of war is brief in some lands, constrained by storms or snow. Depending upon where the Souleaters are, we may only have a small window of opportunity in which to act, if military action is needed. And

I believe it will be. The young queen is said to be allied to Siderea Aminestas"—he could see a flicker of distaste on several faces as he mentioned the name—"and she is a savvy and powerful woman, who may have nearly unlimited witchery at her disposal. Wherever she is, it will surely take more than a handful of Guardians to defeat her." He paused. "It may take an army.

"Time will be required to muster such an army, and to transport troops and supplies without sorcery." He stressed the last two words slightly; they were both a promise to pursue this war in keeping with Penitent beliefs and a reminder to them all that Penitent beliefs were an impediment to military efficacy. "I believe we should begin preparations now, so that when our enemy is finally located, we will be ready to move into action immediately.

"Your Eminences: I am Penitent. I am *lyr*. I am High King. In me, faith and blood and political power are combined. Who should lead such a campaign, if not me? Who else in the Church could play such a role properly, so that in the aftermath of battle men would understand that it was not the hand of man alone that saved them, but the mercy of the Creator?

"This battle will not only save the world, but it will change it. We will not only safeguard the Second Age of Kings, but we will turn it back to penitence and faith. Surely that is what God intended when He sent His demons back into the world to test us."

He drew in a deep breath. The expressions of the primi betrayed no emotion, but one could sense the intensity with which they were listening to his every word.

"I come here today," he said, "to ask for your support. I need the facilities of the Church behind me. I ask for the support of our witches, and any of our warriors who have special skills pertaining to the Souleaters. The armies of Aurelius are vast, but my soldiers are merely men, and mere men cannot fight these creatures. And I will need supplies. Not because food and water can't be conjured on the battlefield, but if we mean to wage this war without relying upon Magisters, the cost of that would be measured in human lives. Penitent lives." He paused. "And I will need these things immediately, so that all our people can be properly trained, and so they will all be in one place when the time comes to move out, and thus can be mobilized expeditiously."

His presentation concluded, Salvator waited for a response.

A brief eternity passed in which the primus just stared at him. His dark eyes, narrowed in concentration, offered no hint as to what was going on inside his mind. Salvator said nothing, merely continued to wait.

Finally Soltan said, "Let me make sure I understand this properly. You're asking for all the faithful who are skilled in witchery to come to your side, and to place themselves beneath your command. *All* our witches, from all corners of the earth, wherever they may be found. Our most skilled warriors should come to you also, to be trained by your people. Presumably to fight alongside the pagans of the north, yes?

"All this for a battle in which you do not know where the fighting will take place, or even when. You don't know what the size or makeup of the enemy army will be, the kind of terrain you will be fighting on, or even how many soldiers—or witches—you will need. In fact, outside of knowing there is one Souleater you have to kill, and probably a witch who will be guarding her, you do not have a single fact on hand about who or what you'll be facing." He raised an eyebrow. "Do I have that right, your Majesty?"

"That's the gist of the matter," Salvator agreed. "Though I do think we should specify that only witches who are willing to die for the cause should be recruited. That will help keep the numbers manageable."

The primus sat down on the throne-like chair behind him. For a moment his eyes disengaged from Salvator's, and they seemed to focus on a point beyond the confines of the sanctuary. The witch moaned softly, rocking back and forth.

After what seemed like an endless wait, Soltan's eyes fixed once more on Salvator. Cold, so very cold. There was no affection in that gaze.

"Will there be Magisters involved in this war of yours?" he asked.

Salvator stiffened. "There will be no sorcery in my campaign."

"But they will be present."

"No man can bar them from the battlefield, Eminence."

"They do not acknowledge your authority."

"They do not acknowledge anyone's authority."

"And the one that is in your palace? What of him?"

Salvator's eyes narrowed. "He is not my Magister Royal, if that's what you're asking."

"But he serves you."

"No. He counsels my mother on matters of ancient lore. His sorcery is forbidden in my house."

"But his *corruption* is not forbidden." The primus stood, his cold gaze fixed on Salvator. "Ramirus' very presence is corrupt. His counsel is corrupt. You come to us asking to be made a figurehead of our faith—to wield our sacred authority in addition to your own—but you can't even maintain spiritual balance in your own house." He stepped down from the dais and walked toward Salvator; his expression was dark. "Who will answer for the corruption of this Magister, Salvator Aurelius? Have you offered penance for Ramirus, so that the blackness of his soul does not befoul the souls of all who would trust in your leadership?"

Lips tight, Salvator reached up to the neck of his damask gown with both hands, grabbing hold of the stiffened collar as well as the linen shirt beneath it. With a quick jerking motion, he then ripped them both open. The buttons of the gown went flying, and the shirt gave way with a sharp tearing sound, strands of linen stretching across his torso before they finally snapped. And then his chest was laid bare for all to see, along with the Penitent sigil that had been seared into it. Angry red flesh marked where a heated brand had been driven into his flesh; the wound was recent, and its edges looked raw and painful.

"This is my penance for Ramirus," he declared defiantly. "And for my own sin, in allowing him into my house." He looked about the chamber, meeting the eyes of the primi one by one, daring them to question his sacrifice. "And I will do penance for all the others as well, if I must. Bring me a thousand Magisters! I will kneel before God and beg Him to lay the sins of each and every one upon my shoulders, that I might offer up penance for all of them." He turned back to Soldan. "Well, Primus Soldan? Am I worthy to lead God's faithful into battle? Or do I still fall short?"

For a moment there was silence in the chamber. True silence. The witch had stopped her rocking, and Salvator sensed that the primi were no longer communicating with one another mentally. All attention was on him.

Slowly he released the edges of his gown. The garment fell partly closed, but the edges did not come together entirely, and a thin line of reddened skin could still be seen. He did not move to cover it up.

"Danton Aurelius had the spark of greatness in him," Primus Soldan said quietly, "but he was constrained by his personal ambition. A man cannot reach his full potential until he submits to a cause greater than his personal glory." His eyes met Salvator's. "You have that same spark in you, King Salvator. And because you are willing to surrender yourself to God, then yes, you are worthy to lead men in His name."

He held out his hand toward Salvator. On his forefinger was a ring of carved ruby with the sigil of the Church etched into its surface. It was clear what he expected. In the monastery such obeisance would have been frowned upon, but Salvator knew that outside those walls it was common practice. The primi were the highest authority in his Church, God's spokesmen on earth. Formal acknowledgment of their authority was seen as a gesture of submission to God's will.

But he was a king now. Submitting himself to the Church's authority in this way had new implications.

The primus waited.

There was no past history to guide him here. No Penitent had ever wielded secular power on the scale that he did. Whatever happened between him and Soltan would stand as precedent for every king who came after him.

You knew there would be a price to pay when you called them here, he told himself. *He submitted himself to your authority when he answered that call. Did you think that would go unchallenged? You cannot deny him now.*

Slowly Salvator reached out to take the primus' hand in his own. He stared at the man for a small eternity and slowly, formally, lowered his head. His ritual kiss barely brushed the ring, but the carved ruby burned his lips like a hot brand. If he looked in the mirror now, would he see the sigil of the Primus Council seared into his flesh?

When he raised his head up again, the primus nodded solemnly. "The Church will give you what you need." He put a hand on Salvator's shoulder and squeezed it gently; coming from such a formal man, it was a disarmingly intimate gesture. "May the Creator look with favor upon your cause."

Not my cause, Salvator thought. *Ours.* But he simply whispered "Amen" and watched in silence as the primi filed out of the chamber.

CHAPTER 25

DARKNESS.
  Throbbing heat.
Struggling toward the surface of a black sea. Black mirror surface, unbreakable. Suffocation. No air to scream.
Must breathe. Must think. Must breathe. Must breathe.
Pain.
Body out there somewhere. Must find it. Reconnect. Reconnect . . .
After an eternity of failed efforts, Kamala finally opened her eyes. The darkness that surrounded her was thick and hot, but a trickle of light coming from somewhere at least confirmed that her eyes were really open. It seemed nothing short of a miracle.
Where was she?
She tried to move, but could not. A limb trembled somewhere in the distance, but she wasn't sure which one. Sweat trickled down her inner thigh. Otherwise, her body would not obey her.
What had happened?

She tried to draw upon her athra, to craft a spell that would help her comprehend her situation, but the mere effort sent pain lancing through her head, and the light began to spin around her. Bile welled up suddenly in the back of throat. She tried to bend over to vomit, but she found that she could not move, so she had to fight back the nauseating wave lest she choke on it.

Finally, after what seemed like an eternity, the sickness receded a bit, and the light grew more steady. It was not a real light at all, she realized; she was seeing the residual power in this place, made visible by her Sight. Whispers of forgotten spells too subtle to notice in the full light of day became visible in such darkness, and also told her where she was. Still in Tefilat, apparently.

She was not sure if that was a good thing or a bad thing.

What in the name of all the gods had happened to her?

Shutting her eyes, she tried once more to summon forth sorcery. But the power slid from her mental grasp like a hagfish in slime. It was as if her very mind had become incapable of organizing anything more complex than a simple thought. Sorcery required much more than that.

She was hungry, she realized. And thirsty. And her arms hurt. A lot.

She dreamed of a woman chained by her wrists, suspended naked from a ceiling high above. Her wrists were covered in blood from where the iron shackles had cut into them. She was hung with her toes barely touching the ground, so that if she strained with all her might she might be able to shift enough weight to take some of the pressure off her arms. At least for a few minutes. But the effort was exhausting, and she couldn't keep it up for long.

Or maybe it wasn't a dream. Maybe it was something worse.

———

The bird flies over the canyon, unsteadily at first, then with increasing confidence. At the outskirts of the city it lands on a ledge high up the canyon wall, out of sight of the city below. Placing a small talisman by a crack in the rock, it uses its beak to push it in, until only the edge of it is visible.

It cocks its head for a moment, as its tiny brain tries to process what it has just done. Surely the shiny talisman would look better adorning its nest than it does in this desolate place. But the thought is only a fleeting one, and after a moment the sorcery that is controlling it wins out. Leaving the talisman behind, it heads out across the desert once more, to pick up its next assignment.

———

The shadows withdrew slowly, painfully. Kamala was more aware of her surroundings now. Also more aware of pain. Her arms felt as if they had been jerked out of their sockets. She struggled to reach the ground with her toes and push up, to relieve some of the pressure on her arms. Blood from her wrists was trickling all the way down to her shoulders now, mixing with the sweat that slicked her body. The chamber was hot. So hot. She could smell her own fear.

"The secret is that it must work quickly, of course."

Startled by a voice that came suddenly from behind her, she lost her balance for a moment. Pain lanced through her arms as she struggled to get her footing once more. Once she accomplished that, she tried to crane her head back to see where the voice was coming from, but her strained neck muscles spasmed from the effort, and she had to face forward again.

"A Magister can cleanse his body of any drug, and needs only a moment to do so. So a drug meant for a Magister can have no warning signs. It must do its job the first moment that it becomes active, or else it is useless."

A figure in black robes walked around her. Magisterial black. It took up a position in front of her, then raised up its head so that the dim light shone upon its face.

Lazaroth.

"I tested it on myself," he said. "Very unpleasant, but you can't trust other people for things like that." He walked up to Kamala, until he was so close that she could feel his breath on her face; with the shackles raising her up high, her face was level with his own. "Do you find it . . . effective?"

Her mouth was so dry she could barely get the word out. "Why?"

He put a hand to her cheek and stroked it gently. The motion mocked that of a lover, but his expression was cold and cruel. "Because you invaded my territory. Because you spoiled my game. I do not take such offenses lightly, Kamala."

"Tefilat is . . . yours?" A thin rivulet of sweat began to trickle down between her breasts, making her acutely aware of her nakedness. Such a thing had never bothered her before, but somehow, in front of this man—this Magister—she felt ashamed.

"I did not mean Tefilat," Lazaroth said.

She struggled to make some sense of that, but the act of trying to think made her head pound. "Kierdwyn? Or . . . something else?"

He did not answer her. Instead he ran his hand down her body, fingers sliding along her sweat-slicked skin, from her throat down to her breast and then to her stomach, feeling the curves of her form as if she were some curious statue. She tried to draw back from him, but the chains would not allow it. She wanted to kick out at him, but she knew she did not have the balance or the strength necessary to make the blow meaningful. And it would just make the situation worse if she did. Right now there was still a chance, however slim, that she could talk her way out of this situation. The minute she spat in his face there would not be.

"I could smell the sorcery on you," he murmured. "The others couldn't, but I could. Fools! They were so convinced a female Magister couldn't exist, they failed to see what was right in front of their faces." He looked into her eyes; something in the depths of his gaze chilled her to her very core. "Never looking deeper than the surface," he whispered. "Never asking the questions that need to be asked."

Kamala's mouth was so dry it was hard to form words. "If I had known you didn't want me in Kierdwyn, I wouldn't have gone there."

A strange, dark smile flickered across his face. "Ah, Kamala. Do you think that's what this is about? Or perhaps I should say . . . do you think that's *all* this is about?" He shook his head and made a tsk-tsk noise. "Like the others, you can't see what's right in front of your face. A pity. I expected more of you."

He glanced to one side and the light in the room grew brighter. "Your lover is all wrapped up neatly and ready for delivery. He would have been in Queen Siderea's hands by now if I could transport him safely from here. As it is, someone is being sent to come get him. No doubt he will find the ride . . . interesting." He shook his head. "You would never have found him, Kamala. No sorcerer can find him now, nor can they free him. Siderea wove a trap out of the substance of his own body, and there's no force on earth that can banish it without destroying him in the process."

"You're working with her? With the Souleaters?" Kamala blinked. "Why?"

Again the chilling smile. Lazaroth said nothing, but he walked slowly around her. She twisted her head to watch him until it hurt too much to do so, then faced forward once more. Listening with dread as he came up behind her, feeling the cloth of his robes brush against her from the rear, praying to gods that she had abandoned long ago.

His hand slid forward over her hip, serpent-like, seeking the place where her legs parted. She tried to jerk away, but that only pressed her more closely against him.

"A female Magister." He whispered the words into her ear, his breath hot against the side of her face. "What does that mean? Is *female* a quality of the flesh or of the spirit? If you alter one of those, does the other change also?" His fingers sought out the most sensitive parts of her flesh, and he stroked them roughly, brutally, a mockery of pleasure. "Does it mean to be weak?" he whispered fiercely. She gritted her teeth, refusing to give him the satisfaction of a response. *I have survived worse than this*, she told herself. A cold and terrible comfort.

And then, without warning, pleasure exploded in her loins. A false heat conjured by sorcery raced through her veins, causing her body to respond as if to a lover's touch. No! she thought, struggling to resist the tide of unnatural pleasure, horrified by the thought of responding to his abusive touch. *I will not allow this!* But his sorcery had taken control of her flesh, and she had no choice but to respond. His hand reached up to cup one arely process what she

His voice had been appearance.

k in. "Others . . .

an? Who have order to call y guard their what you're u compre-

ters," she

pain, and she felt a

ing against him

uggling to

while wave

ging tears of

r shackles, grateful

se it would disguise

oment, then took hold

x, hard enough that her

ackles, drawing fresh blood.

e paused for a moment, then

's tone, "What makes you think you are the a?" He paused. "Or even that you are the first?"

Slowly he walked and her, until he stood in her full view once more. "What m kes you so sure there are no other women who have the power? Who have taken on men's bodies, perhaps, and who live men's lives in order to be able to wield their power openly? Abandoning the identity that nature provided them, to claim the one that men control?"

Reaching up his hands to the collar of his robe, he jerked it open. Beneath it he was naked. His body was hard and lean, with a thin line of black hair leading down his chest to the thick patch of curls at his loins. Then, as Kamala watched in fascinated horror, his male parts shrank and disappeared. The hair on his chest faded. His body grew soft and took on curves. Breasts with dark nipples swelled to fullness on his chest, while his face . . . that hardly changed at all. The hair grew longer, the jawline perhaps a bit narrower, but the eyes remained the same. Hard and cold.

Numbed by the drugs, Kamala could b[...]
was seeing. "You are . . . a woman?"

"So it would appear," Lazaroth said. [...]
altered as well—*her* voice—to suit her new [...]

The shock of it was just beginning to sin[...]
are there others?"

"Other women who have the power, you m[...]
taken on men's bodies and lived men's lives i[...]
themselves Magisters? There may be. But if so, th[...]
secret closely. There is no 'secret sisterhood,' if that'[...]
asking." The dark eyes narrowed. "Now, perhaps, y[...]
hend my politics."

Kamala shook her head. "Siderea hates all Magis[...]
whispered.

"She hates the ones who betrayed her. The ones who played
at being her lovers while using her like a cheap whore, and then
left her to die when her usefulness expired." The black eyes
glittered dangerously. "Don't you think they deserve to die for
that, Kamala? Wouldn't you hate them if they did that to you?"

The room spun about her head. It was all too much to absorb.
"Why me?" she gasped. "I'm not your enemy."

Lazaroth's expression darkened. "Aside from the fact that you
invaded my territory? Threatened my masquerade? Wound up
on the wrong side of a war that I'm committed to winning?"

She walked up to Kamala and took her face in one hand.
Her fingernails had become long and sharp, and they dug into
her cheek hard enough to draw blood.

"I have spent three hundred years living a lie. Three hundred
years! Not by choice, but because that's what I had to do to
become a Magister. And then you come along, strutting your
wares like a cat in heat, proclaiming to one and all that the

sacred, immutable laws of our brotherhood have never been more than a crock of shit. *Three hundred years, Kamala!* What is my lie worth now? My sacrifice? I buried my true identity so deeply that it would take another three centuries to dig it out. What did I do that for?"

Her body began to transform once more: thickening, lengthening, sprouting hair. His voice dropped in pitch with each word. "Would it have been so very hard for you to do the same?" he demanded. "Make yourself a cock, put on a bit of beard stubble, and no man need be the wiser. It's not hard to do. The structure of the thing is simple enough." He gestured down at his own emerging organ. "But no, it's far more important that you strut like a whore among these men. Shattering the masquerade that protects us all. Very well, then," he growled. "Play the whore, Kamala. I will help you."

He grabbed her arm and spun her around, yanking her hard against her chains. Pain shot through her arms, and the room began to spin about her as he grabbed her by the hips and pulled her back against him, hard.

"So how do you want it?" he whispered in her ear. A lover's tone. "With pleasure? With pain? Because I can go either way, Kamala."

"Fuck you," she whispered.

"All right, then." She could feel him nod. "Pain it is."

Shadows shrink along the canyon floor as the sun rises higher into the heavens, until only a thin line of darkness lies at the foot of the eastern wall. And then that too is gone. The sun is directly overhead now, and golden light floods down into the canyon, banishing all but the most tenacious shadows.

In a shallow crevice, the polished edge of a golden talisman catches the sunlight at last. Power sparks to life, shimmering about the precious metal. Drawing substance from the sunlight, it expands out into the canyon. Strands of power, bound to an unnamed purpose.

In another shallow crevice, another talisman activates.

And another.

And another.

The strands begin to weave complex patterns about Tefilat, a webwork of power that no human eye can see. Sometimes a strand will falter as it encounters the turbulent currents of Tefilat, but for each one that fails, another takes its place. A gleaming tapestry of power is being woven, its patterns as fine as lacework, its design drawn from a hundred ancient cultures. A scholar of sorcery might read meaning into its patterning if he studied it long enough, but interpretation would not come quickly. Perhaps he might even figure out what it was meant to do, if he worked at it hard enough. And long enough. And concentrated on nothing else . . .

———

Footsteps. Steady but rapid. Lazaroth returning? Kamala tried not to cringe at the thought.

Light flooded the room as the door opened, seemingly from all directions at once. After the hours she had spent in near-darkness—perhaps days?—it was blinding. She squeezed her eyes shut, but she could not block out the light entirely. Spots of fire danced behind her lids.

She trembled as she heard footsteps approach her. Hating herself for her weakness, and for letting that weakness show. But exhaustion had finally broken down the barriers that physical abuse alone could not. She would have sold her soul to a demon for a chance to lie down and sleep. Just for an hour.

"Well. This situation becomes more interesting by the moment."

The voice was startling in its familiarity. Opening her eyes, she squinted against the light, trying to bring the figure before her into focus.

Ramirus.

He was dressed in a manner she had never seen before, in a jacket and breeches not unlike Colivar's usual attire. His white beard no longer flowed down to his waist but had been clipped closer to his face. The style drew focus to his eyes, which seemed a darker blue than usual. Or perhaps she was hallucinating. Perhaps his beard and clothing were all normal, and her feverish mind could no longer process reality.

Or perhaps it was not him at all.

He looked her up and down, taking in all the details of her condition with the impersonal interest of a surgeon, then reached up to her shackles, summoning sorcery as he did so. It took a moment for him to get the power to do what he wanted, but then the iron bonds shattered in his hands, and she was free. Her legs collapsed beneath her, and she crumpled to the floor like a broken doll. For a moment she just lay there, stunned, barely able to process what was happening to her. Was this real, or was she dreaming?

Ramirus crouched down by her side, looking at the broken bits of iron in his hand with curiosity. "These are not magical. How did they hold you?"

From somewhere she managed to muster a voice. "Some kind of drug. Can't think straight. Can't conjure."

"Ah. Clever." He leaned back on his heels. "Well, I can fix that easily enough. But you will have to let me past your defenses for that. Assuming, that is, you have any defenses left."

The full magnitude of what he was suggesting took a moment to sink in. When it did, she shuddered. If she agreed to such a thing, she would have no way to protect herself. All the secrets she had guarded so carefully since the night of her First Transition would be laid bare for his inspection, if he chose to seek them out.

"Time is short," he pointed out. "The alternative is my leaving you here to fend for yourself. Frankly, I'd rather have you fully functional, as I could use some assistance, but I haven't time to play nursemaid. So what is your answer?"

It cannot be worse than what Lazaroth did to me.

She nodded.

She could feel his power enter her, tentatively—respectfully—then with greater confidence as he saw there was indeed no resistance. She struggled to lock away the memories of her recent violation so that he would not find them, knowing even as she did so that the effort was a futile one. But she had to try. Then fire took root in her veins, a sorcerous flame whose purpose was to seek out one special fuel and consume it: Lazaroth's drug. Shutting her eyes, Kamala trembled as it burned through her body, invading every muscle, every internal organ.. Perhaps it went on for a few seconds longer than it should have. Perhaps under cover of healing Ramirus used a more subtle sorcery on her as well, searching for hidden knowledge in her mind. There was no way for her to know.

Finally the fire subsided. For the first time since she had been struck down, Kamala found she could think clearly. Tentatively she bound a bit of power to heal the bloody mess the shackles had made of her arms, and to restore the rest of her body to full functioning. It was difficult for her to bind her athra properly, but there was no way to know whether that was the result of her weakened condition or of Tefilat's malevolent influence. The sweat on her body was banished, along with other fluids too foul to mention. The psychic foulness of Lazaroth's touch would be harder to get rid of.

She looked up at Ramirus, and found him gazing at her with the kind of intensity that a hawk reserved for its prey.

"You will want to call in your favor now." He said it quietly, but there was no mistaking his meaning.

How much did he know about her? He would have known the truth of what she was as soon as he made contact with her soulfire, but had he learned about the murder of Raven from her mind as well? Or was that something he had always suspected and had just needed to confirm? Either way, it was clear from his expression that he knew there was a price on her head.

"Protect my life," she said.

His eyes narrowed. "Here and now. You haven't paid me enough to ask for more than that."

She nodded.

With a brusque nod he stood and offered her his hand. As she rose to her feet, some clothing appeared on her body, a reasonable simulacrum of what she had worn in Kierdwyn. Evidently he had seen how she was struggling to control her power and decided to take care of that himself.

"Where is Colivar?" he asked her.

She shook her head. "I don't know. Lazaroth said he was here but that no one—"

"Lazaroth?" The look of naked surprise on his face was unmistakable. *"Lazaroth?"*

So. Apparently he had not claimed all her secrets. "He's allied to Siderea. He said he was holding Colivar until her people got here."

"Son of a bitch," he muttered.

She looked at him curiously. "How did you get to me without going through him?"

"I conjured a complicated distraction to occupy the mind of whoever was master of this place. It won't last forever. Lazaroth knows my resonance better than most; it won't take him long to realize he's been had. Fortunately, the same spells will warn me when he comes back—"

"No, they won't."

A white eyebrow arched upward.

"Trust me. They won't."

Curiosity flickered in the depths of his eyes, but he was no longer inside her mind; her secrets were her own once more. After a moment he nodded sharply, accepting her statement at face value. "Then we have to find Colivar as quickly as possible."

"Lazaroth said that sorcery would not be able to detect him."

He nodded. "I tried when I first arrived, and the only trace I was able to pick up was yours. I thought it might be the chaotic resonance of this place that was to blame. But perhaps not." He shook his head. "We'll have to search for him by physical means, then."

"Maybe not." She drew in a deep breath. The mere thought of working sorcery right now was daunting—her soul still felt raw and tender—but she thought she knew how she might locate Colivar without actually having to search for his person. That might circumvent whatever spells Lazaroth had used to hide him.

Closing her eyes, she reached out with her sorcerous senses into the underground complex surrounding her. Not only the chambers themselves, but the walls of those chambers, the air that flowed through them, the very stone that surrounded them.

And she searched for any kind of anomaly. The heat that a human body might generate, lying against cooler rock. A bit more moisture in one room than another, where human sweat had added its burden to the air. The subtle vibration of a heart-beat beating against some solid surface. Signs of the presence of a living body that were not dependent upon its metaphysical signature. It was hard to focus on such minutiae in her current state, and she had a few false starts, but at last she thought she detected clear signs of a living creature elsewhere in the complex.

It was not far away from where she had been taken. If she had gone a bit further in her earlier search, she might have found Colivar.

"This way," she said.

They walked quickly through the labyrinth, checking every chamber they came to, with sorcery as well as human sight. Kamala explained to Ramirus what sort of life signs she had detected, so he knew what to look for. While they moved, she kept looking about herself nervously, even though she knew that if Lazaroth wanted to approach them unseen, it would be a wasted effort. If Lazaroth was truly a woman and bore the seed of a queen within him—within her—then he would share in Kamala's ability to mask her presence from other Magisters.

I should tell Ramirus what he really is, she thought. But that would be of little help to him. She wasn't about to reveal to any Magister the full extent of her power, which she would have to do in order to explain Lazaroth's. She would just have to guide Ramirus through this trap as best she could without that, feeding him what he needed to know when he needed to know it.

Could she stand up to Lazaroth after what had passed between them? The mere thought of having to do so made her knees feel weak. But she had her sorcery now, not to mention a personal score to settle. It was possible to feel violated and unclean and still kick a man in the balls when you had to.

Assuming he actually had balls when you did that.

Down a narrow staircase they went, single file, down into the depths of the earth. Ramirus maintained the sorcerous light that allowed them to see where they were going, but it flickered now and then as currents of untamed power eddied about it, and once it almost went out. This was not a good place to be trapped in the dark. It had the feel of a prison about it, and she was not surprised when they got to the bottom of the stairs and found a heavily barred door blocking their way. Locked, and probably warded as well. Ramirus considered it for a moment, then put his hand on the nearest wall. Sandstone crumbled to dust at his touch, pooling about his feet. Within minutes he had an opening large enough for a man to squeeze inside. A few minutes more and his tunnel opened out into a dark space from which warm, fetid air flowed.

And the smell of human sweat.

Heart pounding, Kamala followed Ramirus into the room. It was a small space, and the shackles affixed to the walls left little doubt about what purpose it had been designed for. But the shackles hung empty, and the body that lay in the middle of the floor did not seem to be restrained in any way.

Colivar.

He lay upon one side, curled in on himself as if in pain. His outstretched hand had bloodied fingernails, where he appeared to have scraped them along the coarse sandstone floor. But otherwise he was still. Deathly still. His eyes were open, but they were empty, and he gave no sign that he was aware of their approach, or of anything else around him.

"What's wrong with him?" she whispered.

Ramirus shook his head and knelt down by Colivar's side. While he was using his sorcery to inspect the man, she used her Sight. And what she saw chilled her to the bone. For there was nothing but a body in front of her. No living essence reson-ated from Colivar, nor any hint of power. Both should have been discernable, if only faintly. A sorcerer was never without such things until the day he died.

She focused all her senses on the physical rhythms of his body and was relieved to discern faint signs of life. A rasping, tortured breath. The feverish pounding of an overworked heart. The scent of fresh sweat on his skin. But outside the boundaries of his flesh it was as though the man did not exist.

"We don't have time for mysteries right now," Ramirus said. "Let's get him out of here. We can worry about his condition later." He reached down to pick up the body. It was not limp, not in the way that dead flesh should be limp, and it was hard for him to position it over his shoulder.

"Can you transport us out of here?" she asked. Given the nature of the currents in this place, she was certain that her own skills were not up to the task.

"Bad idea in this place. Doubly so when dealing with unknown sorcery." He indicated Colivar. "Let's get some distance from this cursed place, first."

With Colivar's body over his shoulder, Ramirus barely fit through the tunnel he had carved. Kamala could see Colivar's arm scrape against the rock, tearing the fabric of his sleeve, and she thought she heard him moan softly. It was a sound more of horror than of pain. What if this wasn't even Colivar? she thought suddenly. Without being able to read his essence, they had no way to confirm his identity. For all they knew, this might be a goat that had been crafted to look like Colivar, the ultimate joke on any rescuers.

But it's the only living creature I detected in this place, she thought. *So we won't be leaving Colivar here, regardless.*

At last they came out into the main chamber. Ramirus' light expanded to fill every corner of the room as they entered. He attempted to bind it so that it would not shine into the corridor beyond, advertising their presence, but his spell was imperfect, and a few trickles of light seeped through. Little wonder he didn't want to invoke sorcerous transportation until they got a safe distance away from Tefilat. One wrong move in conjuring a portal, and your body could wind up splattered across half the desert.

"I cut a tunnel coming in so that I could avoid any wards on the main gate," he told her. His voice was pitched low now, little more than a whisper. In any other place he would have trusted to sorcery to keep others from hearing it. "We can use it going out."

He turned toward an opening at the far end of the chamber and gestured for her to follow him. It was then that she felt a sudden shiver along her spine. Something in the chamber had shifted. A silent, secret, metaphysical *something*. She could not even say where that knowledge came from, but she knew her own instincts enough to trust it.

Had Lazaroth returned?

The concept that he might be in the room even now, watching her, made a wave of sickness come over her. Fear and shame and loathing churned in her gut, and for a moment it was all she could do not to vomit. And in that moment she hated herself for feeling that way, for being so weak, almost as much as she hated him.

Hated *her.*

She put a hand on his Ramirus' shoulder. He was startled when she did so; Magisters didn't usually touch one another. But it gave her a connection whereby she could channel a message to him without need for speech.

Lazaroth is here, she thought to him.

He nodded almost imperceptibly to indicate that he'd gotten the message. He did not look around the room in a physical sense, but she was sure that he was doing so via sorcery, trying to pick up any clue as to Lazaroth's location. It was a hopeless task. Even Kamala couldn't have picked Lazaroth out in this big empty space, devoid of any landmarks to focus on. And Ramirus had no experience whatsoever in dealing with a queen's power.

Her one consolation was that she was pretty sure Lazaroth did not want Colivar dead, which took a number of things off the table. But it still left a lot of unpleasant options. Kamala strained her senses to the utmost as she and Ramirus hurried across the room, trying to catch any whiff of sorcerous intentions, any change in the metaphysical balance of the space surrounding them—

Suddenly sorcery blazed up directly in front of them. The light of it was blinding to Kamala, and she shielded her eyes with one hand as she cursed the sensitivity of her Sight, expecting that at any moment Lazaroth would strike at them.

But he did not.

The light faded. Her eyes adjusted.

The exit was gone.

They turned about quickly, to see what had become of the other doorways. All gone. The rock had healed over all of them, like flesh closing over a wound. Sandstone stripes coursed across the walls in fluid perfection, as if men had never sliced through them. Even Kamala's Sight could not pick out the place where the doors had once been. It was as if she and Ramirus were standing in a chamber that had never had—and never would have—exits.

Instinctively they moved to the nearest wall and put their backs to it. One less direction to worry about. *You can cut off a Magister's head with a single sword stroke,* Ethanus had taught Kamala, *so long as he does not see it coming.* Wasn't that how Kostas had died? Facing off against anyone other than Lazaroth, they would not be in such danger. His sorcery would be visible, even if his person was not, and that would give them at least a moment's warning if he launched an aggressive spell at them.

But the power of a Souleater queen changed that equation completely. And Ramirus didn't know about it. He'd be watching for conventional warning signs. Conventional sorcery.

We have to get out of here, Kamala thought desperately.

Sorcery was beginning to shimmer about the walls and ceiling of the chamber. She saw Ramirus furrow his brow as he bound enough athra to read its purpose . . . and he drew in a sharp breath as he did so. She looked upward and did the same.

The chamber was being sealed off. Not impermeably—no Magister could cut himself off from the outside world entirely, lest he lose his connection to his consort—but with a barrier no transportation spell would be able to pass through. Lazaroth was making sure they would have no avenue of escape before taking further action.

They could not afford to be trapped here.

Shutting her eyes, Kamala reached out to the barrier with all her power. Ramirus was attempting to break through the thing by sheer force, and for a moment she joined her sorcery to his, to help him. It was important that Lazaroth think they were both thoroughly engaged in that effort, so that he did not question what else she might be doing. And then—quietly, carefully—she disengaged from Ramirus' sorcery. Slipping tendrils of her own power through the weakest points in the barrier, she extended them into the layers of sandstone beyond. A plan was beginning to take shape in her mind, and she desperately tried to remember everything Ethanus had ever taught her about the mechanics of sorcery. Particularly about how quickly it worked. You could only wield sorcery as quickly as you could summon forth athra from your soul and mold it into the proper shape, but a spell that was crafted in advance, and required only a trigger to set it in motion, might be all but instantaneous in its action. Yes?

Pray that I am remembering correctly, she thought to her distant mentor. *Or else your prize student may soon be no more than a messy splotch on the ground.*

Trusting to Ramirus' defensive efforts to keep Lazaroth distracted, she began to transform the rock surrounding them. She left the inner surface of the chamber walls untouched, so that the change would not be visible to Lazaroth, but she transformed everything beyond that. Sandstone into sulfur—into charcoal—into saltpeter. It seemed she could feel the weight of the rock pressing down on the chamber now, no different in volume than what it had been before, but infinitely more volatile in potential.

And then, trembling with anticipation, she returned her awareness to her body. Ramirus had failed to break through the barrier, and it was nearly complete now; as soon as it was done she had no doubt that the next phase of Lazaroth's assault would begin. She reached out and grasped Ramirus' arm, holding onto him tightly so that even if everything went to hell in a hand-basket, they would not get separated. He looked at her in surprise.

"Transport us," she whispered fiercely. Praying to all the gods that he would trust her and just do it.

For a moment he stared into her eyes, and apparently whatever he saw there satisfied him. Grimly he nodded and proceeded to summon the power that would be needed. As his sorcery took shape around them, she saw that he understood her intent, for he did not attempt to fashion a portal in front of them, that they might step into—the normal configuration—but rather to conjure one right where they were standing. The risk of that was immense in this place—any flaw in such a spell would kill them all—but if Lazaroth's barrier faltered for even an instant, they would be in motion before he could repair it.

"Keep trying," she whispered. Squeezing his arm tightly. "Keep trying!" She hoped it would sound to Lazaroth as if she were merely desperate and was urging Ramirus to try to force his way through the barrier by brute force. Good. Good. The more he thought he understood what they were doing, the less likely he was to realize what she really had planned.

Muttering a prayer under her breath, she reached out with her power again, into the rock she had transformed, and sparked a fire in its depths.

With a deafening roar the walls of the chamber exploded: ceiling, walls, and floor, all shattered in an instant. There was no way any sorcerer could respond to such a thing in time to save himself.

Unless a portal was already in motion.

Lazaroth's spell had been anchored to the rock walls, and as they shattered, so did his barrier. Even as an avalanche of rock rushed at them from all sides, the portal that Ramirus had conjured lurched into activity, severing them from their current location and sending them—where? What arrival point had Ramirus chosen? As Kamala felt the sickening wrench of power, she realized that she didn't know. And didn't care. Rocks pelted the three of them even as they began to vanish, and it seemed the whole world went mad in that instant, as they were transported—

Somewhere.

Chapter 26

THE TRANSPORT spell manifested with a deafening crack, vomiting the three of them out upon a gritty sandstone surface. Debris spewed forth as Ramirus and Kamala stumbled through the doorway between *here* and *there*, Kamala falling to her knees as they landed, Ramirus nearly dropping Colivar. Shards of rock followed them, hurtling like crossbow bolts on all sides—and then suddenly ceased to fly, as the portal vanished as quickly as it had appeared.

And then there was silence.

With a grunt, Ramirus lowered Colivar to the ground. Several rocks had struck him during their exit, and thin lines of blood were trickling down from his forehead. He raised a hand to the wounds, healing and cleaning them with a touch, then did the same for his abraded palm. Kamala checked her own body for damage, repairing what was necessary. It was clear from the nature and the number of their wounds that the three of them had barely made it out in time.

"You certainly don't do things by halves," Ramirus muttered.

Blinking her eyes against the sudden intensity of full sunlight,

Kamala saw that they were now atop a narrow mesa, formed of the same reddish stone as Tefilat itself. A sigil had been carved into its surface, presumably as a focus for transport. For all his concerns about conjuring a portal in Tefilat, Ramirus had apparently prepared an escape route in advance. In the distance Kamala could see a plume of dust rising, and she guessed that it was coming from Tefilat . . . or what remained of Tefilat. The ground seemed to tremble beneath her feet, and she could hear a sound like an explosion in the distance. A new plume of dust gushed up into the air, spreading out over the desert. Collateral damage from her assault, no doubt; the weakened cliff face was giving way piece by piece, as each collapse triggered a new one. There would be little left of Tefilat once it was all over.

Ramirus knelt down by Colivar's side. If he had hoped that getting him out of Tefilat would improve his condition, it was clear that was not going to happen. The black-haired Magister lay still, insensate, his eyes gazing into nothingness. Periodically they shifted focus, as if he were struggling to see something clearly, but whatever he was focusing on was invisible to Kamala. His face and chest had been protected from the explosion by his position over Ramirus' shoulder, but thin rivulets of blood trickled out from under where he lay. How strange it was, to see such an ancient and powerful creature rendered as helpless as a newborn child. How unnerving.

"What's wrong with him?" Kamala asked.

"Some sort of containment spell," he said, a grave expression on his face. "I've never seen anything like it."

Rising up from her knees, trying to clear her head enough to walk steadily, she came over to join him.

Ramirus had his hand on Colivar's chest, and it was clear he was summoning power. She watched with her Sight as tendrils of sorcery, refined and delicate, began to explore Colivar's body. She tried to still the queasy feeling she got as she watched, remembering the feel of Ramirus' sorcery invading her own person. No sorcerer capable of resisting would ever allow another to do such a thing to him. But Colivar was helpless now, much as she had been back then. Gods help him if Ramirus took advantage of that, as he had with her.

As last the Magister sat back on his heels, his white brow furrowed in thought.

"What is it?" she asked.

"There's a barrier between Colivar and the outside world. Not like the one that Lazaroth was trying to conjure, which would block only a particular type of spell; this one was meant to block them all. An impermeable shell through which no sorcery can penetrate." He gazed down at his rival with a strange expression on his face. Pity? "Obviously, it was not entirely successful, or he would no longer be alive."

For a Magister to be cut off from the outside world meant being cut off from his consort. From the very source of his life. A witch could exist in such a state, but a sorcerer could not. Kamala's skin crawled just thinking about it. "You think they were trying to kill him?"

"No. I think they wanted to neutralize his sorcery so that they could take him prisoner. I'm guessing that he's been fighting it ever since, struggling to keep at least a minimal conduit open. Like a drowning man struggling for air . . ."

The words trailed off into silence. Why? He had talked to her in Tefilat about her calling in his Oath. Only a Magister could do that. So he knew what she was now, and discussing such sensitive matters should not be an issue. Did he still have doubts? Or was he just having problems internalizing the fact that the woman he was talking to was one of his own kind?

Looking down at Colivar's prone form, the red dust of Tefilat turning the sky to blood behind him, Kamala thought, *We're past the point of playing this game.*

"If he loses contact with his consort," she said, "he'll die. So no doubt he's shut down all outside awareness, to focus on the internal struggle. It's what I would do." She met Ramirus' eyes defiantly. *I am what I am. Come to terms with it.* "So the question is, can the spell be removed from him?"

Ramirus hesitated. "I'm not sure. It doesn't appear to be an external conjuration, as one would expect. Rather, it seems to bear his own resonance, which makes no sense at all. Why would a man do such a thing to himself?"

"Lazaroth told me that Siderea wove the trap from the substance of his own body, whatever that means. He said that no one could banish it without killing him."

"Aye. It appears to be part of him, not something separate. How that was managed I have no idea. 'His own body?' Colivar isn't the sort to leave parts of himself lying around." Lips tight, he shook his head; it clearly frustrated him to have gone through so much effort recovering Colivar and still be unable to free him. "I see no way to remove it from him. And I don't think I can get into his mind to gather information. Even if I could break through by sheer force . . ." Though he did not complete the sentence, Kamala knew what he was thinking. Any act that might distract Colivar from his immediate struggle for survival might prove fatal to him. His tie to his consort was a thin, fraying thread right now. They dared not do anything that would stress that connection further . . . and attempting to break into his mind would certainly do that.

Lips tight, Ramirus raised a hand over Colivar's body, to conjure what information he could from the spell itself. Power flowed forth from his fingertips and swirled in the air over the prone body. Colors gathered together in the still, hot air, but they were slow to coalesce; whatever the spell was that was wrapped so tightly around Colivar, it was not going to give up its secrets without a fight.

Finally hazy images began to take shape. Not as substantial as with a normal conjuring, but clear enough for them to make out some general details. Kamala saw Colivar moving through an underground passage, then coming out into a chamber with richly carved walls. Her Sight could pick out the glimmer of power that lay hidden in the deepest portions of that relief, and she leaned forward, trying to get a better view of it. But all she could make out was that something was clinging to the walls that was not supposed to be there, something far more organized and malevolent than the normal resident energies of the place.

And then that *something* whipped forth from the walls—all the walls at once—assaulting Colivar from every side. For a moment she thought she could detect its form—some sort of net or web, made of filaments so thin that the light passed through them. A spiderweb of power. It wrapped itself about Colivar as if it were a sentient creature, and she saw him cry out in surprise and pain as it adhered itself to all the visible portions of his skin. Where the sorcerous strands fell upon his clothing, they seemed to pass through it, or perhaps they were absorbed into it. The vision was not clear enough to tell.

She watched as Colivar fell. His body shook violently as he began to wrestle with the power, struggling to keep open a channel through which the life-essence of his consort could continue to pass. A lifeline to the outside world. While that battle was being waged, it would not be possible for him to do anything else.

Ramirus' vision faded. "So that's the trap he walked into. Designed for him." He shook his head. "He should have seen it coming. That much power . . . you can't disguise such a thing. He should have known walking into that room that something was amiss."

"Tefilat is a metaphysical mess," she pointed out. Not wanting to tell him that Lazaroth's sorcery might be uniquely undetectable, because then she would have to explain why. "The signs of a single spell could get lost in all that."

Leaning down close to Colivar, Kamala studied the portions of skin that were visible. Her Sight could pick out faint remnants of the original web, lines of power from which the spell emanated, crisscrossing his body. There must have been some physical structure to give it that shape originally, she thought. A material anchor that Siderea had imbued with power, which had affixed itself to Colivar's skin. Normally such a thing would have a different resonance than his own flesh did, which is what you could use to remove it. But if she had really made it out of his own body somehow, that would explain what Kamala was seeing. The webwork shimmered against his skin as if it had grown there organically, as much a part of him as his hair or nails, indivisible from his flesh. How did you remove such a thing without destroying the man himself?

Reaching up to the neck of his shirt, she parted the material to see what lay beneath. Colivar flinched reflexively as she touched him. So he was at least peripherally aware of what was going on, even if he could not respond to anything. She wasn't sure if that was a good or a bad sign. The pale skin beneath his shirt appeared at first sight to be unblemished, but as her Sight came into focus, she could see that it, too, was crosshatched with the same mysterious patterns of power. She reached out a finger to touch one of the lines; it seemed to vibrate beneath her fingertip.

"You have the Sight?" Ramirus asked, watching her closely.

She nodded.

"What can it tell you that sorcery does not?"

She narrowed her eyes, considering the question. "I can see where the anchor lies. It has merged with his flesh, but its power hasn't dissipated into the rest of his body. It's still localized."

"You're talking about the web we saw."

"Yes." She shut her eyes for a moment, trying to process all that she had seen. Testing solutions in her mind. "Destroy the web, and it might be possible to banish the spell that is anchored to it."

"If it has become one with his flesh, how do we destroy one without the other?"

She opened her eyes again. "We destroy that portion of his flesh it is anchored to and spare the rest."

Ramirus drew in a sharp breath. "You can make out its shape clearly enough to do that?"

She hesitated for a moment, then nodded.

"You know that such an assault on his person may well disturb his focus. If there's any delay in banishing the spell after that, he may die."

"He'll have a few seconds," she reminded him. "A Magister who goes into transition doesn't die immediately. Hopefully that will be enough time." She looked up at him. "How quickly can you banish the thing, once I detach it?"

How strange it felt, to talk about transition in front of him like this! As if there were nothing at all remarkable about the fact that she knew the Magisters' darkest secret.

"As quickly as is needed," he told her.

Sitting back on her heels, she prepared to gather the full force of her power. *So your life is in our hands now, Colivar. Can you hear what we're planning? Would you advise us not to try this, if you could?*

Drawing in a deep breath, she focused her attention inward, to where the source of her own power lay. Cold, stolen athra, which had been robbed of its living heat long ago. She must mold it into a force that could not only destroy the flesh surrounding the invasive anchor, but cauterize the area as well. Otherwise Colivar might bleed to death from a thousand wounds before he could summon enough power to heal himself.

She knew of no gentle way to begin.

Forgive me, Colivar. You've always treated me well, even if your motives weren't altruistic. I wish there were a better way to do this.

When she thought she was ready at last, she opened her eyes. The web that had melded itself into Colivar's flesh seemed to blaze in her Sight, silver lines shimmering like mercury as they rippled across his skin. She could feel the power rising up from the thing, like heat lapping at her face. Not sorcery, but not simple witchery either. Something hot and poisonous and boiling with hatred, that was a twisted amalgam of the two.

"Now," she whispered.

She released her power into the web. Sorcerous flames blazed to life, searing all flesh that they touched. She heard Colivar scream as they traveled down the lines of power, until they engulfed his entire body. The sickening smell of burning flesh filled the air as he convulsed in pain, his back arching with such force that it seemed his spine must surely snap. Still the fire raged on, hungry to devour the alien anchor in its entirety. Channels were seared deep into his flesh, their walls cauterized by fire. Now that the anchor was being destroyed, she sensed Ramirus adding his own sorcery into the mix, struggling to banish the containment spell before it could attach itself to some new part of Colivar's body. If it did that, then it would not be the spell that killed him; Kamala's own sorcery would spread across every inch of his body in pursuit of it, frying him to a cinder.

But at last the fire seemed to run out of fuel, and after a final few sputtering flares, it was extinguished. And then there was silence. The body lying before them was a gruesome spectacle now, with charred and bloody lines cross-hatching every visible surface. Even Colivar's face had deep channels running across it, and where one of his eyes had once stared into space there was now only an empty hole with blackened edges. Spasms of pain rippled through his body as wild, unfocused sorcery flickered in fits and starts along his skin. Was he trying to heal himself? Or was he fighting off remnants of Siderea's spell, that they had failed to banish? Beads of sweat appeared on the few patches of skin that were still undamaged, and tremors ran through his body as his soul wrestled with unseen enemies.

Then: "It is done," Ramirus told her.

Perhaps it was his pronouncement that quieted Colivar, or perhaps it was some more private revelation. Either way, the tremors finally subsided, and for a moment the wounded Magister lay still on the ground, barely breathing. And then, slowly, he began to heal himself. The edges of charred skin curled in on themselves and began to take on living color. Channels that had been gouged deep into muscle filled with blood, then with strands of spongy wet flesh, and finally with solid meat. The empty eye socket shed its lining of black cinders, revealing a newly formed lid beneath ash. And that in turn opened, revealing an eye that was shot with crimson, but clearly functional.

When the healing was done, Colivar lay still upon the sandstone surface, too exhausted to even try to get his bearings. Ramirus and Kamala waited in silence. Finally the bloodshot eyes seemed to focus on Ramirus, then on Kamala, then on Ramirus again.

"Why?" he croaked.

"You are useful," Ramirus told him.

Colivar shut his eyes. The crusted detritus of his healing turned to dust and a strong breeze swept it away. "What the hells happened?" he whispered.

"You walked into a trap. One that appears to have been designed especially for you." He paused. "It seems you underestimated your enemies."

Raising himself up on one elbow, Colivar looked about the mesa. Then, slowly, he got to his feet. Kamala could see how hard he was struggling not to let his ancient rival see just how weak he was, but it was a losing battle; his legs trembled as he forced them to support him.

"Sulah betrayed me," Colivar said hoarsely. "Perhaps not deliberately. Perhaps he was just a fool. Siderea is adept at manipulating fools. Either way, she played him like a puppet."

"He's the one who alerted me to your disappearance."

"That may have been part of the game." He paused. "What of Lazaroth?"

"Dead. We believe."

"We hope," Kamala said.

Colivar glanced at her. A spark of black amusement flickered in his eyes. *Have you killed another Magister, my dear?* He was about to speak when Kamala spotted something in the distance, circling the dust cloud that was Tefilat. She stiffened.

"I believe your transportation has arrived," she told Colivar.

The two men turned to look. As he saw what she was pointing at, Colivar growled in his throat. It was not the sort of sound one expected to hear from a human being, but it seemed strangely appropriate.

In the distance was a Souleater. It banked toward them as they watched, its wings catching the sunlight. Jeweled colors glittered against a backdrop of red dust, beautiful and deadly. Even from this far away they could feel the creature's mesmeric power lapping over them, and Kamala could feel the same sickening sensation she had experienced at Danton's castle, the desire to surrender herself to this creature and allow it to feed upon her.

Then the creature turned in its flight and began to head directly toward them.

"If he sees us . . ." Colivar began.

"He won't," Kamala assured him.

How little effort it took now, for her to wrap the power of a Souleater queen around them all! A witch might be able to see through it, if she tried hard enough, or Siderea herself, but no male Souleater would be able to do so. Nor any man bound to a Souleater.

And indeed . . . this Souleater did not see them. It circled the area twice as they watched, but it did not come any closer to them. Colivar never took his eyes from the creature, Kamala noticed, but Ramirus . . . Ramirus kept his eyes on Colivar. Lips tight, eyes narrow, icy blue gaze drinking in the other man's every motion, every expression. Every breath.

Then the glittering wings finally turned south, and within a few minutes the Souleater was out of sight. Kamala let out a breath she had not realized she was holding.

"Colivar." Ramirus' voice was quiet, but there was no mistaking the cold strength behind it. "The time for secrets is over now. Do you understand? We can no longer afford to play these games." When Colivar did not respond, his expression darkened. "It's time for you to surrender your secrets. And remember, I'm old enough to guess at just how many you have, so don't think I will be diverted easily."

Still Colivar said nothing. His eyes remained fixed on the horizon as he ignored the request . . . and its speaker.

Stepping forward suddenly, Ramirus grabbed Colivar by the shoulder and spun him around to face him. The movement was so unexpected that Kamala instinctively took a step backward.

"You *failed*, Colivar." Ramirus' expression was black with scorn. "Do you understand that? Failed! Your prize student set you up, and you never saw it coming. Your morati lover laid a trap for you, and you walked right into it. A Magister of half your power and less than half your intelligence held you prisoner, and you could not muster the strength to raise a hand against him. And finally, yes, your greatest rival had to carry you away from danger, like a helpless baby in his arms." The disdain in his voice was palpable. "You are weak, Colivar. *Weak*. Unfit to lead others. It's time to stop pretending you are otherwise."

He stepped back two paces, making room between them. Then he pointed to the ground before him. "Kneel to me."

Colivar did not move. His dark eyes narrowed—fury blazed in their depths—but he said nothing.

"Acknowledge your weakness before it consumes us all,"

Ramirus insisted. His voice, his expression, were merciless. "*Kneel.*"

Sensing the storm that was about to break, Kamala began to step forward. "Ramirus, don't—"

"*Silence!*" A cold and terrible fury was in his eyes as he turned to her. "*You* have brought us to this pass, as much as he has! Fool! What did you think our Law was? A simple legal code? A fancy written contract, perhaps, with pretty illumination about the edges?" He drew in a sharp breath. "It was *sorcery*, woman! A grand conjuration that we all submitted to, in order to safeguard our human souls. So what did you think would happen when you trampled upon that compact? That we would just erase a clause and move on?" He shook his head sharply. "Your actions have compromised our security more than any mundane treachery ever could. And any Magister who fails to prosecute you for your crime—including myself—helps to undermine it. The reasons one gives for it won't matter. Sorcery doesn't give a damn about reasons. The compact that kept us all human has begun to crumble, and it will continue to crumble for as long as the Law remains compromised." He turned back to Colivar. "Am I wrong?" he demanded.

"No," Colivar whispered. "You're not wrong."

"We have played by human rules for a very long time, you and I," Ramirus told him. "But now that game is falling to pieces, and we must fall back upon more ancient rules. The alternative is chaos." He drew in a deep breath. "So you tell me if I'm wrong about what all that means, Colivar. You tell me if I am wrong about what is required of us now."

For a long moment the black-haired Magister just stared at him. Powerful emotions blazed in the depths of his eyes: Indignation. Defiance. Hatred. The energy between the two men was so charged that Kamala could feel it raise hairs along her skin. She stepped back from them, fearing what might happen if any of that energy were channeled into sorcery.

Then a terrible exhaustion seemed to come over Colivar; the worst of his emotion seemed to dissipate. "No," he whispered. "You're right."

And to Kamala's amazement he lowered himself to one knee before his rival. And then lowered his eyes as well, in a gesture of formal submission.

Ramirus gazed down at him in silence. There was no sense of triumph in him, she observed. No pleasure in finally besting his rival. The very necessity of this whole scene seemed to repel him. But that didn't mean he was any less determined to get the answers he sought, and his voice was harsh as he demanded, "Who was it that first crossed the Wrath? The traitor you spoke of, who brought us this power, and with it the curse of ikati madness. Who was it, Colivar?"

Kamala held her breath. For a moment it seemed that time itself was suspended, as Colivar considered the question. Under normal circumstances he would never have answered it, she knew that. But these were no longer normal circumstances.

"I am the one who flew through the clouds of ash and poison," he said at last, "hunting my rivals. I tasted the bite of the arctic wind against my face and felt their hot blood bathe my consort's talons. I battled them in the wake of a queen's flight and claimed my reward over the corpses of my conquests. And in the end I lay on a bier of bloodied snow, with all the ghosts of the Wrath screaming inside my head, and begged the gods for death." Slowly he raised up his eyes to look at Ramirus; his gaze was hollow and terrible. "Is that the confession you wanted?" he demanded. "Yes, I sought obliteration, and I returned to this world instead. Now you know. For what good it may do you. May the gods curse you to the vilest of hells for awakening those memories in me."

"Who is Nyuku?" Ramirus demanded.

Colivar shut his eyes. "He's the one responsible for my exile," he said. "Though he didn't think he was doing that at the time. He just thought he was leaving me for dead." He paused, then whispered, "The gods can be cruel in their hunger for amusement."

"An enemy, then."

"We were all enemies," Colivar said. "No other relationship is possible when one is bound to an ikati."

"And now?" Ramirus pressed.

Slowly, Colivar stood. It was obvious as he did so just how weak he was. It was also obvious how hard he was trying not to let that weakness show.

"Now he's in *my* world." His voice was hard and cold. "The advantage is mine."

"How so?"

"He's a Kannoket upstart by birth. Not a witch. And once he claimed his consort, he had no reason to become a witch. The ikati are concerned with eating, killing, and mating. Nothing else matters to them. And there's very little power to spare in that wasteland. One doesn't expend precious resources just for sport. So while he always had the potential for great power, he never learned how to channel it properly. He may be many things, but he is not a Magister."

"Much time has passed since you left," Ramirus pointed out. "You changed. Siderea Aminestas changed. Perhaps he did also."

"Perhaps," he whispered.

"What is she to you, Colivar?" But the man did not answer.

After a moment Ramirus asked, "Why did you come to Tefilat alone?"

"I've always walked alone," he said quietly. The walls were back up.

"It was foolish."

"Perhaps."

"Maybe the fact that there's a queen involved has something to do with it? You're closer to the ikati than any of us. Maybe Siderea's situation speaks to you in a way it doesn't to the rest of us. Maybe you hunger for her in ways we can't understand."

A muscle along his jawline tensed. "I'm human now, Ramirus."

"But you were once something else, were you not? Let's not pretend those memories have no power." He paused. "The best way for you to get back at Nyuku would be to claim the Souleater queen for yourself. Would it not?"

Colivar's expression darkened; a dangerous edge entered his voice. "I know what the Souleaters mean to do to this world, Ramirus. Unlike you, I *saw* what they did to it the first time. Do you think I would allow that to happen again?"

"You allowed it to happen the first time," Ramirus said bluntly.

Colivar stiffened. Fury blazed in his eyes—and then transformed itself into sorcery, a whirlwind of raw, unfettered emotion that poured forth from him in waves, red-hot in Kamala's Sight. For a moment she wondered whether he was going to strike out at Ramirus. But he turned away, took a few steps away from them, and directed his rage at the mesa instead. The ground in front of him exploded with a roar, sending huge chunks of rocks flying out over the mesa's edge. For a moment the air was so thick with dust that she could not make anything out; then, as it cleared, she saw that a whole section of the mesa had been blown away, leaving Colivar on the edge of a newborn escarpment, open air lapping at his feet.

"Things were different then," he growled.

"You were human back then," Ramirus pointed out. "Since then, you've been other things. And the madness in you was always stronger than in the rest of us. It's probably what gave you the strength to cross the Wrath and to find a way to survive in this world once you returned, but it's also what makes you vulnerable. The spirit of the ikati speaks more powerfully to you than it does to the rest of us. The ancient instincts have a firmer grasp upon your psyche. That may have been your strength once, but it is a weakness now. Your judgment is compromised. You must trust to others to lead the way." He paused. "And to invoke our ikati heritage when they must, in order to establish their authority. Or was I wrong about that heritage, Colivar? Did I mistake what was required in order for us to work together?"

A hot wind blew across the mesa. It left a film of dust on Kamala's lips.

"No," Colivar whispered. A terrible emptiness had come into his voice. "You were not wrong." He paused. "Will you tell the others?"

Ramirus shrugged. "Lazaroth is dead. Sulah is a fool. Whom else would I trust with such knowledge?" He looked at Kamala. "This witch, however . . ." His mouth twitched slightly. "This *Magister* is your problem. Though clearly she knows how to keep secrets when she needs to."

"And will you keep my secrets?" Kamala demanded. "Or will you tell the others about me?"

Ramirus walked a few steps toward her. Though her first instinct was to back away, she stood her ground. The fact that Colivar had offered him submission didn't mean that she had to.

"An interesting question," he mused. "Any Magister who learns what you are—and *who* you are—must then bear the burden of either killing you or violating the Law himself. Which weakens the Law even further. Considering how important it is that we all remain human," he said, glancing back meaningfully at Colivar, "I think that would be a bad idea."

His expression was grave as he turned back to her. "I am bound by my Oath, which is also part of the Law. It would defy the spirit of that Oath for me to pay it off by saving your life and then take that life myself a few minutes later. So you've put me in an awkward position, where no matter what I do, I will wind up offending against our compact. Given that . . ." He paused. "You seem to be useful. *He* thinks you are useful." He nodded toward Colivar. "And in that, I do trust his judgment."

He took a step back from her. "Sometime in the future we must have a chat about how you became what you are. Assuming you survive this war, of course. And the wrath of the other Magisters. Though the fact that you killed a man they all despised will certainly play in your favor."

He bowed his head ever so slightly in formal leave-taking. A shadow of a dry smile played upon his lips. "Until we meet again . . . *Magister* Kamala."

Then a dust cloud gathered around him, and she had to shut her eyes to protect them from the flying grit. When she finally opened them again, he was gone.

She and Colivar were alone.

She walked to where he stood by the mesa's edge—the mesa's new edge—and took up a place beside him. Sharing his exhaustion and his silence. Were he morati, she might have offered some words of comfort. But neither of them were morati, and she knew it was not appropriate. That same part of her that recognized the necessity of what had just taken place also understood the part she must play in it. Offering her support to Colivar right now would compromise his submission. Among ikati—and therefore Magisters—such things were sacrosanct.

But she was also human, and so she stayed by his side until the sun set, and the first moon rose, and then they began the long flight home.

CHAPTER 27

"WHAT DO you mean, *He escaped?!!!*"

"As I said." Nyuku's voice was steady, but frustration echoed in its depths. "He was not in Tefilat. Not bound, not free, not even dead."

Siderea wanted to break something. Or perhaps someone. For a moment she looked around her to see if there was something suitably fragile at hand other than Nyuku himself . . . and then she took a deep breath, trying to still the pounding of her heart so that she could think clearly again. The queen's rage was a fire in her soul, hard to overcome. And she was not all that sure she wanted to overcome it.

He failed you! The ikati thought to her.

"Tell me," she ordered Nyuku.

"Tefilat has been destroyed. The canyon was filled with rubble when I arrived, the dust still rising. I used the talisman you gave me to try to locate him. Nothing. You said that it would find him if he was alive or dead, so . . ." The words trailed off into eloquent silence.

"You searched carefully?"

Anger sparked in his eyes, but only for a moment. He dared not express any emotion that might displease her. She could see a muscle along the line of his jaw twitch as he fought for enough self-control to keep his voice steady, and not voice his own frustration at the current state of affairs. "I made several circuits, flying in as close as I could. The land itself was still unstable, so I couldn't enter the canyon. But that shouldn't have mattered to your talisman."

"No," she muttered. "It should not have."

Colivar had escaped. By all the devils in all the hells! She had invested her greatest treasure in this enterprise, molding his hair into an anchor for her trap, and now that was gone. And the loss was Nyuku's fault. He knew it and she knew it. If not for his request to deal with Colivar, she could have had the man killed in Tefilat and ended the whole affair then and there. One Magister down, a few dozen more to go. Clean, neat, and efficient.

But would she really have done it that way? she wondered. Or was Nyuku just a convenient excuse? Death was too merciful an ending for Colivar. She wanted him to suffer as *she* had suffered, dying by inches while others stood by and watched. Alone and abandoned, fearing death, betrayed by those he had once loved. The way *she* had been meant to die.

Why do you hate him more than the others? the queen asked. *They're all equally guilty.*

But the other Magisters had merely been callous bastards. Colivar had actually pretended to care about Siderea, and that was far worse. Yes, she hated them all, and in time she would see that they all suffered for abandoning her, but Colivar's offense exceeded theirs a hundredfold. And so would his punishment.

"What of Lazaroth?" she asked.

"He failed to meet me as arranged, and there was no message

at the drop point. I remained in the area for a day, rather visibly, so that he would have a chance to contact me by other means if he was there. Nothing." He paused. "If he was true to his word, and remained in Tefilat . . . no man could have survived what happened there, Lady Consort."

"Well," she murmured, "at least he died quickly. If he'd come to Jezalya as planned . . ." She chuckled darkly. "It would not have been pleasant."

Surprised, Nyuku said, "I thought he was your ally."

Yes. Lazaroth thought that, too.

What a fool that Magister had been! She'd thought because she had been born a woman, there would be a natural confluence of interest between her and Siderea. After all, she'd argued, it was different with her than with the other Magisters. *They* had used Siderea like a cheap whore, then abandoned her when she needed them most. Lazaroth could understand why Siderea would hate them for that. It was the kind of indignation only a woman could understand.

But the other Magisters didn't think there was a way to save me, Siderea mused. *I hate them for not even trying—and for denying me comfort in my final days—but only for that. Whereas Lazaroth knew with utter certainty that I could become a Magister in my own right and knew how to make it happen. And instead she chose to let me die. I was not her lover, so I was not her concern.*

I hope she died painfully.

"Lazaroth was useful," she said shortly. "And I would have kept him around for as long as he remained useful."

Nyuku's mouth twitched in a smile. He had clearly perceived the Magister as a rival and was pleased to hear him so roundly rejected. "So what comes next, Madame Consort? What do you require of me?"

She did not miss the hidden message in his words. For a brief moment she considered sending him away, if not as punishment for his failure, then simply to make sure that he understood his place. Humiliation could be a powerful tool when ikati instincts were in play. But he, too, was useful. Perhaps more useful by her side, seething with anticipatory energy, than at a distance, nursing his wounded pride.

"You said that Colivar must come to me. That he cannot help but come to me. Is that still the case?"

"For as long as he lives," Nyuku assured her.

She wanted to ask him why, but she knew he would not answer. *Later.* "We will wait for him here, then."

He drew in a deep breath. "*We*, Lady Consort?"

A faint smile. "You will help me entrap him, won't you, Nyuku? I do so value your assistance."

There was no mistaking the mix of emotions that flashed across his face. Surprise. Relief. And of course, suspicion. He had failed to bring Colivar back to her. Why would she want him to remain by her side now?

Because that is the key to controlling you, she thought. *And I must have control of you by the time my queen declares her flight, so that if and when you establish your sovereignty over the Souleaters, we both understand who is really in charge.*

"Of course," he said. Bowing his head stiffly in obeisance. "Whatever you require of me, you know you have but to ask."

Except to share your secrets, eh, Nyuku? But that will come, in its proper time.

You will surrender it all to me, in time.

RECKONING

CHAPTER 28

COLIVAR SAID, "Welcome to Coldorra."

The plain spread out before them was vast but unimpressive. It was flat—simply flat—for nearly as far as the eye could see, with little variance in elevation that Kamala could discern. There seemed to be some hills far off on the horizon to both the north and south, but they were so mist-hazed and uncertain that they might have represented no more than wishful thinking on Kamala's part. The plain itself was bare of any life save for scattered clumps of grass, which might once have looked passably green had something not eaten them down to the nub.

"So much blood was shed here in past ages it's a wonder the grass isn't bright red," Colivar said. "Though most of that was before my time."

"Doesn't seem like the sort of place one would fight over."

"Danton's southern expansion stopped here. It's the only place his ambitions were ever frustrated, so it has considerable symbolic value. At one time he and Anshasa were fighting over this stretch of land so often, it's said that when the inhabitants woke up each morning, the first thing they did was check to see which king they owed allegiance to. Most of them eventually moved away. As would I. It will be interesting to see if anyone returns now that Danton is gone."

"Salvator controls it now?"

Colivar nodded. "Farah hasn't challenged him for it yet. I expect that he will some day. But he needs to learn what Sulah can do for him first. The parts of the Law that limit our participation in morati warfare are a veritable labyrinth for a Magister Royal to negotiate, and each sorcerer interprets them a little differently."

Kamala noticed that his expression darkened slightly when he referred to his former student. "Sulah will be here?"

"I expect so. It would be odd if he weren't."

"Are you are worried about him and Siderea? That he might still serve her?"

Colivar shrugged stiffly. "Siderea tricked him to get to me. It failed. Now that he knows what she's up to, he won't be as easy a target. She'll move on to other strategies."

She said it softly: "You're sure he didn't betray you deliberately?"

Colivar started to answer—and then hesitated. "No," he admitted. "No, I'm not. But that's to be expected. We are what we are."

In the center of the great plain there were tents. Large tents, small tents, plain and opulent tents: a veritable city of cloth. The ones to the north were much grander in scale, with a great peaked pavilion the size of a respectable manor house in the center of the field. The great golden finials that topped its support poles were shaped like double-headed hawks, and long silk pennants were clutched in their talons. The tents to the south were simpler in structure, low and broad in the desert style, with tasseled ropes that could be used to gather up the walls if ventilation was required. Farther out on both sides of the field were the strictly functional tents of a military encampment, rows and rows of them in perfect alignment, stretching out as far as the eye could see. Salvator and Farah had agreed to a limit of a thousand troops on each side, but there were at least that many servants and attendants present as well, some of whom might be soldiers in disguise, so the entire encampment was immense.

Gods forbid any king should ever travel without an army of retainers at his back, she thought.

The situation was a powder keg, and she knew it. One wrong word and the two men for whom this whole spectacle had been arranged might suddenly find themselves in the midst of a pitched battle.

"Come," Colivar said. "They'll be starting soon."

But not without us, she thought. It was a heady concept. Of all the thousands of men and women who had come to attend this meeting, she and Colivar were two of the most important. True, it was unlikely their input would be needed today—they'd been asked to attend as witnesses so they could offer their counsel later—but if these negotiations went well, Kamala might wind up playing a much larger role in what was to come. Possibly even a public role.

I'm officially part of this now, she thought. Not quite sure if that should please her or frighten her.

Colivar had summoned horses for them so that they could approach the encampment in morati fashion. That was one of the conditions that Salvator had insisted upon. No sorcery was to be used on this plain for as long as the meeting between the two kings was taking place.

Did that mean that Salvator himself had come here on horseback, traveling hundreds of miles like a common morati? Unlikely. Supposedly he had a hundred Penitent witches who were ready to expend the last drop of their life-essence in his service, and any one of them might have transported him here. Apparently Penitent witches went straight to heaven if they died in the service of their faith.

Convenient for the kings who ruled over them, Kamala thought dryly.

Urging her horse into motion, she set off across the great plain with Colivar, heading toward the center of the encampment.

Deep breath, Salvator.

It was hard to shut out the bustle of the camp, but he knew he had to in order to prepare his mind for this meeting. Shutting his eyes, he struggled to turn his thoughts inward, using a passage from the *Book of Meditations* as a focus.

> *Savor the quiet voice of your soul, for the spirit of man knows its Creator. The truth shall come from within you.*

"They are ready for you, your Majesty."

Drawing in a last deep breath, he nodded. Overhead two pennants snapped in the wind: one with the arms of House Aurelius emblazoned upon it, one with the arms of House Farah. Identical in height, identical in size, they answered to the wind in perfect unison. Hopefully, it would serve as an omen.

Farah was waiting for him. He was a husky man of swarthy complexion, with dark, piercing eyes that reminded Salvator of his father's. He was dressed in a curious combination of plain tribal garments and heavy gold jewelry, with so many rings on his hands that he might be carrying enough gold on him to cast a new crown for Salvator. A strange amalgam of opposites, but he was clearly a man of consequence.

It was clear from the Anshasan's expression that he had serious doubts about this whole event, but he nodded to Salvator in a manner that was respectful, if not warm. Good enough. It had been decades since the leaders of their two warring nations had last tried to meet face to face, and that attempt had been a disaster. Given the weight of history, every positive gesture today was significant.

They fell in side by side, entering the grand pavilion together as a herald announced them. Farah's name was offered first, because Salvator had the honor of being the host of this meeting. Thus had their diplomats arranged, after much wrangling, in order to make sure that when the day's tally was finally figured, neither monarch would have been given preference over the other. It was a delicate dance indeed, with so many subtle nuances that it made Salvator's head spin.

The interior of the great tent was shadowy and cool; it took Salvator's eyes a moment to adjust. The interior had been outfitted like a formal reception hall; it even had a set of stained glass windows set into frames in its cloth walls. But none of that really mattered. There was only one thing here of consequence: the heavy table set dead-center in the room, with throne-like chairs of perfectly equal opulence at either end. Behind the table eight people now stood in formal silence, waiting respectfully as the two kings approached. Favias, Ramirus, Colivar, Kamala . . . Salvator didn't recognize the people Farah had brought, but the man standing nearest the Anshasan's chair was dressed in the unnatural black robes of a Magister, so he guessed that to be Sulah, the new Magister Royal.

There were uniformed guards, of course, flanking both royal chairs. A token presence. Any Magister here who wanted to kill Farah—or Salvator—could do so before guards would be able to lift a finger. But they wouldn't do that, of course. Their quixotic Law didn't allow it.

Salvator felt a pang of guilt, knowing that the only reason Sulah was prohibited from killing him was his mother's contract with Ramirus. He hadn't sanctioned the contract, but he was benefiting from it.

Forgive me, my Creator, for profiting from the corruption of others.

The kings took their seats with formal solemnity. The rest of the attendees lined up along the two sides of the table as their choreographers dictated, Salvator's people on one side and Farah's on the other. Colivar and Kamala stood with the former as counselors to Ramirus, who was in turn counselor to his mother . . . an indirect tie to Salvator, to say the least, and of course those two owed him no particular loyalty. Gwynofar had convinced Salvator to include them despite his misgivings; Salvator had yet to decide whether that was a good decision.

When everyone was properly settled, Salvator turned his attention to his royal guest. "King Farah. You do my House great honor by your presence."

There was a brief pause before Farah spoke. It was possible he didn't speak the northern tongue—or didn't speak it fluently— in which case someone had clearly provided a spell to assist him. That was standard practice among monarchs. What was not standard practice was using a witch to provide that spell, instead of a Magister Royal. Yet, judging from the pace of his speech, that was exactly what Farah had done. A Magister could have placed knowledge directly into Farah's brain as he spoke, and translated the man's own thoughts into suitable language as soon as he wished to voice them. Such a spell was undetectable when it was well performed. But it was also a complex undertaking, and a mere witch couldn't afford to waste power on that scale. Farah's witch had probably provided him with a external spell, perhaps something that conjured whispers inside his ear, which he had to listen to and then repeat. The fleeting pause before each statement was noticeable.

He respected my request not to use sorcery, Salvator thought, *even though I might not have detected it.* The gesture pleased him.

"Your invitation does me equal honor," Farah responded with formal gravity. "It has been a long time since the High Kingdom evinced any desire to *speak* with my people. I am curious to know the reason for it."

Salvator sat back in his chair, trying to look more relaxed than he felt. So much was riding on this meeting that it was hard for him to hide his anxiety. "Our countries have been at war for a very long time, King Farah. Sometimes openly, sometimes covertly . . . but ceaselessly, for decades now. It drains both nations of energy that could be used for other things. Things that might be more important in the long run than who owns what piece of land along our common border, or who controls what port in the Sea of Tears."

Farah's eyes narrowed briefly at the reference to a common border; his unspoken message was clear: *Easy words for you, as Coldorra is yours.* But his tone remained congenial as he responded, "Are you interested in some sort of peace treaty between Anshasa and the High Kingdom, then? That would be an interesting experiment. I am not sure how successful it would be, given our history. Of course, that is something we would likely have years to work out, as it would probably take our negotiators years just to work out the starting details."

Salvator allowed himself a faint smile. "A year begins with a single day, your Majesty."

"Indeed it does," Farah allowed. "For which reason, I am open to hearing your proposal." Despite his casual tone his eyes were sharp and alert, Salvator noted. Cold steel in a velvet glove. "So is that what you wish us to discuss today? Terms for a possible peace treaty? Your messenger hinted at some pressing interest. Peace, while admittedly desirable, is hardly a pressing need, given that we are not currently at war."

For a moment Salvator was silent. Studying him. He knew that he would be taking a great risk to broach his business directly. Normally this kind of negotiation would take months to launch, as diplomats danced around peripheral issues, only slowly edging their way toward the one that really mattered. Making sure that all the proper diplomatic wheels were greased before the cart started rolling. But Salvator didn't have months. He didn't even have weeks.

"What do you know about the Souleaters?" he asked, leaning forward on the table.

Farah's face did not betray a flicker of emotion. "As much as any man does, I expect. Civilization was once destroyed by them. Now it appears they are returning. No one knows how to fight them, or even where they have gone." He paused. "I hear you are hunting them. Is that true?"

Salvator nodded.

"Well, then, if you have half your father's capacity in warfare, I pity the poor creatures. So is that what all this peace talk is about, then? You do not want to have to worry about your southern border while you are hunting these creatures?" His eyes gleamed with subtle amusement. "Given that Anshasa will ultimately benefit from your efforts, along with every other human kingdom, that is a goal I would consider supporting."

Salvator nodded solemnly. "Your gracious offer of support is appreciated and accepted. As for the peace treaty . . . that is, I regret, only one part of what I seek."

Farah raised an eyebrow.

"What do you know of Jezalya?" Salvator asked.

Farah narrowed his eyes suspiciously. "I know the name. A trade city in the southern region. Older than the sands themselves, I am told. What is your interest in it?"

"Is it under your sovereignty?"

"No. It lies farther south, in the heart of the great desert. Anshasa did claim a bit of that region once, but the nomadic tribes there proved to be more trouble than they were worth." He leaned forward on the table, his posture mirroring Salvator's own; his gaze was a challenge. "What is Jezalya to you, Aurelius?"

Salvator drew in a deep breath. "I believe that is where Siderea Aminestas is hiding."

Sulah looked visibly startled at the pronouncement, which was certainly interesting. Meanwhile, Farah muttered something in his own tongue and glanced at one of his morati attendants. Also interesting. Salvator had been told that Farah knew about the Souleaters and was fully aware of Siderea's connection to them, but since that information had come to him through a long chain of second-hand sources, including several Magisters, Salvator had been hesitant to rely upon it. This certainly confirmed that Farah knew a lot more about the situation than he'd been letting on.

He didn't know about Jezalya, though. No one had been told

about Jezalya save the four people sitting on Salvator's side of the table and Gwynofar. Until now.

"How do you know this?" Farah demanded.

Salvator nodded sagely. "Those who have the power to see things across great distances have seen her."

Farah scowled. "That is damned vague, Aurelius."

"Apparently she can hide her presence from all but the most skilled observers. And even those who can see her can't focus on her very well. So that is all we have."

Farah sat back heavily in his chair. It was clear the information didn't sit well with him. "You know what you are suggesting, do you not? That one of the most dangerous creatures in all the human kingdoms is sitting just south of my border. And you are hunting her. So you want to send men down there to deal with her, is that the idea? Which would put me between your armies in the south and your armies in the north? Not to mention all your people having to travel through the heart of my kingdom to get there." He snorted. "A plot worthy of Danton Aurelius, to be sure. Did you seriously think I would agree to it?"

"There is no need to travel through Anshasa," Salvator said quietly. "We will go to Jezalya directly."

Farah raised an eyebrow. "This, from the man whose god commands him not to do business with Magisters? Transportation is costly magic. Many witches would die, to provide you with such a service."

"Many may die," Salvator agreed. "But in service to God, not to me." He folded his hands on the table before him. "Our enemy has wings, King Farah, not to mention witchery. She would see any forces approaching by conventional means long before they got there. And then she would flee, and we would have to start all over again, searching the world for her. So even though it's unlikely we can surprise her, we must do everything within our power to attempt it. Even if that requires a greater sacrifice than witches would normally provide."

Farah leaned back in his chair. For a moment he just looked at Salvator. Taking his measure. "You know I cannot just accept your word on all this. My own people will have to confirm it."

"Of course."

"And if they do? What then? What is it exactly that you want from me? Men? Supplies? There must be something specific, or you would not have asked me here."

"What I need right now is the same thing you do: information. Magisters and witches can't seek it out for us, because Siderea may be able to detect their spells. We can't take any risk that she might find out we know where she is. So we need morati who know that part of the world, speak the language, and can pass for natives. Men whose presence wouldn't be questioned if they visited Jezalya and took a look around. You can provide such scouts, King Farah." He spread his hands wide. "I can't."

Farah considered it for a moment, his expression grave, then finally nodded. "Aye, I could do that. It would take a few days to set in motion, even with sorcery. And there would be travel time involved, since the scouts would have to approach Jezalya by mundane means. The results might not come in as quickly as you'd like."

Salvator's lips tightened. "Time is a very precious commodity in this matter."

"I am aware of that aspect of the situation," Farah assured him.

"We'll also need a metaphysical anchor for Jezalya, so that

our witches have a proper focus when it's time for us to go there."

Farah's eyes narrowed. "I am not going to give you anchors from anywhere near my territory until I am satisfied that the situation is what you say it is. And if I do it, then, I will expect safeguards enough that I do not wind up with your armies crawling up my ass when this business is over."

A corner of Salvator's mouth twitched. "Understood."

"I will arrange for the spies we need. Meanwhile, you draw up a draft of your proposed peace treaty for me to look at. Nothing vague or open-ended, or I will throw it in the fire, and you and yours can walk to Jezalya." He snorted. "I remember Danton's treaties."

"I am not my father," Salvator said quietly.

"No," Farah agreed. "And rest assured, if you were, I would not be agreeing to any of this, Souleaters or no Souleaters."

Farah rose from his chair. Salvator followed suit. The others rose to their feet respectfully, some more quickly than others.

"I assume we will be leaving this encampment in place?" Farah asked. "For our next meeting?" A dry smile quirked his lips. "Our people can practice being good neighbors until we return."

Salvator nodded. "That was my thought."

"Very well, then." Farah exhaled noisily. "This has certainly been an interesting meeting, to say the least. Doubtless future historians will write volumes trying to analyze it. Assuming that enough remains of human civilization for there to be any future historians."

"That is our goal," Salvator said solemnly.

"And one that I share," Farah assured him. "Though how it

is best to be achieved . . . well, let us see what my scouts have to say before we get into that, shall we?"

Walking the length of the table, Salvator offered his hand to the southern king. Farah stared at it for a long moment, a curious look on his face. As if it were some strange creature whose habits he didn't know, that might piss on him if he handled it wrong. But when he finally accepted it, his own grip was sure and strong, a good match to Salvator's own.

"No," Farah observed. "You are not like your father, are you? I find that most refreshing."

CHAPTER 29

"THE MERCHANT delegation is here to see you, your Highness."

Nasaan nodded. "Send them in."

In truth, it was a hot day even by Jezalyan standards, and he had little appetite for administrative duties. But trade was the lifeblood of his new city, and these were the men who kept it flowing. So he reached for the goblet of crushed ice that his *djira* had conjured for him—now half melted—and held it against his neck while he waited, savoring the feel of the chilled glass against his skin.

The merchant families that oversaw business in Jezalya weren't overtly hostile to one another, but they were fierce rivals, and outside the city it was rare that they cooperated on anything more complex than "who gets to go through the gate first." Inside Jezalya, however, was another matter. The most powerful families in this region all had representatives in his city, and they were not shy about offering Nasaan their counsel. Since ultimately they had the same goal that he did—increasing Jezalya's influence and prosperity—he had been open to such conversations thus far, provided his authority was properly acknowledged.

But in all their prior meetings they had chosen one representative to speak for all the families; never before had they come to him in a group like this.

As they entered the room, he saw that there were half a dozen of them, and each appeared to be from a different family. That didn't surprise him. Most of the merchant caravans passing through Jezalya were controlled by extended family groups, and the men in charge usually chose wives from among their own relatives in order to maintain control over inheritance rights. The result was that it was fairly easy to pick out the more influential merchant families by their common features. Nasaan had dealt with them often enough by now to recognize that the six who stood before him represented the so-called Great Families, vast tribal networks whose elders effectively controlled all commerce within Jezalya. That each one had sent a blood relative to this meeting, rather than agreeing upon a common messenger, was not a reassuring sign.

"Thank you for receiving us, your Highness." The lead speaker was a man Nasaan actually knew quite well. Hatal et Sarosh had been one of his secret agents in the city in the days before his conquest, and had helped him plant the rumors he'd needed to undermine support for Dervasti. They kept their distance from one another in public now, so few people knew of the connection, but occasionally Sarosh slipped him a choice bit of information, and now and then Nasaan slipped his family a choice bit of royal favor. A man could never have too many loyal agents.

"The masters of trade are always welcome here," Nasaan

responded. "Though I'm not used to seeing such a large delegation."

The men looked at each other. It was not hard to pick up that they were ill at ease about this interview. Since Nasaan had never been one to punish the messengers of bad news, that made him even more wary.

"News has come to the Great Families that they believe might be of concern to the Prince of Jezalya." Sarosh folded his hands in front of him as he spoke the last phrase; it was the signal they had established for him to warn Nasaan that serious trouble might be on the horizon. *As if I hadn't already figured that out*, he thought dryly. "Each felt that they should provide a representative for our meeting."

Witnesses, then, Nasaan thought darkly. *The one role none of the Families would trust an outsider to fill*. Eyes narrow, he sat back in his chair, his battle-roughened hands steepled before him. "Speak, then. What's your news?"

"There is word of trouble in Bandezek." Sarosh told him. "Rumors of the Black Sleep are circulating. Though we are told no actual cases have been verified yet."

Bandezek was an oasis town two days' ride from his own city, a place that he had earmarked for his future military expansion. The place was not nearly as large or as prosperous as Jezalya—few towns were—but by the measure of the wasteland surrounding them it was worthy of notice. For the terrible wasting disease to come to Bandezek would be a disaster on many fronts, not least of them the fact that many desert folk believed the best way to protect themselves from the Black Sleep was to burn everyone and everything that could possibly be infected. Which usually translated to *everything in sight*.

"You say there are no confirmed cases," Nasaan said. "This is only rumor?"

"At this point," Sarosh replied.

It was not necessarily comforting. Towns had been burned to the ground for less.

Sarosh looked to his companions, then back to Nasaan. "There's also some kind of unknown disease spreading among the nomads. It brings on a terrible weakness, like the Blood Sweat does, but it lacks all the other signs of that illness. Several families are said to have disappeared from the region, though of course with nomads it's hard to confirm that kind of thing. But if it's true . . . then they might have died of the sickness, or else been killed by others who feared infection. Either way, it is not a good sign."

Indeed, it was not. Nasaan was silent for a moment as he digested the information and considered its implications. Such problems might all have a common source . . . and one that was uncomfortably close to home. That was a very dark thought indeed, and he took great care to see that his expression did not betray the true tenor of his reflection, lest one of these men guess at the cause.

"This is all taking place outside my borders, yes? None of my people have caught the sickness yet?"

Sarosh's eyes narrowed slightly. "If you mean, is this happening outside your sphere of influence? Beyond the territory controlled by the tribes who have vowed their allegiance to Jezalya? Yes." There was a slight edge to his voice now. "No one who owes fealty to you has been affected."

"Then at least it will be clear to all that I can protect my own."

One of the other merchants drew in a sharp breath. Nasaan

looked at him. He was a tall, thin man with narrow features, someone Nasaan had never seen before.

"Begging your pardon," the man said, when he saw that the Prince's eyes were upon him, "but that is exactly the problem."

"And you are who?"

The merchant stiffened. "Duat et-Ahal, your Highness."

"Well, then, Duat et-Ahal, tell me. Clearly my witches are strong, and clearly they're able to hold this sickness at bay. Anyone who is willing to accept my protection need only ask for it. So Jezalya is safe, and all the people in it are secure. Why is that a problem for you?"

"Sire, Jezalya may be safe, but it's her connection to other cities that makes her great. Without trade caravans to bring the wealth of the world to her gates she would wither away and die. And if the masters of those caravans hear that there's a terrible wasting disease running rampant in this region, and that until they reach your gates they will not be safe from it, they will take their goods and go elsewhere."

"That would be a foolish move," Nasaan suggested, "as there are no other major trade routes within a hundred miles of here. Surely the Great Families would suffer."

The merchants looked at one another. Finally one ventured, "Highness, the elders of my family are already talking about abandoning our traditional rounds, even if it costs us business in the short run. Having a buyer for your goods means little if the seller dies before the sale can be concluded."

"That's why we came here today," Sarosh told him. "To tell you about what was being planned, so that you would have time to address the problem."

Nasaan raised an eyebrow. "What do you recommend I do?"

For a moment there was silence. Not the simple absence of

sound, but something more significant: a tangible sense that certain specific things were deliberately not being said.

"You have witches at your disposal," Sarosh said finally. "And other resources as well, I'm sure. If your people are strong enough to protect a city like Jezalya, then surely they can do more than that. Have them seek out the heart of the disease, even if it's outside your walls, and eradicate it. Yes, that will benefit some people who haven't yet sworn allegiance to you, but it will also prove you to be a magnanimous prince, worthy of men's allegiance in the future." He paused. "Jezalya needs this, your Highness."

"As do we," et-Ahal added.

Ah, Nasaan thought darkly, *but it is not all as simple as asking a witch to perform a healing spell.*

"What kind of time frame are we talking about?" he asked.

"If the Sleep appears in Bandezek, the caravan activity in this region will cease immediately. On this all the Great Families are agreed. Otherwise . . ." Sarosh looked at the other merchants before answering, waiting for a subtle signal of assent from each. "It depends on how much time the Families spend discussing this matter. Which in turn depends upon how much we, as your advocates, genuinely believe that the situation might improve."

Nasaan nodded tightly. "I understand." He looked at them one by one, making eye contact with each. He hoped he looked more optimistic than he felt. "Then I hope your discussions take a while. In the meantime, I'll talk to my witches about what can be done to address the situation."

Sarosh bowed his head. "Thank you, Highness."

Nasaan stood. It was hard to look calm and confident when inside his head there was a storm of conflicting emotions; he wondered if such dissembling would ever come naturally to him.

"I'm grateful to you all for coming here today. Grateful for your counsel. Such consideration from the Great Families will not be forgotten."

They bowed respectfully one by one, saying the kind of things that must be said in order to take proper leave of a prince. But he wasn't really listening to them anymore. His mind was elsewhere.

When they were finally gone—when the doors of the chamber had closed behind them, and their footsteps had faded out of hearing beyond it—a figure slipped out from behind a carved wooden screen.

"You heard," Nasaan said quietly.

"I heard," Siderea confirmed.

"Am I correct in guessing that you have more to do with this situation than simply *protecting Jezalya?*"

There was a moment of silence.

"Has your territory not doubled since you claimed the throne?" she asked. "Do the tribes not turn to you for protection?"

"That wasn't the question."

"True, my Prince." Her voice was like liquid silver, but for once it lacked the power to move him. "Do you really want to hear the answer?"

He shut his eyes. Not until he was sure his voice would be steady did he speak. "The strategies that once served this city now threaten it."

"Are you so sure of that?"

He glared at her. "I seem to recall the authority here was mine?"

She spread her hands. Delicate rings glittered on every finger. "Things have been set in motion. It's not easy to change them so late in the game."

"Then it will be difficult," he snapped. Suddenly out of patience with the whole situation. "Or are you telling me you're not up to the challenge?"

Something flashed in her eyes that was neither sycophancy nor seduction; he found it oddly refreshing. "I'm saying the matter isn't as simple as curing a handful of sick peasants. There's a reason for what's happening out in the desert. I can't just make it all go away."

"Then change something!" he ordered her, all his frustration welling up inside him suddenly, then pouring out with numbing force. "Change where the disease strikes! Change who it affects! There are hundreds of nomads out there in the desert who will never be seen by anyone save camels and vultures. No one cares if *they* get sick. No one will notice if a camp full of them disappears tomorrow. So whatever it is you're doing right outside my city—and you're right, I don't want to know what it is—take it to them. Or somewhere else." He struck out suddenly, slamming his fist into a nearby table. "*Anywhere but here!*"

He turned away from her, breathing deeply. A part of him recognized just how unreasonable he was being. This *djira* had helped him claim his throne. She had brought several fiercely independent tribes to his side and frustrated others who might have opposed him. It was the height of hypocrisy to condemn her methods now, when he had been so happy to applaud them earlier.

But conditions change, he thought. *Strategies must adapt. That is the way of war.*

"I will do what I can," she said.

The tension in his shoulders eased slightly. He had always wondered what would happen if his agenda and hers ceased to coincide. Whether she would accept his authority over her, in that case. Apparently so.

At least for now.

"See to Bandezek," he ordered her. "Protect its people the way you would protect mine. Jezalya will pay a heavy price if that place burns."

"I will not let it burn," she promised him.

Back when they had first discussed the terms of their bargain, she had told him that if the day came when he no longer valued her counsel, she would leave him. But she had made no promise to leave Jezalya altogether. More likely she would target Nasaan's city the way she was now targeting the nomads, to punish him for his rejection. The *djiri* were not known for their forgiving natures.

This would be good enough, he told himself. It would *have* to be good enough. At least for now.

He left without looking back at her.

The House of Gods was illuminated by two dozen immense oil lamps suspended from the ceiling, and their flames sent drops of light dancing along the gleaming surfaces of metal, jeweled, and polished stone idols, lending them an almost animated aspect. It was easy to believe there were spirits active in such a place and that the gods would take a special interest in protecting the city that housed them.

A statue of Alwat stood at the far end of the chamber. Nasaan could feel the power of the war god's presence as he walked up to face it. This was his patron deity, the god who had inspired him to dream of conquest back when he had been no more than a simple warrior. It was Alwat who had taught him to hunger for power, Alwat who had pointed him to Jezalya, Alwat who had urged him to claim this city for his own.

Alwat who had witnessed his bargain with the *djira*.

He heard footsteps come up behind him. He did not turn around. "Tell me," he said. "Spare me nothing."

Sarosh came up beside him. "There are some who whisper that your Lady Consort is a demon. And not some minor sand spirit, either, neatly bound to your service. Something even darker than a *djira*, with a purpose all its own. It's been suggested that the sickness outside the city comes from her. That she visits disease upon the tribes for her own purposes and cares nothing for Jezalya." He paused. "Or for you."

Anger and frustration welled up inside Nasaan, and since there was nothing in the room that he could break without earning the wrath of one god or another, he had a sudden mad impulse to strike at Sarosh. As if the merchant were responsible for the mess he was currently in.

"None of that is true," he growled. Forcing the moment's anger to subside.

"With all due respect, Highness . . . the truth does not matter. Gossip has a power all its own."

Yes, Nasaan thought darkly. He remembered the rumors he himself had spread prior to his conquest of Jezalya, which had helped topple the former prince from power. *And it can be a dangerous tool in the hands of one's enemies.*

With a snort of frustration he turned back to face Alwat. The god's eyes shimmered in the lamplight like living orbs, watching him. Was all this Nasaan's reward for trusting a war god to guide him? After all, from a purely military standpoint, his *djira* had done nothing wrong. Men feared him. His army was growing. Soon he would be ready to send his army out across the sands to expand his empire. It was everything he had prayed to Alwat for, everything his *djira* had promised to provide.

One could not expect a god of war to give a rat's ass about commerce. Or gossip.

Yet both can be as powerful as the sword, he thought soberly. *And both can bring down an empire.*

"I'm sorry," Sarosh muttered.

"Don't be. I pay you bribes so you'll tell me the truth."

"There are also rumors of dark creatures circling this city, out beyond the view of the watch. I'm not sure if anyone has actually seen one, but the nomads are convinced they're there. Sickness is said to follow in their wake."

Nasaan's chest tightened. "Winged creatures?"

"Yes."

He remembered the thing he had seen on the battlefield the night he claimed Jezalya. Black-winged, immense, and clearly not a natural creature. Were there more of its kind out there? If so, what was their relationship to his *djira*? Were they her allies? Her servants? Or something even more alarming? He was suddenly acutely aware of how far out of his element he was. He needed a priest to help him sort it all out. But there was no priest that he trusted enough to share this with.

"The merchants speak of these creatures?"

"Not yet. Only the nomads." He paused. "But that will change, if this goes on long enough. And if the tribes panic—*when* they panic . . ." He let the word trail off meaningfully.

Then there will be chaos, Nasaan thought. *And the gods may well decide to strike down the one who brought it to their doorstep.*

Drawing in a deep breath, he tried to settle the storm of frustration in his gut. Or at least to look as if he had settled it.

Reaching to his belt, he nodded stiffly. "I understand, Sarosh. Thank you. Your counsel is valuable to me, as always."

He pulled a small purse loose from his belt and handed it to him. The merchant did not look inside as he took it, but weighed it briefly in his palm and was apparently pleased by the results. "It is an honor to serve such a generous prince," he said, bowing his head respectfully.

He turned and headed toward the entrance. Nasaan listened to his footsteps receding for a moment, then said, "Sarosh."

The footsteps stopped.

"Bandezek will be safe from this plague."

There was a pause. "Our families will be glad to hear that, your Highness."

Then the footsteps passed over the threshold, leaving Nasaan alone with his gods.

CHAPTER 30

THE MAP was in eight pieces, and each one had been folded several times. Even with rocks holding down the corners it was hard to keep them all flat. How little sorcery would it have taken to flatten them out? Or to bind the pieces together into a cohesive whole? Though Colivar once might have disdained Salvator for his stubborn refusal to accept the use of sorcery, these days, with the spirit of a Souleater clawing at his own soul from the inside, he did not view Penitent beliefs in quite the same light.

Gwynofar had joined them at this meeting, along with one of Farah's marshals, a swarthy man introduced to them as Kaht. There was also a young woman named Shina, who had been put in charge of organizing the Seers and the Penitent witches into a united fighting force. Everyone watched silently as Farah laid out his papers, trying to derive meaningful information from the hastily scrawled images.

"The city is small by northern standards," Farah told them. "The eastern quarter is given over to the House of Gods, here." He pointed to the drawing of a round, domed building. "The palace is in the center of the city, here. The city is walled, solid stone on the outside with tempered earth at the core. Every witch that comes to the city is asked to contribute a spell to its reinforcement. That has been going on for twenty or thirty generations now, so locals believe that nothing short of a direct strike from the gods themselves could harm it. Probably true."

"Underneath?" Favias asked.

"Also reinforced, my scout says. It would appear that all the mundane routes of invasion have been guarded against." Farah folded his arms over his chest. "The current prince is a tribal warrior named Nasaan, who took the city by force a few months ago. He commanded a rather sizable army for this region—nearly a thousand men—but also relied heavily upon spies within the city to infiltrate its defenses. Locals now joke that every third person in the city answers to him, so trying to establish spies in the city would be risky business.

"He has a consort, supposedly a witch of some sort. Few people have seen her." He looked at Salvator. "It is rumored she is not human, but some kind of demon. It is also rumored that she controls Nasaan. Neither is sitting well with the populace."

"Siderea Aminestas," Salvator muttered.

Most likely, Colivar thought. It was hard for him to associate the name with an enemy who had nearly taken his life, rather than a lover he had once known. Images of the two were too tangled up inside his brain for him to separate them cleanly.

"Is it possible she really does control him?" Gwynofar asked. "Perhaps in a magical sense?"

"I'm sure he still has his free will," Colivar said dryly. "She delights in seducing men into obedience. There'd be no sport to it if they couldn't resist."

"A weakness," Salvator muttered. Clearly adding it to some mental checklist he was assembling. "So is the city loyal to this Nasaan? Do we know?"

Farah shook his head. "My scout said that the citizens don't seem to care much who rules them . . . though the inhuman-witch-consort thing has them a bit on edge. They've weathered a few violent coups in the past, and most just try to keep their heads down until the trouble passes. Nasaan offered to spare the city if it surrendered, and the majority of its residents went along with that." He paused. "His warriors are another matter. Tribal culture is fierce and bloodthirsty, and they consider dying in battle to be a sacred honor. If you met them in combat, you'd have to kill them to the last man before they'd give up . . . and maybe not even then.

"Outside the city is a strip of no-man's land, and beyond that, that great desert itself. It's populated by nomadic tribes, who gravitate to—and fight over—whatever stretch of land will feed their animals. The nearer ones have all sworn loyalty to Nasaan. The tribes that are farther out . . ." He hesitated. "There are strange rumors, my scout said. Some sort of wasting disease running rampant there. He even heard tales of human sacrifices being offered, in an effort to get the gods to intervene."

That is a Souleater's influence, Colivar thought. *Or more than one.* The thought brought back memories from so long ago it was like viewing another man's life. Images flashed before his eyes: whole towns with the spirit sucked out of them. Men and women who lacked the strength to feed themselves. Children abandoned by parents who had lost the capacity for human affection. "Where is this sickness supposed to be?"

Farah sketched out a wide circle on the map. The eastern side of it intersected a narrow line of mountain ridges, arranged in perfectly parallel lines. They looked as if some great beast had rent the earth with his claws.

"That's where they are," Colivar whispered. "The Souleaters."

Ramirus looked at him. "How many, do you think?"

His eyes narrowed as he considered the question. "If there were approximately three dozen to start with . . . minus the ones who were left to guard the queen up north, which she killed . . . which was probably only a token force, as they were clearly planning to move their focus down south . . ." He paused. "We should plan for two dozen. At least."

Sulah whistled softly. "That's a lot of Souleaters."

"I don't think we have armaments to take on that many," Favias said.

"Steel will work on them," Colivar assured him. "It's just not as effective."

Ramirus stroked his beard thoughtfully. "The primary challenge, as I understand it, is getting them to come to ground."

"The primary challenge with that many Souleaters," Colivar said dryly, "is figuring out a way to avoid having all your soldiers lie down on the sand and beg to be eaten. Everything else is secondary to that."

"I remember that," Kamala said quietly. "At Danton's castle, when—" She glanced at Salvator. "When Andovan died. I remember . . . wanting to be devoured."

"And that Souleater was little more than a mad beast," Colivar reminded her. "These won't only be sane, they'll have access to higher intelligence—and human allies to tell them when and how to best apply their power." He looked at Favias. "Allies who may be able to keep them from responding to your call as a wild Souleater would. We must allow for that possibility."

"The queen that I fought was bound to a human," Gwynofar pointed out. "And she responded to my challenge."

"She was bound to a child who knew nothing of strategy. And who was likely not strong enough to control her on a good day." He shook his head. "That won't be the case here."

Some of the riders they were about to confront might be survivors of the Great War. Those men had been powerful witches in their own right even before Souleaters had come into the picture. But he had no way to explain how dangerous they were without explaining how he knew that, so he kept his silence.

Some of them might even be men he knew. That wasn't a new thought, but the reality of it was only now sinking in. If he participated in this battle, he might well come face to face with those he had once lived with, fought with . . . and betrayed a world with. And then there was Nyuku. Hatred surged within him at the mere mention of the name. He had thought that all the centuries he'd put between them would have blunted the edge of that hatred, but apparently not.

Salvator looked at Farah. "What of the anchors? Did your man take care of that?"

"Aye," Farah said. "He planted them here, here, and here." He indicated points on the map just outside the no-man's-land. "And he says that he buried one behind the House of Gods as well, in case anyone needed to go straight there. Assuming you don't think the gods would mind," he added dryly.

"Very well," Salvator said, gazing down at the map. Colivar could almost hear his mind churning as he struggled to reduce all the information he'd just been given into some kind of cohesive strategy. "We have one goal that matters here, and one goal only. If the young Souleater queen is killed, then the rest of the species can be hunted down and destroyed at leisure. If she escapes, she may have a chance to create new queens before anyone can stop her. Once that happens there will be no practical way to eradicate them. Everything else must be planned with that in mind."

"Does she differ from the males in any way that matters to us?" Gwynofar asked.

Colivar could see Kamala hesitating. He nodded slightly in encouragement, but she was clearly nervous about contributing information to the conversation. As someone who had spent centuries concealing how much he knew about these creatures himself—and having had to dance a veritable tarantella around the subject in recent months—he was sympathetic to her misgivings.

Not to mention, revealing the nature of the queen's power would reveal her own. Though they won't understand that.

"She can mask her presence through misdirection," she said at last, "to a degree the others can't. No one will be able to see her unless she wants to be seen. And probably no sorcery can be focused on her while her defenses are up." She glanced at Salvator. "Or witchery."

"So we'll have to draw her out," Salvator said.

"Siderea's not a fool," Colivar pointed out. "At the first sign of trouble she'll flee Jezalya, taking the ikati queen with her."

Salvator nodded. "Then the first issue is making sure she can't do that."

Shina offered, "It should be possible to raise a spell that would hinder transport. But the power that would be required to do that, if we don't know exactly where she is . . ."

"You'd have to cover all of Jezalya," Ramirus said. "And since you can't set up camp directly outside city walls, that means a lot of extra territory would have to be included."

Favias pointed to the places where Farah had indicated anchors had been placed. "If witches came in at these points simultaneously, they could spread out from there. Shina?"

"Six focal points surrounding the city would be enough to establish a stable containment field," she said. "Mind you, that wouldn't prohibit all witchery. But it would cut short any attempt at magical transportation."

"So Siderea would not be able to escape, with or without her ikati."

"Six focal points for your witches means six points of weakness for an enemy to attack," Farah pointed out. "Kill one witch, break the circle. You are surrounded by tribes who answer to Nasaan, and possibly to her as well. Too easy."

"Our Seers can pool their energy into a single conjuration," Favias told him. "Removing one of them might weaken it, but the spell wouldn't collapse completely in any one place."

"But weaken it enough, and Siderea might be able break through," Salvator pointed out. "So everyone conjuring the spell will need cover, both military and metaphysical."

"You have enough witches for all that?" Farah asked, raising an eyebrow.

Salvator glanced up at him. A faint smile twitched his lips. "God provides for the faithful, King Farah."

"We still have two dozen Souleaters to deal with," Favias reminded them. "They'll see us as soon as we arrive, and if they have human intelligence, they're going to figure out what we're up to. Any one of them could lay waste to a witch and her bodyguards without missing a wingstroke. So we have to deal with them first or the rest is all meaningless."

"But if we do battle with them first, then Siderea will know that trouble is coming, and she'll likely flee. Along with our quarry." Salvator rubbed his forehead; it did nothing to ease the pain in his head. "What weapons can be used against these creatures? Besides the obvious?"

"Witchery—like sorcery—requires that one focus one's attention on the target," Ramirus said. "So we can't rely on that being available."

"I fought one," Kamala reminded him. "Outside Danton's castle. I focused on him well enough to use . . . witchery."

Colivar shook his head. "That one had been mentally unhinged by the death of its human consort. It could barely think straight, much less defend itself in any meaningful way."

Salvator looked at him suddenly. "Do they all respond like that when their human partners are killed?"

For a moment Colivar was silent. He was considering what he should or should not say . . . and what memories these words might awaken. Then, very quietly, he offered, "My understanding is that it depends on how long the bond between them has existed. For those who are newly joined, the death of one's Souleater's simply returns the human mind to its former state. A disorienting experience, to be sure, but not necessarily a crippling one. But the longer a bond endures, the more interdependent the two minds become. The sudden loss of half one's soul can be a devastating blow when you have forgotten any other mode of existence. And then for a Souleater, there is also the sudden loss of higher intelligence . . . which in some cases will be the only thing holding their bestial instincts in check." He looked at Salvator. "If you kill their human partners, the ikati may turn upon each other. Or they could turn on Jezalya. Or on you. There's no way to predict what will happen."

"So how do we take out their partners?" Favias asked. "That sounds like the most realistic strategy."

Colivar shook his head. "Souleaters never stray far from their human consorts. You won't be able to attack either group without the other moving in to defend it."

"What of Siderea herself?" Salvator asked thoughtfully. "If her Souleater were killed, would she go mad?"

Colivar hesitated. "That bond is very recent, so she should be able to weather severance fairly easily. But her queen may be another story. Depending on exactly how young it is, and when Siderea bonded to it . . . the creature may never have had to think for itself, except in the most primitive terms. In which case . . ."

". . . It may not be able to function at all," Salvator observed.

Colivar nodded. "Exactly."

"So if we destroy Siderea, the queen may be an easy kill."

"That's only speculation," Colivar warned him.

"I understand that."

Folding his arms across his chest, Salvator gazed down at the map. "It all hinges on the Souleaters, then, doesn't it? Without them in the picture, everything falls neatly into place. With them there, we have no starting point." He shook his head, clearly frustrated. "There must be a way."

"Majesty," Favias said, "I'd like a chance to confer with my fellow Archivists on this. With all this new information, they may be able to come up with a new strategy to deal with the creatures. Immobilize them perhaps, even if we can't kill them immediately."

Salvator considered, then nodded. "Very well. We could all use some time to digest this information, I think. Let's adjourn until first thing tomorrow morning; you can brief us then." He looked at Farah. "I thank you so much for all you've done for this campaign. If we're successful in this, it will be in good part because of your efforts."

"You flatter me, your Majesty."

"Do you have the anchors with you?"

Farah reached into a small pouch hanging from his belt and drew out four slender pieces of bone. Each had a broken end and was incised with a symbol from the map. "The other part of each of these is buried at the arrival site, in one of the places I indicated. Magister Sulah said that organic material would provide the best trace, so that's what we used."

"I'm told that is indeed the case," Salvator agreed. He held out his hand to receive them.

But Farah did not give them to him immediately. Instead he turned them over in his hand as if studying them; a gilded fingernail scratched one gently. "These have a price, King Salvator."

Colivar saw the High King stiffen. "What manner of price?"

"Something worthy of the hundreds of lives these will save. Perhaps whole nations, in the end. That is what is at stake, is it not?"

Salvator's eyes narrowed in displeasure. "The Souleaters are on your front doorstep, Farah. If they're not dealt with now, your kingdom will be the first to fall."

Farah chuckled softly. "Oh, I feel quite secure, King Salvator. I have seen your dedication and that of your followers. I have utter faith that you will triumph in the end. So the only question is . . . how much witchery must you waste along the way? Because witchery translates into lives lost, as you know." He folded his hand over the bones; his expression grew hard and cold. "Without these, you would have to pass through my kingdom to get to Jezalya. There is no other route. Did you

CELIA FRIEDMAN

think there would be no price for that? And even if you managed to somehow establish anchors of your own . . . then what of the journey home, after the battle ends? Will you ask your witches to sacrifice even more of their life-essence for that?" He shook his head. "No. Not you, King Salvator. *Penitent* King Salvator. You will want your people to return home by mundane means. Which means traveling through Anshasa." He nodded toward the anchors in his hand. "A reasonable investment for so many lives, I think."

"What price are you asking?" Salvator asked tightly.

Farah spread his hands wide. "Only what is rightfully mine, which was taken from my people years ago." He nodded toward the door of the tent, indicating the vast plain beyond. "Coldorra."

Salvator hissed softly. Colivar could see Ramirus stiffen. "Out of the question," the High King said coldly.

Farah's expression darkened. "Think well before you speak, Salvator. Time grows short for this campaign. Did you not say so yourself? How many witches would you have to sacrifice to find another way to get down there in the proper time frame? I believe I am offering you a bargain, under the circumstances."

Seeing Salvator's lips tighten into a thin, hard line, Colivar had to repress a smile. *Ah, Farah, I thought you were going down too easily. Glad to see you had something up your sleeve after all.* The High King would have to give in, of course. His religion left him no other choice. Whereas Farah would not have hesitated to order the death of a hundred witches, if that was the price of war.

"No," Salvator said.

Gwynofar looked at him, startled. Even Ramirus drew in a sharp breath.

Farah's eyes narrowed. "Are you sure, King Salvator? So many lives, measured against one small stretch of land." A faint, cold smile flickered across his face. "I would think a Penitent king would have better priorities."

"The answer is no," Salvator said coldly. "And it will remain no. I will not be blackmailed into diminishing my kingdom." He raised a hand in dismissal. "I believe our business is done here, King Farah. I thank you for the amount of assistance you were willing to provide. I will take it from here."

He began to turn away.

"Salvator."

He stopped, but did not turn back.

"Your people are from the north. From the far north, for the most part. Do you really think that you can just march them into the desert—in full armor—and wage war as though you were still in the High Kingdom?" Farah shook his head disdainfully. "They will not last a day. Some will not even last an hour. I have seen foreign armies halved by the desert's heat before the fighting even began."

Salvator turned back to him slowly. "What are you suggesting?"

"They will need time to acclimate. A safe place to work off their first sweat. Training in how to deal with the desert. What if your witches all die in battle? In that case, the rest of your people will have to come home the long way." He paused. When Salvator still did not respond he added, "You should have a guide who speaks the local languages. Someone who knows the lay of the land and will be able to parley with any hostile tribes you run into."

"Are you offering to supply these things?" Salvator asked quietly.

Farah glanced at Kaht, who lowered his eyes almost

imperceptibly. It was the smallest motion a nod could possibly be reduced to and still exist.

"Bring your people to my southern border," Farah said, "and I will provide shelter and supplies for them. Set aside five days—three for hard training, then two to rest and recoup before you engage the enemy—and I guarantee your chance of success in this venture will improve." He paused. "The desert gods are cruel, Salvator. Only a fool underestimates them."

"You spoke of training. And a guide."

Again Farah looked at Kaht, who nodded again. "Marshal Kaht will see to the training of your men. I will provide a guide," Farah said.

"And safe passage through your realm, coming and going?"

"Of course."

Salvator seemed to consider the offer. Finally, nodding slightly, he stepped around the table and approached Farah. When he was within an arm's length, he paused for a moment, then extended his hand, palm up. "You will not bring your armies into Coldorra. I will arrange for my own observers to make sure of it. If you breach that condition of our agreement, all the rest is nullified, and Coldorra returns to my control." His gaze was steady and cold. "We have a peace treaty now, so there is no longer need for armies at the border."

Farah's nostrils flared, and for a moment it looked as though he might offer an edged retort. But then he just chuckled softly, and he reached out and dropped the bone fragments into Salvator's outstretched palm, one by one. "You must have merchants in your bloodline, Aurelius."

"And you must have devils in yours," Salvator answered, smiling slightly. The tension level inside the pavilion dropped palpably as he looked at the bone fragments for a moment, then tucked them into his doublet. "I will see that everything you require is properly signed and sealed before we leave this camp. How long before your training site will be ready for us?"

Farah looked at Kaht.

The marshal considered the question for a moment. "Five days to get all the supplies delivered and set it up right, with no one but me and a few handpicked officers knowing about it, and with witches masking the whole place from scrutiny. I could make it three days if we risked bringing in a few more people, but I would advise against that."

Salvator nodded. "Five days it is. Have confirmation and a suitable anchor delivered to me when you're ready for my people to arrive." He turned to Farah. "You had no objection to my marching an army through your territory; do you have any objection to a decoy army doing so instead? We'll mask it with enough witchery that it will be hard for Siderea to detect, which will make it look convincing. If she thinks she's discovered a hidden army marching south to take her by surprise, she may not look as hard in other places."

A faint smile crept across Farah's face. "I will see that a few key people know there is something along the route that we don't want people looking into too closely."

"Excellent." Salvator sighed heavily. "All the rest must wait on the Archivists' report, it seems. So I suggest we call it a day, and set the scribes working on the necessary agreements."

"A most productive afternoon," Farah agreed. He nodded his head ever so slightly. "Until morning, then, King Salvator."

He left the pavilion, Kaht and Sulah following silently in his wake. As soon as they were gone, Favias exhaled noisily. "That was one hell of a gamble. If he had really walked out on you—"

"He would not have walked out," Salvator said calmly. "The

minute he walked in with Kaht by his side, I knew he was here to bargain, and I had a pretty good idea of what he planned to put on the table."

"Coldorra is quite a prize," Colivar said quietly. "Did you anticipate that request as well?"

Salvator shrugged. "Coldorra is a piece of land, nothing more. I am not my father, who measured his greatness in acreage. Our quarry is on the far side of a hostile kingdom, and that is a problem that isn't going to be solved cheaply. Land is the most acceptable of the available options." A faint smile flickered across his lips. "Why do you think I arranged to have our meeting here, if not to make sure that Coldorra was front and center in his mind?"

"She will figure out where your people are," Colivar warned him. "Whatever you do, and however many witches or sorcerers you assign to keep it hidden, that kind of power leaves its mark. She need not look for your men, only for the spells that are hiding them. A witch of her caliber will know how to do that."

"Precisely. Which is why I have set up two decoy operations. The first is simply there to make the second look genuine. In actual fact, we will be using witches to send our people directly to Jezalya, even while visible preparations are being made for their reception in Farah's domain. If Siderea does indeed catch a whiff of magic out there and investigate, she'll discover that everyone involved genuinely expects us to arrive at Farah's camp in five days' time."

"I presume, then, that you expect to be in Jezalya within five days," Ramirus said. "Because after that, Farah will know something is wrong . . . and so will all his men."

Salvator nodded. "We'll be leaving directly from here, as soon as Farah departs. Our camp is much more complex than his, so it will of course take longer to strike. An innocent reason to remain behind. By the time his rear scouts quit the area, our witches will have begun preparing portals to Jezalya. If all goes well, we will be out of here before Farah has time to give his first orders back home."

Colivar raised an eyebrow. *So your Penitent witches are already here in the camp, and your Guardians as well. Disguised as soldiers, perhaps? While the massive size of the encampment gave you an excuse to move in supplies in quantity, with no one asking questions about it. Very clever.*

Ramirus coughed lightly. "There is one more issue, your Majesty. With all due apology, I know how important your faith is to you . . . but we must have a Magister in Anshasa. There is simply no way around that."

Salvator's face darkened. "Why?"

"Siderea knows there's a cadre of Magisters hunting her. If your diversion doesn't have the faintest whiff of sorcery about it, she'll know this trick for what it is and keep searching elsewhere for her enemies."

Salvator was silent for a moment, his eyes narrowing as he considered the philosophical issues involved. There was a time when Colivar could have guessed how he would respond, but lately the young king had proven quite unpredictable. And surprisingly interesting.

"I don't think God would have a problem with a Magister guarding empty space," Salvator said at last. "Can you find someone to go down there?"

Ramirus turned to Colivar. "I suggest Sulah."

Colivar saw what was in his eyes and nodded. "I agree." *Nicely played, Ramirus. I don't trust him either.*

"Which leaves only the assault itself," Salvator said, "and the problem of two dozen Souleaters." He sighed heavily. "On the plus side, the fact that they're there means that Siderea may have made no other arrangements to protect herself, since they could be expected to take down any witch, Magister, or mortal army that came calling. On the minus side . . ." He shook his head in obvious frustration. "Well, there are two dozen Souleaters. And if we don't figure out how to get rid of them, the rest of this is all empty conversation. They are the key to everything."

Gwynofar offered, "Let's see what the archivists have to say tomorrow, shall we?" She glanced at Favias. "They may have suggestions. For now, I think we've done all we can."

"Aye." Salvator sighed again. "We have indeed."

He offered his arm to escort his mother out. As she took it, he nodded a polite leave to his guests. Even to the Magisters, Colivar noted.

The High King became more and more unpredictable every day.

And more and more interesting.

CHAPTER 31

KAMALA FOUND Colivar far from the main encampment, gazing at the rising moon. She stood next to him silently, watching as the full disk eased its way over the horizon, while the twilight sky surrounding it slowly faded to black.

"They didn't have human intelligence back then," Colivar said. "They couldn't gather in large numbers. They feared fire. And with all that in our favor, we barely managed to defeat them. Thousands of witches died. *Thousands*. We don't have that many to start with. How can we possibly do this?"

"We have Magisters," Kamala reminded him. "If Salvator can be made to listen to reason . . ."

Colivar shook his head. "Can't rely on Magisters. What if the ikati portion of a sorcerer's soul grows stronger in their presence? What if he surrenders control to it? Even having Ramirus and myself there will be a risk. Each additional Magister you add makes it that much more likely something bad will happen. What happens if we wind up turning on one another, as the Souleaters do? There won't be anything left in the desert by the time that fight is over."

Yes, Kamala thought, *and you are the most vulnerable of all. Which makes you the most dangerous.* "Give me some more information about these creatures, Colivar."

He looked at her. "You heard everything I told the other Magisters. What more do you want to know?"

"Tell me about the mating flight."

"Why? Siderea's queen is still a juvenile. No matter how fast she's maturing, she won't have the size or the strength needed for her first flight this soon. As long as we move quickly we should be fine."

"Indulge me," she said softly.

He shut his eyes and sighed. For a moment he just stood there, so still in aspect that it seemed his mind had left his flesh. Then, very quietly, he began to speak.

"It begins with a call. The queen takes to the sky and declares her intent; the sound of it carries for miles. It's somewhat like the cry that the Guardians imitate, but it's not a call to combat. There's also a smell that fills the air, like her own natural scent but ten times more powerful; it can be detected by Souleaters a hundred miles away. Their response is instinctive. All-consuming. Wherever they are, whatever they are doing, male Souleaters will put their business aside and come to her. The summons is woven into the very fabric of their being, and not even human intelligence can override it.

"And so they are all drawn to the same place, at the same time. Back when the species was wild, that alone was enough to get many of them killed. Much blood was spilled before a flight even began. These days the creatures are marginally more tolerant of one another—and they may have improved further in that regard since last I saw them—but it's still a dangerous time. Bloodthirst and sex are so closely allied in that species that it would take more than mere human will to separate them."

"Are their human partners with them during all this?"

"Gods, no! Getting caught in the middle of that chaos is dangerous enough with spikes and claws; a man would not last five minutes. No, the men generally try to find somewhere safe to wait it out, preferably far away from each other. Channeling that kind of energy doesn't do good things to human relationships. Often they will go into a sort of trance, opening themselves up to the full sensory experience of their Souleater's flight. You don't want rivals around when you do that." He paused. "Not unlike a Magister's fear of having rivals present when he goes into transition.

"Finally, when enough males have gathered, the queen takes flight, and they pursue her. She is lighter and faster than they are, so if she keeps to open skies, none of them can catch her. Ostensibly it's the strongest and most capable one who will lead the pack and eventually be rewarded with mating rights. But the males are known to swipe at each other along the way, to try to gain advantage, and sometimes actual combat breaks out. A queen may even encourage that, doubling back and forth in such a way that the paths of her suitors cross." He shrugged stiffly. "As I said . . . bloodthirst and sex.

"The fact that she can turn their attention away from her allows her to elude any unwanted suitor who gets too close. It's difficult for her to hide herself fully at that point—their attention is too firmly fixed on her for true invisibility to be possible—but she can cause them to become disoriented, which has much the same result."

"What happens when she does that?"

He looked at her. "What do you think happens when all the

energy that was centered on pursuing a mate suddenly has no proper focus?" He shut his eyes; a tremor seemed to run through his body. "I have seen fields of snow turn to crimson in the wake of such a flight. I remember one time we lost nearly a third of the colony."

"It sounds like a good way to get rid of a few Souleaters. Not to mention draw them away from Jezalya while the battle is going on."

"It would be," he agreed. "But as I said, Siderea's queen is still a juvenile. There'd be no way to get her to declare a flight, much less actually fly it."

She said it softly: "I wasn't talking about the Souleater queen."

It took a moment for her meaning to sink in; when he realized what she meant, his eyes widened in alarm. "Surely you can't be suggesting what I think you are."

"Why not? You told me I had the essence of a Souleater queen within me. I know I can tap into her power. Why can't I mimic her form as well? Then I can summon the males to a mating flight myself and draw them away from the battleground. Hopefully long enough for Salvator's people to do what they need to." When he said nothing, she pressed, "Wouldn't that solve the problem?"

"Kamala." His voice was very quiet. "This isn't a simple shapeshifting experiment we're talking about. There is a part of your soul for which this form is natural and human flesh is alien. Thus far that part has been buried deeply within you, manifesting as little more than a metaphysical echo, but there's no guarantee it will stay that way. What happens when you give it the freedom it hungers for and the body it longs to possess? Are you so sure you'll be able to change back after that?"

"Colivar." She reached out a hand to touch his cheek. She

could feel his tension beneath her fingertips, muscles tightly controlled as he sought to keep his expression from revealing too much to her. "I understand why you're so concerned, but remember . . . I'm human. I've never been anything but human. If this . . . this Souleater essence . . . takes on a life of its own, then I will fight it off as I would fight off any other possession. Do you doubt my tenacity in such a contest?"

In answer he reached up and took her hand away from his cheek. She thought that he hesitated a moment before releasing it, but it was hard to be sure. "Ignoring for the moment your boundless self-confidence, there are practical considerations here. Think back to when you first learned to shapeshift. Do you not remember how you stumbled the first time you had to walk on four legs? Or how the wind buffeted you about the first time you took on winged form, until you learned how to ride it properly? Each form carries within it the instinct necessary for it to function, but that doesn't mean we can access it right away. It takes time and practice. The more alien the form is to our own, the harder it is to adapt, and the longer it takes.

"The Souleaters are unlike any creatures you've ever replicated before. The nature of their flight has nothing in common with that of birds or bats, so the fact that you've mastered those forms won't help you at all. The subtle currents of air and heat that a bird rides are meaningless to an ikati; its wings stir up currents independent of the wind, powerful enough to lift that massive body without need for forward motion. Different muscles. Different dynamics." He shook his head. "You wouldn't have any time to practice. Your very life would depend upon your ability to fly perfectly from the start, and you can't do that without prior knowledge of how an ikati body functions."

"No," she said softly. Her voice a whisper. "I would need to get that knowledge from someone who already possessed it."

It took him a moment to realize what she meant. When he did so, he recoiled as if he had been struck, and all the color drained from his face. "You cannot ask that of me."

"Who else has what I need, Colivar?" When he didn't respond she pressed, "Who else has smelled the perfume of a mating queen—who else has heard the call to flight as a Souleater performs it—has felt the beat of those great wings, the flexing of the muscles that drive them? Or do I mistake the nature of the bond you shared? Did you not experience those things along with your consort?"

"You don't understand the risk," he whispered fiercely. Turning away from her.

"I just need to share your memories," she told him. "Nothing more. You wouldn't be transforming into an ikati. Or inviting one into your brain. However terrible your memories may be— whatever instincts you fear they may awaken in you—surely they're still just that: memories."

"They're *not* terrible," he whispered. "That's the point."

"And are you telling me that you haven't ever dreamed of that time? That you've never surrendered to those memories in your sleep, so that for an hour you thought you were back there? Yes? Didn't you awaken after that? Shaken, perhaps, but still human?" She paused. "You won't be able to escape the ghosts of your past until the last of the Souleaters is gone, Colivar. And this may be the only way to get rid of them." When he still said nothing, she pressed, "Do you have a better suggestion?"

For a long moment he stared out into the distance. "No," he said finally. "No. I do not."

Slowly he turned back to her. "Once," he said. "I will do this only once. If that's not enough for you, you'll need to find some other source of information. Or come up with another plan."

She nodded solemnly. "Agreed."

He lifted a hand to her face and placed it against her cheek; his sorcery should not require such a thing, but she guessed he was doing it to help him focus.

"You will have to let me in," he whispered. "I'm sorry."

She nodded, closed her eyes to shut out all distractions, and tried to take down enough of her defenses for him to make direct contact with her mind. It was harder than it had been with Ramirus. She'd been battered and weak back then, and she had needed to submit to him in order to survive. Now she was strong, and her survival instincts rebelled at the mere thought of letting another Magister into her mind. Even Colivar.

But if she wanted to be able to draw off the Souleaters, then she had to do this. And so, squeezing her eyes tightly shut, she turned her awareness inward and stripped herself of all the spells that normally protected her from others of her kind. She could feel his sorcery taking its place, moving into her soul, and she gritted her teeth as she struggled not to resist it.

Then the memories came pouring in.

Clouds like icy knives score his flesh as he plunges through them—

Rivals on every side screech their mating challenge to the wind—

Teeth pierce through his tail. He shakes them off. His own tail whips through the air, driving its blades into the offender. His serpentine body twists in its flight like an agile dancer, compensating for the motion. Wings shift their angle. Flight is steady once more.

He howls out his own challenge, rage and lust and bloodthirst combined, but does not look back. His lead over the others is fragile, and one moment's inattention might cause it to be lost. He must stay ahead of the others. He has no choice. He must fly faster and harder and higher than all of the others, even if he expends the last ounce of his strength in doing so. Even if he dies in doing so. There is no other action possible for him.

How hard it is to fly in the cold, dim sunlight! Frozen muscles struggle to move the great wings; flight that should be fluid and painless is torment. His lower wings beat the air with frenetic energy, creating roiling whirlwinds to support him. His upper wings stretch out into the frozen sky, struggling to stabilize his flight. The scent of the queen surrounds him, envelops him, maddens him. Her cry resonates in the air, stirring his blood. In the wake of such things no rational thought is possible. Hunger pounds in his veins, more terrible than anything he has ever known, and he must satisfy it or die in the attempt—

The flow of memories ceased so suddenly that it left Kamala gasping for breath. For a moment her mind could not adjust to the shift in reality, and she stumbled. Strong hands grasped her by the arms, holding her upright. She trembled, overwhelmed by the sensation of being human once more. Already it seemed an alien thing to her.

Shaken, she looked up into Colivar's eyes. How dark they were, how haunted! So much pain in their depths. And desire. So much desire. The madness of the ikati had faded from his mind, but she could sense the human hunger that had taken its place. For a moment they just stared at each other, wordlessly aware of how close they were to one another, equally loath to move away.

"I didn't expect the pain," she whispered.

"They need the sun on their wings. We trapped them in a

place starved of sunlight. The ones that were born there have never known anything else."

The moon was rising. It reflected in his eyes.

"Do you have what you need now?" he asked. *Because I cannot go there again*, his expression said plainly.

She nodded. In truth, it was not as much as she had hoped for. But it would have to be enough. She would make it enough. She would replay the memory in her mind, over and over, until she knew the feel of the ikati's body as well as she knew her own. Until the motions of its flight were as familiar to her as breathing, and the scent and cry of a queen's flight were second nature to her.

"Yes," she whispered. Raising a hand to his face, brushing back a lock of jet-black hair that had fallen across it. His cheek was warm, and it seemed to her that he trembled slightly as her fingers brushed against it. So much hunger. So tightly controlled. What had it been like for him in the first days of his exile, when human memories had been no more than a distant echo? How did a man hang on to sanity when his soul and his flesh were no longer in agreement?

We are the harvest of your madness, she thought.

For a moment he did not respond to her. Then he reached up to catch hold of her hand, drawing it away from her cheek. His heart was pounding so hard she could feel the blood pulse in his palm, but in his eyes there was only sadness. He put her hand down by her side and let go, then moved back from her ever so slightly, so they were no longer close. A single inch. A thousand miles.

"Why?" she asked.

A shadow of pain flickered in his eyes.

"Because I'm not sure which part of me wants you," he told her. "Or why."

Before she had a chance to respond, he transformed himself. Black wings flurried in the air before her—a single feather brushed her cheek in passing as he rose up—and then he was gone.

She watched him head out over the plain, his wings rising and falling in a simple rhythm, until the currents of the evening wind carried him out of sight.

CHAPTER 32

MASTER FAVIAS and the High King were together when Shina found them, conferring in a small tent near the edge of Salvator's military encampment. Just before entering it, she stopped for a moment, closed her eyes, and tried to bring the fluttering of her heart under some semblance of control. Not until she felt she was calm enough to do what she had come to do did she continue on to the tent itself and greet the guards outside.

No one liked to bring bad news to a king.

In the distance, to the south, one could hear the sounds of Farah's camp being struck. The Anshasans were working quickly and efficiently, and soon all his people would be gone, leaving nothing in their wake but trampled tufts of grass stubble and a line of earthen mounds where the cesspits once had been. Salvator's men seemed to be having trouble with their work and were well behind schedule. With as many grand and complicated tents as the High King had brought with him, some of his people would probably be at the site long after the last of Farah's men had departed.

She felt a tightening in her gut at the thought that within a day or two—as soon as Farah's people were all gone—they would be moving out to Jezalya. And because of her failure, a key element of the campaign could not be brought into play.

The thought of delivering that news to Salvator made her sick inside.

The two men looked up when she entered, and they seemed genuinely pleased to see her. For some reason that made it worse. There was a camp table between them with papers they had apparently been going over. She did not look down to see what they were.

"Your Majesty," she said, bowing her respect. "Master Favias."

Then she drew in a deep breath and said, "I bring news from the witches."

"Ah, good." The High King pushed the papers away and picked up a metal cup that had been sitting beside them. "Let's hear it."

Shina had always found the High King intimidating. They had put her in charge of the witches because she was the most skilled of all the Seers, but her life in Kierdwyn had not prepared her for the frenzied world she was suddenly part of, or for the battle-scarred priest-king who lorded over it.. The three deep claw marks running down his face gave his expression a fearsome aspect even when he was smiling—which he did not do often—and while the clarity of his faith was a thing to be praised, its intensity unnerved her. She was not used to dealing with fanatics. Or with giving them bad news.

"Majesty," she said, "We have been unable to teach our spell-song ritual to the Penitent witches. It appears . . ." She paused. Did she look as nervous as she felt? "It appears they are incapable of learning it."

The silence that followed her pronouncement was not what she'd expected. It was worse.

Salvator turned to Favias. "How important is this ritual?"

"Important." Favias' expression was grave. "This is very bad news."

Salvator turned back to Shina. "Most of the witches in the world know nothing about this trick, and they seem to function well enough. The witches of the Great War didn't have it, and they dealt with the Souleaters quite effectively. I understand why it would be a good addition to our arsenal, but what makes it such a pivotal element?"

Shina looked to Favias to see if he would take the burden of explanation from her, but he nodded for her to continue. With a sigh of resignation, she turned back to the High King. "The spellsong ritual allows a number of witches to pool their efforts, so that all their energy can be combined into a single spell. We use it mostly to share the cost of witchery amongst ourselves, but there are other advantages, which we'd hoped to apply here . . ." How much did he already know, how much did she need to explain? Neither man was giving her any kind of clue. "Normally, if a dozen witches wanted to raise a barrier about Jezalya, each one would have to conjure a section of that barrier by herself, then all the segments would be joined together. The problem is that if one witch were killed, her section would then collapse. But if those same witches were to pool their efforts as the Seers do, then the entire barrier would become a single spell, drawing its strength equally from each of them. Then, if one witch were killed, the spell would grow weaker overall, but there would be no single point at which it failed completely. And the whole of the barrier would be stronger, also . . . but that is not the part that matters most." She shook her head.

"Without this we are very vulnerable, your Majesty. A single well-placed arrow could break the barrier wide open. We might compensate through redundancy, erecting several barriers . . . " She let her voice trail off, certain they could fill in the rest themselves. *Time lost. More witches needed. More life-essence sacrificed.*

Salvator nodded; it was clear from his grim expression that he was beginning to grasp just how serious the problem was. "You say the Penitent witches can't learn this trick?"

She bowed her head. "It appears so, your Majesty."

"Why not?" he demanded.

She shook her head. "None of us have ever seen anything like this before. We had anticipated that maybe the two groups would turn out to be metaphysically incompatible, given that they draw their inspiration from two such different paradigms, but that should have resulted in two unified collectives instead of one . . . not an unlimited number of people who can't connect to each other at all."

"Are there prayers involved in this ritual of yours? Or any religious references? The polytheism of most *lyr* is anathema to our faith. References to such beliefs might keep Penitents from making the kind of spiritual commitment that would be required."

Shina shook her head. "The incantations that we use rely upon metaphors of unity and common purpose. Nothing that should give offense to any god." *Even your infamously intolerant Creator*, she thought. "But we did ask the question anyway. So one of your Penitent witches translated our incantations into the language of your own faith, glorifying your god, so that the ritual would be a true Penitent undertaking. And then they tried it among themselves, without any of us in the circle. But even that didn't help." She hesitated. "I'm told that several of your people offered up penance to the Creator, whatever that means. Just in case they had been sinful enough that their god was displeased by them, and that's why he wouldn't let them master the ritual. But that didn't help either. Something about the Penitents simply makes it impossible for them to learn this technique, and we don't have a clue what it is. I'm sorry, your Majesty."

Salvator stared at her in silence for a moment. His gaze was daunting. Then he turned back to Favias. "Do we have enough Seers to conjure the barrier without Penitent assistance?"

"Minimally," Favias said. "We had counted on linking them up to your people. It will be a much weaker construct without them."

"But we can get the barrier up. That's the most important part, yes?" He turned back to the Seer. "Keep trying," he ordered. "Up until the minute that we leave for Jezalya, keep trying. And if you come up with any clue as to why this problem exists, come talk to me. If it's something connected to the Penitent faith, perhaps I can help you figure out how we can compensate for that. Meanwhile . . ." His lips tightened into a hard line. "Time is too precious here. Once the fifth day arrives and our people don't show up at Farah's training camp, it will be clear to all what's really going on." He shook his head tightly. "We cannot delay this. We move out at dawn as planned. Do your best to solve the problem before then."

What if it is Penitent beliefs that have made your witches weak? she thought. *What if they're not strong enough spiritually—or magically—to do what's being asked of them?*

But that was something she would never say to the High King. Not even in her sleep.

"Yes, your Majesty." She bowed her head respectfully. "I will certainly do that."

At dawn, she knew, she would probably be reporting her final failure.

———

"The Queen said you wished to see me."

Salvator put aside the pen he was holding and waved for the servants to leave them alone together. "Yes, I did. I felt there was something we should discuss before we left Coldorra." As the last of the servants left the pavilion, his expression took on a solemn air. "The question of sorcery in Jezalya."

Ramirus' expression did not waver, but Salvator could see a muscle along the line of his jaw tense slightly. "With all due respect, your Majesty, I've made a commitment to the Queen Mother, and I must protect her. If sorcery is required to do that, then I will use sorcery. Even your sovereignty can't override a Magister's contract."

Salvator raised a hand to silence his protest. "Magister Ramirus. Please." When he saw that he had silence, he lowered his hand. "It's rare that a Magister comes up against anything that has the capacity to kill him. But these Souleaters undoubtedly can do that, and Siderea may be able to as well. Yet you and Colivar have offered your support in this venture, and shortly you may risk your lives to assure its success. *He* certainly is risking his life. That's the kind of thing no man does lightly, and for one who can hold death at bay indefinitely if he's careful enough . . . it's an extraordinary act.

"It would be ungrateful of me—and unreasonable—to expect you to do that with both hands tied behind your back. Would it not?"

Ramirus' expression was wary. "I would not presume to judge your character, Majesty."

"No." He smiled faintly. "Not while I'm around to hear it, anyway." He shook his head. "Understand, I do expect you to respect the beliefs of the Penitents and not use your power upon myself or my witches. Death with honor is preferable to corruption, in our eyes. And since the gift of the *lyr* shows signs of being incompatible with sorcery, you should refrain from using your arts on them as well, lest their power be compromised. A purely practical matter. Other than that . . ." He paused, then said quietly, "I will not place restraints upon your actions. Or Colivar's. So you can concentrate on the matter at hand without worrying about my sensibilities."

Ramirus just stared at him for a moment. Salvator could not recall any other time when he had seen the Magister look surprised; it was oddly satisfying. "Majesty, I . . . don't know what to say."

"There is nothing to say, Ramirus." Salvator picked up his pen again and focused on it, not wanting to meet the Magister's eyes any longer. "Send the servants back in on your way out, please. And let Colivar know."

When Ramirus was gone he put down his pen and sighed. *You will do whatever you want once the battle starts, and so will Colivar. Don't you think I know that? This way, at least you may respect my prohibition when you can, as opposed to writing it off entirely.*

Maybe if he repeated that often enough, he would believe it.

Gwynofar found Salvator at the edge of the field, almost alone. Now that Farah's people were finally gone, he was allowed to walk more than ten feet away from his guards without them protesting, but they were still watching him, albeit from a respectful distance. She felt a pang of sympathy in her heart, knowing how much he valued the quiet solitude of meditation. But until they went home again, this was as close as he was going to get to being alone.

"Salvator," she said gently.

He turned to her.

"I heard about the witches," she said.

He sighed and shut his eyes for a moment. "Why would their love of God make them incapable of learning?" he whispered. "Is it my fault? Have I offended against the Creator somehow? Is this His punishment for me, to send me into battle with my forces hamstrung?"

"Surely he wouldn't do that to one so faithful."

"I vowed obedience to His will, and I have fallen short. Time and time again I've compromised His law for political expediency, or else just to please others." *You being one of them*, his expression reminded her. "Now I sit at a table with Magisters and listen to how they will play a part in this war, as if they were no more than morati marshals. Not all the penance in the world is enough to cleanse that stain from my soul," he said bitterly.

"Salvator. You are a king. A Penitent king. If your god wants such a creature to exist in the world, then He must make allowances for the things a king has to do."

He sighed heavily. "I told Ramirus I wouldn't forbid him from using sorcery."

She said it softly: "I heard that too."

"What other choice did I have? He's not going to restrain himself for my sake, if he perceives that his life is at stake. So I can play the fanatic and pretend that isn't the case, insist that he go into battle on my terms rather than his, and then watch as he blithely disregards my authority . . . or I can put on a show of compromise and hope that the few conditions I do insist on—the ones that really matter—will be respected."

She put a gentle hand on his arm. "It was a wise call, my son."

"Then why are the Penitent witches failing?" he demanded. "What if He doesn't want us to fight this war at all, Mother? What if He brought the Souleaters back to punish mankind for its sins, and He doesn't want us destroying them until they've finished their job? Might he not give us one last warning, in that case? One last warning to withdraw from this affair of our own free will, before He takes matters into His own hands?"

"The leaders of your Church sanctioned this campaign," she reminded him. "If your god didn't want this to happen, don't you think he would have sent them some kind of sign before this?"

"Perhaps He did. Perhaps they missed it. The entire First Age of Kings misread the will of the Creator, didn't they? The Souleaters were sent as a warning, and they never understood that. So their world was destroyed. If the leaders of my Church repeat their mistake, doesn't it stand to reason that the same penance might be applied to them?"

"Would your god destroy a whole world for the sake of a few?"

"My god is the Creator, from whom all life descends. He fashioned this world as an act of divine love, and He gave mankind all that he needs to prosper. My god is also the Destroyer, whose job it is to cleanse the world of sin. If mankind's spiritual corruption becomes so great that mere prayers and penance can no longer address the problem, then it is His duty to step in and wipe the slate clean, so that man can start over. As He did once before."

Gwynofar sighed. *Your god demands a perfection of man that is not in his nature,* she thought. But she squeezed his arm gently and said in her softest, most comforting voice, "I know nothing about these things, my son. All I know is that come daybreak we'll be heading out to Jezalya, and you need a good night's sleep before that. For better or for worse, we're committed to this now. Try not to torment yourself with doubts that have no practical purpose." She paused. "Have one of the witches help you sleep if you need to." When he didn't respond she prodded him gently with her finger. "Promise me."

A faint, pained smile flickered across his face. "I promise, Mother."

She drew him down to her and kissed him gently on the forehead. Then she quietly took her leave. As she headed back to the encampment, she whispered a prayer to her own gods. Not to any one of them in particular . . . just anyone who cared to listen.

Help me, she begged. *I know he's wrong. He has to be wrong. Give me the tools I need to prove it to him, so he can go into battle armored in the confidence of his faith, not weakened by doubt.*

The wings of the Throne of Tears are dark and silent, inviting Gwynofar into their embrace. She trembles, remembering her first experience with the artifact, and one hand moves reflexively over her stomach, mourning the child who was lost that day.

The ancient knowledge of the lyr is linked to this artifact. Surely she can find the answers she needs here.

But her legs feel weak beneath her as she steps up onto the dais. She can see where her crusted blood still adorns the grotesque chair. Wasted, all of it wasted, until the ultimate sacrifice was offered. If she had known what would be required of her, would she have followed the same path? Or would she have given in to a mother's strongest instinct and backed away from the Throne, protecting her unborn child at any cost? Even if that meant that all the others in the tower would have to die? The question has haunted her ever since that terrible day.

How merciful the gods were, to have removed the choice from her hands.

Trembling, she lowers herself down onto the throne, resting her arms along its deeply carved arms. Her fingers curl down naturally over the ends, fitting themselves in between the polished claws, fingertips brushing the faceted crystals they hold. A single flake of dried blood, dislodged by her motion, falls to the floor.

Show me the way, she prays to her gods. Show me what I am here for.

The gods respond.

This time she is prepared for what the Throne will do to her, but even so, the raw force of the power that surges into her leaves her breathless. Molten ecstasy and pain and fear and despair and yearning: a maelstrom of living energy. It bursts forth from her and reaches out to all the other lyr, connecting her to all of them, connecting them to each other, not only on a personal level but through every social network that exists. Man to woman, family to family, bloodline to bloodline . . . a burning web starts taking shape around her, with a point of searing light at each intersection. Some points are brighter than others, and some lines of connection are stronger than others, but overall its purpose is clear: it is a map of her people, charting their metaphysical connections. The overall pattern matches the faceting of the black crystal, as if that stone were an attempt to capture the essence of this vision in material form.

Then she catches sight of something between the lines of power.

Shielding her eyes from the glare of the supernatural display, she struggles to see what it is. After a moment she can barely make out a dim point of light, almost invisible beside the brilliance of the lyr network. Looking about the map, she finds one more. And another. They are all over the place, filling the darkness between the glowing strands. If the points of bright light represent the lyr, are these meant to symbolize the people who are not lyr? How sad they seem! Isolated fragments of humanity that have no connection with one another, no existence outside of their own identity. The strands of the lyr web brush past them, but do not connect; in the midst of all the network's thrumming power they remain dim, isolated, eternally disconnected from the power that the Throne has awakened . . .

Gwynofar's eyes shot open. For a moment she just lay there, heart pounding, as her mind struggled back to full waking consciousness. Then, in a hoarse voice, she called for her maidservant.

The girl who appeared a moment later had obviously been roused from a sound sleep. "Majesty? Is everything all right?"

"Go get Shina," Gwynofar whispered. "Now." She sat up and reached for her dressing gown. "Tell her that I know what we must do."

CHAPTER 33

THE STORM over the Sea of Tears arrived with no warning. One moment the sky was clear and bright—a perfect summer day—and a moment later clouds swept in. Dark thunderheads reared up like stampeding horses, blotting out the sun, casting the beaches of the Free States into shadow and turning the sea black as ink. Below the clouds, in an increasingly choppy sea, sailors struggled to make it to the safety of a port—any port—before the storm worsened. But it was already hard to navigate. The wind seemed to shift direction back and forth repeatedly, a bizarre and unnatural pattern that made the sailors doubly afraid. It was as if nature itself had gone mad, forgetting all the rules that usually governed storms.

By the time the sun set, the entire sky was almost entirely black, and bands of rain whipped across sea and shore in a pounding rhythm. One thin band of orange light that managed to work its way into the storm was caught up by the rain, making it seems as if liquid fire were raining down on everything.

Then lightning began. Flashes of blinding light raced across the heavens one after the other, accompanied by ear-splitting cracks. Most of the bolts did not strike downward, but rather traveled from cloud to cloud, as if great storm gods were dueling among themselves. So frequent and bright were the flashes that the entire sky seemed to pulse with light, and the thunder was so loud at times that it made the sailors' ears ring.

On the shores of the Free States, in the ports of Anshasa, on board ships that were struggling to stay afloat in a world gone mad, desperate prayers were voiced. For surely a storm such as this was not natural, and nothing less than a god's intervention would be required to end it. Yet even as the sailors prayed, they noted that the seas were not as high as they should be, given the ferocity of the winds. It was as if some outside force were keeping the waves artificially low while the heavens went wild overhead, so that their ships would not capsize.

Eventually the terrible display subsided. The lightning became less frequent, and the clouds began to thin. When they finally parted, one could see that night had fallen during the storm, and a single crescent moon now glowed in the heavens like a beacon of hope. Fearfully, men and women who lived by the sea eased their shutters open, hesitant to trust that the unnatural storm had passed. Many left candles burning on their family altars until dawn, just in case.

The Magisters who saw the storm did not pray. They watched it with quiet interest but not with any sense of wonder, for they instinctively sensed its cause. They didn't know the names of the Magisters who had conjured it, or even how many of them there were—clearly it was the work of more than one sorcerer— but they knew what its purpose had been. Weather-working was one of the most costly and difficult arts in a sorcerer's repertoire, and no man undertook a project like that unless there was a purpose to it. Somewhere in the world, one or more consorts had been deliberately drained of their final soulfire. Somewhere else in the world, the same number of new consorts had been claimed, fresh and vital. The only thing the Magisters who were watching did not know—and wondered about—was what sort of monumental effort was about to take place, that required more than one of their kind to be at the peak of his strength.

By morning, the sea was still once more.

CHAPTER 34

THE WITCHES gathered in the chill of early morning, as the sun was just beginning to rise. The thin band of light that played along the eastern horizon was not yet enough to see by, so torches had been lit, and their flickering light illuminated nearly a hundred expectant faces.

Penitent faces.

"They are all here," Salvator said.

Gwynofar nodded. She could feel the force of their strange faith like a glowing warmth against her face, defying the morning's chill. Not faith in her gods, perhaps, but still a powerful sacred energy. She stood still for a moment, letting the sensation envelop her, drawing strength from it. Salvator waited patiently by her side, respectful of the moment's solemnity.

Finally she nodded. He held out his arm to her, and together they stepped up onto the dais. A sea of faces looked up at them, and it seemed to Gwynofar all the shapes and colors of mankind were represented in this gathering. *As it must have been during the Great War*, she thought. That army had been made up of the last survivors of their age, coming together to pool their resources in a final desperate attempt to save their world. This time the strike would be preemptive, but the act was no less universal.

When she saw that all eyes were upon her, she drew in a deep breath, trying to still the fluttering of her heart. All the paths they had traveled thus far had led to this one place, this one moment. It was impossible to be here and not feel the weight of destiny upon one's shoulders.

Mankind's destiny begins or ends with us.

She unhooked the padded leather pouch at her side and withdrew the precious item it guarded. Holding it up before the crowd, she turned it in her hand so that its black facets caught the torchlight. It seemed to her she could feel energy thrumming within the ancient crystal.

"This is the blood of the ancient martyrs," she announced, "safeguarded down through the generations by the Protectors, preserved by witchery until the day of our need. It is the living essence of men and women who came together to fight when it seemed all hope was lost, and who ultimately sacrificed their lives to save a world. From each of them a single drop of life's substance was taken, and with it a trace of that person's spirit. Courage. Faith. Sacrifice. All bound together into what you see here so that it might come down to us intact and strengthen our spirits in the darkest of hours." She turned the sphere so that its facets caught the torchlight.

"This is your inheritance. Your birthright. Bequeathed by men and women of courage to their spiritual descendants." She breathed in deeply. "What more precious gift can there be than the essence of one's own life? What greater wisdom can there be than to foresee the trials that are yet to come, and to prepare the tools your children will need to face them?"

She held the sphere up high, so that all could see it clearly. "Know that these men and women, your ancestors in spirit, divided their most precious knowledge into thousands of pieces, and scattered those pieces all across the earth, not to make it hard to find, but so that tyrants hungry for power would look past it. In their wisdom and foresight they wove their knowledge into songs—into prayers—into prophecies—so that even the burning of all the world's books would not have the power to destroy it all. And they trusted that if darkness ever fell again—*when* darkness fell again—their descendants would search out all those fragments and learn how to reassemble them.

"This we have done."

She lowered the sphere. "Tonight you become family to those men and women in body as well as spirit, so that their last and most precious gift can be shared with you."

Shina had been waiting quietly in the shadows to one side of the dais. When Gwynofar nodded to her, she approached, offering her a large silver chalice. Gwynofar took the chalice in her free hand and positioned it in front of her, holding the black sphere directly over it.

"Return it to its original form," she ordered.

Shina shut her eyes for a moment. Gwynofar could see her lips move as she recited the incantation that would help her focus her power. When she opened them, a strange light seemed to shine forth from her. Not a physical light, Gwynofar thought, but a mystical one.

Shina reached out and touched the sphere. A shiver of energy ran up Gwynofar's arm as the crystal began to dissolve in her hand. Black became red; stone became liquid; smoothness became heat. Holding it high, she let the scarlet fluid stream down between her fingers into the cup. There it mixed with the wine that Salvator had prepared, until the final drops filled the cup to its brim exactly.

Holding the chalice before her, she stepped back and nodded for Salvator to take her place.

The young king was wearing full armor with a priest's stole over it, and he had a leather-bound book in his hand. "Fellow Penitents." His voice carried to the back of the assemblage with natural ease. "By the word of the Primus Council, I have been restored to the station of Priest for the duration of this campaign, so that the sacraments of our faith can be performed."

He opened the book before him, paged over to where a golden marker lay, and in a clear, strong voice began to read:

Lord God, Creator of the world
Lord God, Destroyer of the world
Lord God, Source of all wisdom
Lord God, Judge of all men
Hear our prayer:

In humble penitence we turn to You, our eternal Judge, and beg for Your blessing upon our mission. Not because we seek glory for ourselves, but because we would glorify You. Grant us Your divine mercy this day, and forgive us our many sins, so that we may enter battle with a clean soul, free of the burden of our past failings. Remove all fear of death from our hearts, for life is the ultimate possession a man can offer You, and sacrifice the greatest of all prayers. Lo, he who dies in Your

*service is doubly blessed, for the measure of his faith
has been taken, and his sacrifice will ransom the souls
of his fellow men.*

*Therefore do we consecrate our bodies and our souls unto
Your service this day, trusting to Your mercy and Your
wisdom, and we beseech You to give us Your blessing for
the coming battle, so that we may fight in Your name.*

As he closed the book, a servant stepped up onto the stage
and handed him a second chalice, with the symbols of his Church
etched about the upper edge. And he waited.

Shina ushered one of the Penitent witches up to the dais.
The woman looked a bit hesitant, and she glanced at Salvator
for reassurance; he nodded with regal grace, which seemed to
settle her spirit. She bowed her respect to Gwynofar, then took
the chalice from her hands and sipped from its contents. There
was no visible change in her, but in Gwynofar's mind she could
imagine the essence of ancient *lyr* warriors coursing through her
veins, adding a single crucial note to the spiritual symphony of
her own soul.

Shina stepped forward then, and took the woman's hand. For
a moment the two of them just stood there quietly, eyes closed,
and Gwynofar could hear them murmuring something in unison.
Then, suddenly, the witch gasped and pulled back. Trembling,
she stared at Shina, astonishment clear in her face.

Shina turned to Gwynofar, her own face glowing. "It works,
your Majesty."

The rest of the witches followed: some hesitant, some eager,
some clearly awed by what was taking place. One by one they
accepted the chalice from Gwynofar's hands and sipped a single

drop from its contents. One by one they came before Salvator, each one kneeling or standing according to the custom of his home culture, and he anointed each with a spot of consecrated oil in the center of the forehead, while murmuring prayers in an ancient tongue that Gwynofar did not recognize.

When all the witches had shared in the dual communion, Gwynofar looked out upon the field of them and felt a deep satisfaction. Closing her eyes for a moment, she imagined she could see the ghost of her child standing among the witches. His face looked serene and content, and for the first time since Alkali, the knot that had been in her heart loosened up just a tiny bit. When she opened her eyes again, he was gone.

As they handed the chalices to servants, Salvator took off his priest's stole and gave it to them as well. Then, dressed only in the armor of a king, he looked out over the crowd. Men and women who had been watching from the sidelines had begun to come over as soon as they'd seen the ritual was ending, and now there was a mixed crowd of Guardians and Penitents before him, intermingling without any self-consciousness. Hundreds of them. Their energy was a tangible thing, that heated the blood and strengthened the spirit.

Salvator raised his hand for silence, and as soon as he had it, waved toward the open field to the south of them. "The time has come. I want the portal teams ready by sunrise. As soon as they're in place, the first group will move in. We only have a couple of hours of good combat weather to work with, so I want to get as much done in that time frame as possible. And remember, the goal of this mission is to take out the Souleater queen. Everything else is secondary to that." He paused. "May God watch over you all."

Or gods, Gwynofar thought.

As the men and women in the crowd ran off to their various stations Salvator saw Colivar and Kamala, and he waved for them to come over to him. The former had abandoned his black garb for more inconspicuous clothing, Gwynofar noted; from a distance one would not suspect that he was anything more than a common workman. Kamala was wearing the men's garments she seemed to prefer, but in muted shades of brown and tan.

Salvator stepped down from the dais and approached them. Unexpectedly, he reached out and clasped Colivar's shoulder briefly, then Kamala's. "I want you to know I respect you both greatly for your courage today. Without the services you have volunteered, none of this would be possible."

Their surprise could not possibly have been greater than Gwynofar's own.

As the two of them hurried off to their posts, Gwynofar looked up at her son. Dawn's early light had made a silhouette of his profile, emphasizing his hawk-like Aurelius features. The image brought back memories of Danton, and she knew that if her husband were here, he would approve of the leader his son had become.

Filled with pride, she whispered a prayer of thanksgiving under her breath and then added a plea for the gods of the north to watch over Salvator and keep him safe. Just in case his own god wasn't up to the job.

CHAPTER 35

KAMALA STEPPED through the portal braced for trouble. Her own inspection of the anchors had indicated no malevolent intent attached to them—certainly no trickery by Farah's people—but that didn't mean that Siderea's people hadn't figured out what was going on and set a trap of their own. Not to mention that it would take very little effort for a witch of Siderea's caliber (or was she a sorcerer now?) to alter a scout's memory so that he reported falsehoods without knowing it, or overlooked the obvious in his reconnaissance.

But when she stepped through the portal, there was no hostile army waiting for her, nor any sign of a sorcerous trap. She summoned her power quickly, wrapping herself and her immediate surroundings in the gift of the ikati queen so that neither human eye nor superhuman power would be able to detect her. But when the portal had first appeared, there had been no such protection, and whoever or whatever was standing guard in this place might have taken note of it. So she was doubly wary, and she scoured the land and sky with both her physical and her supernatural sight, alert for any sign that someone had taken an interest in her arrival.

It appeared that no one had.

The land surrounding Jezalya was flat and desolate, with a few stark ridges of black rock to the east—were those the mountains?—and little else to look at. The sun had not yet risen here, and the predawn light gave the entire landscape a hazy gray quality in which it was hard to make out details. Not that there was much to see. The utter starkness of the empty plain made the badlands surrounding Tefilat seem downright festive by comparison, and as Kamala shivered in the chill morning air, she wondered why anyone in their right mind would choose to live in a place like this.

When she was finally satisfied that no one had detected her arrival, she conjured a message to let Colivar know that all was well. A moment later a second portal appeared, considerably larger than her own. Salvator's people began to come through, each new arrival moving out of the way quickly to make way for the next. Last of all came the High King himself. He nodded as he took note of the markers Kamala had set up, indicating the boundary of her protective spell. As long as they all stayed within that area, no one on the outside would be able to detect them.

Or so they hoped. But Kamala herself didn't know the exact range of her ikati power, so nothing was certain.

She wondered if Salvator would have forbidden her from using that power if he'd known she was a Magister. She was the only one in this crowd—possibly the only person in existence—who could guarantee them true invisibility, to the point where even Siderea's power would be unable to detect them. Without Kamala's sorcery the invaders would have been unable to arrive on this plain before the actual moment of attack, so they would have had no chance to take stock of their surroundings or establish a base camp before engaging the enemy. Would that have been enough to justify the use of sorcery in his mind? Or would even that have fallen short? She was a survivor by nature and could not conceive of throwing a good tool away just because the wrong person had provided it.

She could hear Salvator and Favias giving orders to the small cadre of soldiers and witches who had arrived with them, as they unpacked supplies and began to erect a canvas awning over the arrival site. The size of the first team had been kept to a minimum in respect of her sorcerous boundaries, but even so, there suddenly seemed to be a lot of people in the desert. Salvator and Favias had arrived to command the overall campaign, Shina to direct the witches, Gwynofar to bolster the *lyr's* special abilities, and Ramirus to protect Gwynofar. Small teams of witches and warriors stood ready to take up positions surrounding the city as soon as they were given the word to move out. The witches were all carrying silk scarves and jeweled trinkets from the box that Colivar had once given Kamala, treasured possessions of the Witch-Queen that presumably still carried her resonance. Using those items as anchors, they would be able to focus their witchery on Siderea herself, instead of wasting time and energy on more generalized conjurations. Even Ramirus carried a bright pink scarf tucked into his belt, its beaded ends tinkled as he moved. The utter incongruousness of it would have been amusing had its purpose not been so lethal.

She saw Colivar standing some distance from the others, staring out into the darkness. She didn't know how to reach out to him, or even if she should. He must be afraid—what man wouldn't be, given his role in this campaign?—but if he wouldn't even acknowledge that fear to himself, how could anyone help him address it?

She came up to where he was standing, and for a moment just gazed silently out into the darkness beside him. A faint gray shape was slowly becoming visible in the center of the great plain. Colivar turned one of the bone fragments over in his hand as he stared at it, his fingers unconsciously tracing the symbols etched into its surface. Kamala knew that the other half of this anchor was buried outside the House of Gods, but no more details had been given to them. Whoever used this to open a portal into Jezalya would be traveling blind.

"There must be another way to do this," she said to him. Speaking quietly, so the others would not hear.

"The witches will need time to take up their positions and perform their ritual before they can raise the barrier. But the minute they move out from under your protection, Siderea will be able to detect their presence. So someone has to distract her, at least for those first few minutes, or none of this will work. My presence in the city will accomplish that."

She said nothing. They had discussed this at length in Coldorra and no one had come up with a better idea. Whatever fantasy she'd had that they would come up with an alternative at the last minute was fading along with night's darkness.

"Siderea wasn't trying to kill me in Tefilat," he reminded her. "She wanted me taken prisoner. So it stands to reason that even if she manages to get the upper hand now, she probably won't kill me immediately."

"And if her plan was to torture you?"

She could see his jawline tense. "Well, then, that will succeed in distracting her, won't it?"

Kamala started to open her mouth to say something, but he

turned and put a finger to her lips. "Shh. No more." He took off the silver ring he was wearing and placed it in her hand. It looked like the same ring he had lost in Tefilat; her hand tingled briefly as she held it, remembering Lazaroth's poison. "I won't be able to send a message to you without her detecting it. So you'll have to gather the information you need from here. If I die, then launch the operation without hesitation, and let's hope she is preoccupied enough with my death to give you the time you need." He folded her fingers over the ring. "The others will wait upon your word, Kamala. I've arranged it with Salvator. You are the one who must tell them when to begin."

"I will," she said. Closing her hand tightly about the ring. "But only if you promise me that you'll return safely."

It seemed to her that a terrible sadness came into his eyes.

"I made this mess," he whispered. "So long ago. Another lifetime. Now I must help clean it up."

Stepping away from her, he glanced back at Salvator for approval. The High King nodded. Colivar shut his eyes for a moment and concentrated. The air directly in front of him began to shimmer, and a portal the size and width of a man formed. Without looking back, he stepped into it. The air rippled like water in the wake of his passage, then grew still once more as the portal vanished behind him. The small piece of bone fell to the sand behind him; Kamala walked over and picked it up, tucking it carefully into her doublet.

She knew that the odds of Colivar coming out of this alive were slim. Surely he knew it too. If he had been morati, she would have thought that he was resigned to his death. But such a state wasn't possible for a Magister. So this was something more complex than simple self-sacrifice. A desperate bid for freedom, perhaps. A chance to cast off the shadows of the past,

CELIA FRIEDMAN

after so many centuries he could no longer remember what it felt like to live without them. The most rare and precious thing any man might fight to possess: a chance to start over.

Any man might be willing to risk his life for that. Even a Magister.

If she had believed that there was any god who cared about the welfare of Magisters, she might have prayed for Colivar. As it was, she could do no more than slide the ring onto her right thumb—the only finger it fit—and wait.

———

Siderea dreamt that the gods were angry at her. It was a dream she'd had before, but not one that usually worried her. If there really were divine entities in Jezalya who had an issue with her presence there, thus far they had proven too impotent—or simply uninterested—to do anything about it. By which she judged that her nightmares were merely nightmares, and had no greater significance.

But today's dream felt different.

She woke up with a sense of dread that was both compelling and unfocused. As if she knew that something in her immediate environment was *wrong*, somehow, but didn't know what. Lying still in her bed, she tried to focus on the feeling, to determine its cause. There didn't appear to be anything amiss in the bedchamber itself, nor in the rooms beyond it, nor anywhere surrounding the palace. She reached out to her ikati consort to see if perhaps some agitation from that creature had bled through to her awareness, but the ikati queen was still asleep, her presence no more than a dull, warm weight in Siderea's mind.

All seemed well enough.

And yet it was not.

Gathering her power to her, Siderea extended her senses out into Jezalya itself, searching for any anomaly that might explain her disquiet. For the most part the city seemed quiet. A local witch had been hired to keep rats away from the meat market; another was establishing travel wards on a merchant's wagon that would urge thieves to choose some other target. Other than those few sparks of witchery, this dawn seemed as quiet as any.

It was not. She knew that.

Closing her eyes, Siderea summoned the nearest bird to come to her. A dove arrived at her window a few moments later, its iridescent blue wings identifying it as one of those she had received as a gift from a sycophantic merchant. She had set them loose in her gardens, knowing that there were few places in the hot, dry city for them to escape.

Gently she extended her consciousness into the small winged creature. It was a trick that was becoming more and more difficult over time; apparently her tie to a great predator made herbivorous birds loath to accept her essence. But she was practiced in the art, and soon she was able to slide her mind into the tiny creature, allowing her to direct its motions and see through its eyes. If a flutter of avian panic attended the action, it was not enough to distract her.

She headed out the window and began to fly over the city. Dawn's light was just beginning to spread out across the heavens, which meant that the city was beginning to stir. She ignored all the people who were going about their normal business, searching for any pattern of activity that seemed out of the ordinary. But she could find none. As far as the residents of Jezalya were concerned, this morning was just like any other.

When she was satisfied that the rest of the city was functioning normally, she headed toward the House of Gods. The

patina of residual energy hanging about the place made it
hard for her to make out any meaningful patterns there. Traces
of prayer clung to the ancient walls, along with the residue
of countless rituals, some of them magical in nature. Spells
had been affixed to many of the idols for one purpose or
another, and foreign energies swirled and eddied about them.
A minor spell worked in such an environment would be all
but undetectable, and there would be no way to see it from
a distance.

Yet as soon as she approached the ancient temple, she
realized that the source of her disquiet was indeed here. For
a brief moment she worried that it might be coming from
within the House itself (what if the gods really *were* angry
with her?), but as she circled the plaza, she was able to make
out a place nearby that seemed to resonate as if a powerful
rite had just been performed there. It was within a small
copse of trees that flanked the prayer plaza, the only place
within sight where a man could hide himself . . . or his
magic. She circled the area warily at first, looking for any
sign that the perpetrator was still present, but apparently the
place was empty. So she settled her avian body on an upper
branch of one of the trees and folded its wings, preparing
to concentrate all her attention on the task at hand. Then
she reached within her soul for power, molded it into a spell
of inquiry, and cast it out over the area. She could not pick
out any personal traces of the person who had been here
while possessing another creature; the focus required to maintain control of its body detracted from her ability to focus
her power on fine details. But the spell he had performed
here was another thing. The kind of magic that could tear
a hole in reality was not easily obscured, and the metaphysical

scar that it left behind when it closed was something no well-trained witch could mistake. She could not tell who had made it, or what kind of power had been used, but its purpose was clear.

A portal had been conjured here.

She withdrew her mind from the dove, hearing it squawk in surprise as its body was suddenly returned to it. For a moment she lay still upon her bed, considering the ramifications of what she had just experienced. Though she had established wards all over the city to warn her of any foreign magic being used, she had not done so in the area immediately surrounding the House of Gods. Such a spell would have been triggered ten times a day by the priests and pilgrims who performed their rituals there, becoming effectively worthless. So the conjuration of a portal right next to the House of Gods should not have triggered any of her metaphysical alarms, and it should not have awakened her from sleep. Something else had done that. Had someone tried to get through her personal defenses? Perhaps whoever had arrived through the portal?

Don't jump to conclusions, she warned herself. Many a powerful witch had died as a result of misreading such situations; she did not intend to join their ranks.

She sent out a spark of power to awaken one of the palace witches, a young woman named Hameh. By the time the girl arrived, Siderea had put on a silk dressing gown and had applied a whisper of magic to smooth out her sleep-tousled hair. No one in the palace was ever allowed to see her at less than her best; that was part of her mystique. The same could not be said of the young woman, who was rubbing the sleep from her eyes as she responded to the summons.

"Milady." The witch bowed deeply in the southern style, hands before her forehead. "How may I serve you?"

"A portal was used outside the House of Gods. I need to know if one of our own people was involved. And I need to find that out discreetly, Hameh. Can you do that for me?"

The girl bowed again. "Of course, milady. Though if you really need discretion, I'll have to wait a bit. If I wake up the city's witches to ask them questions, they'll know that something's amiss."

"That's fine." Siderea wasn't happy about the delay, but there were other avenues of investigation she could apply while waiting for Jezalya's witches to wake up.

After the witch departed, Siderea called for her servants to come and dress her. Not because she needed help, or even wanted help, but because that custom was a standard part of royal protocol, and questions would be asked if she did otherwise.

In the distance the ikati queen awoke and stirred, wondering aloud at the agitation she sensed from her consort. *Are we in danger?* the creature asked.

Siderea hesitated. *I don't know yet.*

It was always possible that the portal wasn't significant. Someone who had needed to leave Jezalya quickly had hired a witch to send him elsewhere. Someone who had wanted to visit the city hadn't been in the mood for a long desert trek.

But magical transportation was costly enough that such things were never done casually. And a legitimate traveler would have no reason to depart from the one place in Jezalya where local energies would mask such a spell. Not to mention the fact that an innocent portal would not have awakened her from a dead sleep, no matter how many wards it had triggered.

Farther in the distance, the leading edge of the sun breached the horizon at last.

———

Nasaan awoke from sleep the moment the door to his bedchamber creaked, and he had a weapon in his hand by the time it was fully open. Battlefield reflexes. His visitor was clearly startled, and hesitated on the threshold. By the dim light of early dawn he could see it was one of the palace witches, a young woman named Hameh. Normally he wouldn't respond well to such a furtive entrance, but this was someone he had entrusted with unusually discreet business. If she was coming to him at this hour of the morning, and was not even willing to knock on the door for fear of alerting the servants, she must have significant news.

Sheathing his sword in the hidden place beside his bed—another battlefield habit—he waved for her to approach him. "What news?" he asked, his voice pitched low enough that no one outside the room would hear it.

She offered a hurried gesture of obeisance. "You wanted to be informed if the Lady Consort did anything unusual."

"Yes." *Unusual* was a subjective term, of course, and he'd already had a thousand useless bits of information delivered to him by agents who thought they were doing him a favor. But he paid for it every time. Better too much information than too little. "What happened?"

"She said that a portal had been conjured outside the House of Gods. She doesn't know who's behind it yet. I'm supposed to help her find out."

Of course you are. The witches of the city didn't trust Nasaan's consort, so the *djira* wouldn't be able to question them directly. "She doesn't think it's normal business? A local witch doing . . . well, local witch things?"

"She's not certain yet, Sire. We are checking on that first. But I assume she would not be giving us secret orders if she didn't feel there was a good chance it was something more than that."

A portal.

He cursed under his breath as he swung his legs over the edge of the bed. A portal could be bad news. Someone might be in his city now who was not supposed to be here. Or else someone who normally lived here might be traveling secretly to other places. Either possibility could spell trouble for him. He had begun his own conquest of Jezalya by planting agents inside its walls, and any enemy worth his salt would do likewise. Just as any enemy worth his salt would know that a portal spell was uniquely conspicuous magic that might be detected by his witches. If someone was conjuring one now, it meant that time mattered to him more than secrecy.

Also not a good sign.

"Send word to the outlying tribes," he told her. "Tell them to have scouts scour their territory and report anything unusual to me immediately. If a lizard so much as blinks in the wrong direction, I want to know about it. And have their men arm up and be ready to fight; there may be trouble in the wind."

"Yes, Sire." Her eyes were wide, and he could see the concern in their depths. Nasaan rarely asked his witches to expend their life-energy simply to deliver messages. If he was doing so now, that meant that he believed there might not be time to have a man on horseback do so in person. Or perhaps that he feared a trap might have been set for mundane messengers. "Shall I follow the Lady Consort's orders after that?"

"Aye. But I want any information you gather to be brought to me first."

His *djira* could stop an invading army in its tracks, Nasaan knew that. But she would only do so if it suited her personal agenda. And he was no longer certain how confluent that was with his own.

A man should not rely upon the aid of demons, he thought.

As soon as Hameh was gone, he barked out an order for his guard to attend him. The man entered with his hand on his weapon, and the first thing he did was look about the room for any sign of danger. Evidently something in Nasaan's tone had made him think there was some kind of threat present in the bedchamber.

No man would risk conjuring a portal in the early stages of an infiltration, Nasaan thought. *If some greater plan is being set in motion, its final stage is probably underway.*

"Bring me my armor," he commanded. "And tell my private guard to suit up and be ready to move out. Ask them to be as quiet about it as possible; I don't want the city to panic. If anyone asks, it's for a training exercise."

Should he be more afraid than he was? Was it wrong of him to feel a rush of pleasure at the thought of combat, every bit as intense as the moment of release inside a woman?

I will kill someone before the day ends, he thought with satisfaction.

Colivar's portal had brought him to a small thicket of trees at the edge of a plaza. Given how little light there was, he thought it unlikely that anyone had seen him arrive, but he bound a bit of sorcery just to make sure of it. It seemed to be unnecessary. In the distance he could hear the sounds of people starting to move about, but no one nearby was stirring. This corner of town was all but deserted.

Giving thanks for the foresight of Farah's scout, he wrapped a layer of protective sorcery tightly around himself and slipped out from among the trees.

Nearby, in the center of a great plaza, was a circular building with a dome of polished gold. That must be the House of Gods, home to the idols of the city. There were two priests at the door, ready to receive any visitors, but they looked only half awake, and his sorcery was not hard pressed to push them over the edge into true slumber.

A short distance away, a line of close-set buildings offered him comfortable shadows to slip into. Once he was safely away from the portal site, he molded some athra into a spell to find Siderea and sent it coursing out over the city. Whether it actually located her or not was irrelevant. He knew from past experience that she had good metaphysical defenses, and the subtle prodding of such a spell would not go unnoticed. Soon enough she would know that there was a Magister in Jezalya. And Colivar had left enough subtle signs for her to figure out which Magister it was.

He hadn't told Kamala about that part of his plan. She would have declared him a fool, and rightfully so. Ramirus might even have forbade his doing it, which—barring a successful challenge to his dominance—he had the right to do.

But any other path was greater folly.

Colivar still remembered the trap that Siderea had set for him in Tefilat. He remembered it not only in mind but in his body as well; the pain of it was seared into the very substance of his flesh. If her defenses in Jezalya entailed something like that, he would not be able to approach her by surreptitious means. And while he was willing to risk imprisonment and even torture to aid Salvator's campaign, being imprisoned and tortured by a mindless spell while Siderea went about her business undisturbed—perhaps even unaware that he was there—would accomplish nothing. If Colivar's purpose in Jezalya was to distract Siderea, then he must somehow draw her attention to him. And he must *know* that he was drawing her attention, so that the next stage of the plan could be set in motion.

What better way to do that than to have her seek him out?

He watched as a small blue bird appeared, its bright coloration incongruous against the dull sandy hues of the surrounding architecture. It circled the plaza twice and then dipped low over the place where his portal had appeared. He found himself holding his breath, and only an extreme act of will kept him from directing his sorcery at it, to learn its purpose and identity. If it was serving as a conduit for Siderea's power, establishing any kind of direct sorcerous connection might be dangerous.

He watched as the brightly colored bird circled the area once more, then headed back the way it had come, toward the center of Jezalya. A short time later two witches approached and headed straight for his arrival site. No doubt they had been sent to gather more information for Siderea. In bird form it would have been hard for her to read his traces clearly, but these two witches should have no problem with it. The mark of his sorcery was impossible to miss; even an untrained witch would not mistake its cold essence for anything else. They would know—and they would report to Siderea—that a Magister had come to Jezalya. And, if their skills were good, they would tell her which one.

So far, so good.

———

"You wished to see me, Lady Consort?" Nyuku was clearly pleased to have been summoned, but when he saw the grave look on Siderea's face he grew wary.

As well he should, she thought. The time for games was over.

She spoke simply, because any attempt to elaborate on the truth would have lessened its impact: "Colivar is in Jezalya."

His back grew rigid. His nostrils flared. Emotions stirred in the depths of his eyes that were probably not human in source. "You are sure?"

"There are remnants of true sorcery outside the House of Gods. What other sorcerer has business in Jezalya? And he left traces of his presence on the ground when he passed. He tried to disguise those things, making them hard to identify, but I'm as adept at ferreting out secrets as he is at hiding them." When he said nothing she added, "You don't look surprised."

"I told you he would come to you. And that was even before you tried to entrap him in Tefilat. Now he has two reasons."

"Yes." Her eyes narrowed dangerously. "You did say that." Her tone grew disarmingly soft; any man who knew her well would recognize that as a warning sign. "You've said a lot of things about him, in an indirect sort of way. Hinted at mysteries enough to keep an oracle employed for a lifetime. And now we have come to the moment when that particular game is ending. I am going to be the one who writes the rules for this round." Her expression darkened. "*Why* must he come to me? How did you know that would happen?"

He opened his mouth, then closed it again without saying anything.

"There is a hostile Magister in my city," Siderea said harshly. "He's not here for the scenery. So you will tell me what I need to know to deal with him, or so help me, all the gods in Jezalya will not be enough to guarantee you victory in my queen's flight."

Something black and cold glimmered in his eyes. His words were edged in ice. "That isn't your decision to make."

"Isn't it? The fact that queens have always submitted to the strongest suitor in the past doesn't mean that my queen will have to. Or that the contest can't be fixed in other ways." Her expression darkened. "I'm not one of your helpless little girls, Nyuku, who has never been anything more than the eleventh wing of a Souleater, too ignorant to question the rules of the game she's playing. And I understand about the vested interest of my advisers as well, in choosing what parts of the game they will tell me about." She could see by the look on his face that she had guessed right; they had been misrepresenting the queen's flight to her, or at least withholding information. A dark satisfaction filled her heart as she thought to her ikati, *You see? It is as I told you.* "Don't test me, Nyuku. You won't like where it leads."

If she'd been a man—or a woman whose favor Nyuku did not need—he might have responded in an acerbic manner. But he did need her, so he breathed in deeply to steady his spirit and said, "What is it you want to know?"

"Why will Colivar come to me? What drives him?"

"The same thing that drives the rest of us, my lady."

"*Us*, as in . . . the riders? Why? He's not one of you. Is he?"

A faint smile appeared, as if something about the question amused him. "He was joined to an ikati once, as we are. He

shared in its hungers, as we do. And he will be drawn to the
last living queen for the same reasons that we are, though he
will doubtless come up with other reasons to explain it to himself.
Human reasons. But those will be just excuses. It is the spark
of the ikati that drives him . . . and perhaps the hunger to regain
what he once lost."

She drew in a sharp breath. "You're sure of this?"

"Absolutely."

"And your personal issue with him?"

The brief flicker of hatred in his eyes was more eloquent than
any words he could offer. "We have . . . unfinished business."

He did not need to say anything more. She had seen enough
men in rutting mode to recognize what kind of business they
shared.

Let them fight over us, the young ikati whispered in her mind.
It is what they want. It is what their blood demands.

It was apparently what Siderea's blood demanded as well, for
she could feel a rush of heat warm her loins at the mere thought
of such a contest. "Very well," she said. "I'll give you a chance
to finish your . . . *business* . . . before I deal with him."

Nyuku scowled. "So I must spare his life again? With all due
respect . . . aren't we past that point?"

In truth, Siderea doubted that Nyuku could take Colivar. The
rider might have the fire of ikati passion in his veins, but as far
as she knew, he had never had any kind of magical training. All
the athra in the world did you little good if you didn't know
how to channel it properly.

But she was not pleased with Nyuku at the moment. He had
failed her in Tefilat. And while his masculine arrogance might
be appealing to a Souleater queen, it was starting to wear thin
on her human nerves.

If he kills Colivar, he will serve my need in doing so. If he fails, then he will be dead, and another will take his place. Either is acceptable.

"Very well," she said. "I will place no constraints upon you. If you're capable of killing him, then do so. If you can't, then I'll deal with him myself. Either way," she promised, "this will be Colivar's last battle."

How good those words sounded. And how gracious of Colivar to come to her city and give her the chance to say them.

For the first time that morning, Siderea smiled.

———

Something in the theater of war had changed. Ramirus could feel it. Nothing so concrete as a spell that he could point to, or any single phenomenon he could give a name to. Call it a ripple of potential. A subtle shift in probability. Things were being set in motion that had little significance on their own but that might set off significant events farther down the road. His divinatory sorcery could detect the greater pattern, but it could not put a name to its cause.

Was this part of Colivar's plan?

There was no point in warning the others yet. Salvator wouldn't trust any information garnered by sorcery. Favias and Shina would need more specific facts before they could act, and he didn't have those to offer. Whereas Gwynofar . . . she didn't understand how severely the Law constrained his actions. She didn't know that once sorcerers had thought nothing of slaughtering whole armies for sport, and that the Law had been formulated in part to keep such things from happening again. A Magister might guide the course of a war by advising its leadership, lending subtle advantage to one side, or perhaps fiddling with the environment where a battle was taking place. But he could not lay waste to a morati army by his own hands, no matter how much the outcome of that battle mattered to him. So while Ramirus could and would protect Gwynofar, there was a limit to how much he could do for her beyond that.

He had already broken the Law once, with Kamala. Now he could feel bestial instincts lapping at his mind again, as they had not done for centuries. He remembered what it had been like in the early days, when he had been less than human. He remembered how hard he had fought to reclaim his humanity, after First Transition had stolen it from him.

He would stand by while a thousand human armies perished before he would allow himself to be reduced to that state again.

But that did not mean he couldn't take precautions. And so, shutting his eyes, he extended his sorcerous senses out into the desert. Across miles of sand and scrub brush and wind-scoured rock, so much athra pouring into the effort that his sleeping consort probably dreamed of death. He tasted the flavor of the wind and the shifting of the sand dunes. He drank in the moisture in the air above the oases, the breath of wild camels, the breezes stirred by the wings of vultures as they launched themselves into the morning sky. He measured the golden creep of dawn's light across the barren landscape, and sipped from the wave of blinding heat that crested just behind it. He tested the traces of human emotion that clung to the sand: passion and fear, anger and hope.

With that much knowledge of the surrounding environment he could bargain with Nature herself if he had to. He hoped that such extreme tactics wouldn't be called for, but war was full of surprises, and the more weapons you had in your armory, the more likely it was you'd have the right one available when trouble came calling.

I hope you know what you're doing, Colivar.

———————

The palace was white, pure white, and its central dome was tall enough that the rays of the rising sun played across it before reaching the rest of the city, setting it aflame. Its columns were made of white marble, with thin lines of color coursing just beneath its surface, like delicate blue veins beneath a woman's skin. Such stone was precious anywhere, and doubly precious in this place, hundreds if not thousands of miles from the nearest marble quarry.

Which, of course, was the point.

Colivar gazed at the building for some time, trying to settle his spirit. On all sides of him the city was now stirring to life, and the palace guards were keeping a wary eye out for anyone who approached the palace too closely. Had Siderea told them he would be coming? Was she the one who had conjured the summoning spell that even now tickled the edges of his mind? It was such a faint thing that it was hardly compelling, and it wasn't making a very concerted effort to get through his defenses. Call it more an invitation than a mandate. If he could be sure that it came from her personally, then nothing more would be needed; having her focus enough attention on him that she was sending spells out to find him would satisfy the tactical needs of Salvator's people. But this spell was so faint and indistinct that he couldn't make out any kind of signature: a mere whisper of magic, so insubstantial that he could not determine whose trace it bore.

Passing his hand over his garments, he exchanged his

camel-hued travel wear for crisp black clothing. No need to
hide what he was if he was going to march in the front door.
Then he let his sorcery drop, so that morati eyes were no longer
forced to turn away from him. Startled by his sudden appearance, the guards drew their weapons. Then, after studying him
for a moment longer, they sheathed them again.

He walked up the broad stairs with a casual air, as if this
were a mere social call. But inside his head his mind was racing:
binding power, molding spells, gathering all the information he
could about the palace and its inhabitants. It appeared to be a
new building, and it did not have the kind of residual witchery
that came from a long history of defensive spells. But Siderea's
mark was clearly on it, and her power was no small thing.
Especially now that the athra available to her was, for all intents
and purposes, infinite.

One of the guards snapped his fingers as he reached the top
of the stairs. A young woman emerged from the shadows of the
doorway and bowed her head to Colivar, indicating for him to
follow her into the building. He took note of a subtle power
that seemed to emanate from the area they were approaching,
but he could not make out its exact nature without stopping to
concentrate on it. Gods willing, it was not a trap like the last
one.

Breathing deeply, he repeated to himself all the things he had
told Kamala: *Siderea doesn't want to kill me. Distraction is all we
need. Make sure the battle goes on if I die.* The ikati spirit within
his soul beat its wings suddenly at the suggestion that it might
die, raging against the mere concept of submission. He had not
felt its presence so strongly in centuries, and he struggled to
force it back down into its accustomed bondage so that he might
think clearly. This was not a time to lose control.

But you are about to confront an ikati queen, he thought. *How successful can you be in denying what you really are, in her presence?*

The servant brought him to an empty chamber and gestured for him to wait. It was a large room with little furniture in it: a few benches, a narrow table set against one wall, and several wooden racks with an assortment of weapons in them. He was tempted to inspect the latter, but past experience suggested that handling unknown items in Siderea's home might be a bad idea. He moved close enough to see that there were numerous swords of different makes and other handheld weapons of a variety of types. The half dozen spears in one rack had bronze heads inscribed with the images of gods; they looked as though they had tasted their share of blood. Not practice weapons, any of them. He wondered if they were normally stored here, or if they had been placed for his benefit; for a minute he was tempted to read the traces in the floor, just to see how long the racks had been present. But that was just the kind of trap that Siderea had set for him last time. He would not be foolish enough to fall for it again.

"So good of you to come visiting," a man said behind him.

In Kannoket.

He whirled around, athra surging in readiness. Though there was a part of him that recognized that voice, the shock of suddenly seeing its owner standing before him was like a physical blow that drove the breath from his lungs.

Nyuku.

He was far cleaner than Colivar remembered, but otherwise he was much the same. Sharp Kannoket features in a weathered face, skin etched with harsh lines from squinting against the cold, eyes so dark that pupil and iris bled into one another, black as the arctic night sky. And, of course, the armor. Layers of Souleater skin molded into close-fitting garments, cobalt highlights shimmering along their surface like rainbows on an oil slick. He wore a necklace made of polished chips of Souleater tail blades strung on a cord of seal gut. Trophies from vanquished rivals, perhaps? The fact that each chip invoked images not only of a dead Souleater, but also of a consort gone mad, made it a truly macabre adornment.

Ever since Colivar had learned that Nyuku was still alive, he had been preparing himself for this moment. But it had not been enough. Nothing could possibly have been enough. Memories rushed up from a black pit within his soul, not coherent images but waves of raw emotion, images from a forgotten life—a life he had struggled to forget—

Scream, scream rage into the twilight winds
Wings beat wildly against the blistering cold
Hatred is ice on the tongue
Pride becomes strength, fury becomes fuel, where is the sunlight?
Claws rend ice-air and flesh, hot blood froths like surf
Hatred, hatred, hatred on the wind, consuming all thought
Madness
Screaming pain madness fear hunger
Beg the gods for surcease
Beg the gods for obliteration
This, this is the cost for betraying mankind—

"The human world has not treated you well," Nyuku said. "You reek of weakness."

Colivar gritted his teeth against the tide of memory. The wounds in his soul throbbed mercilessly. "And you reek of arrogance, as always."

He chuckled softly. "Is it *arrogance* to celebrate the downfall of a rival? If so, then I'm guilty. But you—surviving such a loss—that is no small accomplishment." The black eyes glittered coldly; there was cruelty in their depths. "Tell me, what is it like to feel your consort killed while you're riding him? To feel half your soul being torn away and be helpless to do anything about it? That must be a unique sort of impotence."

Suddenly Colivar could feel the loss of his ikati as though it had just occurred, that terrible instant when his human identity had been ripped to bloody bits. He wanted to scream as a wounded animal would scream, as he had once screamed in the arctic: mindless agony, utter despair. But instead he balled his hands into fists by his sides, trembling as he struggled to maintain some semblance of composure inside himself, even while he feigned loss of control on the outside. Squeezing his eyes shut for a moment as though Nyuku's words had completely overwhelmed him, he struggled to focus enough power to detect any active spells in the room. It wasn't a difficult task. The entire chamber resonated with power. Its walls, floor, and ceiling had been warded so that no sorcery could affect them, and the air in the room had apparently been fortified as well. Which would explain why the shutters were all tightly closed; fresh air coming in from the outside would dilute the effect. Colivar didn't dare take the time to inspect the weapons closely, but it was a good bet that they had some power attached to them as well, perhaps even primed to respond to Colivar's own touch, as the traps in Tefilat had been.

"Don't do this," he whispered. Pouring as much pain into his voice as he could, hoping Nyuku would take such pleasure in his humiliation that he would stay his hand for another moment, giving him a few precious seconds more in which to assess the situation.

He wouldn't be able to use sorcery on the room itself, he thought desperately. Nor could he use it directly on Nyuku without risking a fatal connection to the man's ikati. No, he realized with a sinking heart, the only thing he could use his sorcery on in this room was his own body, and the only safe weapon he had was his own intelligence. But the latter was no small advantage. Nyuku was an ignorant barbarian at heart, who had been raised up to power by forces beyond his comprehension. He might have learned to play the part of a sophisticated nobleman, but he lacked even a peasant's education to back it up. Whereas Colivar had been a witch and a healer long before ever meeting the ikati, and he understood how the human body functioned.

It was his only possible advantage.

It would have to be enough.

Slowly he looked up at Nyuku. It didn't take sorcery to sense the energy tightly coiled inside the man, or to see the rage of his ikati shining through his eyes. He might have been successful in claiming leadership of the colony from Colivar years ago, but clearly he regarded the Magister's survival as a personal affront. He would give no quarter.

"Do you remember that day?" Nyuku said. His voice was a mockery of seduction, crooning insults to Colivar's pride in the tone one might use with a lover. "Because I do. I remember the taste of your consort's blood. The sound of him screaming and thrashing as he died. The sight of you lying in the snow, helpless as a child." Clearly it was his intent to goad the ikati portion of Colivar's soul into such a rage that he would be forced to surrender to it. And he was succeeding.

Wrapping his arms around himself, Colivar tried to stay focused; he knew he might have only a few seconds of sanity left, and he had to make them count. Sorcery rushed through his body with unnatural speed, driven by desperation. Muscles expanded. Bone thickened. The chemistry of his blood transformed. Organ by organ, fluid by fluid, his body was transformed—not in rational order, as it would normally be done, but in a chaotic whirlwind of mutation that left each living cell in agony.

And Nyuku smiled. Arrogant egotist that he was, he assumed there was nothing more happening than Colivar suffering. He was pausing for a moment to enjoy his rival's pain.

His mistake.

His last mistake.

Then the transformation was complete, and Colivar's self-control crumbled. The beast came roaring up out of the depths of his soul, hungry for vengeance. And everything turned crimson.

———

Hands gripped Kamala, holding her steady. Sand shifted beneath her knees. Her head felt as if it were on fire.

"Are you all right?" Ramirus asked. "What happened?"

It took Kamala a moment to realize who was talking to her and to remember where she was. Her concentration had been so tightly focused on Colivar that she had lost all sense of the world surrounding her. And then the storm had come. Blinking, she looked up at Ramirus, not sure how to answer him. Salvator was beside him, she saw. Equally worried, though likely for different reasons.

"Is it time?" the High King asked.

Was it?

Using Colivar's ring as an anchor, she had been able to pick up faint traces of his emotional state. She knew that when he arrived in Jezalya he had been calm but apprehensive. She had been able to taste the subtle shadows of fear that played about the edges of his mind after that as he analyzed the threats surrounding him in a rational, controlled manner. And then, in an instant, everything had changed. A storm of violent emotion seemed to fill the very air around her: fury and hatred and frustration and pain . . . and then it had all exploded. A crimson mist seemed to hang about Colivar's ring now. Was that a metaphorical vision, or something real?

But the mere fact that Colivar's soul was in turmoil said nothing about their mission. The combined armies of Jezalya might have descended upon him with swords drawn, and still that might have no immediate relevance to Siderea. Nothing mattered except the moment in which *she* turned her attention on him, so that she stopped paying attention to other things. How was Kamala supposed to know when that happened if she had nothing more than these unfocused signs to interpret? For all she knew, Colivar had run into Siderea already, and that's what this storm of emotion was about. Or not. She couldn't use her sorcery to get more information without running the risk that Siderea would detect her efforts. Nor could Colivar contact her directly, for the same reason. How on earth was she supposed to find out what was happening to him?

She was suddenly angry at Colivar, but the feeling had more to do with frustration and fear than actual rage. Gods *damn* him for putting her in this position! If he managed to come out the other end of this alive, she was going to wring his neck.

Is it time for the witches to move out? Somewhere in the distance Salvator was asking her questions. *Is Siderea's attention fixed on something else?*

I don't know, she wanted to say. I don't even know how I'm supposed to figure it out.

But an army could not be led that way. It required certainty from its leadership . . . or at least the illusion of certainty.

"No," she said quietly. Feeling her words resonate across the desert sands, "Not yet."

Cursing Colivar under her breath—and fearing for him—she waited.

———

Nasaan was just buckling on his sword when a servant came running in. Clearly the prince hadn't put on his armor a minute too soon.

"In the east wing, Sire." The servant was breathing hard, though it seemed to be more from agitation than exhaustion. "There's some kind of fight going on, Nyuku and a stranger—"

Cursing under his breath, Nasaan was in motion before the end of the sentence could be voiced.

Nyuku was one of the Lady Consort's sycophants, and Nasaan's least favorite. Left to his own devices, Nasaan wouldn't trust the man to clean out a chamber pot. It was hard to say just why he felt that way, since Nyuku had never actually said or done anything offensive—that Nasaan knew about—and he generally respected all the proper protocols in dealing with the royal household. If anything, his obeisance sometimes bordered on excessive, almost as if the whole thing were a joke to him. But as soon as he walked into a room, Nasaan could feel all the hairs on his neck prick upright, and his muscles tensed in the way they did during battle. There was a sense of challenge about the man, all the more irritating for never being voiced openly, that stirred Nasaan's blood in ways he did not fully understand.

The *djira's* insistence that this unpleasant creature have free access to Nasaan's palace was one of the few real points of contention between them. His witches had told him that Nyuku's aura was not entirely human—whatever that meant—and as Nasaan had made a contract with only one supernatural creature, he was under no obligation to allow another one into his house. So Nyuku barely had permission to visit, and he certainly had no permission to be raising his hand against anyone within these walls. Nasaan found himself hoping that the man had finally transgressed in some major way, so that he would have an excuse to throw him out for good. And to hells with the Lady Consort if she did not like it.

By the time he got to the room where the altercation was taking place, several members of the palace guard had assembled outside, wary of entering without some kind of instruction from him. From inside came the kind of sounds one would expect from combat, though it didn't sound as though metal weapons were being used. Nasaan wasn't sure if that was a good or a bad sign.

"The Lady Consort said we should remain outside—" a servant began.

He did not wait for the end of that sentence either, but drew his sword and pushed his way through the half-open door. The room had been stripped bare of all its normal decorations, he saw, and racks of weapons from the armory had been arranged against one wall. The sand shutters were tightly closed, reducing the early morning light to a bare minimum, and the few lamps that had been set up in the four corners of the room did little to dispel the shadows. There was indeed a fight going on, between Nyuku and a tall, black-haired man, and while no weapons had been drawn, it was clearly more than a simple wrestling match. Gouts of flame accompanied blows that were struck faster than a human limb should be able to move, and shadows and smoke swirled in the air between the two contestants, only to be quickly extinguished. Blood appeared, then became a cloud of crimson mist, then was gone. He could hear bones cracking under blows so forceful they seemed to make the whole room shake, but the one who had been struck would simply glance at his shattered limb and then reengage his opponent.

Thus do demons fight, he thought darkly.

He saw Siderea in one corner of the room. Her eyes were bright and moist as they followed the fight, and her full lips were parted in an expression that was both sensual and disturbing. When she saw him enter, she waved him over to her, and she put her hand on his free arm as he drew close. "They can't see or hear us," she said quietly, and he saw no reason to think that she was lying. Her pulse was hard and rapid, like a woman in the throes of pleasure, and the scent that rose from her skin was something that belonged in a bedroom more than an armory. It made him more wary than the battle itself, and he pulled away from her, putting enough distance between them that the scent of her arousal was less intrusive.

"What is this all about?" he demanded.

"What it's always about," she answered. Nasaan watched as Nyuku grabbed hold of his opponent in what might have been a death-grip among normal men, but the black-haired stranger simply altered his form into a more flexible shape and slipped from his grasp. He left behind him a sheet of blue flame that clung to Nyuku everywhere the two had made contact, but that was quickly extinguished. The action was almost too fast for Nasaan to follow, but he had the impression there was much more going on than was visible to the human eye. "Power," she continued. "Lust. Dominance." She paused; her lips curled into a smile that was warm on the surface but utterly chilling in its essence. "Courtship."

He remembered the last time he had seen that smile. He had been on a battlefield then, and she had stood within a circle of death, the blood of living men falling about her feet like rain. He had feared what she was capable of, even as he'd lusted for what she was offering him. That formula had never changed.

She had toyed with whole armies that night, for her pleasure. Tonight it was only two men, but the hunger driving her was clearly the same. And for the first time since he had known her, its nature was undisguised. Nasaan could read the truth in that cold, predatory smile. He could smell it on her skin. And as two men attempted to tear each other to pieces in front of her, he knew for the first time exactly what the name of that hunger was.

Or perhaps he had always known. Perhaps he had simply not wanted to acknowledge it.

Let them die for me, her expression proclaimed.

Speed and strength. That was what mattered. Speed and strength enough that Nyuku would be forced to respond in kind. Nothing else offered hope.

Colivar clung to that thought, even while fear and despair pounded in his veins. Fighting with a sorcerer was futile. He knew that. He had been alive in the days when Magisters were still allowed to kill each other, and he knew how it had to be done. By surprise. By stealth. Nothing else worked. When you were dealing with a man who could heal any wound with a single thought, and who could protect himself from any attack he saw coming, the only way you could take him down was to give him no warning and allow no time for healing. And since a skilled Magister could detect hostile intent in an enemy, that meant you couldn't even plan out your actions in advance. How often did all those elements come together?

But refusing to fight was not an option. The beast within him had risen to the surface, and its rage was not to be contained. Memories of past pain and humiliation welled up inside him, awakening a hunger for vengeance so powerful that all other thoughts were simply swept aside. All of his being was focused upon one thing and one thing only: taking down the man who had bested him so many years ago, driving him into the embrace of madness.

The chamber they were in restricted their sorcery, forcing them to fight as morati would fight—strength against strength, speed against speed, a primitive physical contest. Sorcery flickered about them, but they were too evenly matched for it to make a difference. Flames engulfed Colivar, but he doused them before they could ignite his clothing; poisonous smoke shot into Nyuku's lungs, but the Kannoket neutralized it with a thought. The fact that neither of them could transform the air or summon foreign elements into the chamber made it next to impossible to conjure any malign force of consequence; even a fireball, lacking proper fuel, would extinguish itself within seconds. But their own bodies were fair game, and Colivar was quick to realize the potential of that. The sweat on his skin could be transformed into an acid mist. His own breath easily became toxic smoke. But conjuring such effects entailed considerable risk, and Colivar knew it was something that must be done carefully lest he poison himself in the process.

And then there were the weapons.

Colivar dared not touch them for fear they were entrapped,

but Nyuku was under no such restriction. With one wild gesture he levitated all the swords from their rack and sent them hurtling toward Colivar. The Magister transformed the natural oils of his own skin into an impermeable shield—just in time, for in that fraction of a second in which he was distracted Nyuku transformed his fingers into an ikati's talons and swiped at his throat. What an inept fool, using the same sort of physical assault that Colivar had just established protection from! As it was, the swords slammed into Colivar from the side, but they did not pierce his skin; Nyuku's blue-black talons skittered across his body as if it were made of stone.

Out of the corner of his eye Colivar could see that the swords that missed him continued on in their flight until they struck the wall. All save a group of three, which stopped in midflight as if some giant hand had grabbed hold of them, then dropped to the floor with a clatter. So. Apparently there was an unseen audience that did not wish to be skewered.

He could not tell how long they fought, but thin rays of sunlight soon began to lance through cracks in the shutters, and the air about them was warming. Good. Nyuku would be at a disadvantage in the full heat of day, and more likely to make mistakes. Already Colivar could see that his opponent was tiring, and once or twice the man seemed to stumble. Was that exhaustion, or something more significant? It was clear that Nyuku was enhancing his own strength and speed to match Colivar's, which was what he had been pressing for. If such a transformation wasn't done properly it could destroy the very body it was meant to protect. The thin, porous bones and slender ligaments of a normal human body were not sufficient to anchor what their muscles were becoming, and the unnatural exertion was pouring toxins into their flesh with every moment. Colivar had made allowances for all that. Had Nyuku? If the Kannoket's body failed him from the inside, that would be one precious instant in which he would have to focus on healing while Colivar still had full use of his sorcery. It would only provide a moment's advantage, but one moment could mean the difference between life and death in a contest like this.

Colivar grappled with Nyuku, hands shifting into claws as the Kannoket's flesh reshaped itself to break free, forcing him to exert himself beyond any human limits . . . and he could feel the break as it occurred. Not the simple crack of a limb that resulted from blunt force impact, but the shattering of a bone from the inside, after it had finally been stressed to its breaking point. He could hear Nyuku's grunt of surprise and could feel him withdrawing his concentration from their grapple as he focused all his attention on weaving his broken flesh back together.

And in that precious instant Colivar lifted him up and heaved him against the stone wall, headfirst, as hard as he could. He didn't expect he'd be able to crush the man's head so easily—though it would have been nice—but his action forced Nyuku to shift his focus from internal healing to external defense so quickly that he could not pay attention to his environment at the same time. At what point would he realize that Colivar had chosen an impact point just above the rack of spears? He could save his head or control his fall, but he could not do both at once.

One second of confusion. That was all Colivar needed, one extra second in which to conjure his weapon of choice, in the way that it needed to be done. Now he had it. The instant he released Nyuku, he bound the sweat on one hand, transforming it into an inert, impermeable surface that covered his hand like a glove. Then he touched his palm to his forehead, picking up a few drops of sweat, and he transformed those as well. He trembled slightly as he did so, for he knew just how deadly this weapon was, but he might not get a second chance to try this.

Nyuku twisted in midair, and even as he hit the wall he began using sorcery to melt the spears beneath him. Colivar could not have asked for more. He lunged toward Nyuku and grasped him briefly in a place where he was unarmored, so that the substance coating his palm was pressed tightly against the Kannoket's bare skin. The rider's body shuddered, and it crashed into the rack of weapons before they were fully blunted. Most of the blades were deflected by his ikati armor, but one that was directly beneath him punched through, and Colivar could hear Nyuku moan in fear—not from the pain but from what else was happening to him.

Then he tumbled to the ground and fell silent. The body twitched a few times, but it was clear that he had no control of it. Or over his mind, apparently. For a moment Colivar just stood there, waiting for some movement that might indicate his plan had not worked. But at last it was clear that Nyuku was fully unconscious. Their fight was over.

The beast within Colivar screamed for him to rip out his rival's throat and consummate their vengeance by drinking his blood, but he shook his head and focused on his sorcery once more. Pain lanced through his transformed muscles, exacerbated by physical exhaustion, as he carefully banished the substance he had spread across his palm, making sure that not even a single bit of it remained. The poison that Lazaroth had used on Kamala was far too volatile for any Magister to handle safely. Thank the gods he'd had the foresight to study the traces of it that remained on his ring when he had rescued it from Tefilat.

Banishing the layer he had conjured to protect his hand from the stuff, he turned to face his audience. Knowing with certainty who must be there, but no less shaken to see her.

Siderea Aminestas.

She was dressed in an opulent gown of deep purple silk, with some kind of crown resting on the thick dark curls of her hair and a necklace of golden drops trickling down between her full breasts like rainwater. Her scent was a mixture of human arousal and the spicy-sweet smell of a Souleater queen; he trembled as it filled his nostrils, stirring memories anew. Nyuku was no longer a threat to him, but his body was a trophy of conquest. An offering to be laid before her. He remembered other bodies in other times, dead warriors in their blue-black carapaces, which he had laid at the feet of various queens. He struggled to control the sudden flood tide of memory, but the battle with Nyuku had opened the door to his past, and he could not force it shut. He had been a queen's mate once. Nyuku had stolen that from him. Now he would reclaim what was rightfully his.

There was a man standing next to Siderea. For a brief moment Colivar wondered if he would have to fight him as well. But though the man was armed, and clearly wary of Colivar, the same energy was not there. This man had never known the glory of flight, nor surrendered to an ikati's hunger. He was as relevant to their business as a pet dog would be.

Now it was time for Colivar to answer to that hunger. Time for the ancient ritual to be completed at last. Slowly, muscles aching, he went down on one knee, and bowed his head. He could hear Siderea's sharp intake of breath as he did so; he thought he could feel the pounding of her heart echo within his own chest.

"I have killed for you," he whispered.

Flying in icy skies, drunk on the scent of the queen . . . tasting the enemy's blood in his mouth . . . this, this is my offering, this

is my strength, this is my worth . . . I have killed for you, my
queen!

————————

Kamala's eyes shot open. It took her a moment to remember
where she was. The images being channeled from Colivar had
been so powerful that it was hard to focus on anything else.

Then she realized why that was happening.

She turned to Salvator. "He's with her." She could taste the
truth of the words on her lips even as she spoke them. "Go!"

The High King signaled to the lead witches, who moved into
position and began to concentrate. Six portals appeared in neat
array. Silently, efficiently, the teams that had been waiting
patiently in place for nearly an hour began to step into them.

Two witches would establish a traditional barrier at each
arrival point, by the fastest method possible. Two more would
perform the spellsong ritual, a lengthier process; they would
weave a more permanent construct once linkage was solidly
established. Other witches would protect them from supernatural
assault while they worked. Soldiers would stand guard against
more traditional attacks. And when everything was in place and
the final barrier was sealed, so that Siderea could no longer help
her Souleater queen escape the trap, the secondary teams would
transport in to help protect everyone.

Then it would be Kamala's turn.

Her heart pounding, she tried not to think about Colivar. He
had played his part, and now she must play hers. She needed
to focus on her own role in this campaign and not be distracted
by worrying about him.

But something in that last series of images had been
deeply disturbing. Not the overwhelming sense of an ikati

presence—though that was truly daunting—so much as what had been missing. There had been no human element in that vision. No human element in him. Gods willing, that was no more than just a quirk of the spell she was using to connect to him, reducing his mindset to its most basic elements. Gods willing, he had not surrendered his human self entirely.

Because once he did that, she was not sure he would ever be able to find his way back.

Wrapping her arms around herself, she stared out at the desert, using her Sight rather than her sorcery. Shimmering sparks seemed to play about the edges of a vast circle with Jezalya at its center as the witches took up their places one by one, casting their spells. Kamala could see the shimmer of witchery take shape over various portions of the landscape, gleaming in the sunlight like vast plates of glass. The sections were not uniform in nature but differed in their depth and luminosity, and where they met, the power shimmered and rippled like air over sun-baked sand. Slowly, piece by piece, a dome of power was being erected with Jezalya at its center, and presumably a matching dome was being established underneath the sands as well, enveloping the city above and below in a perfect globe. It was a powerful but unstable construct, with too many different minds feeding into it; Kamala's Sight could pick out tremors of energy coursing through the dome at irregular intervals, and they crashed into one another at the seams where the different conjurations met, sending thin sprays of witchery into the air.

She consulted Colivar's ring briefly to make sure that Siderea was still within the city walls. Judging from his state of mind, she was. She nodded to Ramirus and Salvator to let them know that. So far so good.

Now the spellsong was being established, and Kamala could see the barrier being transformed by it. The tremors of power that had roiled across the dome's surface grew quieter, then ceased; the fracture lines between the segments faded and then disappeared; a soft, measured light began to emanate from the whole of the dome, no brighter or dimmer in any one place than another. Where there had once been wild currents and eddies of power and the collision of mismatched planes, there now was a single, uniform whole, as clear as a flawless crystal. It seemed to Kamala that it had not merely been improved in its visible aspect but that it was stronger in its substance as well. Such a construct might well succeed in binding a powerful witch . . . or even a Magister.

And Gwynofar was a part of it. Kamala had never fully understood the nature of the special relationship she had with the lyr, which helped her link them all together, but it was clearly visible now. The same arcane light that shimmered from the crystal dome surrounded her as well; the same sense of balanced power that gave it strength resonated in her aura. No creature with supernatural sight could possibly mistake the fact that she was central to this undertaking, if not the metaphysical keystone for the entire project. The shimmering dome of witchery was a visible extension of her person.

Then Ramirus met Kamala's eyes, and she knew that her turn had finally come.

Raising up her arms, she bade the power come to her. Athra rushed into her soul, drawn so swiftly from her unnamed consort that it still carried a whisper of life's warmth about it as she molded it to her purpose. Holding the image of a Souleater queen in her mind, she surrendered herself to transformation. This was no easy change, as adopting the form of a familiar creature would be, but it required that she create her new body by conscious effort—crafting it scale by scale, cell by cell, even as she fixed Colivar's image of the queen within her mind. As she did so, she imagined she could feel the ikati essence within herself stirring, expanding—exulting in its new horizons—and she surrendered herself to that as well. If she was to call the others to flight successfully, and keep them engaged after that, she would need every ounce of ikati instinct in her soul to be active.

Never mind what would come after her flight, or how a human soul might be altered by such an exercise. If Colivar was willing to surrender to his own personal demons to make this campaign succeed, she owed him equal courage.

When the last gleaming scale was in place and the last bit of jeweled-glass membrane was stretched taut across insect-veined wings, she took to the air. Sunlight blazed along her wing membranes as the ground dropped away from her, and she could feel it feeding strength to her body, warming her blood and increasing the strength of her heart.

Below her the conjured dome still glowed, albeit dimly; apparently the Souleaters were able to detect metaphysical energies.

Then the shadow of something winged rose up from the nearby mountains, and she knew that one of the Souleaters had seen her. It was time.

Drawing a breath into lungs so vast they seemed endless, she cried out across the desert as she had heard the queen cry out in Colivar's memory. A single long, keening note that rose and fell with the wind. She could see the humans on the ground looking up at her, and she was sure that all the people in Jezalya were watching as well. Including Siderea.

She had no idea how her new body was supposed to spread

its mating scent, so she simply created the smell herself, with sorcery, and let the wind carry it eastward. Soon it would be blowing into every crack and crevice in the rocky range, all the places where men and Souleaters might hide. Then she wrapped herself in the ikati queen's power—far easier to do in this form than as a human—and waited for the Souleaters to rise.

One by one, they did so. Rising from the crevices and caves where they had been hiding, spreading their glorious wings in the morning sunlight like a flock of freshly decanted butterflies. Whenever two of them came too close together, one of them snapped at the other, and several encounters drew blood before the combatants parted. Once or twice she heard the same sharp cry that Rhys had used to call the Souleater outside Danton's castle, which she knew was the challenge of a male in full combat mode, inviting others to test his strength. Unable to see the queen that had called them, they were turning their energy on each other. If Kamala left them to their own devices, they might even kill each other off eventually. But that would not serve her purpose, which was to get them away from Jezalya as quickly as possible.

There were not quite two dozen of them in all; more must have expired in the north than Colivar had allowed for. A few of them seemed to notice the human armies on the ground, but the intensity of their mating rituals apparently allowed for no distraction. If their human consorts were aware of what was going on, they were clearly not in control; there was no sense of anything driving these creatures other than blind bestial instinct. For perhaps the first time since arriving at Jezalya, Kamala found herself truly afraid. Up until now this whole enterprise had seemed unreal—even her transformation and flight had possessed a dreamlike quality—but the cries of the males were waking her up from that dream into a chilling reality. She was fully committed to the game now, and if she did not play it well many people might die.

She might die.

Concentrate, she told herself. The first task at hand was to get the Souleaters away from here, so they could not interfere with Salvator's people. One thing at a time.

Dropping her sorcerous shield, she allowed the Souleaters to see her.

The response was immediate. Awareness shot through the air like lightning, and even those Souleaters who had not been facing her wheeled about in midair, suddenly sensing her presence.

As soon as she saw them heading in her direction, she turned west and began to fly, with as much strength and speed as she could manage. The advantage was hers in that arena. Her body was lighter than that of her pursuers, in part because it lacked the specialized combat appendages that the males required. The wind flowed smoothly over her sleek body, with no spikes or armor ridges to interrupt it. No male could catch up with her unless she allowed him to.

Over an empty expanse of desert she flew, as fast as her broad wings could carry her. They followed. Several times she heard screeches of rage from behind her, and once it seemed she caught sight of a dark, crumpled shape falling toward the earth. But though a real queen could probably have managed to look behind her while flying, swinging her long serpentine neck around without missing a wingstroke, Kamala was not so confident in her skills. She kept her gaze resolutely fixed on the skies ahead of her, using sorcery to bolster her hearing, so that if any males drew too close to her, she would not fail to detect it. Everything was now riding on her success in evading them, at least until Salvator's people had a chance to bring the true queen down.

But she remembered what Colivar had told her about the queen's flight, and when she finally reached a place where there was nothing but empty sky and sun-baked sand visible on all sides of her, she began to alter her course, adopting a sweeping curve toward the south. The Souleaters who were directly behind her continued to follow blindly, wholly fixed upon the prize just out of reach, but those who were farther back and had a better view of the overall picture set their course at an angle, meaning to head her off. Heart pounding in her chest, she turned back even more sharply, encouraging them in their strategy . . . and headed directly toward what promised to be a violent collision between the two groups. The Souleaters following behind her howled out their challenge, seeing her head toward their rivals, and they whipped the air so violently in their frenzied attempt to catch up with her that she felt as if a storm were battering at her rear wings.

And then, just as the two groups of Souleaters seemed certain to crush her between them, she disappeared. Summoning the ikati gift that would hide her from their sight, she pulled in her wings tightly against her sides and turned her carefully controlled flight into a heart-rending plummet. If any Souleaters had been able to see through her obfuscation, they would still be unprepared for the suddenness of her move.

And the two groups of Souleaters crashed into one another, drops of blood flying through the bright morning sky as they began to vent their fury and frustration on each other. A few individuals broke free of the chaos and circled the area, searching the sky for their lost quarry, but they all searched the skies at the normal elevation for ikati flight; none of them thought to look down to where she was coasting, mere yards above the sand.

A strange satisfaction filled her as she craned her head upward to watch the chaos, one that was not wholly human in its tenor. Yes, she had fulfilled her primary goal in drawing the Souleaters away from Salvator's forces and keeping them distracted, and yes, she was managing to get them to turn on each other, which might get rid of some and would weaken more than a few. But there was more to it than that. The patterns playing out overhead struck some nerve deep in her psyche, fostering a sense of satisfaction more intense than anything she had known before. This was right. This was as it should be.

The ikati were starting to sort themselves out now, and though a few were still focused on tearing their rivals to pieces, most were now searching the skies for her. As she considered what course of flight would cause maximum bloodshed the next time, she noted that the ikati who had come out of the collision unscathed were not the ones she would have expected to. This contest was not about size or strength, she realized, least of all raw aggression. The more intelligent ikati had been better prepared to analyze her flight pattern and gain advantage from it; the ones with the most self-control had managed to escape the maelstrom of violence and remained undamaged. A simple flight might favor brute strength over intelligence, she realized, but a complex one rewarded other qualities.

No wonder the species had become so strong.

Fixing her next flight pattern firmly in her mind, she banished the power that protected her from their sight and began to climb into the air once more. Drops of blood pattered down on all sides of her as she did so, raising tiny dust clouds as they landed. Crimson rain in the desert.

Come on, boys. Let's see just how smart you are.

———————

This moment is perfect, Siderea thought.

Nyuku lay crumpled against the rack of weapons, effectively humbled but not yet dead. It was a suitable penance for his failure in Tefilat, she mused. The Magister she hated most had been forced to his knees by the power of ikati instinct and was at her mercy. And Nasaan now understood just how powerful she was: He had seen two of the world's most powerful men vie for her favor like dogs in a fight ring. The only thing that could have possibly made this moment better was to have a man inside her right now, to drive her raging blood to climax and release . . . but that would come in time.

She stared down at Colivar in quiet satisfaction for a few moments, reveling in her triumph. Then she turned to Nasaan, who had not yet spoken. "Prince Nasaan." She bowed her head to him graciously. "Permit me to present Colivar to you. Once Magister Royal of Anshasa, now . . ." She shrugged. "Unaligned. Apparently he came to visit Jezalya without being properly announced. I called him to the palace so that he might explain himself."

"So I see," Nasaan said quietly. His expression was unreadable. She guessed that he was not pleased by the situation—what prince would be?—but he said nothing more. She had known him long enough now to know that only a fool would mistake such silence for passivity.

Her own eyes narrowed as she turned back to Colivar. "You've

killed one of my servants," she accused. "Not to mention made
a mess of my hall. Did you expect all this to please me?"

She expected him to respond with at least a spark of defiance,
but all the spirit seemed to have been leached out of him. It
was clearly more than mere physical exhaustion. His expression
was haunted, his eyes gateways to a terrible spiritual emptiness.
Whatever had passed between him and the Souleaters in the
past, it had clearly left deep scars upon his soul. And now she
was rubbing salt into those wounds.

*Thank you for giving me that weapon, Nyuku. It seems you were
of some use, after all.*

"Your servant challenged me," Colivar said dully. "If you know
the ways of the ikati, then you know I had to answer him." A
fleeting spark of defiance played weakly in his eyes. "Did you
expect me to just let him win?"

She was about to answer when she felt the queen stir within
her. She let the queen see the current scene, and she felt the
creature picking through her mind for enough details to understand what was happening. Finally an unvoiced question took
shape within her mind: *This is the one you hate most?*

Yes.

Why?

*The other Magisters merely failed to help me. This one came to
gloat over my death, under the guise of sympathy.*

She could feel the ikati gazing down at Colivar through her
eyes. He seemed to sense her presence as well, for his eyes
widened in surprise. His nostrils flared, and Siderea realized
that he was testing the air, seeking the scent of the ikati queen
that clung to her skin. When he detected it, she could see a
flicker of fear in his eyes . . . and desire.

He is yours now, the ikati thought.

Yes.

"That does not excuse you, Colivar." She folded her arms sternly across her chest. "I believe I am due compensation."

A flicker of concern suddenly sparked in her brain, not from within her but from outside. She sensed some kind of confusion in her queen's mind, and a shadow of apprehension. She held up a hand for Colivar to be silent and was beginning to turn her senses inward when a terrible cry filled the heavens and exploded inside her head simultaneously. Part of her knew what it was—what it must be—but the greater part of her could not accept the truth. *Her* queen had not made that sound. Where had it come from?

She could sense the fear rising in her consort, and she knew if she did not find a way to ameliorate it she would quickly be overwhelmed.

Be steady, she thought. *I will come to you.*

She glanced at Colivar—who had not moved—and then Nasaan. "See to them," she ordered the prince. There was no saying what he would make of that order, but she had no time to stay and explain things to him. She summoned her power and created a portal, so that she might join her queen in the mountains and comfort her—

And nothing happened.

Stunned, she tried again.

Nothing happened!

Ikati panic was pouring into her brain now, making it impossible to think clearly. *There cannot be another queen here! No other queen exists!* Siderea ran to the window and jerked open the heavy shutters, letting outside air pour into the room. Maybe the spells she had placed in the chamber had backfired and were inhibiting her power as well. But the air carried with it a scent that made every hair on her body prick upright. Once more she tried to summon a portal . . . and once more she failed.

She whirled back to confront Colivar. He had risen to his feet and looked considerably more composed than the last time she had looked at him. "What have you done?" she demanded, and when he did not answer she repeated, with increasing fury, "*WHAT HAVE YOU DONE!!!*"

"I invited some friends," he said quietly. A corner of his mouth twitched into a smile. "I hope you don't mind."

She struck out at him blindly, channeling her ikati's rage as well as her own into one blazing, unstoppable wall of power. It slammed into him with so much force that she could hear his bones snap, and it threw him across the length of the room, directly into a stone wall. Then, drawing in a deep breath to steady her spirit, she reached out into the desert with her supernatural senses, to see what was happening.

She saw witches.

Armies.

An unknown Magister.

Salvator!

She tried to strike out at them, but they seemed to be protected from her direct assault, so she reached out past them, into the tribal encampments that were loyal to Nasaan. Their own scouts must have spotted the foreigners already, for their warriors were armored and getting ready to move out. She relayed to their witches the information they would need to locate the invaders and one simple order: Kill them all. Then she returned her attention to the invading forces and addressed herself to finding a way around their protective magics, so that she could crush them all like insects.

"Not bad for a slave."

The words broke her concentration. She returned her awareness to the room, where she saw Colivar standing once more. Whatever damage she had done to his body had been repaired.

"Given your origins," he continued, "I would never have expected you to get this far. Quite impressive, really."

For a moment she was too stunned to speak. She took a few steps toward him without thinking, then stopped herself. "What do you know of my origins?" she whispered.

"Not much," he admitted. "It was hard to research. You covered your tracks well. But I did find records that spoke of an Elanti slave who had been working her way north, owner by owner, just about the time you showed up in Sankara." He glanced at Nasaan. "The Elanti were a line of slaves especially bred and trained for sexual service. Very popular in some regions. This one was supposedly quite skilled."

"This is of no interest to him!" she exclaimed, shaking with a new sort of rage now.

"The curious thing about this slave," Colivar continued, "was that her owners all died mysteriously. Reasons were always offered, of course—one had an unfortunate accident, another died of a lung ailment, a third was killed by bandits while traveling—and the slave was invariably purchased by someone more affluent after that. So I suppose it was just good luck."

"This is of no concern to anyone now," she hissed. Fingers flexing as though they had claws at their tips.

"Eventually one of them became enamored enough to free her, and he brought her to the Free States on his arm as a free woman, intending to make her his wife . . . what a pity, though. He died also. Touch of summer fever, I hear." He shook his head. "That slave seems to have disappeared about the same time you arrived in Sankara. There wouldn't happen to be a connection, would there?"

For a moment the rage was so hot inside her she could not speak. Her ikati did not comprehend what was wrong, but she could not spare the time to explain it to her. Focusing inward, she drew forth her power again—

—and heard the whisper of steel through the air one instant before the sword hit her neck—

—and darkness.

———

The two men stood there for a moment in silence, staring down at Siderea's headless body. Then Nasaan reached down and wiped off his sword on her gown. Returning it smoothly to its sheath, he looked at Colivar. "If I'd known she was just human I would have done that a while ago." After a moment he added, "Thank you."

Outside the window the cries of Souleaters could be heard, fading into the distance as Kamala led them away. Colivar had not heard the ruckus when it first began. The game he had been playing with Siderea had been a delicate one and had consumed all his attention. But his final gambit had paid off. Her sudden realization that her past history was known, in all its murderous glory, was enough to break her concentration on whatever she'd been trying to do. Long enough for Salvator's people to do what they came here to do. And long enough—unexpectedly—for Nasaan to kill her. *Foolish woman. I uncovered your secrets years ago. Mysteries are a Magister's greatest passion; did you forget that?*

Colivar looked about the room, now splattered with blood from one side to the other, and caught sight of Nyuku lying in a heap by the weapons rack. Not dead yet, despite Siderea's assumption. Fresh hatred welled up inside him, and with it the atavistic desire to rip out the man's throat with his teeth. But he still had unfinished business with Nyuku.

He looked at Nasaan. "Don't kill him. Not yet."

The prince raised an eyebrow, then nodded.

Colivar leaped up onto the windowsill. Outside the palace a crowd had gathered, drawn by the sound of combat, but they were keeping a safe distance. Or what they thought was a safe distance. He stood for a moment on the broad stone sill looking down at them, knowing what a sight he must be to them in his bloodsplattered clothing, his long black hair unbound and whipping free in the wind. He found it perversely pleasing.

Are you sure you want to do this? he asked himself. For a moment he shut his eyes, and a shudder ran through him, and he was not certain at all. In fact, this was possibly the stupidest thing he had done in his life. Only a madman would even consider it.

Then looked back, saw Nyuku lying there, and he remembered the night the man had killed his ikati. He remembered walking into the Wrath, his arms held out as if inviting its embrace, tears frozen on his cheeks as the screaming voices of murdered witches filled his head, as he begged them for death . . . and the last vestige of his doubt disappeared, drowned out by a hunger for vengeance more primitive and powerful than any human doubt could possibly be.

The gods have given you this opportunity, he told himself. *You cannot pass it by.*

Bolstering his courage as best he could, he stepped off the sill, into the open air. A few of the spectators gasped, but he shapeshifted so swiftly that he had no chance to hit the ground. It was not a difficult transformation; his soul remembered this form as though it had actually been his own. All he had to do was shut down every part of his mind that was human and let the ancient memories possess him utterly. Surrendering everything he had become in the last few centuries and returning to the one state he feared—and hungered for—the most.

Those few locals who hadn't run screaming in terror when they first saw him change now watched as a large and powerful Souleater rose up over their city. It flew one wide circle above the desert plain surrounding it, then headed out to the west, following the scent trail of its brothers. And soon was out of sight.

———

Two dozen Souleaters screeching their mating challenges overhead was a sound piercing enough to bring pain to human ears. The creatures seemed oblivious to the human presence beneath them, and occasionally one even dropped down low enough that the turbulence from its wings rippled the sand at their feet. Ramirus saw some of the witches cringe when they got that close, but the Guardians were eager to do what they had come here for, and they kept looking at Salvator and Favias, hoping to get permission to fire. But no one was going to sanction an attack on the ikati until Kamala had made her attempt to draw them away from Jezalya; a wounded Souleater might well focus his attention on his attacker and thus get left behind.

Much to all their relief, the Souleaters did follow Kamala when she finally reappeared, and she led them off on a chase to the west; their cries of lust and fury echoed across the landscape with decreasing volume until they could be heard no more.

After such painful cacophony, silence was welcome.

Ramirus had conjured a spell of his own to supplement that

of the witches, using Siderea's scarf as a focus. It hung about the barrier like a thin mist now, ready to detect any spell of Siderea's that was sent out into the desert. Now, even as Ramirus watched, his sorcerous construct responded to something. Apparently many small spells had been sent out at the same time, and they pierced the witch's barrier—and his own creation—simultaneously. He could see his spell ripple briefly as they passed through it, like water into which a handful of pebbles had been cast; by the time the surface settled down again, he had determined what the spells were and the purpose behind them.

His expression was dark as he turned to Salvator. "The tribes have all been alerted. They've been told to head in toward Jezalya immediately, and to kill anything in their path that doesn't belong there. In short, us."

Favias cursed under his breath. "How far out are they?"

Ramirus shook his head. "Don't know yet. I got a mental impression that she expects them to be able to move in pretty quickly, so we should assume the worst until reconnaissance says otherwise."

"They'll be coming from all directions at once," Salvator muttered.

It was not an unexpected development. In fact, it was the reason that they had brought so many common soldiers with them, just in case something like this happened. But that did not mean that an attack by the tribes wouldn't put their people in danger, not to mention complicate the portions of this operation they had yet to launch.

We must find the Souleater queen quickly, Ramirus thought, frustrated by the new complication. *This is all a wasted effort otherwise.*

Salvator opened his mouth to speak . . . and then closed it. A dark shape was rising up from Jezalya, and the sudden realization of what it must be appeared to have banished all other concerns.

The queen was rising.

Ramirus could hear the Guardians preparing to fire at her, archers nocking their arrows while witches prepared to lend added velocity to their fire. But something was wrong. It took him a moment to realize what it was, but when he did, he called out *"Hold!"* with all the power his voice could muster. Apparently Salvator trusted him to make such a call, for the High King held up his hand and nodded his approval of the termination. Shina shut her eyes, presumably to begin to pass the message along to the Seers at all their relay points. Thus far not a single arrow had been fired.

"It's not a female," Ramirus said.

It wasn't a real Souleater, either. Its body looked proper enough, but its presence lacked that disquieting power that was a hallmark of the species. And he could see that the Guardians were having no trouble focusing their attention upon it, which would not have been the case with a real ikati.

The false beast circled low overhead, following the circumference of the witch's barrier. Ramirus held his breath, hoping he had not made the wrong call. Then, just as it passed over the royal party, a wind whipped up about Ramirus' feet, raising enough sand to blind them temporarily. But his sorcerous senses still functioned, and he was able to catch a glimpse of the power that had conjured the wind, as well as the metaphysical signature of the man behind it.

The Souleater was Colivar.

Ramirus was torn between being furious with him for his

insane recklessness and being afraid for him. Had he discovered something in Jezalya that merited taking this kind of risk? Or had he simply lost his mind? Ramirus remembered back to the Colivar he had known back in the days before the Law, so close to a wild beast in manner and spirit that others had remarked upon it. Now that he understood the reason for it, he knew that the last thing Colivar should be doing was taking on the very form that would encourage his ikati side to express itself. What if, after knowing such freedom, it did not wish to return to the shackles of human existence?

When the great beast turned away from Jezalya and began to head west, Ramirus looked down at the place where Colivar's wind had scoured the ground. A map had been impressed into the sand, he saw, with Jezalya at its center and the mountains on two sides. A wide circle had been drawn around the city, no doubt representing the witch's barrier. Outside that were a dozen cryptic marks, each one a cluster of tiny imprints such as a fingertip might make, arranged in neat rectangles. Troop markings, Ramirus realized. Much too close for comfort. There would likely be fighting soon, and a lot of it. He looked closely at the mountains and saw similar imprints there, but they were single points, arrayed in no particular pattern.

Below the map were two hieroglyphs. They were from the written language of a culture that had died out so long ago that few men knew how to read them. Ramirus did. So did Colivar.

"What does it say?" Salvator asked him.

"The first one signifies a woman in power. The second signifies death." He looked at the High King. "It would appear that Siderea Aminestas is dead."

"Good news if it's true, but who sent this to us?"

Ramirus drew in a deep breath. "I believe that was Colivar, your Majesty."

It said much for Salvator that he didn't look as surprised as he must have felt. Or perhaps he wasn't surprised. Perhaps his faith had prepared him for the thought of a Magister turning into a Souleater. Didn't they both stem from the same corruption, in his eyes?

Favias looked up from the map. "If Siderea just died, shouldn't her ikati be going insane right now?"

"That is the theory," Ramirus agreed.

They had all hoped that if Siderea were killed her Souleater would appear right afterward. Screaming in rage or anguish, as her cousin had done outside Danton's castle, perhaps even attempting to attack Siderea's killers. That's what precedent suggested would happen. That's what they had prepared for.

Not this silence. Not this mystery.

The queen is young, Ramirus reminded himself. *Colivar guessed that she would be dependent upon the bond with Siderea because she'd had next to no life experience before it. But what if youth in fact makes her more adaptable? Humans can learn some things easily in childhood that they must struggle to grasp when they are older.*

"We have to find her," Salvator said. "And if we can't find her—" He bit his lip and did not continue. Gwynofar was ready and willing to challenge this Souleater queen as she had done in the Spinas, but Salvator loathed that option and would only consider it as a last resort.

We may come to that point soon if the queen does not show herself.

"What are these things?" Favias asked, indicating the isolated spots in the mountains.

"Most likely the places where riders are hiding," Salvator said. "If so, we need to send in troops to deal with them. If what

Colivar told us is true, they won't be in shape to resist right now. Send witches in also, to search out any who aren't accounted for on the map. We must get them all."

Ramirus looked westward, remembering the flock of maddened Souleaters who had set off after Kamala. If their consorts could be killed, so that the Souleaters lost their human intelligence, she would be in much less danger. Was that a good or a bad thing?

"With the tribes so close—" Favias began.

"I can hold off their warriors," Ramirus told him. "You see to the riders, and focus on finding the queen."

Salvator's eyes fixed on him. There was a question in them. Ramirus did not flinch, but nor did he answer. After a moment the High King nodded gruffly and turned away.

You are learning, High King.

———

The warriors of the Tukrit tribe were thundering across the sands when their leader suddenly pulled up short and signaled for the others to do the same. Their compact, tightly muscled horses had been bred for maneuverability, but even so they were hard pressed to come to that quick a halt in neat array; the sand that was stirred up by their hooves was taken up by the wind, veiling the air in a gritty mist as the man who had called the halt peered off into the distance.

Then they heard him curse under his breath, a long and picturesque curse that combined unclean animal parts and the sexual habits of enemies. Even the horses knew him well enough to know that was not a good thing, and several pawed the ground nervously.

Then he said simply, "Sand," and they all understood the cause.

It was barely visible to the east, masked by the brightness of the rising sun, but those with the most perceptive vision could just make it out: a thin gray cloud in the distance, stretching from the land upward to the sky, and as far from side to side as the eye could see. It was moving quickly toward them, which was not a good sign. In fact, it was the worst possible of all signs, short of the earth opening up and sending them hurtling down into the Abyss. An option that some of the warriors might have preferred.

No orders were required, because only one course of action was possible. Dismounting, the men began to force their horses to the ground, their flanks to the east. The animals sensed what was coming and jerked nervously at their reins, but it was a token defiance; this was not an operation in which there was any room for compromise or delay, and deep inside they seemed to understand that.

The storm moved swiftly, a demon of sand and wind that towered over them as it approached. If any of these men had ever seen the sea, they might have likened it to a massive wave, whose rolling crest seemed poised to crash down upon their heads. But these men knew only the shapes of sand and heat. And they knew that there was no way to fight such a storm, or run from it, or do anything other than take shelter as best they could, until this demon of the desert passed them by.

By the time the first sand-laden winds struck, the men were huddled down behind their horses, wide desert robes spread over the animals' heads as well as their own bodies, to offer what protection they could. But the wind whipped about them with typhoon force, driving sand into every possible opening and crevice; even with fabric held before one's mouth it was impossible to breathe without inhaling some of it. Those who could draw enough clean breath to speak muttered prayers under their breath, asking the gods to dispel the storm. But few expected their appeals to be answered. For such a storm to come upon them just as they were riding toward Jezalya was a clear sign that the gods of the city did not approve of their mission; only a brain-damaged child could mistake a message like that.

Apparently the gods were not yet content with their understanding, for the sand demon that had come upon them with such great speed now settled down over their huddled forms and did not move on. And it seemed to some of them that in the sound of the wind there was laughter.

———

The scent of ikati rivalry hung heavy in the air, leaving a clear trail for Colivar to follow. The conflicting odors of two dozen males were spread across an area half a mile wide, each one as distinct to his ikati senses as a human name. A few seemed vaguely familiar to him, though he could not remember them clearly enough to identify their owners. But it was very possible that some of the ikati he was chasing now were among those he had flown with—and fought with—before. The thought was both exhilarating and unnerving.

Rising above all those odors was the rich, musky-sweet scent of a queen in flight. Breathing it in awakened memories that he would rather not surrender to, but there was no way to deny them now. In taking on this form he had opened the floodgates of recall and thrown away the key.

It is worth the price, he told himself stubbornly. The words had become a mantra to him as he flew, a mental drug with which he subdued the human portion of his soul. The ancient hungers that were stirring in him now threatened to drown out his human awareness, but he did not resist them. He let them fill him and drown him and drive him to the edge of madness, because he knew there was one hunger that must be satisfied—that he had waited centuries to satisfy—and there was no other way he could do so.

Today he must become ikati.

Sunlight played across his wings, fostering a pleasure so intense it bordered on pain. It was a sensation he was not prepared for. He had known all along that the Souleaters thrived on sunlight, but that knowledge had been a thing of human words, sterile of personal experience. His own ikati had been trapped in the north for so long it had forgotten the feel of tropical sunlight on its wings. Even at the peak of the arctic summer, when the sun never set, fear of the long arctic night lurked about the corners of ikati consciousness, filtering that sun through a veil of fear.

But now! Sunlight blazed across the jeweled panels of Colivar's wings and lent him strength—it warmed his blood and bolstered his heartbeat—it intensified his senses so that every breeze that touched his skin made him tremble. Flying in the sunlight sent his spirit soaring to heights that human experience could not hope to replicate. If his faceted eyes had been capable of tears, he would have wept from the sheer pleasure of it. What human passion could begin to compare with this?

What fools he and the others had been, to search all over the world for the ikati! Of course the creatures would come to a place like this in the end, to bathe in this glorious sunlight! Why had Colivar not realized that from the beginning?

As he flew, he began to alter his ikati flesh, altering it in much the same way he had done just before fighting Nyuku. If Kamala was leading the males in a straight path away from

Jezalya, it would take every sorcerous trick he could muster to catch up to them. If, on the other hand, she had fallen into the flight pattern of a true queen—if she had picked up enough details from the memory he'd shared with her in Coldorra to realize just how complex the mating flight could be—then the whole colony might have turned in another direction entirely, or at least lost some time weaving tangled patterns in the sky before moving on.

Tangled patterns . . .

Memories from the past washed over him, images from forgotten flights crowding about him like the ghosts of jilted lovers. The last queen he had known had been a master of the dance, and she had led her suitors along a serpentine path whose essence was beauty and death combined. How could Colivar ever explain to a mere human the maddening arousal that came of such a flight, so far beyond any simple concept like *lust* or *bloodthirst* that one lacked words to describe it? Human language could not possibly do justice to such a transcendent intimacy.

Now he could hear a murmur on the wind, mating cries muted by distance. He could feel his heartbeat quicken at the sound, and fire shot through his veins. This was not mere lust-born energy, but something even more driving. Lust was an ephemeral thing. Finite. The hunger he was feeling now was so much more than that. It had gnawed at his heart for centuries, without any hope of surcease or satisfaction. Until now.

Soon he could see dark shapes moving in the sky before him. Many of the males seemed to be engaged in one-on-one combat; apparently Kamala had figured out how to turn them against one another. That she had been able to do so with no more than a snatch of his memory to learn from filled him with awe.

How appropriate it was that such a woman should be the one to drive the Souleater colony to its final destruction!

He did not see her anywhere, but that did not concern him right now. She was not the one he was looking for.

Heart pounding, he hovered a short distance from the melee, trying to make out the features of individual ikati. Would he even recognize the ones he had known in the north, after so many years had passed? Their smells were all mixed together on the wind, a maddening elixir of lust and hatred, and he could feel his body responding to it despite his attempt to stay focused.

And then one of the largest males suddenly broke out from the flock. It was a broad-chested creature with spikes half a span longer than those of its fellows, and its flanks were crosshatched with the ragged scars of past mating contests. Colivar watched as it looked about to find the queen and then, when it failed, let loose a mating challenge of such arrogance and anger that it seemed to shake the very sky.

Colivar remembered that cry.

His body remembered it.

He answered.

The creature wheeled about to confront him. Did it recognize the body Colivar was wearing? He had done his best to replicate the appearance of his lost consort. Was the sound of his challenge familiar to it? The last time this ikati had heard that cry, they had been above the ice-fields of the far north, so close to the Wrath that one could hear its ghostly screams in one's brain.

By unspoken accord they began to fly upward, seeking a place far enough from the general fracas that they would not be interrupted. The air grew thinner and colder with each passing minute, and their layered wings had to beat twice as hard to maintain altitude, but that was just part of the challenge. A weaker ikati would have fallen back at this point, panicking as his breath grew short and his maneuverability was compromised. These two did not waver. They were among the strongest of their kind, and both knew the value of staging their fight in a place where none could follow them.

When they finally reached an elevation that suited them, they faced off against one another and began to circle. Colivar felt his forward wings stiffen even as his rival spread his own; jeweled membranes stretching wide on both sides of his neck, providing a fearsome backdrop for the snake-like head. The sight of his rival's display made the blood rush to Colivar's head, awakening a hunger that no human soul could contain, but he embraced it without reserve, even as he embraced the inevitability of this glorious moment.

The two great serpentine bodies began to circle one another, a delicate and deadly dance in which each one sought to create an opening whereby he might gain advantage. Tails with razor-sharp blades at their tips feinted toward fragile wings; talons flashed when a sudden shift in position brought the two bodies close together for an instant . . . but not close enough. The concentration required for such maneuvering was absolute, and Colivar could feel all the rest of the world fading from his consciousness. He let it go. There was no way to win this challenge other than to be wholly subsumed by it, and if that meant abandoning his humanity, so be it.

It was worth the price.

Suddenly the ikati struck out at him, its tail whipping sideways through the air with such speed that it was rendered nearly invisible. Colivar pulled in his wings so that gravity yanked him out of range, then caught the wind again and lunged upward, catching the sinuous tail in his teeth just as it reached the end of its trajectory. He bit down into the heavily muscled flesh and felt it spasm against his teeth; the blood of his enemy filled his mouth. But the ikati managed to pull free before Colivar's jaws could close completely, and it quickly put distance between them. Not without cost, though. There were deep parallel gouges in his tail now, and drops of blood sprayed into the wind as it moved. Such damage would not be enough to kill the creature, Colivar knew, but it might hamper its mobility.

Apparently the ikati thought so as well, for it turned and lunged directly at him. Colivar tried to twist out of the way, but in dodging the deadly teeth he miscalculated and came within range of the talons. He managed to pull his wings out of the way at the last minute, but two of the claws scored his flank before he could dodge them.

Whipping his own tail upward, he wrapped it about the ikati's own. It was a move better suited to mating than to combat, and it took the creature by surprise. Colivar now had a python's grip on his opponent's tail, and he used it to pull the creature off balance. For a brief moment the ikati had to focus all its attention on remaining airborne, and in that instant Colivar struck. His teeth closed on one of the creature's lower wings and ripped through its membrane, tearing loose a fragment as long as its leg and releasing it into the wind. Now the ikati was bereft of half its lift on one side; it struggled to save itself, but Colivar's weight dragging down on its tail made it impossible for it to establish the equilibrium necessary for flight. Nor could Colivar's wings, angled upward for the assault, support them both.

Locked in a serpentine embrace, they began to plummet toward the earth. A chill wind roared past Colivar's ears as he twisted desperately about, seeking a way to deal a deathblow before the fall killed them both. The ikati clawed at his flanks, trying to force him loose, but he did not let that distract him from his purpose. Wounds meant nothing at this point. Pain meant nothing. Even his own death meant nothing, if he could destroy this creature on his way out.

Then his talons slipped between the ikati's wings, and he lashed out with all his strength, rending to pieces every bit of flesh, bone, and membrane within reach. The creature howled in pain and began to struggle wildly, trying to free itself from Colivar's deadly embrace. And now Colivar let it go. His tail unwrapped from about the ikati's and, dodging the great beast's claws one final time, he pushed himself away from it, seeking enough distance to be able to spread his wings wide so that he could stop his own fall.

It was over.

Breathing heavily, blood trickling down his flanks, Colivar watched as his opponent spiraled down toward the earth. Faster and faster the great creature fell, and it was clear it would be unable to save itself. Lacerated wings beat frantically at the wind, but that only tore the delicate membranes further; by the time the ikati reached the earth, there was little left of its wings but broken struts, and Colivar imagined he could hear them snap as the massive body struck the ground. Sand rose up in plumes from the force of the impact, and a single piece of glistening membrane drifted from the sky, coming to rest beside the still, broken body.

Colivar watched to see if the ikati would move, and then, when it did not, he let out a howl of triumph that could surely be heard as far away as the Sea of Tears. The torment of all his lost centuries resounded in that cry, and even the ikati who were sparring beneath him paused in their fighting and looked up, wondering which one of their number had made such a terrible sound.

And then there was silence.

Colivar gazed down at Nyuku's Souleater with a strange sense of humility, for he knew just what this death would mean to the Kannoket. Only someone who had experienced that madness himself could comprehend its full horror. But he felt no pity. Not an ounce of pity. This was the way of their kind. Nyuku had played the game and lost.

Now we are even, he thought with satisfaction.

He turned to take one last look at the Souleaters . . . and then hesitated. All about him he could hear cries of challenge and triumph being released into the wind, and they resonated within his soul as well as his flesh. A part of him knew that he was supposed to head back to the human encampment now, but the reason for that was no longer clear. Why was he leaving this place? He had proven himself among the Souleaters. They would recognize his dominance now. Wasn't that what mattered?

With a last puzzled glance toward the eastern horizon, he spread out his wings to catch the wind and headed back down to join the others of his kind.

The Guardian who came through the portal had blood splattered all over his armor, and as soon as Salvator saw him, he waved for one of the healers to attend to him. But the blood was apparently not his own, and as the man walked the short distance from his arrival point to the base camp, it was clear from his steady stride that he had suffered no major damage. Of course, that revealed nothing about the battle that had just taken place; the company that Salvator had sent into the mountains to hunt down the Souleaters' riders had included a contingent of Seers, skilled enough in the healing arts to handle any wounds his people might suffer.

Between gritted teeth he had muttered, As a last resort, then, I will consider it. But only as a last resort. When every other option has been exhausted. Not one second before that.

They were not at that point yet, he told himself. Not yet.

"There are two possibilities as I see them," Favias said. "One, that she fled the area as soon as she saw trouble coming, or right after Siderea died. In which case she is now beyond our reach, unless we do something to call her back. Two, that she is hiding somewhere nearby. Maybe the sight and smell of another female scared her so badly that she's just not going to come out until that scent is gone from the area."

Shina said, "We can banish that."

Salvator nodded. "Do so."

She moved off to comply.

Ramirus said quietly, "There is a third possibility, which is that she is still here and still quite sane, and knows exactly what is going on. She may even have been watching this campaign play out, albeit from a safe distance."

"You speak of her as if she were still highly intelligent," Favias said. "But her human partner is dead now, and Colivar said that she would be even more vulnerable than the others because she had bonded to Siderea before her own mind was fully developed. He said that would make her even more dependent on her partner than the other Souleaters, and less stable once her partner died."

"With all due respect for Colivar's omniscience," Ramirus said dryly, "let us not forget that was only speculation. What if he were mistaken? What if being nurtured from childhood by a mind like Siderea's could affect the development of the Souleater's own mental capacity? So that even after her human partner died, an echo of higher intelligence would remain? What then?"

In that case, Salvator thought, even baiting her would not work. She would see the trap for what it was and keep her distance from us.

Feeling the frustration that was welling up inside him about to reach the breaking point, he walked away from the others for a moment, just to get some space around him. The sense of futility in the air made him feel claustrophobic. Never has a campaign accomplished so much, he thought bitterly, and had it mean so little. If there had been a piece of furniture around that he could strike out at, or even a sizeable rock to kick, he would have vented some of his anger on it. But nothing other than sand was nearby, and kicking sand would just not be satisfying.

He thought of asking Gwynofar what she thought of all this, but her opinion didn't really matter, did it? It was more important that he watch the western sky for something that might happen there. Like Kamala's return. Or Colivar's. Or that of the other Souleaters. Or maybe the spell that Ramirus had cast to hold off the tribal warriors would collapse, in which case he should be watching for signs of enemy soldiers approaching from that direction . . .

He shook his head, aware that something was wrong but not sure what it was. Looking back at the others, he saw them all staring in the same direction he had been, as if something to the west of the camp had drawn their attention. But even though he looked back and squinted into the distance, he couldn't make out what it was. He thought of asking Gwynofar what she thought, then realized that her input was not important. He needed to stay focused on things that really mattered.

But she had been standing with the others a minute ago.

It took all of his effort to make himself turn around. His mind might have decided that he needed to look for Gwynofar, but his body clearly didn't agree. He was aware enough of the disparity that it lent new strength to his efforts, even as a new kind of fear took root in his soul.

She had left the base camp and was standing out on the empty plain, alone. She had picked up a spear along the way—no one was allowed to take a step outside the sheltered area without a weapon in hand—but it hung limp in her grasp, the shaft horizontal. Useless. She seemed to be staring at something in the sky. No. She was staring at nothing in the sky. Her eyes were turned upward, but he sensed that they were seeing nothing.

He followed her gaze. A dark shape seemed to come into focus that had not been there a moment before, and an odor filled the air that was cloyingly sweet, insufferably foul. Even before he could make out details of the creature, he knew what it was. What it must be.

A Souleater.

It was plummeting down at her from a bright, clear sky, its long talons extended, like a hawk about to snatch up a field mouse. Though Gwynofar's face was turned up toward it, he knew with sickening certainty that she did not see it at all—at least not in any conscious sense—and that she could not act to save herself.

He yelled at her as he sprinted across the sand, a sound that might have been meant to be her name but that came out of his mouth as an inarticulate cry of despair. He grabbed up a spear as he ran, knowing even as he did so that he was going to be too late. The thing was too close—it was coming down too fast—and she was too far away. For the first time in his life he wished that he were a witch, so that he might sacrifice his life's own essence to increase his speed. But all he had was prayer, so he offered it.

Let this be my sacrifice, not hers!

Great jeweled wings filled the sky overhead as he dove the last couple of feet, transforming sky and sand into a mad cacophony of color. He reached Gwynofar even as the talons were about to close on her head and tackled her down to the ground, desperately trying to brace his spear in some kind of defensive position. She was as limp as a rag doll and offered no resistance. It seemed that he could feel a breeze upon his back as the great talons snapped shut just inches from his skin, and the ikati screamed in rage so loudly that it made his ears ring. Could the others hear it too? Or were they still entranced by the creature's power as he had been, and blind to its presence?

Rolling over on his back, he thrust the spear upward with both hands, not even caring where his target was at that moment, just trying to win himself some room to maneuver. The mass of the great body overhead seemed to blot out the sun, and its musky-sweet scent filled his lungs like noxious smoke. He had to fight the urge to gag as he struggled to get to his feet, while staying near enough to his fallen mother to protect her.

Where were the others? Were they going to help? Even if they couldn't see the creature he was fighting, surely they could see that he was engaged in combat with something, and maybe fire their weapons into the space it so clearly occupied. But even as he gripped his spear in both hands and braced himself to strike at the creature the moment it came within range, he knew with a sense of utter despair that the queen's power didn't work that way. The others wouldn't be able to help him because their attention was fixed on other things. Tribesmen attacking. Souleaters returning. Maybe even a sandstorm moving in. Each of her mesmerized victims would come up with his own reason for not looking in this direction, without ever realizing he was not doing so.

Salvator was on his own.

The Souleater's great wings beat the air mere yards overhead, whipping the sand about him into a frenzy. His hair blew wildly across his face as he feinted with the long spear to keep her at a distance, trying desperately to remember the key facts of Souleater anatomy, to figure out where to strike. The body of this one was longer and thinner than the ones in the diagrams Favias had shown him, and a few of the landmarks he'd been told to look for, to locate major organs, were absent. But he knew he might only get one good shot at her, so he had to make it count.

Suddenly she lunged down at him with her great triangular head, teeth bared. He thrust the spear forward aggressively, so that she would have to impale herself on its point in order to reach him. She pulled back, frustrated, and great jaws snapped shut several feet short of his head. She was so close now that he could taste her breath on his tongue, sickening sweetness with an aftertaste of decay. The great black eyes reflected his own sweat-streaked face back at him in its thousand uniform facets, and he realized suddenly that if he moved quickly enough, he might be able to blind her before she withdrew. With a muttered prayer on his breath he angled his spear—

—And pain exploded in his side without warning. He felt himself flying through the air, and he hit the ground with such force that it drove the breath from his body. For a moment the entire world went red; sand mixed with blood in his throat, and he tried to cough it all up, but the motion sent a sharp pain lancing through his chest. Favias' voice seemed to ring in his head, admonishing him for his carelessness. *They fight with their tails. Don't underestimate their reach.*

Blinking against the pain, he struggled to get an elbow under him, to lever his way back onto his feet. He could feel a dent in the side of his armor where the sheer force of the Souleater's blow had caved in the steel; if they'd been fighting on anything other than sand, he would probably be dead now. Every breath he drew was accompanied by a stabbing pain, and he was sure that one or more of his ribs had been broken. But he couldn't let it end like this. Not after all they had gone through to get this far. He could not let this creature win.

Now his vision was becoming clear enough that he could see his spear lying on the ground to one side of him; he reached out to grab it. But razor-sharp talons suddenly closed about him from behind, locking him in an inexorable vice as they jerked him upward. The pain was so intense that for a moment it blinded him; by the time he could see again, the ground was far beneath them, and his dazed vision could not make out any sign of either city or camp nearby.

The Souleater's talons were like bars of iron around his chest; surely, if Salvator had not been wearing a solid steel cuirass, he would have been crushed to death. As it was, he could hear the ominous creak of steel as the powerful talons tightened, struggling to finish the job. And to his horror he could feel the cuirass begin to give way, surrendering at last to the crushing grip. Bones snapped along one side of his ribcage, sending spears of pain lancing through his side and very nearly driving him into unconsciousness.

I will not die like this! he raged, struggling for every breath. Shadows were closing in about his field of vision. Black spots danced before him as blood seeped steadily into his lungs. Every indrawn breath was agony. *I will not die like prey!*

The only weapon he had on him was a short sword edged with Souleater blades, and he knew that even if he could get it out of its sheath, he could not reach far enough to strike at any vital target. But his hand closed about its grip nonetheless, nails biting into the leather binding as spasms of pain wracked his flesh. He would not pass out, he told himself. He would not give up. He would not stop fighting until the moment that God himself collected his soul from his body, so that all the Souleater carried away was empty flesh . . .

Delirium was closing in on him now, disjointed visions flashing in and out of existence all around him. He saw figures from one of Favias' anatomical charts flying past him, with Souleater vulnerabilities marked in red ink and meticulously labeled. *Look.* Favias' voice was a whisper in his ear. *The artery inside the leg. It is vulnerable at the joint. Slice it open and the result will be as deadly to a Souleater as a cut to the femoral artery would be to a man.*

He tried to twist about in the ikati's grip so he could locate the spot, but just then the talons tightened about his chest, driving out the last of his air and causing fresh pain to explode in his chest. His heart labored as it struggled to push enough blood through his constricted veins to keep him alive. *Blessed Destroyer,* he prayed desperately, *give me strength to finish this one task before I die, I beg You. Let me be the vehicle by which You banish this plague from the earth.*

Gritting his teeth against the pain, he somehow managed to twist his head around just enough to see the joint Favias had described. He could see where the hide was thin where the creature's leg was joined to its body, and he imagined he could hear the pulse of blood coursing beneath its skin, so close to the surface. Fixing his vision upon that one point, he tried to shut out all the rest. Fear was temporary. Bodily pain was meaningless. Soon he would be in the presence of the Creator, and nothing else mattered.

There was a strange kind of peace in such total surrender. The pain in his body seemed to become a distant thing; it did not hurt any less, but it was as if the pain now belonged to someone else. He could feel knife-edged bone shards stabbing into his internal organs as he unsheathed his sword, gripping the handle tightly so that the wind would not tear it from his grasp. The world all about him had faded to blackness, and only a single central point of light remained, focused upon the vulnerable joint overhead. Somewhere a stranger screamed in pain as he raised his sword as high as he could, struggling to reach the vulnerable spot. Somewhere a man was coughing up blood, in spasms so agonizing no human soul could bear it.

Guide me, my Creator, for the sake of mankind, whom You love.

Drawing in as deep a breath as he could, he thrust upward with all his strength. The ikati jerked its leg back in surprise; the sudden motion caused Salvator to black out for a moment. When he came to and found his hand empty, he thought for one terrible moment that he had dropped the sword. Despair rushed over him with numbing force. Then he saw it embedded in the creature's leg, the grip hanging down toward him. Despite the depth of the wound, only a trickle of blood was leaking out. He had missed the vital artery.

Unable to draw in a full breath any longer, he hung limp in

the creature's grip, praying for one last moment of strength to do what he had to do. Then, gritting his teeth against the pain, he lurched up and grabbed the leather-bound grip of the sword. The cobalt blade sliced through the Souleater's flesh, and more blood flowed out of its leg, but it was still not enough. The ikati howled in pain and tried to shake him loose, but he managed to twist the sword hard to the left before he lost his grip—and a river of hot blood answered his efforts, as the wall of the artery was finally breached.

And then the ikati queen released him.

And he fell.

Wind rushed by his head, but he could not take any of it in; the crushed steel cuirass held him too tightly in its embrace to allow for breathing. But that was all right. His time on earth was over now. There was no longer need to breathe.

Thank you, my Creator, for accepting my sacrifice in the place of my mother's. May my death serve as penance for any and all sins this company has performed in its mission.

Clearly the Creator was pleased by his prayer, for in His infinite mercy he allowed the High King's consciousness to slip away from him gently, just before the ground rushed up to meet him.

———

The queen was watching.

Colivar could see her in the distance, so far away that at times she seemed little more than a dot on the horizon. At first he thought she was just a vulture in search of carrion, and he paid little attention to her. But something caused him to look more closely, and he realized then that her silhouette was not that of a bird, and she hovered in the air in a way that no vulture could manage. A thrill ran up his spine then as he suddenly realized what she was . . . and who she must be.

None of the other ikati seemed to be aware of her. Was that by her choice? How adept had Kamala become at manipulating the queen's special gift? Colivar remembered past mating flights that he had viewed through the eyes of his own ikati—remembered them beating their shared wings in wild fury when a queen suddenly disappeared, all rational thought driven out of their joint consciousness by a tide of pure animal frustration. Little wonder the males turned on one another! Such energy must have an outlet or it would consume its source.

If she was allowing him to see her, and only him, was that not an invitation? The mere thought of it sent blood rushing to his wings with such force that it was hard to focus on anything else; the jeweled panels twitched in anticipation, hungering to consume the distance between them. When he began to fly in her direction, several of the males tried to get in his way, but he dodged them rather than confronting them, not wanting to take his eyes off that distant winged figure for a moment. Afraid she would vanish like smoke if he did. A few other Souleaters followed his gaze westward, curious to see what it was that he was flying toward with such determination, but apparently they saw nothing of interest there. Only empty sky, a blazing sun, and sand so hot that the air above it rippled like a sorcerous portal.

She was there only for him.

The sensation of flight was so intense that it was hard for him to focus on anything else now. He was acutely aware of each muscle in his body, and the pulse of contraction and release that accompanied each wingstroke sent ripples of pleasure through his flesh. The air surrounding him seemed to shimmer with colors, and the sunlight on his back sent waves of pleasure coursing down his hide like a physical caress. Nothing his ikati had shared with him had ever been like this! Were such sensations normal for this species, and the bond between ikati and human was simply not strong enough to convey them? Or was this something that only a hybrid creature like himself might experience? If so, was Kamala feeling the same things right now? Was the very air alive with energy for her as well, so that every movement, no matter how small, heated her blood beyond bearing?

He was coming close enough to her now that he could see her clearly. Sunlight rippled along her scales as she hovered in midair, her long, serpentine tail coiling and uncoiling suggestively. Just a bit farther and he would be able to twine his tail about hers, feeling that sleek surface sliding against his own rough hide, using it to bring their bodies into perfect alignment. The promise of it was maddening. He could feel his wings falling into a new pattern as he approached her, echoing her own, and he knew that at the moment of pleasure they would share the same rhythm, stacked wings beating in perfect unison. It was an ecstasy beyond human comprehension.

But just as he was nearly within reach of her, she wheeled about in the air and began to fly away from him.

He was startled for a moment, then quickly followed. She was fast, very fast, but his altered body was equally capable of speed, and the stream of turbulence that roiled in her wake only stoked the fire in his blood to greater heights. Yet every time he was just about to take hold of her, she managed to dart away again, leaving him trembling with frustration. Once he was so close that he could have nipped her tail with his teeth—but then she surged forward suddenly into the wind, putting so much distance between them that he was afraid he might lose her.

Miles of sand gave way to stone beneath them, a rocky black plain crisscrossed by sand-bottomed faults. She turned in her flight to head directly over it, then dropped down so low that her talons nearly brushed the ground as she flew. Uncertain of her intent, he followed. She began to fly along one particular fault—and then dropped down into it suddenly, and out of sight.

Startled, he overshot the spot and had to circle about to come back to it. The fault looked much too narrow for a Souleater to fly into; Colivar's own wings would be crushed by the rock walls on either side the moment he tried. So how had she entered it? And why? Hovering over the center of the fault, he could see no Souleater inside.

Only a woman.

She had reclaimed her human form and stood there looking up at him. For a moment he could not absorb what had happened; then the terrible truth of it hit home.

The Souleater queen was gone!

Maddened by frustration, he bellowed his rage to the heavens. His wings beat at the rock on either side of the narrow pass with audible force; one of his smallest wing struts snapped, but he didn't even feel the pain. Gone! She was gone! The hunger for her was an unquenchable fire in his belly, but the creature he lusted for no longer shared his form. There were no wings to beat against his own, no tail to coil against his belly.

"Colivar!"

The sound she made was strange. It took him a moment to realize what it was. Human language. A name.

His.

Hovering above the rock, his wounded wing throbbing, he looked down at her again.

Her body was naked, he saw, and covered with a thin sheen of sweat. Her high, full breasts were flushed with the heat of human arousal, and the perfume that arose from her skin awakened a faint memory within him, of a kind of desire that had nothing to do with either frenzy or bloodshed. Trapped between the hunger of two species, he suddenly found himself frozen, unable to respond in any meaningful way. In some distant part of his mind he knew that his body was wrong for this moment and that he had to change it, but he no longer remembered how.

She began to walk along the sandy floor of the fault, moving slowly toward him. His wings thrummed helplessly against the rock, but they were unable to bring him any closer to her. "Be human again, Colivar." The scent of her filled his nostrils, awakening fragments of human memory. Morati lovers. Languid pleasures. The taste of a woman's sweat-slicked skin, warmed by the tropical sun.

"Come back to me," she whispered. Holding out her arms in invitation.

He bound his power without knowing it, molded it without conscious thought. The change that followed was uncontrolled, and pain shot through his limbs as they returned to their former shape in fits and starts, like a bird breaking out of its shell. Suddenly his wings were gone, and he dropped down onto the sand before her, the breath driven from his lungs by the impact. Two legs. Two arms. No more. That was right, wasn't it?

He looked up. Close, she was so close, and so real. So human. He reached out to touch her, and she did not back away. Her flesh was like silk beneath his fingertips, agonizingly soft. He stood, and his hands slid up her body, following the curve of her thighs, her hips, moving upward to cup the fullness of her breasts. He wondered at how alien her body felt, even as it aroused him. Skin so smooth. So fragile. Where were the scales? Where were the wings? So much was missing!

She moved closer to him, pressing the full length of her body against his own, bringing her lips up to his. Images of pleasure rushed through his head, human and ikati intermingled, and he struggled to find his way back to her world. Then her hands found the focus of his desire and she stroked him, leading the way. They moved down to the sand together, her legs parting for him, and then there was only heat: wonderful, glorious, human heat, and a rhythm that had nothing to do with flying. When she cried out in pleasure, it was a purely human sound, and when his own passion crested, the heat of it was so intense that in a single instant it consumed all moments but this one, banishing every instinct and sensation that was not in perfect harmony with his current self.

And the memory of wings was gone from his mind.

And the memory of ice was gone from his soul.

And when it was over, he lay in the sand by her side, and he wept.

CHAPTER 36

THE SEA of black ink was viscous and bottomless. Salvator swam through it slowly, each stroke a monumental effort, knowing there was a surface somewhere but not knowing how to reach it. Voices murmured in darkness, black ripples of sound without identities attached.

Is he waking up?

I think so.

Call Gwynofar!

And then the surface of the black ocean parted at last. A sea of white assailed his eyes in its place, blinding him. White walls. White linen curtains. White bed. The brilliance of it burned his eyes, forcing him to squeeze his eyelids shut, but even that could not keep all of it out. He was drowning in light.

"Salvator?"

He followed the familiar voice like a lifeline, struggling to resurface. Finally, he managed to open his eyes again, squinting against the blazing light. He could make out the shapes of three figures by his bedside now: a small blonde woman who sat beside him, a middle-aged man with weathered features, and a tall man with a white beard whose long robes were as black as the inky sea Salvator had just escaped from.

He opened his mouth and tried to speak, but no sounds would come out. His body had forgotten how to speak. Finally, with conscious effort, he managed to rasp out, "Is she dead?" The only question that mattered.

The three of them looked at each other. "He means the Souleater queen," Ramirus said. "Yes, she's dead. You killed her."

Salvator closed his eyes for a moment. He felt as if he were floating in a sea of physical and mental exhaustion. But no pain. "Am I dead?" he whispered.

He heard Ramirus chuckle softly. "Does your faith allow for you and I to be sharing the same afterlife?"

Despite himself, Salvator smiled. The expression made his face ache. "How long?"

"Three days," Gwynofar said. "The witches said they were going to keep you asleep until everything was properly healed. They said there was so much to repair . . ." Her voice trailed off but he heard the words that were unspoken. *They were not sure if you would make it.* "The high court has been told you're all right, that you're busy seeing to the political aftermath of battle. Valemar has everything under control. I'm told you're becoming something of a legend in Penitent circles. And soon will be outside of them, I expect." She smiled. The strain of recent events was apparent in a host of new lines on her face. "I wasn't sure if you'd be pleased by that or not."

"As long as they credit God for our victory, and understand that I was but His humble tool." He looked about the room. "Where am I?"

"Prince Nasaan's palace, in Jezalya. He insisted on having his own witches tend to you. He credits you with freeing his city from a plague of demons, and he wants to express his gratitude to you in person as soon as you're up to it." She hesitated, "He said that the Penitent god must be very powerful, judging from what he has done here, and that Jezalya will honor him accordingly. He's going to invite you to place his statue in the House of Gods, which is apparently where the local idols are worshipped." Before he could respond to that, she reached out and squeezed his hand. "Be gentle, Salvator. He means it as an honor."

He said nothing in response, just shut his eyes again. The room was so warm. He could feel it now. Desert heat, seeping into his skin.

"Tell me what happened," he whispered.

It was Ramirus who answered. "None saw the queen but you, until you attacked her. Few saw her even after that, but some of the Guardians managed to focus on her and were preparing to attack. It looked as though she snatched you up to use you as a shield, to keep them from firing at her."

Salvator opened his eyes and looked at Ramirus. "She could have used my mother for that, if all she wanted was a human body in front of her. I was farther away. Why me?"

It was Favias who spoke. "We believe she might have been observing us for some time and figured out you were the leader of the group. So your value as a shield was greater."

Salvator blinked. "Do you realize what you're suggesting?"

Ramirus nodded gravely. "We believe the strike on her Majesty was not a random act. The ikati picked the moment too carefully, waiting until all the rest of us were distracted enough that we were unlikely to notice Gwynofar's departure. That was not an act of rage, but of calculated intelligence. She was hunting us, Salvator. And quite effectively, too. If not for your unique ability to resist her power, your mother would be dead now, and the ikati queen would be somewhere far away from here, preparing a nest for her first clutch."

"But why my mother?" Salvator asked. "She wasn't playing a visible leadership role. She hadn't called the thing to her." He stopped and looked sharply at his mother. "You *didn't* call it to you, did you?"

Gwynofar smiled slightly as she shook her head. "You ordered me not to, remember?"

"Kamala said that her Sight could detect Gwynofar's link to the Seers," Ramirus told him. "We think that the queen may have had a similar ability. If so, she might have believed that your mother was responsible for the spell that bound Siderea. Possibly even for her death." He shrugged. "There's no way to know the truth, at this point. But I think we should all give thanks that this particular Souleater will never have a chance to reproduce."

Salvator leaned back and shut his eyes. The strain of speaking for so long was beginning to tell on him. "So the world is a safe place now?" he murmured weakly.

He heard Ramirus chuckle. "The world is a place of chaos and warfare, rife with bloodshed, betrayal, and every conceivable form of human suffering. As it always has been and always will be. But thanks to you there will soon be no Souleaters in it, which is a noteworthy improvement."

Salvator felt Gwynofar's hand on his forehead, smoothing back sweat-dampened strands of his hair. "Rest, my son. Nasaan will want to talk with you when you feel strong enough."

He nodded. Sleep was already edging its way into the corners of his mind as she leaned down and kissed him on the forehead. Then he heard her leave, and two pairs of heavier footsteps followed her to the door. He knew one stride well enough from his childhood years to hear when its owner was the only one left in the room.

"Ramirus."

The footsteps stopped. Salvator managed to raise the massive lead weights that his eyelids had become and looked at the Magister.

"Who saved me?" he asked him.

A white eyebrow arched upward. "Majesty?"

"No man could have survived a fall like that. Not with all the witches in the world to put him back together afterward. So someone must have intervened before I hit the ground. Yes? Someone who had been tracking the queen all along—following her scent trail perhaps, or the blood I was leaving behind—so that he'd be close enough to act when there was need." He paused. "Who saved me, Ramirus?"

The Magister's expression was unreadable. "The witches have asked that you not be given that information. They don't want any one of them to be singled out for special attention, as they view the entire enterprise as a group effort."

Salvator said nothing, but his gaze did not waver.

Finally Ramirus' eyes narrowed slightly. "You told me that you would rather die than have your life saved by sorcery," he reminded him. "I took you at your word." He chuckled softly. "I trust you will be able to sleep peacefully now, your Majesty?"

"Yes," Salvator whispered. Shutting his eyes once more. "Thank you."

He listened to Ramirus' footsteps leave the room, then slipped into those quiet depths where souls are healed, allowing sleep to claim him.

EPILOGUE

"THEY'RE ALL here," Ramirus said.

Kamala nodded, and took a moment to compose herself before she responded to him. The pounding of her heart was almost under control now. "How many?"

"Nearly three dozen. That's not all of them, but I think most of the important ones are here." He paused. "I can't say I recall so many Magisters ever being together in one place. The energy in the air is . . . interesting."

She raised an eyebrow. "What about when the Law was first established?"

He chuckled quietly. "There weren't that many Magisters in the whole world back then. Partly because we kept killing each other." His expression grew somber once more. "You understand what is at stake here."

She whispered it: "I do."

"The Law is not something we can simply put aside, even if we want to. It has been strained already by the few of us who know your secret, but if this many Magisters were to openly deny its tenets . . . it would shatter, Kamala. And then we would become no better than the creatures we just fought. The Law is the only thing that protects us."

"I understand," she said solemnly.

"I helped you bring them here because I agree that your situation does need to be resolved. My name is respected enough among sorcerers that many came at my bidding who would not respond to any other summons. But understand, Kamala: My debt to you was paid in Tefilat. I owe you no support beyond that. You're on your own from this point on."

She nodded. "I understand. And I thank you for your assistance in arranging this."

He pulled open the heavy door and exited the chamber, leaving it slightly ajar for her. It took her a moment before she could bring herself to step through it. So much was riding on this one meeting! But she was not going to run from these men any longer. Either she would win them to her cause, or the game would end here and now.

Finally she pulled the door all the way open and entered what had once been the greathall of a sizable castle. The building itself had fallen to ruins centuries ago, but the skeletal walls that remained had a surreal majesty, and the patina of age that clung to them suited the nature of her guests. She had reinforced a few of the walls and restored several items that time had devoured—such as the ironbound door—but otherwise she had left the place exactly as she found it. The ghosts of the First Kings seemed to hang about the ruined walls, a reminder both of mankind's potential majesty and its mortality.

Three dozen Magisters turned to face her as she entered the room, and the quiet conversations that had been taking place subsided into silence. She could tell from the surprise in their eyes that Colivar and Ramirus had not told them why they had been called here; clearly, they had not expected a woman to address them. *We are off to a good start*, she thought dryly.

There was a low stone platform at the head of the room, and she stepped up onto it. The little bit of height she gained allowed her to see all the Magisters at once, even those in the back rows.

So many of them! There was enough power in this room to lay waste to all of human civilization, if that was what these Magisters desired.

As they had done in the Dark Ages, before the Law was enacted.

Ethanus was there, she saw. The look of concern on his face brought a pang to her heart. And Colivar was standing in the middle of the crowd. He had helped make sure that all the Magisters who had once been Siderea's lovers were present, without ever asking her why that mattered so much. He seemed to enjoy the mystery of it. Kamala recognized the two Magisters from Gansang as well, far to the back of the crowd, but most of the rest were unknown to her. Were any of them women? she wondered suddenly. If Lazaroth had been masquerading as a man for so long, surely others might have done so as well. It was disconcerting to think that any of the men staring back at her right now might have begun life as a woman, surrendering her sexual identity in exchange for membership in the insular brotherhood of sorcerers. Such a Magister might despise her as much as Lazaroth had, resenting the fact that she openly celebrated the same identity they had been forced to abandon.

She waited until all eyes were upon her and then inclined her head ever so slightly, as she had seen Ramirus do. A gesture of respect among equals, with no hint of submission about it. Thus did sorcerers greet one another.

"Magisters," she said. Feeling their eyes fixed upon her, knowing that their magical scrutiny was focused on her as well. She wrapped her defensive spells tightly about her, hoping that her own power was up to such a test. "I thank you for coming. I trust you will find today's business worth your journey."

There was a part of her that was sorry to be ending this phase of her life. For all of her frustration with having been forced to hide her true nature, she had enjoyed moving secretly among these men and had savored the game of cat-and-mouse she'd played with several of them. Testing her wits and her sorcery against Magisters who had made an art form of ferreting out other people's secrets had been a unique challenge. Given that men like Ramirus had invested centuries in honing their skills in that arena, she had not done badly.

Now that game was ending, and a new one would take its place. And only the gods knew for certain what it would be.

Drawing herself up to her full height, proud and elegant with only a hint of defiance, she spoke the words that would end this phase of her life forever.

"My name is Kamala," she told them. "I am a Magister."

Few of them evinced surprise at her announcement, but she had expected that. Any madwoman could make such a statement, and she knew it would take more than mere words to prove to these men that she was what she claimed, or even that she was worthy of their attention. A few Magisters glanced at Ramirus or Colivar to assess their response to the announcement, but most of them simply looked skeptical.

Eyes fixed upon her audience, a subtle smile upon her face, she ran her hands slowly down her body. Smoothing her clothing over her breasts, around her waist, along the curve of her hips, drawing their eyes to the very features that so obviously made her a woman. As she did so, she transformed the fabric that was beneath her fingertips, replacing its natural hue with the color that only magic could produce: the traditional black of the Magisters. And though she had taken great care to shield herself from their sorcery thus far, she allowed that one transformation spell to remain unguarded, so that they might inspect it at their leisure.

Witchery was warm magic, which vibrated with life. Sorcery was a cold, dead thing, athra devoured and regurgitated: carrion magic. The difference between the two was not always apparent, as they functioned in an identical manner, but no skilled sorcerer who bothered to look closely would ever mistake one for the other.

She could sense their scrutiny upon her now, tendrils of their power licking at the substance of her sorcery, testing its nature. She felt as if the hands of three dozen strangers were roving all over her body, and the memory of past violations made it hard for her to just stand still and accept it. But she knew that this was something she had to do so they would know the truth of her words. No other proof would suffice.

When she thought they'd all had enough time to verify her true nature, she extended her defensive spells to protect herself once more. She found that she dared not look in the eyes of the Magisters directly, for fear that what she saw there might weaken her determination. Her next words would commit her to a path from which there would be no chance to withdraw. She felt as if she were standing at the edge of a precipice, seeking the courage to jump. Below her there was only darkness.

Now, she thought. *Do it.*

"Several months ago, a Magister named Raven was killed in Gansang. I am the one who killed him." She could feel the shock of her pronouncement ripple through the crowd; she waited a moment for it to settle before continuing. "I did not intend for him to die, but the Law of the Magisters does not care about motive. I am the person who set in motion the series of events that ultimately cost Raven his life; hence, as far as our Law is concerned, I killed him."

Now, finally, she looked at her audience. Magisters were well versed in hiding their true feelings from one another, but her words had shocked a few of them severely enough that some honest emotion was visible. Ramirus certainly looked surprised; whatever he'd expected from her, it had clearly not included a public confession. Colivar was staring at her intensely, as if trying to see through her air of defiance to see what lay beneath. As for Ethanus . . . she knew him well enough to read the message in his eyes: *I hope you know what you are doing*. The genuine concern in his expression made a knot form in her throat.

"The Law of the Magisters forbids any sorcerer from killing another," she continued. "Whether a murder is intentional or not is irrelevant to our justice system. That is because the Law exists for one thing and one thing only: to place limits upon our darker instincts, so that we can live as something better than bloodthirsty beasts. The part of our soul that is ikati will devour all the rest if we give it a chance; our spirits must be kept in balance or we will cease to be human.

"The Law was created to safeguard that balance. It is therefore sacrosanct. It is the very bedrock upon which the sanity of our kind depends."

She paused. "It is also incomplete."

She could hear whispers now, pitched low but urgent, but she ignored them to go on speaking. "What was the original purpose of the Law?" she demanded of them. "Not to deny our ikati instincts but simply to channel them appropriately. The bloodthirsty competitiveness of the male ikati was forced into a more 'civilized' mode, but it was not outlawed. The Souleater's hunger for dominance was transmuted into a subtle rivalry that might be sustained down through the ages with minimum bloodshed. Territorial battles were to be fought politically and psychologically, rather than with tooth and claw . . . but they were still to be fought. Only a Law that accepted our darker instincts—that *accommodated* them—could ever hope to bring the two sides of our spirit into balance.

"But what were those instincts?" she demanded. "Did the Law encompass the full range of ikati potential? Or did it speak to only one half of that bloodthirsty species—and therefore to only one half of *our* species?"

She paused. Her blood pounded hot in her veins, driven by a heady mixture of fear and elation. "I am, like you, a Magister. But I am also unlike you, in that my soul contains the essence of a Souleater queen. Those who designed the Law originally did not figure that into their plans, for they did not know a creature such as myself could exist. Yet I assure you, though I am currently the only woman to claim the title of Magister, others will follow me. And in order for the Law to serve *all* the Magisters, as its creators intended, it must be amended so that we, too, are part of it.

"That is why you were asked to come here today," she told them. "To provide that amendment."

She was tempted to shut her eyes for a moment. To concentrate on reading the emotion that must be welling up on all sides of her, hidden behind masks of perfect composure.

"Raven assaulted me," she told them. There was naked hatred in her voice now, and a razor-edged indignation whose source was not entirely human. She could sense her ikati rage stirring the bestial awareness that lay dormant within their own souls, like calling to like, demanding the justice of the open skies. "Had we been ikati, I would have torn him to pieces with my claws and my teeth and scattered the bloody bits before the males of my species as a warning. That is a queen's right. It is *my* right. And it is what our Law must accommodate." She paused "Until it does, that Law is incomplete and cannot rightfully be applied in judgment of my actions."

What were they thinking now? The ikati energy in the room made it hard for her to focus on subtle displays of human emotion. No matter. She was finished now. She had said what she had come here to say and cast the spell that she had come here to cast, and if those things were not enough . . . then the game would end here and now. There would be no second chance.

Sometimes life required such a gamble.

"I leave the matter in your hands," she said quietly. And she stepped down from the stage without looking back, to leave her black-robed colleagues to their deliberations.

———

She was deep in meditation when a fist rapped lightly on the door. Gazing down at the remnants of her latest conjuring (possibly the most important one of her life) she did not turn around. "Come in."

The door creaked open behind her, then closed again.

"It is done," Colivar said.

Day had reached its end long ago, and the candles she had conjured on the sideboard had melted halfway down. She closed her eyes for a moment, shutting out their light. "And?"

She heard him walk up behind her. "The Law will be amended. Granted, that will take a while to arrange. Not quite as simple as scrawling an additional line on the bottom of a contract." He paused. "Raven's death was judged to be outside the scope of the current Law. So you are quite safe, my dear."

She could feel a wave of relief come over her, so intense it made her feel light-headed. "Thank you," she whispered.

"I believe Ramirus was a bit surprised by the verdict. Though not necessarily displeased."

"And you?" she asked. "Were you not surprised?"

He chuckled softly. "Not once I realized that most of the Magisters who were arguing in your favor were Siderea's ex-lovers. The same ones you had sent me running all over the world to find." He paused. "There was never any real doubt about the verdict, was there?"

"There is always doubt," she whispered.

He came up beside her. There was a box on the table before them, ebony with a domed lid. He reached out and opened it. Inside was nothing but a thin layer of ash, featherlight, that stirred in response to his motions. He gazed at it for a moment, then shut the box again. "I admit that when I first told you about Siderea's tokens, I envisioned you using them to bargain with. But this was far more entertaining."

She smiled slightly. "As you said, there was not much power in them. Barely enough to influence a man's judgment. But you don't have to figure out which token belongs to which Magister if you use them all in a single spell."

"Your argument about the Law was not half bad, you know. It might have succeeded on its own merits."

"Perhaps." A faint smile flickered across her face. "We will never know, will we?"

"Do you really believe that more women will join our ranks? That your presence among us has more significance than a quirk of nature?"

He didn't know the truth about Lazaroth, she realized. Well, she would not be the one to tell him. If there really were other women hiding among the ranks of the Magisters, it was not Kamala's place to unmask them. Each one of them must decide for herself what sort of life she wanted to live, now that there were other options available. Some, like Lazaroth, might have invested so much time and energy in their masquerade that they would have a hard time letting go of it. Old habits—and fears—died hard.

She wondered if the women present today—assuming there were any—had argued for or against her execution. No way to tell.

"There will be others," she said softly. "Be sure of it."

Colivar reached up and fingered a lock of her hair. She was not accustomed to being touched in such a casual manner; it was strangely pleasing. "So what will this particular woman do now?" he asked her. "Take up a position as Magister Royal, perhaps? I'm sure there are monarchs who would be pleased to have a sorcerer who is as pleasing to the eye as she is useful on the battlefield."

"I was thinking I might hunt Souleaters," she told him.

A strange look came into his eyes. He said nothing.

"Mad or not," she said, "the survivors are still dangerous. And once they scatter to the four corners of the earth, it will be that much harder to track them down. Favias said the Guardians want to deal with them before that happens, and he asked me if I would help. I can call the creatures to them better than any Guardian can." She shrugged. "It seems a logical alliance."

His said it quietly: "You would risk taking on that form again?"

"I don't think that will be necessary. Now that most of their human consorts are gone, all that's left in them is blind instinct. Easy to manipulate. A few may still have partners, but we can deal with them by other means." She cocked her head to one side. "And you, Colivar? What is next for you?"

For a moment he said nothing. His fingers played with her hair for a moment longer, then his hand fell away. "A few of us will be heading to Alkali," he said. "We'll establish a gateway through the Wrath, and then we will head north, to hunt down any ikati who were left behind in the original invasion."

She breathed in sharply. "Such ikati would still have consorts. And the use of witchery."

A faint, dry smile flickered across his face. "That's why I am not going there alone." His dark eyes shimmered in the candle-light. "Perhaps when that species has been dealt with there will be time for . . . other things."

There was an intensity behind his words that made her breath catch in her throat. She opened her mouth to speak but could not make any words come. And then someone rapped on the door, shattering the mood. She looked at Colivar, a question in her eyes.

"I'm afraid you have one more gauntlet left to run," he said apologetically. "The Magisters all want to meet you."

"Ah," she said softly. "Now, *that* is a prospect more daunting than Souleaters."

He chuckled softly and offered her his arm. "Magister Kamala?"

She accepted the offer, resting her hand upon his arm. Taking pleasure in his warmth beneath her fingertips. And in victory. And in life.

Not to mention the new game that was about to begin.

extras

www.orbitbooks.net

about the author

Celia Friedman has been a voracious reader from her earliest days and began writing at the age of thirteen. At university, she studied maths, then theatre, before following her love of costume design to study and pursue a career in that field. She taught Costume Design at a northern Virginian university and has designed period dress patterns for a historical supply company. She now writes full-time and teaches a creative writing course at a local high school.

To find out more about Celia Friedman and other Orbit authors you can register for the free monthly newsletter at www.orbitbooks.net

if you enjoyed
LEGACY OF KINGS

look out for

THE DROWNING CITY

by

Amanda Downum

CHAPTER 1

S YMIR. THE Drowning City.

An exile, perhaps, but at least it was an interesting one.

Isyllt's gloved hands tightened on the railing as the *Black Mariah* cleared the last of the Dragon Stones and turned toward the docks, dark estuarine water slopping against her hull. Fishing boats dotted Ka Liang Bay, glass buoys flashing in the sun. Cormorants dove around them, scattering ripples as they snatched fish from hooks and nets.

The west wind died, broken on the Dragons' sharp peaks, and the jungle's hot breath wafted from the shore. Rank with brine and bilge, sewers draining into the sea, but under the port-reek the air smelled of spices and the green tang of Sivahra's forests rising beyond the marshy delta of the Mir. Mountains flanked the capital city Symir, uneven green sentinels on either side of the river. So unlike the harsh and rocky shores of Selafai they had left behind two and a half decads ago.

Only twenty-five days at sea—a short voyage, though it didn't feel that way to Isyllt. The ship had made good time, laden only with olive oil and wheat flour from the north.

And northern spies. But those weren't recorded on the cargo manifest.

Isyllt shook her head, collected herself. This might be an exile, but it was a working one. She had a revolution to foment, a country to throw into chaos, and an emperor to undermine with it. Sivahra's jungles and mines—and Symir's bustling port—provided great wealth to the Assari Empire. Enough to fund a war of conquest, and the eyes of the expansionist Emperor roved slowly north. Isyllt and her master meant to prevent that.

If their intelligence was good, Sivahra was crawling with insurgent groups, natives desperate to overthrow their Imperial conquerors. Selafai's backing might help them succeed. Or at least distract the Empire. Trade one war for another. After that, maybe she could have a real vacation.

The *Mariah* dropped anchor before they docked and the crew bustled to prepare for the port authority's inspection; already a skiff rowed to meet them. The clang of harbor bells carried across the water.

Adam, her coconspirator and ostensible bodyguard, leaned against the rail beside her while his partner finished checking over their bags. Isyllt's bags, mostly: the mercenaries traveled light, but she had a pretense of pampered nobility to maintain. Maybe not such a pretense—she might have murdered for a hot bath and proper bed. Sweat stuck her shirt to her arms and back, itched behind her knees. She envied the sailors their vests and short trousers, but her skin was too pale to offer to the summer sun.

"Do we go straight to the Kurun Tam tonight?" Adam asked. The westering sun flashed on gold and silver earrings, mercenary gaud. He wore his sword again for the first time since they'd boarded the *Mariah*. He'd taken to sailor fashions—his vest hung open over his scarred chest, revealing charm bags around his neck and the pistol tucked into his belt. His skin was three shades darker than it had been when they sailed, bronze now instead of olive.

Isyllt's mouth twisted. "No," she said after a moment. "Let's find an extravagantly expensive hotel tonight. I feel like spending the Crown's money. We can work tomorrow." One night of vacation, at least, she could give herself.

He grinned and looked to his partner. "Do you know someplace decadent?"

Xinai's lips curled as she turned away from the luggage. "The Silver Phoenix. It's Selafaïn—it'll be decadent enough for you." Her head barely cleared her partner's shoulder, though the black plumage-crest of her hair added the illusion of more height. She wore her wealth too—rings in her ears, a gold cuff on one wiry wrist, a silver hoop in her nostril. The blades at her hips and the scars on her wiry arms said she knew how to keep it.

Isyllt turned back to the city, scanning the ships at dock. She was surprised not to see more Imperial colors flying. After rumors of rebellion and worries of war, she'd expected Imperial warships, but there was no sign of the Emperor's army—although that didn't mean it wasn't there.

Something was happening, though; a crowd gathered on the docks, and Isyllt caught flashes of red and green uniforms amid the blur of bodies. Shouts and angry voices carried over the water, but she couldn't make out the words.

The customs skiff drew alongside the *Mariah*, lion crest gleaming on the red-and-green-striped banners—the flag of an Imperial territory, granted limited home-rule. The sailors threw down a rope ladder and three harbor officials climbed aboard, nimble against the rocking hull. The senior inspector was a short, neat woman, wearing a red sash over her sleek-lined coat. Isyllt fought the urge to fidget with her own travel-grimed clothes. Her hair was a salt-stiff tangle, barely contained by pins, and while she'd cleaned her face with oil before landfall, it was no substitute for a proper bath.

Isyllt waited, Adam and Xinai flanking her, while the inspector spoke to the captain. Whatever the customs woman told the captain, he didn't like. He spat over the rail and made an angry gesture toward the shore. The *Mariah* wasn't the only ship waiting to dock; Isyllt wondered if the gathering on the pier had something to do with the delay.

Finally the ship's mate led two of the inspectors below, and the woman in the red sash turned to Isyllt, a wax tablet and stylus in her hand. A Sivahri, darker skinned than Xinai but with the same creaseless black eyes; elaborate henna designs covered her hands. Isyllt was relieved to be greeted in Assari—Xinai had tutored her in the native language during the voyage, but she was still far from fluent.

"Roshani." The woman inclined her head politely. "You're the only passengers?" She raised her stylus as Isyllt nodded. "Your names?"

"Isyllt Iskaldur, of Erisín." She offered the oiled leather tube that held her travel papers. "This is Adam and Xinai, sayifarim hired in Erisín."

The woman glanced curiously at Xinai; the mercenary gave no more response than a statue. The official opened the tube and unrolled the parchment, recorded something on her tablet. "And your business in Symir?"

Isyllt tugged off her left glove and held out her hand. "I'm here to visit the Kurun Tam." The breeze chilled her sweaty palm. Since it was impossible to pass herself off as anything but a foreign mage, the local thaumaturgical facility was the best cover.

The woman's eyes widened as she stared at the cabochon black diamond on Isyllt's finger, but she didn't ward herself or step out of reach. Ghostlight gleamed iridescent in the stone's depths and a cold draft suffused the air. She nodded again, deeper this time. "Yes, meliket. Do you know where you'll be staying?"

"Tonight we take rooms at the Silver Phoenix."

"Very good." She recorded the information, then glanced up. "I'm sorry, meliket, but we're behind schedule. It will be a while yet before you can dock."

"What's going on?" Isyllt gestured toward the wharf. More soldiers had appeared around the crowd.

The woman's expression grew pained. "A protest. They've been there an hour and we're going to lose a day's work."

Isyllt raised her eyebrows. "What are they protesting?"

"New tariffs." Her tone became one of rote response. "The Empire considers it expedient to raise revenues and has imposed taxes on foreign goods. Some of the local merchants"—she waved a hennaed hand at the quay—"are unhappy with the situation. But don't worry, it's nothing to bother the Kurun Tam."

Of course not—Imperial mages would hardly be burdened with problems like taxes. It was much the same in the Arcanost in Erisín.

"Are these tariffs only in Sivahra?" she asked.

"Oh, no. All Imperial territories and colonies are subject."

Not just sanctions against a rebellious population, then, but real money-raising. That left an unpleasant taste in the back of her mouth. Twenty-five days with no news was chancy where politics were concerned.

The other officials emerged from the cargo hold a few moments later and the captain grudgingly paid their fees. The woman turned back to Isyllt, her expression brightening. "If you like, meliket, I can take you to the Silver Phoenix myself. It will be a much shorter route than getting there from the docks."

Isyllt smiled. "That would be lovely. Shakera."

Adam cocked an eyebrow as he hoisted bags. Isyllt's lips curled. "It never pays to annoy foreign guests," she murmured in Selafaïn. "Especially ones who can steal your soul."

She tried to watch the commotion on the docks, but the skiff moved swiftly and they were soon out of sight. A cloud of midges trailed behind the craft; the drone of wings carried unpleasant memories of the plague, but the natives seemed unconcerned. Isyllt waved the biting insects away, though she was immune to whatever exotic diseases they might carry. As they rowed beneath a raised water gate, a sharp, minty smell filled the air and the midges thinned.

The inspector—who introduced herself as Anhai Xian-Mar—talked as they went, her voice counterpoint to the rhythmic splash of oars as she explained the myriad delta islands on which the city was built, the web of canals that took the place of stone streets. Xinai's mask slipped for an instant and Isyllt saw the cold disdain in her eyes. The mercenary had little love for countrymen who served their Assari conquerors.

Sunlight spilled like honey over their shoulders, gilding the water and gleaming on domes and tilting spires. Buildings crowded together, walls of cream and ocher stone, pale blues and dusty pinks, balconies nearly touching over narrow alleys and waterways. Bronze chimes flashed from caves and lintels. Vines trailed from rooftop gardens, dripping leaves and orange blossoms onto the water. Birds perched in potted trees and on steep green-and gray-tiled roofs.

Invaders the Assari might be, but they had built a beautiful city. Isyllt tried to imagine the sky dark with smoke, the water running red. The city would be less lovely if her mission succeeded.

She'd heard stories from other agents of how the job crept into everything, reduced buildings and cities to exits and escape routes, defenses and weaknesses to be exploited. Till you couldn't look at anything—or anyone—without imagining how to infiltrate or corrupt or overthrow. She wondered how long it would take to happen to her. If she would even notice when it did.

Anhai followed Isyllt's gaze to the water level—slime crusted the stone several feet above the surface of the canal. "The rains will come soon and the river will rise. You're in time for the Dance of Masks."

The skiff drew up against a set of stairs and the oarsmen secured the boat and helped Adam and Xinai unload the luggage. A tall building rose above them, decorated with Selafaïn pillars. A carven phoenix spread its wings over the doors and polished horn panes gleamed ruddy in the dying light.

Anhai bowed farewell. "If you need anything at all, meliket, you can find me at the port authority office."

"Shakera." Isyllt offered her hand, and the silver griffin she held. She never saw where Anhai tucked the coin.

The she stepped from the skiff to the slime-slick stairs and set foot in the Drowning City.

The Phoenix was as decadent as Xinai had promised. Isyllt floated in the wide tub, her hair drifting around her in a black cloud. Oils shimmered on the water, filled the room with poppy and myrrh. Lamplight gleamed on blue and green tiles and rippled over the cool marble arch of the ceiling. She was nearly dozing when someone knocked lightly on the chamber door.

"Don't drown," Adam said, his voice muffled by wood.

"Not yet. What is it?"

"Dinner."

Her stomach growled in response and she shivered in water grown uncomfortably cold. She stood, hair clinging to her arms and back like sea wrack, and reached for a towel and robe.

The bedroom smelled of wine and curry and her stomach rumbled louder. The *Mariah*'s mess had been good enough, as sea rations went, but she was happy to reacquaint herself with real food.

Adam lit one of the scented-oil lamps and sneezed as the smell of eucalyptus filled the room. The city stank of it at night—like mint, but harsher, rawer. Linen mesh curtained the windows and tented the bed. The furniture and colorful rugs were Assari, but black silk covered the mirror, true Selafaïn fashion.

Adam sat, keeping the windows and doors in sight as he helped himself to food from the platter on the table. He'd traded his ship's clothes for sleek black, and the shadows in the corner swallowed him.

"Where's Xinai?" Isyllt asked, glancing at the door that led to the adjoining room.

"Scouting. Seeing how things have changed. The curry's good."

She tightened the towel around her hair and sat across from him. The bowls smelled of garlic and ginger and other spices she couldn't name. Curries and yogurt, served with rice instead of flat bread, and a bowl of sliced fruit.

"We should find our captain tonight." She stirred rice into a green sauce. "The Kurun Tam may take all day tomorrow."

The *Black Mariah*'s legitimate business would keep her in port at least half a decad, but Isyllt wanted to make sure their alternate transportation was resolved before anything unexpected arose. She scooped up a mouthful of curry and nearly gasped at the sweet green fire. A pepper burst between her teeth, igniting her nose and throat.

The sounds of the city drifted through the window, lapping water and distant harbor bells. Night birds sang and cats called to one another from nearby roofs. Footsteps and voices, but no hooves or rattling carriage wheels—the city's narrow streets left no room for horses or oxen.

"You don't want to be here, do you?" Adam asked after a moment. Shadows hid his face, but she felt the weight of his regard, those eerie green eyes.

She sipped iced-and-honeyed lassi. "It isn't that, exactly."

"You're angry with the old man."

She kept her face still. She hadn't cried since the first night at sea, but emotions still threatened to surface when she wasn't careful. "I know the job. My problems with Kiril won't interfere." Her voice didn't catch on his name, to her great relief.

"I hope not. He'll skin me if I don't keep you safe."

Isyllt paused, cup half raised. "He said that?"

Adam chuckled. "He left little room for doubt."

Wood clacked as she set the drink down. "If he's so bloody concerned, he could have sent someone else." She bit her tongue, cursed the petulant tone that crept into the words. The side door opened with a squeak, saving her from embarrassing herself further.

Xinai slipped in, feet silent on marble. "I found Teoma. He frequents a tavern on the wharf called the Storm God's Bride." Izachar Teoma had made the most of his wealth and notoriety smuggling along Imperial shores, but sailed north often enough to have encountered Kiril's web of agents before. A ship quick and clever enough to escape harbor patrols would be useful if they had to flee the city.

Xinai tossed a stack of cheap pulp paper onto the table. "Newsscrawls, from the past decad or so. The criers will have stopped spreading those stories by now."

"Thanks." Isyllt flipped through the stack—wrinkled and waterspotted, and the ink left gray smears on her fingers, but the looping Assari script was legible. The latest was three days old. She took a moment to adjust to the Assari calendar; today was Sekhmet seventh, not the twelfth of Janus; 1229 Sal Emperaturi, not 497 Ab Urbe Condita.

She often found the pride of nations silly. Trade and treaties between Assar and Selafai had to be twice dated, because the founders of Selafai had abandoned all things Imperial when they fled north across the sea five hundred years ago. But if not for the pride of nations, she'd be out of a job.

She sipped her drink again, watery now as the ice melted. Moisture slicked the curve of the cup. "Did you hear anything about the protest we saw?"

"Not much. The guards ran them off not long after we arrived, it sounds like. There were arrests, but no real violence." From Xinai's tone, Isyllt couldn't tell if she was disappointed in that or not.

Adam rose, taking a slice of mango with him. "Finish your

dinner, Lady Iskaldur." The title dripped mockingly off his tongue. "We'll leave when you're ready."

Night draped the city like damp silk. Heat leaked from the stones, trapped between close walls; sweat prickled the back of Isyllt's neck. The end of the dry season in Symir, but the Drowning City would never be truly dry. Insects droned overhead, avoiding the pungent lamp-smoke, and rats and roaches scuttled in the shadows. Charms hummed around them, soft shivers from doors and windows. *Safe*, some murmured, *home*. Others pulsed warnings—*stay back, move on, look away*.

Shadows pooled between buildings, leaked from narrow alleys; the glow of streetlamps drowned the stars. Voices drifted from taverns, floated up from the canals as skiffs passed. Water lup-lup-lupped against stone and wind sighed over high bridges, rattling the chimes that hung on nearly all the buildings. Hollow tubes and octagonal bronze mirrors flashed and clattered—in Erisín, Selafai's capital, no one left mirrors uncovered and even still puddles were avoided, but here it seemed they were lucky.

The crowds had thinned after dusk, stores closed and shuttered, the last clerks and shopkeepers hurrying home. More than once they passed guard patrols, green uniforms edged with Imperial red—a whispered word kept the soldiers' eyes off them.

A cool draft wafted past Isyllt, and a whisper light and hollow as reeds. Her bare arms prickled and the diamond chilled on her finger. She smiled—the touch of death was comforting, made the city feel less foreign.

She studied Adam's easy stride, the roll of Xinai's hips as she kept pace with him, the dangerous grace with which they moved. At home she worked alone more often than not—probably more often than she ought—but Kiril had insisted she bring backup this time. She could have brought someone familiar, but it was better this way. Too many people in Erisín knew her bitter history with Kiril, offered her sympathy and sad glances. She preferred the quiet solace of strangers. And, she admitted to herself, in this strange place she was glad of their presence.

They crossed a wide canal into the dock district—Merrowgate, the map named it. The Phoenix lay in Saltlace, the tourist and market quarter. The night grew louder as they neared the docks, bare and sandaled feet slapping the stones, laughter and music echoing from taverns, bells tolling to guide ships in the dark. The cloying spice-sweetness of opium drifted out of an alley mouth.

As they passed a narrow walkway along the water Isyllt heard a soft cry, like a child's muffled sob. She paused, searching for the source. It sounded like it came from the water.

Xinai laid a hand on her arm as she leaned toward the black offal-reek of the canal. "Don't. It's a nakh."

"A what?"

"A water spirit. Like your sirens in the north. They mimic children to lure people close to the water, then pull them in."

Isyllt frowned down at the black water. "Then what?"

Xinai shrugged. "Eat you. Drown you. I don't know. I doubt you'd care once you were at the bottom of the bay. The inner canals are warded, but they slip in around the edges of the city sometimes." She leaned over the railing and called out in Sivahran; the word shivered with a weight of magic. Something below them croaked, then splashed and was still. Xinai turned away and Adam and Isyllt fell in behind her.

The Storm God's Bride lay on the far side of the district, nestled between storehouses, with cheap rented rooms stacked above it like a child's precarious block tower. The sound of flutes and drums drifted through the door and firelight fell from the windows in oily-gold streaks.

Isyllt was glad to find the Bride little different from the disreputable dock taverns at home. Smoke and sweat and spilled beer thickened the air, and the tiles were cracked and sticky. Dried plants hung from warped rafters, wards or decoration or something else entirely.

Xinai twisted through the crowd in search of the captain; Isyllt stayed close to Adam, careful not to foul his sword-arm. She ran a surreptitious hand over the hilt of her own knife, though the mood in the room seemed pleasant enough.

Musicians played on a low wooden platform against the far wall, mostly ignored by the custom. Sailors and dock-workers, Isyllt guessed, watching the people slouched on low benches or gathered loudly around the gaming tables. Wiry men and women, scarred and wind-scoured and plainly dressed, bronze skin and ocher, shades of black and brown. Ninayans and Sivahri and Assari alike laughed and gambled and drank bowls of beer, and none seemed less welcome than the others. She even saw a few fairer heads, from Hallach or lands farther north.

Xinai reappeared soon and led them across the room, toward a door beside the stage. As they moved down a narrow corridor, Isyllt heard the rattle of dice. They entered a cluttered storeroom and found a man sitting alone, rolling bones across a scarred table.

She'd known Teoma was a dwarf, but the leather cuff that capped his missing left forearm was a surprise. Dark eyes gleamed under heavy black brows as he glanced up at them.

"Good evening. Here for a game of chance?"

Adam's lips curled. "Since when is there chance in your games, Izzy?"

The dwarf's grin rearranged his creased face; lamp-light winked off two gold teeth. "It's dangerous to accuse a man of cheating." He nodded toward his maimed arm. "Look what happened to me."

He turned his eyes to Isyllt. "But if you haven't come for the bones, what can I do for you?"

Isyllt twisted a red-gold ring off her finger and held it out. "Among blind men—" She gave the first half of the code in Selafaïn.

"The one-eyed reigns," he finished. He reached out to clasp her hand and palm the ring in one smooth gesture.

As his calloused fingers touched hers, a shiver ran up her arm. Isyllt barely managed to keep her face still: no one had mentioned the man was a sorcerer. The sensation vanished so quickly she almost doubted her instinct, but his eyes narrowed as he studied her.

"Well met, I hope. I'm Izachar Teoma."

"Isyllt Iskaldur."

His eyes flicked briefly toward her left hand. "What is it you wish of me, Lady?"

"I want to hire your ship."

"The *Rain Dog* can take you anywhere you need to go."

"Actually. I want you to stay in port. We'll be in Symir for perhaps a month—hopefully it will be a peaceful visit and we'll leave quietly. But it may come to pass that we'll need to leave the city very quickly, and we'll need a fast ship we can trust."

"Ah." Izachar ran a hand over his curling beard. His chair creaked as he leaned back. "I understand. But a month . . . My crew have families to feed, and I'll lose business." A gold tooth gleamed with his smile. "And with the new import taxes, my business is booming."

"We're prepared to compensate you."

Adam slid a purse across the table. Izachar hefted it, listened to the clatter of metal and stones. He loosened the ties and pulled out a coin. Silver gleamed smooth, unstamped.

"I'll keep the *Dog* in port for a decad," he said at last. "My first mate's daughter is sick, anyway, and she'd like to spend some time with the child. After ten days, find me again and we'll negotiate further."

Isyllt nodded. She'd expected no better. "A pleasure doing business with you, Captain."

"The pleasure's mine, Lady." The money vanished off the table.

The door swung open and a dark, scar-faced man leaned in. "Time to go," he said. His hand moved against his thigh, a sign Isyllt didn't recognize. Then he was gone.

Izachar cursed softly. "A raid's coming. Business is booming a little too well." He pushed off his chair and crossed the room, quick enough for his short legs. "We'll use the back door," he said, motioning them on. "It'll be clear for a few more minutes—Desh pays his bribes on time."

Isyllt and Adam exchanged a quick glance and followed the dwarf down the hall. From the main room she heard a door slam, then a flurry of curses and shouting and the clatter of an overturned table. They stepped outside into a dark alley, as empty as Izachar had promised; the last light caught his grin before the door shut behind them.

"Welcome to Symir," he called after them as they escaped into the sticky night.

Xinai moved through her exercises by the light of one guttering lamp. The flame gleamed on her knives, shattered on their razored edges. Her breath hissed through clenched teeth as she thrust and spun and stretched. Normally she flowed like water from one stance to the next, but tonight tension trembled her limbs, made her movements too quick and jerky.

The smell of the canals breathed across the casement: water and waste, eucalyptus and brine and citrus-sweet champa flowers. Beneath it her own sour salt sweat clogged her nose.

She'd thought she could do it. She'd thought she could come home after twelve years gone. On the voyage she'd told herself that the city would have changed, that time would have made her memories bearable.

She'd almost believed it.

The exercise wasn't calming her. She stopped, stretched, and put her blades away. Adam watched her from the shadows of the bed as she stripped off her vest and trousers. He'd asked if she could take the job, one of the rare times he acknowledged all the things she'd never told him about her past. In Erisín, spending the wizard's money on food and wine, she'd said yes. Even the necromancer hadn't deterred her, for all the woman's magic made her skin crawl.

She could do this. She didn't have a choice.

She threw herself down beside Adam and buried her face in a cushion. His familiar scent was a comfort—oil and leather, musk and iron. Nothing that reminded her of home.

He propped himself up on one elbow. "Is it so bad?"

"It's—" Pillows muffled her sigh. "It's the same. Things have changed, but it's still the same."

He knelt over her, running his hands over her shoulders. She grunted softly as he pressed against knotted muscles.

"They think they're lions," she muttered, thinking of the customs inspector with her expensive coat and hennaed hands, her perfect

Assari. The Sivahri soldiers in their red-trimmed uniforms. "Only dogs licking their masters' boots." She gasped as Adam dug his thumbs into her back.

He worked down, calloused hands strong and steady. She forced herself not to stiffen as he brushed the scars on her back. It had been a long time, even after they were lovers, before she let him touch them. Not until the nightmares faded and she didn't wake up gasping, expecting to find her skin slick with blood.

Years of partnership had left his touch as familiar as her own. By the time he reached the small of her back she could breathe easily again, the angry stiffness gone from her limbs.

"It's only a job." He leaned down to kiss her shoulder. "When it's over we'll go somewhere else. Anywhere you like." He caressed the unmarked skin on her sides and she shivered. "You want to be a pirate?"

She chuckled and rolled over, stretching out the last of her tension. "You might be able to talk me into it." But she pulled him down and kissed him before he could try.